The Light Speed Project

Ron Wilk

Accipiter Publishing

ISBN: 978-1-63453-007-1

Cover Design by: Rost-9D

The LIght Speed Project

Chapter One

Tuesday, August 1, 2017

3 A.M.

Nevada

Classified U.S Government Plasma Physics Lab

Scottish born physicist, Gregory McCraken, PhD, had been rudely awakened by a dreadfully loud alarm. A group of twelve scientists, although present during the daytime hours, had been taking turns spending a full week of nights in the underground facility, sleeping in one of the three sparsely outfitted bedrooms. And he had just segued into his second dreamscape, a not unpleasant depiction of a misty, Scottish moor, when the pulsating siren began to wail. He'd jumped from the bed, having never borne witness to the horrid outburst, and ran for the signal board. The board, a series of variously colored and labeled LED lights, had been constructed for the purpose of providing rapid recognition of system failure points. But still in his skivvies, with no one else around to observe or assist, he stood before the board rubbing his eyes, wondering if the colorful display was simply part of an elaborate nightmare.

"This can't be real," he shouted to the empty corridor, as he followed the blinking lights and their suggested pattern of malfunction.

He scurried for the troubleshooting manual and feverishly tore through a series of plastic encased pages, but nothing of this magnitude had apparently been anticipated. And because the project's responsibilities had been equally divided among the twelve highly regarded scientists, there was no single supervisor to query.

"Shit, shit, shit," he hissed, dashing for what he felt to be the initiator of the fault chain, when a flash of light momentarily blinded him, and a sonic boom-like blast nearly shattered his eardrums. A period of unconsciousness, that may have been perceived as an eternity, but actually lasted less than five minutes, had been followed by brief confusion. Seated on the cold, concrete floor, his ears dripping bright red blood onto his shoulders, the persistent siren could be felt more than heard. Struggling to arise, his balance severely impaired, he dragged his body upright and slithered along the wall to the origin of purple, number one LED. What he saw caused him to gasp.

"A plasma burst, that was a plasma burst," he half shouted and laughed. "We've done it ... I have to call the others but..."

* * *

He awakened hours later to find himself in unfamiliar surroundings, half submerged in an ice bath. Where am I, he wondered, struggling to exit from the stainless steel vat that threatened to freeze him like a supermarket flounder. But then a buzzer sounded and the door at the foot of the tub opened. His life was about to change in ways he could never have imagined.

***

Wednesday, August 2

7 A.M.

Dr. McCraken's sixty-five year-old hands were still trembling from the unsolicited deep freeze, when he attempted to dress in the khaki toned scrubs that had been left at the foot of his bed. The metal cot had been bolted to the floor in one corner of the twelve by twelve foot, windowless room. And aside from a wall mounted mirror and prison-like, open-air commode with its attached stainless sink, the room was devoid of furniture. He lugged his muscular, six foot frame to the mirror and examined the graying stubble that covered his face, his dark brown, almost black eyes staring back at him. A lock of silver hair had slipped before his eyes and he blew it upward, just as he contemplated unsealing the plastic encased razor that sat on the sink's edge. But a blast of cold air distracted him, as the door to his confinement swung open.

"Good morning doctor, I trust you had a wonderful night?" a dark suited man inquired, as he stood in the archway.

Gregory slowly turned to face the newcomer and growled, "Who are you and where am I?"

"Both good questions but, first, I have questions of my own," the man said, fiddling with his black, funereal tie.

Gregory padded back to the cot and took a seat on the edge of the thin mattress. "Go ahead," he said, repeatedly fighting with the unruly lock of hair perched over one eye.

"What do you recall of the events leading up to this?" he asked, gesturing about the cubicle.

"A siren."

"Nothing more?"

"No."

"What about the nature of your project?"

Gregory glared at the man, and spat, "It's classified."

The man reached into his jacket and withdrew a plastic encased government ID card that he displayed at a distance. "Surely you can tell me," he said.

"Not another word, until you tell me where I am and

how I got here."

The man frowned, spun about on his leather heels, and left the room.

What the hell's going on, he asked himself, noticing a stinging sensation emanating from his back. He stretched behind as far as his arms would allow and grimaced when he'd reached his shoulder blade. Tearing off the loose scrub top, he approached the mirror. What he observed caused him dismay. The skin covering the visible portion of his back had turned a reddish purple. I've been burned, he questioned. And it was at that moment that he'd recalled the blinding flash of light that had likely led to his curious predicament. He continued to examine what could be seen of his posterior, when the door to his room once again opened.

"Have a seat," the dark skinned, white coated man said, more a demand than a request, while his similarly attired female assistant carried a stainless steel tray containing gauze pads and other unfamiliar items.

"What the hell's going on?" Gregory seethed, as he slowly lowered his body to the edge of the cot.

"You've received some nasty burns," the man replied.

"How did that happen," he asked, suspecting that it had had something to do with the flash of light.

"Not for me to say," the man, whose coat displayed the embroidered name of William F. Black, MD, drawled.

"Then get me someone who can answer my questions," he demanded.

"We have to cleanse your wounds," the female insisted, as she pulled on a pair of surgical gloves and unwrapped a disposable scalpel.

"You're not touching me until I get some answers," he shouted, his back now facing a blank wall.

The doctor turned to face the woman, shrugged, and gestured for her to leave the room. The nurse apparent lowered the tray to the cot and departed, but Doctor Black stood his ground. "Allow me to have a look at your back, it could easily become infected," he advised.

"At least tell me where I am," Gregory pleaded.

The doctor hesitated, but replied, "You're at the University Medical Center's burn unit."

"And where is that?"

"Las Vegas."

"Any idea how I got here?"

The doctor gazed about, as if searching for eavesdroppers, and replied, "I believe you'd arrived in a FedEx container."

"I hope you're a better doctor than you are a comedian,"

he sneered.

"Lay on your belly and let me do my job," Doctor Black demanded.

Reluctantly, Gregory did as requested. But as the Doctor began to gently debride the wound, he said something that made Gregory's unscorched skin crawl.

"What did you say?" he returned, still on his stomach.

"You're in great danger, and not from this fairly substantial but superficial burn."

"What do you mean?"

The Doctor finished what he'd come to do, lifted the tray from the cot and left the room without another word.

Gregory, his back now covered with a patchwork of gauze, pulled the khaki top over his head and stood facing the door. Was he trying to get back at me for being an asshole, he wondered, when he considered the Doctor's warning, or is there something else going on.

He tried the door, but it had been locked from the outside. And he was about to return to the bed, when he heard a knock.

"Yes?" he called out.

"Are you decent?" a female voice inquired.

"Depends upon who's asking," he spat.

Without further adieu, the door opened and in walked

an over six foot tall, not unattractive female Amazonian dressed in military fatigues.

"I am Major Fuentes," she announced, stopping uncomfortably close to the still standing physicist.

"And I'm getting tired of the dog and pony show. What the hell is going on?" he shouted.

"Do you recall the agreement that you'd signed when you'd come onboard with your project?" she said.

"Y-e-s," he answered, tentatively.

"Then you're aware of whom you are working for."

"If I recall, it's a division of the DoD (Department of Defense)."

"Correct."

"So?"

"There was a secrecy clause..."

"And I've honored it," he interrupted.

The Major relaxed her stance and half smiled. "Can you prove it?"

Gregory carefully lowered his buttocks to the cot and frowned. "Not sure how to prove a negative," he said, dejectedly.

"Word of your *accident* has gotten out."

"What accident?"

"We're beyond game playing. You know what I'm

talking about," she advised, with a stern facial expression.

"Look, I was the only one on duty at the time of the so-called, *accident*. Maybe it was someone who was remotely monitoring the cameras," he suggested.

"The cameras had been rendered nonfunctional."

He gazed at her askance and a thought came to mind. "Which branch of the service did you say you're with?"

"I didn't."

"So you're an intelligence agent," he offered.

The Major cracked the knuckles of her dark skinned fingers and Gregory winced, anticipating some form of physical attack. But instead, she turned and left the room.

What is it with these people, he asked himself. They can't seem to complete a thought, or perhaps their scripts are incomplete.

Chapter Two

Wednesday, 1 P.M.

Gregory had spent the better part of the morning and early afternoon alternating between the cot and pacing the tiny room. There had been no further inquiring visitors or medical personnel to interrupt, or to add to his already considerable confusion. But the alone time had afforded him the luxury of introspection, and it was now clear that something entirely beyond his understanding had transpired at the time of his injury.

I recall the blinding flash, he pondered, and I'm not certain, but there may have been some associated heat. Nothing else ... wait a minute, it may have been the effect of the intense light on my retina, but I think I remember seeing something blue before I passed out. And I'm absolutely confident that I'd been alone that night. But the fake major had claimed that the cameras had been deactivated. However, we'd been told that the surveillance cameras had been hardened to the extent that they could not be tampered with or damaged by our equipment, so what took them out, he wondered. It couldn't have been a power spike, since the facility has a surge protected, redundant backup system. And a plasma burst would have been contained within the the physics lab's three foot thick concrete walls and ceiling.

At 1 p.m., the door to his room sprung open to allow entry for a food cart. But there was something odd about the cart and its driver. He could not tell if the presumed bearer of food was male or female, because the individual was dressed from head to toe in a surgical gown, cap, gloves and a full facial mask. The large cart, on the other hand, contained a small, transparent container of what had appeared to have been green Jello, as well as a rectangular, covered stainless steel tray that seemed out of place for a food cart.

"Is that what you people call lunch?" he jeered.

Suddenly, and without warning, there was a prick to his neck, followed by the sensation of floating on a bed of marshmallows, and then nothing. Later, he would recall seeing the server's green cloth covered arm coming at him like a speeding arrow, before his lights went out in a not unpleasant fashion.

***

He awakened hours later in a long, rectangular room, the entire expanse of which had been covered with mattresses. He called for help, but the mattresses had effectively soundproofed the room, his voice appreciable only to himself. It had taken several tries to arise from the structure's floor, as each attempt had resulted in a fall back to the soft flooring. But he eventually managed to gain a semi-secure foothold, and it was then that it had become apparent that the sound deadened environment was actually the interior of large trailer truck that had been locked from the outside.

First the locked hospital room, and now this, he fumed. "What the hell does the government want with me?" he cried out, almost in tears. He rubbed his eyes and dried them with a swipe of the now blood stained Khaki scrubs, while looking for a way out. The mattresses covering the double, rear doors had been installed in such a fashion as to allow for free movement of the lever/lock. A sliver of light pierced the narrow gap where the doors met, and while the opening did not allow for a view of the exterior, it did not prevent the passage of external sounds. Hmm, sounds like traffic noise, he thought. And I can just make out some voices—sounds Oriental. Just then, the trailer shook with a jolt and he froze and he watched as the lever preventing his escape began to move. Seconds later, one door swung open and a short statured, middle aged male entered carrying a tightly wrapped package that resembled the product of a Chinese laundry. He tossed the package to the floor and stood glaring at his captive.

"You are Dr. Gregory McLaken," the man announced.

Gregory winced at the bizarre mispronunciation of his name, and screeched, "I'm finished with this nonsense, and unless you tell me what's going on, I'm shutting down. That means, no more conversation."

The man aimed an index finger at the package and demanded, "You put clothes on."

He wondered if the man had understood what he'd said, but since his current outfit had taken on all kinds of odors, he ripped open the brown paper, removed the freshly starched, long sleeved white shirt and jeans, turned his back to the visitor and dressed.

Apparently satisfied that his order had been complied with, the man departed without closing the door. And as Gregory was about to make a running dash for the outside world, two men and a young woman entered the container carrying a collapsible chair. One man placed the chair at the extreme, closed end of the trailer, while the other issued a command to sit. The two men then positioned themselves at the door, leaving the black clad woman standing only a foot before their now seated guest.

Gregory focused on her long, black, shiny hair and thin, gleaming, bright red lips. And while under normal circumstances she would have been considered quite attractive, her demeanor and aggressive posture caused Gregory to sweat.

"I will not waste your time and you will not waste mine," she said, in perfect English, continuing, "you will give me what I require."

"What's in it for me?"

She hesitated, and growled "This is not a negotiation."

Gregory McCraken, PhD., born in Glasgow, Scotland, had come to the United States on a student visa for the sole purpose of continuing his education in plasma physics at Princeton University. As one of Princeton's oldest students, his plan had included an eventual return to Scotland, but upon receipt of his PhD he had been approached with an offer that he'd found difficult to refuse. And some four years had passed since he'd signed on to the U.S. Government sponsored, Light Speed Project.

Gregory had never been an emotional man, and the decision to leave Scotland had not been fraught with the usual anxiety of leaving one's family behind, particularly, since he had no family to speak of. He'd resigned himself to a life of solitude, as his existence in America had been consumed with study and work, leaving little time for the opposite sex. And aside from the occasional group gatherings with fellow scientists, there had been sparse social interaction. That's not to say that he'd been a complete misanthrope but, rather, a focused individual devoted to his career. But one aspect of his younger years had served to set him apart from his scientific community, and that related to the five year interval in his twenties, during which he'd been engaged in martial arts training.

Gregory clenched his fists, but remained seated. With the exception of the flash of light that had somehow led to his current predicament, nothing had made sense. Somehow, he'd been removed from the sealed, underground facility by unknown individuals that, to the best of his knowledge, could not have known about his plight if the cameras had been inoperative. He'd been semi-interrogated by presumed government operatives and now this, a mattress covered container and a bunch of weirdos that could have come straight out of a cheap, Oriental action movie. He shook his head and said, "It sure as hell is. You want something, and I want something—that's a negotiation."

She ignored his rant, and spat, "Give me your project passwords."

"They change every twenty-four hours," he laughed.

The apparently unexpected revelation caused her to turn and gaze at her male escorts. Gregory took that as his only chance for freedom and he leapt from the chair, wrapped his right forearm around her throat in a sleeper hold, and shouted, "Out of my way, or she dies."

One of the men reached inside of his suit jacket, presumably for a weapon, but the other slapped his hand away and nodded for him to relax. Both men stepped aside and allowed their captive to slowly approach the exit, as he dragged the thin, unconscious body of their leader across the mattress covered floor to the open air. Down the makeshift stairs they went, her high heeled shoes clacking as they bumped along the steps until they'd reached the asphalt covered ground. He eased her to the pavement and began to run, but he hadn't gotten more thirty yards from the trailer when an older, black, Cadillac limousine blocked his path. And before he could change direction, a pair of stubby, automatic machine guns were pointed at his torso by two muscular Orientals. They held him at bay, apparently waiting for reinforcements, or further orders. Gregory gazed about for an escape route, but found himself surrounded by scrub brush, cactus and dirt as far as the eye could see. The patch of asphalt that was home to the trailer, however, continued for a considerable distance in two directions, with markings suggestive of an airstrip. This can't be good, he thought, as he stared down the barrels of the approaching weapons.

With his hands held high in the air, he stood in place and watched in amazement, as a sleek, corporate jet began its approach. He could hear the screech of rubber striking asphalt as it touched down. But then, something totally unexpected unfolded. A single AH-1Z Viper gunship (helicopter) appeared out of nowhere and opened fire with the earsplitting chatter of its 20-mm three-barrel cannon. The landing jet's fuselage was cut to shreds, sending metal and fuel spilling over the narrow runway. One wing tank exploded, turning the tarmac into a ribbon of flames and black smoke. This is my chance, Gregory thought. But the gunship's unknown origin, coupled with its incredible firepower gave him pause, and he ran back toward the trailer and took cover on its blind side. Glimpsing around one corner of the metal enclosure he could see, but barely hear the sound of his oriental captors returning fire. They must have assumed that the tall column of black smoke would hide their position, and that the flames would obfuscate their heat signatures to the helo's presumed infrared technology, Gregory mused. But the Viper simply pivoted around the flames and pointed its nose at the men standing beside the limo. Their machine guns continued to spew bullets into the air, and just as the Viper let loose with a Sidewinder missile, the helo began to smoke. The missile impact vaporized the limo and launched the two thugs into the air, their body parts raining down upon the ground as if they'd been expelled by a meat grinder. But the helo was too low for autorotation to have much effect, and it fell to the ground with a thud. The doors flew open and the occupants exited, running from the smoking aircraft as if their lives depended upon it.

From the distance, Gregory could see the characteristic U.S. Military markings on their flight suits, and he breathed a sigh of relief ... a little too soon.

"On the ground, face down, hands behind your back," the pistol pointing airman shouted.

"Don't shoot," he screamed, his voice muffled, as his lips pressed against the coarse pavement.

The airman quickly zip-tied Gregory's wrists and forced him to a standing position. "State your name," the man demanded.

"Gregory McCraken," he stuttered, fearing that his ill-fitting gifted trousers were about to make their way southward.

"I have orders to take you into custody."

"What is the charge?"

"Start walking."

Gregory gazed about for the second pilot, and spotting him seated back inside the helo, realized that his options for escape were limited. But a thought came to mind. "I need to pee," he said.

The pilot stopped his pushing from behind and replied, "Go ahead."

"I can't imagine that you'd want the smell of urine in your shiny helicopter. There's no place for me to run ... why not release my hands so I can do it like a man?"

Gregory noted that the pilot appeared to hesitate, but he pulled a pair of wire cutters from his flight suit and snipped at the plastic ties. With his hands free, and the pilot's pistol holstered, he sprung at the man with the force of an unleashed, tightly wound spring. The airman, taken by surprise, was thrown off balance. Gregory lunged for his pistol, but the man's military training had already kicked into gear and he launched a roundhouse kick at Gregory's midsection. Gregory sidestepped, and the man's kick went astray, leaving him open for a reciprocal attack. And as he ripped the pistol out of his opponent's holster, the second pilot came running, sending two misguided rounds streaking in his direction. With the pistol now firmly gripped in his right hand and pointed at the first pilot's head, he held up his left arm and said, "I think it's time for an honest conversation."

Chapter Three

Thursday, August 3

3 P.M.

Pentagon

Office of General Enoch Louder

There are three known main levels of DoD security clearance: Confidential, Secret and Top Secret. And while there are various subcategories, the most noteworthy of those mentioned is the latter. General Louder, given his flag status, had been receiving TS/SCI (Top Secret Compartmented information) for several years. But despite his apparent access to government secrets, there had been questions that had remained unanswered, leaving him to suspect the existence of one or more levels that remained beyond his reach.

The late afternoon sun was a glaring ball of fire, as the General stared through his deeply tinted glass window. Something unexpected had occurred at an underground laboratory that fell within his aegis, and he'd been kept out of the loop. The limited facts that he'd been privy to, and the lack of concrete details, had caused him great angst. And now, he'd been informed that one of the laboratory's prime investigators had been kidnapped, taken from a government facility by foreign agents.   He called his immediate subordinate to the office for interrogation.

Enoch Louder, the progeny of a wealthy family, had led a privileged childhood.   He'd attended a private preschool, an elite prep school and later, Princeton University, eventually departing the institution   with a masters degree in electrical engineering. He'd joined the Marines a short while after leaving Princeton and gradually inched his way up the ladder of advancement, cultivating connections at every opportunity.   His posting to the Pentagon had come as a big surprise, and had coincided with the receipt of the gleaming stars that now occupied his shoulder boards.

His wish list had never included an office job, as he'd termed it, but as time went by he came to realize that more could be accomplished from the seat of his thick leather chair than on a battlefield. And of course there were the perks of the job that included a driver if he so chose, a healthy living allowance, access to the best available healthcare, and more.   And given his rather exalted position he had access to contacts that would not have been otherwise possible.

But the post had its downside as well.   Despite the

availability of health club facilities and the insistence of medical professionals, Louder had gradually added considerable weight to his previously lithe body. High blood pressure had arrived on scene four years after his initial posting and two years later, a nasty case of hemorrhoids that would wield its ugly head at the most inopportune moments. And then came the allure of alcohol, the best that he could afford. His consumption had remained slightly below what could have been deemed to have been true alcoholism, but there had been occasions when he'd come close to crossing that fine line.

The General's social life, however, had not been as glorious as one might have expected. With the exception of a brief relationship with a shady intelligence agent, and a few one night stands with women that he'd encountered during episodes of alcoholic excess, he'd remained a lonely, graying, sixty-seven year-old man.

Colonel Bradley Duke sat before the General's immense desk with his legs crossed. He was a large man, taller and wider than his boss, with deep ebony skin contrasting against his olive toned uniform. As a college graduate with a background in several Oriental languages, he'd rapidly ascended the Marine Corps ranks. But despite his linguistic abilities, his personality had been lacking in certain social skills, and during his very occasional appearances at Pentagon functions he'd rarely smiled or conversed with other officers. And for that reason, his name had never appeared on the party guest list of fellow officers. But the General had a different take, viewing the Colonel as a loyal pet who would follow his orders to the last detail, without question.

"Something stinks around here," the General announced, with the bang of his fist against the desktop.

Bradley sniffed the air, taking the General's words in a literal sense. "Smells OK to me, sir," he replied, his thick lips barely moving.

"And when did you obtain a sense of humor? the General sneered.

Bradley tilted his head, as if questioning the General's remark.

"Two days ago, there was a mishap at the Nevada lab..."

"The underground facility, sir?"

The General glared at him, as if to say, *what other lab are we babysitting?* "Only one person was allegedly present at the time, and now he's missing," he informed.

"Missing?"

"He somehow disappeared from a guarded hospital room," he explained, holding back the exact nature of the disappearance.

"Do we have intel on the nature of the mishap?"

"Not a clue. I want you to fish around and see if we can get some answers."

"Why not set up our own investigation?"

"I've received strict orders to stand down."

"But it's your project, sir."

"In name only. I'm the guy who eats shit if all goes south. And I'm beginning to feel the heat."

"Am I allowed to ask who's really in command?"

"You can ask, but I can't give you an answer because I really don't know."

Bradley's face assumed a stupefied expression, and the General, taking note of same, replied, "There are some things that are above a general's pay grade, and this is one of them."

Bradley scratched his shiny forehead, and offered, "I'll put out some feelers, but you know how the others react to me."

The General pushed back in his chair, drummed his fingers on the armrests, and said, "I know about your college buddy at the NSA."

"We were roommates, but I wouldn't describe our relationship as being terribly close."

"You speak with him on a regular basis, I'd call that close."

"He calls me."

The General exhaled, an act of exasperation, and replied, "Pump him for intel. I want to know who took the scientist, why, and what's being done about retrieval."

"He's an analyst, he won't..."

"Bravo sierra (bullshit), he's a spook. I know that for a fact. If he doesn't have first hand intel he can get it."

Bradley's eyes widened, as if he'd been struck by an epiphany. "Do you think the NSA owns the project?"

"Wouldn't be surprised, but it's beginning to smell bad."

"Sir?"

"Deep black, Bradley, deep black."

"Makes sense. It would explain why, with the exception of its first day of operation, visitations have been discouraged."

"And that's suited me fine, until now."

"But why would they risk the exposure of a black project by involving us?"

"I can only guess that it has something to do with

funding."

"But I'd bet that they've got all kinds of backdoor cash, sir."

"Doesn't matter right now. Call your friend and squeeze hard."

Bradley left the office feeling somewhat out of sorts. I've never seen the General so agitated, he said to himself, as he cruised the corridor at high speed, heading for his own cubicle. I can call Dominic, but I don't know how far he'd go for his old roommate. And given the General's reputation, if I don't come through I could find myself in Afghanistan.

He sat at his desk staring at the phone, when he realized that all calls were likely recorded, or monitored. He rose and headed for the parking lot with his questionably secure cellphone in hand.

Chapter Four

Thursday, 4 P.M.

Vandenberg Air Force Base

Holding Cell

Gregory's conversation with the Air Force pilots hadn't gone well, and despite his martial arts prowess he'd been outnumbered and overcome. And seated on the ground, his hands secured behind his back with zip-ties, one of the airmen had returned to the chopper to call for assistance. Help had taken the form of four dark suited men in a pair of black SUV's that promptly placed a felt hood over his head and wordlessly carted him off to the unknown.

The sound deadened room that he'd been led to contained a solitary metal chair. The fact that there was no bed or toilet suggested that it had not been intended for protracted internment, so he took a seat and waited. The past few days have been full of this nonsense, he said to himself. All kinds of people have made me their prisoner and I haven't the slightest clue as to why. But I hope someone shows up soon, or there's gonna be a yellow pond on the floor.

He didn't have to wait long. The door opened, and with a pained expression he gazed up at one of the dark suited men who had taken him into custody.

"I have to pee real bad," he announced.

"That's your problem," the man bellowed.

"In a minute it's gonna be yours as well."

The man appeared to consider the prisoner's predicament, pivoted, and left the room. He returned moments later with a urinal and a pair of wire cutters. He quickly snipped the zip-ties, placed the urinal at Gregory's feet and nodded.

"That's better," Gregory sighed, pushing the filled urinal off to one side.

"State your name," the man ordered.

"You already know who I am, otherwise I wouldn't be here."

"Your name," the man repeated, angrily.

"Doctor Gregory McCraken, and you are?"

"What did you pass on to the Chinese?" he roared, ignoring the question.

"Chinese?"

"Answer the question."

"To the best of my knowledge, my only recent contact with anything Chinese was at a barf worthy restaurant."

"This isn't a joking matter. Answer the question."

"Look, I've been knocked unconscious, burned, almost

blinded, taken—without my consent—to what I assumed was a hospital, and then kidnapped by some Orientals. That's all I know."

"Then you admit to conspiring with the Chinese."

"I said, Orientals, but they could have been from anywhere in Asia."

"Be aware, espionage is a very serious crime."

"I've done nothing of the sort."

"Can you prove it?"

"How do you propose I do that?"

"I'll make it real simple. Tell me what you've told them about your project and we'll consider a lesser charge."

"There was no exchange of information."

"You expect me to believe that they went to the trouble of taking you from a secure facility for no reason at all?"

Gregory's level of tolerance had reached the red zone. I'm a victim, he thought, not the perpetrator of a national crime. "I demand to speak with General Louder," he spat.

"Is he part of this cabal?"

"That's it, I'm through talking," he hissed.

***

* * *

Midnight

In the absence of a bed or other suitable sleeping paraphernalia, Gregory had fallen asleep on the hard, concrete floor. And shortly after midnight he was awakened by a gentle shove from an unknown shoe. A single overhead fluorescent light had been ignited and he rubbed his eyes in the presence of the harsh, unexpected brightness.

"Dr. McCraken? General Louder sent me," the tall, black man announced.

Gregory sat upright, startled by the presence of Colonel Duke's imposing figure standing only inches from his trembling and aching body. "How did...?" he stuttered.

"We'd received a call that you'd been brought here. I commandeered the first available military jet."

"I've been handed back and forth so many times during the past seventy-two hours. How do I know you're not one of them?" he said, gesturing toward the door.

"Them?"

"The men in black, or whomever they are. And, by the way, what do I call you?"

"Colonel Bradley Duke, and I'm not one of them," he grinned, flipping his uniform's lapel.

"Where the hell am I?"

"Vandenberg Air Force Base."

"And why am I being accused of espionage?"

"I'm not aware of any accusation."

"Then I'm free to go?" he said, attempting to rise from the floor and falling back to the concrete.

"Not exactly."

"So you just dropped by to say hello?"

"It's complicated."

"Great, where have I heard that before," he mumbled.

"Apparently, you were found in the midst of some really bad actors. And given the sensitive nature of your work there are security concerns."

"Yeah," he sighed. "Already been down that road with a guy in a dark suit."

The Colonel tilted his head, rubbed his chin, and out of context, asked, "Do recall seeing anything odd the night of the mishap?"

"Odd? The whole event, as well as everything that's happened to me since has been damn odd."

"No, I mean, really strange."

"Gregory scratched his chin and replied, "Just a bright light." But during his brief, uncomfortable nap, he'd revisited the scene in a dreamlike fashion. And there had indeed been something terribly troubling that had flashed before his eyes between the appearance of the bright light and his apparent loss of consciousness. However, he wasn't willing to share the frightening vision with someone whose credentials had yet to be verified, and he wasn't entirely convinced that what he'd experienced had been anything more than an embellished fantasy.

"Let me see what I can do about having you released into my custody."

The Colonel left the room. Gregory heard the click of a lock, and the room returned to silence. He perched himself upon the metal chair and wished that he'd never left Scotland. But as he shifted on the chair's hard, gray surface, he was revisited by the startling image that had appeared in his dream. It was alarming, alluring, and so brief in duration that it'd strained his imagination. It's nature was just within reach, but a clear mental image was not. What did I see, and did I really see it, he wondered. He closed his eyes and tried to force a command performance, but it was not happening. And then the door opened, and he was thrust back into the world of sequestration.

Colonel Duke had returned, but he could see the shadow of another just outside the still open door. "Looks like you're going to be here awhile longer," he advised.

"Any special food requests?"

"Are you serious?" he shouted, jumping from the chair.

The Colonel frowned.

"This is no way to treat an employee."

"I'm sorry, but the Chinese thing is still a problem that we've yet to resolve."

"Shit," Gregory hissed, adding, "what about a bed, bathroom and a change of clothes?"

"A room is being prepared as we speak."

"What about the project?"

"It's been temporarily shut down."

Gregory did his best not to show concern, so he bent his head toward the floor. If they've sealed the facility, I'm not the only one who saw something. The female major had said that the high definition cameras hadn't been working, but I'd bet that she'd lied to cover up what they'd observed. There's no way they would have left their baby in the hands of one nighttime scientist without oversight. But like myself, they might not be able interpret what they'd seen, and they're probably taking the time to analyze the images.

"Oh," he replied.

"I'm due back at the Pentagon, and I'll discuss your

situation with the General."

"So I'm to remain the prisoner of, let me guess, the NSA?"

The Colonel gazed about the room, bent close to Gregory and whispered in his ear, "Task Force Orange."

"Never heard of it."

"Not surprised. This isn't their usual purview."

"Guess that makes me special."

"Here's the deal. If the Chinese are involved, there could be some operational implications, and that *is* their ball of wax."

"I don't understand anything you've said."

"Better that way. And you didn't hear any of it from me," the Colonel whispered, as he left the room.

Moments after the Colonel's departure, two men dressed in green, hospital scrubs entered, handcuffed him and guided him down a corridor to what he likened to a windowless, dormitory room. They unlocked the restraints, wheeled in a cart containing various food selections and a change of clothes, and without a word left and locked the room.

Chapter Five

Friday, August 4th

8 A.M.

The Pentagon

General Louder had been carefully thumbing through a classified report, when Colonel Duke gently knocked on his door. The General had been informed of his subordinates' imminent arrival and he looked up and called out, "Yes?"

"Colonel Duke, sir," he announced through the closed door.

"Get your ass in here, son," he replied.

The Colonel entered, stood before the familiar desk and waited.

"Well?" the General growled.

"I spoke with my contact…"

"I don't need that crap, Bradley. Just give me the facts. Is it the NSA?"

"Not directly."

"What the hell does that mean," the General blasted.

"Task Force Orange has him."

The General flew out of his chair and shouted, loud enough to be heard through his thick walls and into the outside corridor, "What the fuck do they want with him?"

"I don't know, sir."

"They're battlefield operations, and this has nothing to do with a war."

"All they would share is a Chinese connection."

The General took a deep breath, popped open a small, brown bottle of white tablets and swallowed two. "Did you ask your NSA friend about their involvement?"

"Yes, sir. "

"And?"

"He thinks it goes deep."

"C'mon, Bradley, I'm not a mind reader. What the hell does that mean?"

"He confirmed the existence of the NSA's no name subdivisions, and he thinks that it could belong to one of them."

"Not good enough. I need actionable intel before I steamroll into their domain and ask for help."

"What should I do?"

"Alright. Let's take a leap and assume that LS (Light Speed) belongs to one of their no names. Tell him to make it known that the Orange people have taken a project scientist, and we want him back, ricky tick."

"Can they make it happen?"

"Let's hope so."

"What about the Chinese?"

"Fuck-em."

"But..."

"Our guy, as well as the other scientists, have been vetted from every angle possible. He's not a spy."

The Colonel left his boss' office in a huff. He hadn't appreciated being treated like a child, despite having been forewarned about the General's outbursts before taking the position. But he knew that he had to suck it up, particularly since he hadn't been entirely truthful with his boss, and had neglected to mention his meeting with the scientist. He could feel the sweat on his palms as he walked the corridor, angry, yet grateful for the access he had been given to the General. Back in the day, he told himself, a black man would never have reached such an exalted position. But times had changed and, to some extent, political correctness had found its way into the military. He nodded to several officers as he continued his jaunt, wondering if their smiles had been transmitting a sense of oneness, or ridicule. Regardless, he thought, my mission objective is of primary importance.

Forty-five year old Bradley Duke had been born in Detroit Michigan. His parents, having taken the Christian family name of Duke at the time of emigration, had originated from Egypt prior to his birth. Despite their feigned Christianity, they had enrolled their young son in the Michigan Islamic Academy, claiming to anyone who'd asked that it had offered a superior educational experience, while their motive had been entirely centered around indoctrination. Like their parents, the Duke's had been raised Muslim. Bradley's father—Abasi—a believer and follower of a rather distorted interpretation of the Quran, had been employed by the Mukhābarāt (Egyptian Intelligence). A radical sub-faction of that organization had enticed Abasi to join their coalition. And since their views had dovetailed with his own, he had agreed. Together, they'd devised a plan to infiltrate the *Devil Nation*—the United States—at its highest level. There had been no timeline for the initiation of their plan, but Abasi had wasted no opportunity to impregnate his wife with the hope that their offspring could carry on where they could not. And to their surprise and joy, along came a male child who Abasi would indoctrinate into his own brand of Islam.

And now, as he carried his more than six-foot, dark skinned frame through the halls of the Devil Nation's seat of power, he smiled inwardly, as his deceased father's wishes were closer to fruition than ever.

Chapter Six

Friday, August 4th

8:15 a.m.

Gregory had spent the night undisturbed, save for the delivery of food and a change of clothing. He had been pleased to find that the accommodations were not unlike those of his underground facility, his prisoner status not withstanding. He had hoped that the conversation with General Louder's assistant would have gained his release, but as the hours passed he'd become ever more depressed. He had already moved the breakfast tray off to the side of the room, and was wondering how he would spend the remaining hours, days, weeks, or more, when there was a knock at his door.

"Yes?" he called out, as if the prisoner within controlled the comings and goings.

The door opened and a familiar face entered.

"Hi Greg," Iliana Franks, a red headed project co-worker and sometime squeeze said.

"What are you doing here?" he breathed.

"You're not happy to see me?" she replied, the sound of crackling coming from her ever-present chewing gum filled mouth.

He shrugged.

She took a seat on the edge of his cot and said, "I'd heard that there'd been an accident and you got burned."

"That's what they've claimed, but I feel OK."

"Want me to have a look?" she blushed.

"They sent you in to pump me for information, didn't they?"

"You took my shift, it could've been me," she grimaced.

"Not your fault."

"So, what happened?"

"I think there was a plasma burst."

"And you were too close."

"Seems so,"

"They told me that you were caught with some foreign nationals."

"That's it, small talk is over? And you believed them," he mumbled.

"People do all kinds of things for money," she shrugged.

"I'm not one of them. I was taken against my will. And why aren't you at work?"

"The lab is on lockdown since the accident. But tell

me about the Plasma burst. What did you see?"

He gazed at her askance, thinking, she knows what a plasma burst might look like. Only one reason she'd ask. She's wearing a recorder. He pointed to her chest, and lightly ran his hands over her clothed body.

"They made me do it," she mouthed, her eyes tearing up.

He motioned for her to rise from the bed. Feigning an affectionate embrace, he felt for the equipment and gently tore it from her chest, placing the miniature device between the cot's mattress and metal springs. He then whispered in her hear, "I need a favor."

"Anything," she returned.

"We're about the same height, I need your clothes."

"You want to trade places?" she giggled.

He nodded a yes.

"You, wearing a skirt," she guffawed.

"I'm a Scotsman, my people have worn kilts for centuries."

"What about your hair and stubble?"

"Do you still carry that crushable hat in your bag?"

"Of course, never know when a bad hair day will come calling."

"OK, I'll shave off the stubble, put on some of your

lipstick and pull the hat down as far as it will go."

"They'd have to be pretty dumb to buy that disguise, but if you're quick it might work."

"They'll likely want the recorder back, but we'll claim a bathroom emergency and hope for a window."

"And what about me?"

"You can wear my clothes."

"Not what I meant. I don't want to be accused of a Federal crime."

"You can say that I threatened you."

"I guess I owe you that much," she breathed, removing her blouse and long, black skirt, adding, "but have you considered that we're on a military base and that there are guards all over the place?"

"I can't stay here—I've gotta try."

The two sometime lovers switched clothes. She applied lipstick and a touch of makeup to his freshly shaven face. He pulled the hat down over his forehead and said, "Moment of truth," as he knocked on the door to be opened.

From outside, a voice replied, "What do you need?"

"I have a restroom emergency," she called out, quickly scurrying beneath the woolen blanket and turning her head to face away from the door.

"Use the one in the room," the voice returned.

"Not clean," she replied.

The door opened, and with his head down he quickstepped in the direction the guard had indicated. He hadn't had the time or the inclination to try on Iliana's shoes, and he prayed that the guard would not notice his loafers. The bathroom was only thirty or so feet beyond his room of confinement, and he entered and locked the door. He suspected that it had been intended for guests, since it was a single seat affair, rather than the usual military layout. Just as I'd hoped, he said to himself, a window. But the privacy glass insert was of the frosted variety, and he could not see outside without opening same. He flushed the commode several times to validate his presence, and used the palm of both hands to shove the initially locked window vertical. Feels like it's never been opened, he thought, as it eventually gave against his desperate shoving. To his surprise, there was a dumpster just below, and he was able to push through the opening and slide down the four foot distance to the top of the trash bin. The metal had been exposed to the morning sun, and it was hot against his bare legs. But he lowered himself to the ground and surveyed his surroundings. I have no idea where I am, or how to escape the base, he told himself. And the guard will be wondering why I haven't exited the bathroom. Oh crap, I forgot to lower the window.

He inched his way around the building that he'd just left, trying to get his bearings, when he spotted a camouflage attired young man carrying what appeared to be two large, laundry bags. Dirty clothes, he said to himself, ugh. But right now I'd wear anything that'd get me out of here. The airman was opening what appeared to be the back door of a one story hut, and as he scrambled to arrive before the door closed, he could see smoke rising from its roof. He caught the edge of the metal door just as it was about to bang shut, and carefully peeked inside. It looked and smelled like a commercial laundry. There were at least a dozen people inside, but no one paid attention to his presence, as he stood just inside the doorway. The bag carrying airman was nowhere to be seen, but there were tables of folded fatigues traveling the length of the room. He guessed that they were all of different sizes, but he didn't have the time to visit a dressing room, so he grabbed the nearest set and ducked behind a tall wooden crate to change. The shirt was an almost fit, but the pants were a little large, and without a belt they threatened to hit the deck. He'd felt a twinge of guilt for leaving his coworker and sometime girlfriend in the lurch and now, even more so, for disposing of her clothing, after having rubbed his makeup and lipstick covered face all over the black skirt. I'll have to buy her something nice, if I ever get out of this mess, he said to himself.

He left the laundry without consequence, the fingers of his left hand grasping the wasteband. No guards in the laundry, he mused, but I guess there are no secrets in there.

Walking away from the hut as confidently as possible, he spotted an eighteen wheeler parked at a loading dock. The truck was free of military markings, and for all intents and purposes appeared to be civilian in origin. I can see people offloading from its lowered gate, he observed. That's my ticket out of here ... I just have to figure out how to get on board without being seen. But suddenly, the sound of a siren appeared out of nowhere. Assuming that it was for him, he ran for the truck and hoisted himself inside of the now empty trailer. There was literally no place to hide within, but the trucker had been kind enough to leave a pile of musty moving blankets toward its rear, and he hastily wrapped himself inside a dark blue model, dragged the others on top and waited. Ten minutes later, the diesel engine roared to life and it began to move. Huddled beneath the blanket he thought, if they seal the base I'm a goner. And before the truck could reach the maximum speed allowed on base, its airbrakes groaned and it came to a complete halt. Gregory could neither hear nor see what was transpiring, but the urge to defecate came upon him without warning when the trailer's rear doors clanged apart. A pair of armed, helmeted men peered into the darkness as he trembled beneath the pile of blankets. But they'd apparently decided against entering, as they'd slammed the doors shut, followed by the return of the diesel clatter. He breathed a sigh of relief, but realized that his next order of business would involve a fresh change of clothes.

Chapter Seven

11 A.M.

Lompoc, California

The truck had traveled the roughly eight mile distance to the City of Lompoc, where the vehicle had idled for five minutes and then drove onward for another ten or so miles to a filling station. Gregory hadn't considered the risk of being locked inside the trailer, but with the sound of the engine no longer vibrating in his ears it had become a real concern. He tossed the blankets aside and ran for the rear doors, hoping that there was some form of emergency release. But it was dark inside, and he could only feel his way around. Fortunately, however, the Air Force guards had failed to securely close the trailer doors, and he was able use his body weight to force them open. He hit the ground running, not sure where he was going other than far from his captors. But he suddenly realized that he had no idea where he'd landed, other than the fact that he was in the parking lot of a Valero gas station. Assuming that he hadn't traveled very far from the base, and that military garbed personnel were not an uncommon sight, he strode into the office and asked for a map, hoping that the noxious odor emanating from his trousers would be ignored.

He had been experiencing frequent dreamlike flashbacks of the ill defined blue aura that he'd witnessed at the time of the presumed plasma burst. But he was no longer certain that what had led to his current state of affairs had actually been a release of plasma. And his scientific mind was screaming at him that something far more significant had occurred. I have to get back to the facility, he thought, as he left the office with the map in hand. The only way to define the true nature of what happened is to recreate the events that led up to the flash. But if Iliana was truthful, and the facility is on lockdown, there will be armed guards around the clock. However, I still think that they'd lied to me when they'd claimed that the cameras had not been operational. They had to have been functioning for them to have retrieved me so rapidly. And if that's true, they saw what had happened. If I'm right about that blue aura, someone on the other side of those cameras recognized the signature as well. For that reason alone, I doubt that the lab has been shut down. It may be sealed to our team of investigators, but not to the government.

He walked out to the road where his presence was obscured by a large sign. Opening the map, he determined that the distance from Lompoc to Nevada was approximately 585 miles. Hmm, it would take roughly eleven hours by car, he determined. I have no money or credit cards, and that leaves only one option. There were two trucks stopped at the station, the one he'd just departed and a newish cab lacking a trailer, whose driver was filling his tank. He approached the latter.

"Where you headed?" he asked.

The driver gazed up, spat out a dark brown liquid, and replied, "Comin' off a long haul, an' I'm headin' home."

"I need a ride."

The driver examined him from head to toe. "You ain't awol, are yah?"

He realized that the man had made a connection between his clothing and the nearby Air Force base, and he replied, "I'm on leave and my car broke down."

The man looked away, spat again, and said, "Ah'm headin' to Carson City. Will that help?"

"Perfect. You can let me off on the way."

"It's a long ride, could use the company."

Gregory climbed up and into the passenger side of the cab, as the driver paid for his fuel. And while he took a moment to consider his good fortune, a pair of military Hummers rolled into the station. They did not approach the pumps and appeared to be waiting for something or someone. He slid down as far as the seat would allow, when he noticed a well-worn Stetson resting upon the driver's side dashboard. He hesitated, and then reached for it, placing it down over his face as if blocking the sun in preparation for a nap.

"Hope you don't mind," he said, when the driver returned.

"Nah, the damn thing just makes me sweat. The old lady gave it to me for Christmas. Said it was to protect me from the sun, but I think she got tired of lookin' at my bald spot," he laughed, as the engine belched out a giant puff of black smoke and the truck began to roll.

The hat now back on the dashboard, Gregory watched the Humvees from the corner of his eye. And soon they, as well as the filling station, were out of sight. He looked over at the middle-aged driver, a non descriptive male, whose ruddy complexion and protruding belly suggested many years of excessive alcohol and cheap food. But who am I to judge, he thought. I'm just a guy who came to this country to get ahead, and look where I am now—a falsely accused fugitive with shit in my pants.

The driver, who'd called himself Simon, just Simon, hadn't contributed much in the way of conversation. He hadn't commented about Gregory's Scottish accent, nor had he asked about his role in the military, and at some point during the journey he'd stopped talking altogether. Gregory took the silence as his opportunity to get some much needed rest. Eleven hours later, following several bathroom and fuel stops, as well as time out for more greasy hamburgers—courtesy of Simon—than any human should have consumed, he awakened to an increasingly familiar landscape.

***

Midnight

Carson City, Nevada

Gregory had slept through the majority of the trip, the diesel's constant droning serving as a facilitator. He hadn't planned on going all the way to Carson City, but when Simon announced that they had reached the end of the road, they shook hands and parted ways in front of a Greyhound bus station. And as a further act of kindness, Simon had handed the penniless airman a twenty dollar bill for the service that Gregory was allegedly providing for his country. He'd felt a major stab of guilt, but since his pockets were empty he'd gladly accepted the donation.

He hadn't discussed his ultimate destination with

Simon, but he'd guessed that the facility was still a fair distance away. And a review of his map by streetlight had revealed that there were still at least two-hundred and forty some odd miles left to the journey.

The scientists at the underground facility had never been given their exact location, their arrivals and departures having been accomplished in the dark of night, via a van with blacked out windows. But their natural curiosity had brought them to the conclusion that their lab had been built within the confines of a large, abandoned mine shaft. And by a lengthy process of elimination, incorporating time based distance calculations, odors, noise and the absence thereof, they had collectively determined that their location was somewhere in the Battle Mountain region of Nevada.

He stretched out on a bench and hoped that he would not be mugged if he fell asleep. But the larger issue at hand was the distance yet to be traveled. I'm certain that the bus fare will be more than the twenty in my pocket, he said to himself, as he gazed upwards at the star filled sky. And what's the likelihood of crossing paths with another kind soul like Simon, he wondered.

Finding a comfortable position on the bench had been no small task, but in the process he'd realized that the alleged burns that the government doctor had spoken of, assuming that they'd really existed, weren't quite as bad as had been described. He'd felt no discomfort moving about on the wooden planks, felt none of the characteristic itching that accompanies the healing process and, in general, felt just fine. He couldn't recall when, but the bandages had fallen off leaving no obvious raw skin behind. Maybe it had all been a ruse to cover up what had really happened, he said to himself.

Chapter Eight

Office of General Enoch Louder

The General's desk was littered with a mass of documents and folders that he'd been neglecting, as he'd been consumed with the debacle created by his projects' missing scientist. At the onset, he'd been informed that he was to babysit the underground laboratory from a security standpoint, but when he'd inquired about the nature of the research he'd been informed that it was of no consequence to him. It hadn't been a gleeful moment, being told that the knowledge exceeded his pay grade, but he had accepted the responsibility as part of the job description. But the absent scientist, whose name he had only recently learned, had presented a new wrinkle. And his natural curiosity had been shifted into high gear.

If I'm to assume responsibility for Dr. McCraken's disappearance, I damn well should know what in tarnation he was tasked with performing, he thought. I'm not a child. I have a top secret (TS/SCI) security clearance, so what in hell could there be above that, he wondered. And then he searched his memory for the events that had led to his assignment. He recalled that it had begun with a visit from a well respected senator. The man had arrived without an appointment, but due to his involvement with senate finance and appropriations the General had agreed to see him. The senator had spoken of many advanced projects, some of which the General had been familiar with, while others had been entirely foreign. The Senator, by way of simple conversation, had asked the General if he had any knowledge of physics or astronomy, and the General had implied that he did. After all, he'd thought, I have a masters from Princeton in electrical engineering, close enough. The senator, on the other hand, had a degree in astrophysics, and he took the General on a verbal journey that had left him cold, confused and feeling inadequate. But that disturbing discourse had been followed by a proposition, a quid-pro-quo of sorts. If the General would agree to watch over one of the senator's pet projects, the senator would make certain black funds available for something dear to the military. General Louder had brightened at the offer, as it would afford him the leverage needed for the development of a portable railgun that he'd been dreaming about. But now, as he squirmed in the chair—a bout of chronic hemorrhoids rising to a crescendo—he'd realized that he'd never really asked about the nature of the senator's project. The senator had implied that it had something to do with astrophysics, and rather than admit that he hadn't a clue or even a minor understanding of the mumbo jumbo he'd been spouting, he'd simply agreed to take on the responsibility that had been presented as requiring the presence of several armed military guards and no real physical presence of his own. But now his ass was on the line. The Senator had called and left several messages, even going so far as to appear at his office while he was spending more time than he'd wished in the men's room. Thankfully, the senator's schedule had precluded waiting for the General to finish his business. But the man had left a sealed, eyes only envelope on his desk that contained an angry message demanding a meeting. The General had been dreading the inevitable, but it was time to face the music; the senator was due to arrive within minutes. And before he'd had the opportunity to take a deep breath, the intercom announced the senator's presence.

The General rose, opened the door and feigned a smile.

"General," Senator Raymond Washburn nodded authoritatively, as he walked straight for the metal sideboard cart that sat to the right of Louder's desk. He lifted a bottle of Remy Martin Louis XIII Cognac that the

General had received as a gift and had been saving for a special occasion, and poured more than two fingers into a cut crystal glass.

Louder watched in amazement, as the man guzzled the entire glass in one gulp, and said, "How was it?"

"Pretty good," the Senator replied.

"At three thousand dollars a bottle it'd better be good."

"You haven't tried it?"

Louder shook his head with a, no, as he walked toward his desk and took a seat.

"You have a problem," the Senator grinned.

"And what would that be?"

"You know what I'm talking about."

"The lockdown, I assume."

"And the missing physicist."

"I had nothing to do with the facility's closure."

The Senator still had not taken a seat, and he bent across the General's desk until their faces almost touched. "Where the hell is the fucking scientist?" he shouted.

I've dealt with all manner of vile politicians, and if Raymond Washburn thinks that he can rustle my feathers he's got another thing coming, Louder thought, as he raised a brow and said, "I believe that he's with Task Force

Orange."

"What the hell do they want with him?" he growled.

"I was hoping you might have the answer to that mystery."

The Senator backed off of the desk and began to pace the room. But he stopped in the middle, sighed and said, "Things are getting out of hand. I don't have access to them."

"Are you ready to tell me what this project's all about?"

"I can't."

"And why is that?" Louder asked, toying with a yellow number two pencil.

"Because I really don't know."

Louder exhaled, ejecting a whoosh of air that could have blown any loose papers off of his desk, had there been any, and hissed, "You fed me all that bravo sierra about a top secret project, alluded to an offer of funding for whatever, and you had no idea what was going on a hundred feet below ground?"

"Sadly, I am only the errand boy."

"Whose project is it, anyway?"

Senator Washburn lowered his body to a chair, ran a hand across his slicked back gray hair, and said, in a subdued tone, "I'd been approached by someone from the Intelligence community who'd mentioned   that they had something that was too hot for them to handle directly."

"So you'd figured it was OK to burn me?"

"I was told that it was beyond top secret, and that it required a discrete military guard."

"I need to know which agency is behind it," Louder snapped.

The Senator hesitated, rubbed his eyes, and mumbled, "I'm not at liberty to say."

"You've put me in an untenable position, Senator. I can't begin to make sense out of this mess without knowing with whom I'm in bed with," he said, emphasizing his frustration with a fist thrust against the desktop.

"I can tell you that it's not the CIA."

"So now we're playing charade?"

The Senator lowered his head, but did not otherwise respond.

"OK. By your silence I'm guessing that the NSA put you up to this."

"No, not exactly them," he stuttered.

"C'mon, Senator, this room isn't bugged, and I'm tired of playing games with you. Spit it out."

"Are you absolutely certain that there are no listening

devices?"

"The room is swept once a day."

"They don't have a name."

"Who doesn't?"

"The people behind the project."

Louder sank back into his chair, as he glared at the man seated across from him. He didn't tell me anything I didn't already suspect, he said to himself, but hearing the words is still a shocker. And that means that it's a black project and that they were looking for deniability, a scapegoat, if things were to go south. I don't like being the patsy. If I'm going to take the fall for those bastards, I sure as hell need to know what they were doing down there.

He rose from the desk, stared at the now opened bottle of Remy, a ray of sunlight causing it to glow amber in its Baccarat crystal enclosure, and decided to sample his gift. He poured a less generous serving into a tumbler and took a sip. "Not bad," he admitted, turning to the Senator and adding, "want another jolt?"

"No thanks," the Senator breathed.

"So here's how it's gonna play out," Louder announced, emptying his glass with a grimace. "You're going to get in touch with your *intelligence* person and find out what they've been doing in that laboratory, and why it's been sealed. Understood?"

"I'd heard that there'd been an accident of some kind," the Senator offered.

"*Some kind* isn't good enough. I need details."

"I'll see what I can do."

"Remember, we're in this together. If the rain begins to fall, you're gonna get wet."

The normally arrogant Senator left with his tail between his legs, and Louder watched the departure from behind his desk. Well, Louder thought, that asshole needed to be knocked off of his pedestal. And with that thought still hanging in the air, he reached for the phone and dialed Colonel Duke's number.

Bradley Duke answered on two rings.

"Any news?" Louder asked.

"Not yet."

"Getting the intel I need should be second nature for your guy."

There was a brief pause, and then Bradley replied, "He hasn't been returning my calls."

"You didn't per chance leave a voicemail with your request?"

"No sir.'

"Then why would he be avoiding you."

Another pause, and then the bombshell reply, "He hasn't been home for days, and his wife is crawling up the wall."

"Maybe he's undercover somewhere."

"He's not a field officer … as I've said in the past, he's an analyst."

"Believe what you will, but in my book your Mr. North is a spook."

Louder could hear the Colonel's gasp, and then his stuttered reply of, "How do you know his name?"

"We both have our contacts, but mine are more powerful. But in this instance it was a simple process of deduction, and a little assistance from The Twenty-fifth Air Force (previously designated as AFISRA; Air Force Intelligence). And you're wondering why I couldn't obtain the intel by my own means?"

"The thought had crossed my mind."

"Where are you right now?"

"Down the corridor."

"We need some face-time, ASAP."

"On my way."

Chapter Nine

Saturday, 8 A.M.

Carson City, Nevada

Gregory had been awake for the majority of the night, his thoughts shifting from the details of his absurd predicament to the events leading up to it. The notion that he, a dedicated scientist and staunchly honest person, would violate the trust implied by his position was to him, unfathomable. But as the sun began its lazy rise above the horizon, his personal conflict had been replaced by the Battle Mountain quest. Arrivals and departures from the facility had been monitored by armed military personnel, and he had no way of knowing if the alleged shuttering of the lab had been accompanied by the disappearance of the security detail. And then there was the issue of power. If the project has been sealed, he told himself, they may have shut off the power. I can't hope to recreate the events leading up to the flash without power, lots of power. After all, at the time of the incident in question, the accelerator was drawing more power than the entire city of Las Vegas uses in a month. And last, but not least, are those allegedly inoperative cameras. Well, none of that's of concern if I can't find the means to get there.

He rose from the bench for the umpteenth time since he'd claimed it as his own, yawned and stretched. He'd considered calling Iliana to arrange for a wire transfer of funds, but aside from the fact that he wasn't certain that she'd even speak with him after his hasty departure, he'd reasoned that there was a possibility that she was still being held at Vandenberg. No, he'd said to himself, there has to be another way. But after realizing that the twenty dollar bill in his pocket would have to be spent to fill his empty stomach, he began to reconsider the concept of hitchhiking.

He had abandoned the bench and had begun walking in search of breakfast, when he came across the Cracker Box Diner. Scrambled eggs, bacon, toast and two cups of coffee later, he found himself surveying the early morning patrons. Most of the customers had their eyes glued to their food, but one burly, bearded, middle aged male locked gaze with him, and he smiled. Gregory pretended to sip from his empty coffee cup, and smiled back. The beard waved for him to approach, and Gregory questioned his motive, but figuring that there were numerous witnesses to any potential nefarious act, he paid the check and walked toward the man's seat.

The beard extended his right hand and said, "Staff Sergeant Gimmler."

Gregory shook the offered hand, but took a moment before he introduced his fictitious self. He'd had some familiarity with the various ranks in the U.S. Military, and had even befriended a senior airman from Travis AFB before the man had been shipped out of the country. So he replied, "Senior airman, Raymond Gold, sir,"

"You from Vandenberg?" the man asked.

"Uh, no, Travis," he fibbed.

"Did my thing at Edwards ... but that was some time ago," the man said, turning to drain his coffee cup.

Gregory did not know where the conversation was going, so he assumed the silent role and waited for the man to carry the exchange.

"You on leave, Raymond?"

"Sir, yes sir."

"You can cut the sir crap. These days I'm a GC/ carpenter. Live around here?"

This was the opening he'd been waiting for, and he replied, "No. Trying to get back to Battle Mountain."

"You got a wife back there?"

"No, family," he lied.

"You looking for a ride?"

"Yeah, my car broke..."

"Say no more. This is your lucky day, son. I'm just

startin' a renovation out that way—my truck's outside."

"Much appreciated," Gregory grinned.

"Anything for a fellow ground pounder (non flyer)."

The Sergeant paid the check, blew a kiss to an attractive waitress, and left the Diner with Gregory in tow.

***

10.00 A.M.

The Sergeant's truck was a shiny, heavy duty, red dually with a hammer and saw logo painted on the driver and passenger side doors. The interior was about as fancy as it gets and it smelled new.

"What a beauty," Gregory said, running a hand over the pleather dash.

"Thanks, picked her up two weeks ago. This is her first work trip."

"You from Carson City?"

"Nope, LA. But I go where the work takes me. And this month and next it's Battle Mountain."

"Big job?"

"Single family home that needs a second story."

"Just one person to accomplish that?"

"No way," he laughed, adding, "I got a crew, and they

should be arriving on site about now. So sit back an' relax, we got about three or so hours of driving ahead."

Chapter Ten

Saturday, 10 A.M.

The Pentagon

Office of General Enoch Louder

Colonel Duke had just entered Louder's office and had taken a seat before the General's desk. Louder paid no attention to the man's presence, as he rummaged through a stack of folders stamped TOP SECRET in red letters. Bradley, feeling somewhat uncomfortable by the uncharacteristic silence, cleared his throat and said, "You wanted to see me, sir?"

Louder slid the folders into an open drawer and replied, "We need to talk about Mr. North."

"What would you like to know?"

"I'll come right to the point, is he capable of duplicity?"

"Isn't everyone," he said without thinking, instantly regretting the outburst.

Louder's lips formed a wide grin, and he said, "No, only those with hidden motives."

Bradley Duke felt a chill travel down his spine, and he wondered if his grand charade was about to come to a climax.

"I—I meant the..."

"We'll discuss your intent at another time. Right now I'm interested in Mr. North and his motives."

"I've known him for a long time, sir. I never got the impression that he might someday turn."

Louder rose from the chair, his hemorrhoids had become an increasing problem, and at that moment they were itching like hell. He wasn't about to scratch his ass in front of his subordinate, so he marched about the room, hoping that the movement would ease his suffering. He'd been told before that they might require surgical attention, and that time was rapidly approaching. Finally, he stopped before the beverage cart—his back to the Colonel—turned, and said, "The best double agents never make it obvious."

"Sir?"

"I was referring to Mr. North."

"Is there something more that I should be doing?"

"Make a visit to his wife and feel her out. Maybe he just needed a break."

"Sir, if the NSA can't find him, I sense that any further investigation will prove fruitless."

The general returned to his desk, the pruritic attack having subsided, and carefully lowered his weight onto the leather chair. He smiled at the Colonel, and then removed a red folder from a bottom desk drawer and held it several inches above his blotter. "Know what this is?" he asked.

The Colonel hesitated, but replied, "A red folder."

"Cute. But it's a very special folder containing some startling information."

The Colonel felt his pulse rise, as a few droplets of sweat began to form on his forehead. "About Dominic, I mean, North?" he asked.

The General ceremoniously placed the folder onto the desk's surface, all the while maintaining his false smile, and replied, "Even more alarming then your Mr. North."

"I don't understand," the Colonel said, but his intuition suggested otherwise.

The General's right hand disappeared beneath one edge of his desk, and a finger pressed a silent alarm button. Seconds later, the office door flung open and in marched two armed, military guards. The General motioned for them to remain by the door, tapping the folder as he explained, "It appears that you've been withholding critical information."

The Colonel moved forward, toward the edge of his seat and replied, "I've told you all I know about Dominic North."

"Negative. This has nothing to do with Mr. North," he

bellowed, continuing, "and everything to do with you."

The Colonel shook inwardly and prepared for the worst.

"No clue? OK, here's the skinny. Someone has been looking into your security clearance..."

"*My* clearance, sir?" he interrupted.

"It appears that there are some discrepancies."

"Such as?"

"You've claimed to be a Christian, but there's no supporting evidence."

"I-I'd converted."

"We're gonna need proof."

"Why is it so important?"

"You know the answer to that, but in case you're still wondering, it suggests that you've lied. And until such time as you can present credible proof, you're security clearance is inactive, cancelled, mothballed."

The Colonel was speechless. He'd always feared that his house of cards would someday come tumbling down, but he never thought that his religion would be the cause. He had gone through the motions in his hometown of Detroit, and had contacted the local diocese to discuss the requirements for conversion, and the process had been initiated. But for reasons that he could not recall, he had not completed the program. And now it had come back to haunt.

Chapter Eleven

1:30 P.M.

Battle Mountain

The contractor had dropped Gregory off at the Owl Club and Casino in the town of Battle Mountain, a locale that had been lovingly called the Armpit of America. And as he gazed up and down the street he understood the meaning behind the phrase. Since his trips to and from the underground facility had been secretive, none of the scientists had had definitive knowledge of their whereabouts, but there had been clues. However, they had never set foot in the town.

Nice place, he said to himself sarcastically, as he walked along Front Street. I have no real understanding of the local geography, and that's going to make finding the facility a real challenge. Mama's Pizza was down the street from the Casino, and he walked in for a slice.

A man behind the counter quickly hid a magazine that he'd been perusing and said, "What would you like?"

"A slice of pizza," he replied.

"I can sell you a whole pie, but we don't do slices."

Gregory checked the prices, and said, "Forget the pizza, I'll have a Coke."

"You a soldier, or somethin'?" the man asked.

Gregory had become accustomed to the stolen fatigues, and replied, "Air Force."

Pizza stores are usually full of young people, especially at lunchtime, he thought.   Where are all the Armpit residents, he wondered, realizing that he was the only non-employee in the establishment.   He took the drink and stood by the counter, trying to start up a conversation.

"Quiet today?" he noted.

"Nope."

"Is it usually busier at this time?"

"Nope."

"The street is pretty empty, where is everybody?"

The man shrugged, wiped his hands on a leg of his stained, blue overalls and replied, "Workin' at the mine or the Casino. There ain't much else."

The word, mine, had caught his attention, and he said, "What kind of mine?"

"Gold."

"Is there more than one mine in these parts?"

"Yup, but they don't all produce."

"Anything unusual about them?"

The man had a puzzled expression on his face, so Gregory tried harder. "I've got a cousin that works for the government in some kind of secret, underground factory around here. Any idea where that might be?"

The man scratched his chin, a blank expression on his nondescript face, and sat down on a stool behind the counter. "Don't know nothin' about no government thing."

Gregory took that to mean that the man knew more than he'd been willing to admit, to a stranger. Normally, he would have loosened the man's tongue with a few bills, but his pocket was running on empty, calling for a different approach. "Have there been any female, government employees here about town?"

"Your cousin's a girl?"

Gregory nodded affirmatively.

"I woulda' noticed that."

"Yeah, she's a looker. Matter of fact, she's single and you're just the kind of rugged guy she's been lookin' for."

The counterman appeared interested, so Gregory pushed onward with, "I'd introduce you, but I'm not sure where to find her."

The man rubbed his scalp and appeared to hesitate, but his hormones apparently took over and he asked, "How old is she?"

"Twenty-four."

He nodded for him to come closer, and Gregory

leaned across the counter.

"Me and some friends go out huntin' sometimes, an' one time we spotted a couple of mean lookin' fuckers standing out in the middle of nowhere."

"That's it?"

"They was wearin' dessert boots, you know, like yours."

"Where are you going with this?"

"They had big ass rifles as well, like they was guardin' somethin'."

"But there was nothing obvious to guard, you're saying?"

The man nodded a, yes.

"Can you tell me where this was?"

The man withdrew a local map from beneath the register and drew a line from the end of Front Street to the location of his sighting.

"How far is that from here?"

"Twenty minutes if you're drivin', an 'bout an hour on foot."

"By the way, what exactly were you hunting for?"

"Mostly rabbit. But, hey, there ain't nothin' more than a pile of wood sittin' in the sand. So I don't know if that's what you're lookin' for."

"Worth having a look-see."

The man nodded and said, "If you find your cousin, bring her around."

"You bet," he replied, as he turned and left the establishment.

Two guards standing in the middle of nowhere, he pondered, as he walked down Front Street. They weren't out there for a suntan.

Ninety sweaty minutes later he'd reached the designated map coordinates. In the distance he could see a dilapidated shack that appeared ready to fall, but the remainder of the vista was made up of sand and scrub brush, and there were no guards to be seen. He walked another twenty minutes until reaching the shanty, thinking that it might be camouflaging the entry to the lab, but no such luck. It was just what it had appeared to have been, an old, decaying miner's residence. How could pizza boy have missed this, he wondered. But perhaps this is what he'd meant by a pile of wood. And if the military had been here, there had to have been something of importance, he thought, as he kicked the dirt in front of the house. Hmm, this shithole might have been recently created to appear ancient. He reversed course and took another look at the house. Inside, he began kicking at the floorboards until one slat showed signs of movement. He dropped to his knees and, with his only available tool—a tarnished quarter —began an attempt to pry loose one end of the board. This is not going to work, he told himself, as the coin fell through the opening between two boards and disappeared. But the fallen silver disc had made a barely audible clink when it had come to rest, and he sat back to consider its significance.

Either I was hallucinating, he speculated, or the quarter hit something metallic. Of course, given that this was a mining zone, there could be any number of metal items beneath this structure. But since I am sitting roughly on top of the suggested map coordinates, and since there are no guards, I have to assume that this shanty had been placed here to discourage unwanted visitors like myself. These floorboards have to go. But then he had a thought, and he raced outside to examine the foundation, thinking, maybe I can get beneath the boards. Sure enough, the would-be cabin had been supported with concrete blocks, several of which had begun to sink, accounting for the building's slight tilt. But there was just enough room for him to crawl beneath the flooring, the light penetrating from above revealing the quarter's resting place. Due to the soft ground and the weight of the building bearing down upon the blocks, the closer he got to the coin the tighter the space became. The risk was too great. He calculated, that if the structure were to shift more than an inch, he would be pinned down, and would probably spend the next several hours suffocating beneath the hut. He backed out in search of an alternate approach. One hour later, after probing the ground around the site, he uncovered a short metal bar and a broken shovel. He returned to the shack's interior and began hacking away at the floorboards. But just as he was about to remove the second of two boards, the beating of an overhead helicopter —its blades whipping up the dust covered flooring—caused him to freeze. This can't be good, he said to himself, as he resigned himself to capture.

***

Once again, he found himself in the midst of two angry helicopter pilots.

"Hands behind your head," one helmet wearing man ordered.

Gregory complied, and sat with his back against what was left of a wall.

"You Air Force?" the man asked, while his partner

stood at the open doorway.

Gregory hesitated, trying to divine the correct answer. And given his stolen Air Force fatigues, he figured that he had little to lose and replied, "Yeah, out of Travis."

"What the hell are you doing way out here?" the pilot demanded, his body still rigid, his weapon unwavering.

"Lookin' for gold."

"Well, you won't find it in here…"

"Senior Airman Raymond Gold," he chimed in, using the same fake moniker that he'd employed with the carpenter.

"Airman Raymond Gold is looking for gold," that's hysterical, the pilot said, with a straight face.

"Did I violate a restricted area?"

"You sure did."

"There were no signs."

The man shrugged, as his partner stifled a chuckle.

"How did you know I was here, anyway?"

"Ground sensors."

"So now what?"

"We RTB (return to base) and let the MIB (men in black) do their thing."

Gregory wasn't certain that he'd understood the acronyms, but it had been clear from the man's demeanor that he was not home free. Think quick, he said to himself, as the pilot motioned for him to rise from the ground. "C'mon, guys, it was an honest mistake. Can't you give a ground pounder a break?"

The pilot motioned for him to sit tight, while he returned to the chopper. Gregory slid back down to the floorboards and chewed on a fingernail. I'm in deep shit if they take me back to their base, after all, I'm impersonating an airman, I'm officially on the run, and I'm not supposed to be here. But as he was mentally planning for a visit to the brig, or whatever it was they had in store for him, the chopper's blades began to spool up and the aircraft departed, leaving behind a very confused physicist.

Chapter Twelve

Saturday, 3 P.M.

Following his departure from Louder's office, Colonel Duke had mindlessly walked the halls of the Pentagon. He'd been in a daze. The general had given him a difficult, if not impossible task. How can I provide proof for something that had never happened, he'd asked himself, before deciding to leave work and head for home.

At the time of his Pentagon posting he'd been living in an inexpensive rental apartment in Arlington, but soon thereafter he'd acquired a rent to own condo on Arlington Ridge Road, Pentagon City. It had been a two bedroom furnished affair from the get-go, and he had done little to alter its period decor. Friends had always been few and far between, and while he'd presented himself as a Catholic, he'd continued to follow the tenets of the Muslim faith in the privacy of his own home. For that solitary reason, female companionship had been all but ignored. Housecleaning was a chore that he'd never appreciated, and he had considered hiring a cleaning service, but feared that the presence of a stranger might somehow pierce the web of secrecy that he'd constructed around his religious persuasion. Domestic maintenance fell within his purview.

As was his routine, he'd checked the mail upon arriving home. The usual stack of junk mail—solicitations for items of little use—occupied the top of the pile. He unlocked the door to the condo, dumped the load onto an antique table, and headed to the kitchen for a glass of ice water. That accomplished, he checked the time, rolled out his prayer carpet and performed the usual. A shower came next, and following that he flipped through the day's mail. The advertisements went straight into the trash, but beneath the remaining utility bills was an oddity. He examined the envelope. It brought back childhood memories of Detroit, as an old friend's name sat atop the return address label. He carried it into the living room and stretched out on the mustard colored, brocade couch. Shoeless, he tore open the envelope and began to read:

My Dear friend Bradley, or should I say, Akil,

Much time has passed since we last shared a pot of tea and I miss my friend. But I digress. You are probably wondering how I'd managed to locate you. I am not that crafty, but others are. It was never clear why you'd disappeared from our mosque, but it had been rumored that you'd converted to Catholicism, and you must know that there are those that will no longer welcome your presence. But despite the rumor, the Imam has asked me to contact you, he said that it is urgent.

Your friend always, Baba.

Baba Aboud, Akil's junior by less than one year, had arrived in Detroit around the same time as Akil's family. The elder Aboud had been a Syrian mining executive with expertise in phosphate extraction. And he had initially come to the U.S. for the purpose of brokering the sale of his company's production. But a short while after his arrival the Syrian civil war had begun to take hold and he'd applied for asylum.

Despite their different backgrounds, the boys shared a Muslim heritage and they had become fast friends. They'd attended the same Islamic school, played together on an almost daily basis and had confided their dreams and aspirations. However, Akil had been made aware of his father's unorthodox version of Islam right from an early age, and his father had frequently contradicted the teachings that had been impressed upon his young son. But this aspect of his life had been kept apart from his friend Baba, and it had led to frequent bouts of depression and rage for the young Akil.

Baba, on the other hand, had been a happy go lucky child who'd harbored little in the way of future aspirations beyond the Seven-Eleven type store owned by his family.

As young children often do, the friends occasionally fantasized about their grownup futures, with Baba portraying himself as a candy store mogul. Akil, however, had no such ambitions, and had yet to have been made aware of his preordained destiny.

With the recent development regarding my security clearance, I should destroy any evidence of my past life, he reminded himself, as he burned the letter over the stove's blue flame. But the Imam knows the truth that he'd sworn never to reveal. He must be troubled by something of great of importance, otherwise, he would not have taken the risk of contacting me, even through a conduit. I will not reply to Baba, but I must find a way to clandestinely communicate with my mentor.

Chapter Thirteen

Saturday, 4:30 P.M.

Battle Mountain

Gregory dusted off the seat of his fatigues and rose to a standing position. Following the helicopter's departure he had remained in the dilapidated cabin for a good thirty minutes trying to decide whether the pilots had been baiting him, waiting for him to do something that would justify his seizure. But a few glimpses of the outside world had revealed that they and their aircraft had truly taken leave.

Good thing they hadn't made note of the missing floorboards, he said to himself, as he considered replacing them. But he had come with a purpose in mind, and he set about removing two more slats. Wait a minute, he said to himself, the pilot mentioned ground sensors. Could they be hidden around the perimeter of this dump, or are they beneath my feet, he wondered. Well, they already know about my presence, and I don't have the time to look for them, so here goes. He'd removed a total of six boards, creating enough space for him to reach down and clear the dirt and sand from the metal plate that his coin had struck.

This thing is thick, he thought, as his fingers examined

the raised edges. And thick means heavy. But that's not the only problem, he admitted, realizing that the steel panel extended beyond his outstretched arm's reach. This has to be the entrance to the facility's elevator, but I can't move the panel by myself—they must have used heavy machinery to put it in place.

Frustrated, he stared at the dull, gray metal sheet for a few moments longer and decided to cover it back up. He left the shack and headed back to the Armpit.

Even if I could somehow borrow a front loader, how could I get it past the alleged ground sensors and then into the shack without destroying the entire structure, he wondered. Think, Gregory, you haven't really planned this out very well, have you, he chided himself. And whom can I ask for help, when the only person I've encountered is the vacuous pizza guy. We'll, on second thought, he might be dumb enough to lend a hand.

By the time he'd reached Front Street the sun had begun to set. Despite his education and intelligence, he'd been overcome with the notion of finding his way back into the laboratory and, as such, had given little thought to the big picture. His pockets were almost completely devoid of cash, he had no credit cards and no friends to rely upon. I've reached hobo status, he lamented, as he looked about for a safe place to spend the night out in the open. And as he walked the street, acutely aware of its ghostly appearance, he meandered past the pizza shop. The young proprietor was sweeping the floor, so he did an about face, walked in and stood by the counter.

"Gettin' ready to close," the man drawled, without taking his eyes from the floor and dustpan held in his right hand.

Gregory nodded his understanding.

"Find yer cousin?"

"Not yet."

"And the place ah told you 'bout?"

"I think so, but there weren't any guards. Just a beat up shack."

"Weren't nothin' important out there before," the man declared, gazing quizzically at Gregory.

Life out here must be pretty boring, Gregory thought, as he watched the man dump the dustpan into a large trash bag. Let's see if he takes the bait.

"I found something real suspicious," he said.

The man cocked his head and asked, "Like what?"

"Based upon your account, the shack is a recent addition. So you gotta ask, what the heck is a newly placed, yet dilapidated shack doing out in the middle of nowhere?"

The man scratched his head and nodded.

"But there's more. The dump has a false floor and there's a heavy metal plate beneath it."

"Metal plate?" the man repeated.

Gregory nodded, yes.

The man's eyes widened, and he blurted, "Treasure. Gotta be something valuable underneath."

"That's what I was thinking. But the plate is too heavy for one, or even two men to move or lift."

The man hesitated, and Gregory felt that he could almost sense the fellow's limited brain cells going into overdrive. But, finally, he said, "Wanna cut me in?"

"Why should I?"

"I told you where it was."

"Even if I agree, I can't see how we can move that plate."

"How big is it?"

"Just a guess, but I'd estimate it to be ten by ten feet wide, and more than an inch thick."

"Gimme a minute," the man said, as he wandered to the back of the shop.

Gregory leaned against the counter and waited. He hadn't told the fellow about the ground sensors, or his encounter with the helicopter pilots. And there was a good chance that they'd be back if heavy equipment arrived on scene. Well, first things first, he said to himself, as the young man returned.

"Got an idea."

"I'm listening," Gregory said.

"Got a friend who works for a buildin' contractor, and he's got some machines."

"The contractor will allow him to use one?"

"Not exactly, but if a machine were to roll out at night and come back before sunup, who'd know?"

"I'm afraid that any machine large enough to move that plate will destroy the building."

"We'd be workin' in the dark. Ain't nobody gonna notice until the next day, an' by then we'll be long gone."

Gregory extended his hand. The man, apparently unaccustomed to handshakes, stared at it but took the cue and grinned."

"My name's Raymond."

"Jeb," the pizza man exclaimed.

"There are some details that need to be worked out before we proceed. But right now, I need a place to stay for the night. Any suggestions?"

"There's a couple hotels in town."

Gregory frowned and made a gesture to indicate that

he had no cash.

"Guess you could stay at my place. I got an old barn a few yards from the house. It ain't the Ritz, but ah can throw a sheet over a few bales of hay."

"Animals?"

"Nope. I inherited the place from my grandad. The critters are long gone."

"Deal."

***

Well, the kid was right, it ain't the Ritz, he thought, as he surveyed the barn's interior. Jeb had explained that the structure had been built about eighty years earlier, and that he'd maintained it as best he could. A quick survey had revealed that there were three separate stalls, a hay loft, wood slatted flooring and an overpowering odor that he could not discern. Jeb had pushed three, rather square bails of hay from the loft above and arranged them lengthwise to create a makeshift bed. As promised, he'd provided what had appeared to have been a clean sheet and pillow, and had taken off to join friends for a few beers, as he'd put it. He'd made a halfhearted offer for Gregory to join the group, a proposal that he'd politely declined. And as he sat upon the hard surface, wondering how he'd manage to sleep on a pile of hay that was probably older than himself, he was struck with the reality of the arrangement that he'd made with his host.

There's more than a good chance that the arrival of heavy machinery will trigger the alleged sensors, he reasoned. And Jeb did not clarify his construction industry friend's involvement in this scenario, and that could present a problem, especially if he'd offered up the possibility of treasure where there is none. I'll need to deal with that before we get started, which I'm guessing will be tomorrow after dark. And by now, unless he's a complete moron, he has to realize that there will be no female cousin in the sealed, underground cavity. So I guess I'll go with the lure of treasure for the time being. But if the lab is beneath that plate, and we gain entrance, Jeb may have to be dealt with and I don't know if I'm up to the task.

Chapter Fourteen

Saturday, 5 P.M.

Colonel Bradley Duke had considered sending the Imam a text message, but with his phone in hand he'd changed his mind, fearful of an intercept. Instead, he'd packed an overnight bag, changed from his uniform to an old pair of jeans and denim shirt, grabbed a long raincoat and aimed for the airport. He planned to meet with the holy man face to face.

He'd just made it in time for a flight leaving from the Ronald Regan Washington National Airport to Detroit. And as he sat on the aircraft, awaiting departure, he sent off a text message to the General indicating that he'd be gone for a few days while he searched for his baptismal certificate. Maybe the Imam can help with a counterfeit, he thought. After-all, my charade is of his creation. However, he'd never explained my precise role. And when I had inquired, I was told that I'd be informed when the time was right. Well, for me, the right time is now.

He took a taxi to the hotel nearest the Islamic Center of America—the Hawthorn Suites in Dearborn—and rented a room for the night. His plan was to attend the morning prayer service and seek out the Imam. But as he unpacked his overnight bag, he wondered if his appearance had changed since their last encounter, seven years earlier. I must maintain a low profile, he realized, and no one other than the Imam can know that I'm here. To that end, he found his way to BD's Mongolian Grill and helped himself to the salad bar and his own stir-fry concoction. By the time he'd finished dinner, fatigue had taken over and he headed back to the hotel to turn in.

***

Sunday, August 5th

5 A.M.

Following a shower and a hot cup of tea, the Colonel dressed and set out to walk to the Islamic Center. He'd checked the prayer schedule and knew that he'd be early, but hoped that the Imam might be early as well. Catching him before the faithful's arrival would allow some level of anonymity, and following his conversation with the general, he'd begun to worry about his being followed. He had checked the street before leaving the hotel, and had stood silent in the darkness for more than fifteen minutes, listening for manmade sounds and unexplained shadows. When he'd felt comfortable with his surroundings he'd begun the trek, constantly checking the reflections in storefront windows for followers or anything else out of the ordinary. It was still dark when he'd arrived at the mosque. And while he'd recalled its majestic, almost palace-like appearance in the daylight, shrouded in darkness, the ornate building and its ominous appearance caused the icy tentacles of fear to travel down his spine. He stood staring at the entrance, building confidence, before entering. Despite Bradley's more than six foot frame, the Imam had always held the upper hand, his diminutive stature notwithstanding. In earlier years, monster-like, nightmarish visions of the Imam had awakened him from sleep, an image he'd never managed to erase from memory.

The cavernous interior was cool and damp, and as he walked his plan to be the first on scene gradually collapsed before his eyes. But in the distance he could see the Imam walking off toward his private sanctum and he followed suit, and knocked.

"You may enter, Akil," Imam Faaroog Awan called out.

Bradley looked about for a camera that might have signaled his presence but, finding nothing obvious, lowered the lever and stood just inside the doorway. "I'm here because..."

The Imam gestured for him to take a seat, and said, "I know why you are here. I saw you standing outside, deliberating in the darkness."

"This meeting must be kept secret," Bradley advised.

"Of course, of course," the Imam whispered, rising to offer his disciple a cup of tea.

Bradley took a sip of the steaming liquid and asked, "Why am I here?"

"You recall our last conversation?"

"To the word."

"Then you will understand when I say that it is time."

Bradley lowered the delicate cup to a side table and replied, "What do you wish of me?"

"Our followers are gradually saturating the planet. Soon, we will be a dominating and unstoppable force. It has taken roughly fourteen hundred years, but the time has come for us to rise above all others."

Bradley smiled nervously. "And my role?"

"We need an accounting of America's weaknesses."

"I assume that you mean military?"

"Are there others?"

"Too numerous to discuss."

"For now, military will do. Perhaps we can exploit the others when the time is right."

"Is there anything else?"

The Imam frowned, raised his right index finger and proclaimed, "There is one small issue of security."

"Yes?"

"Baba must be silenced."

Bradley gasped.   Kill my childhood friend—is he serious, he wondered.

"You have no response?" the Imam breathed.

"Why?"

"He knows who you've become and where you are employed.   It is for your safety, as well as that of our future."

"Who will do such a thing?"

The Imam poured himself another cup of the now cooling tea, and said, "You."

"There must be another way," he pleaded.

The Imam shook his head, as if to say, no.

Bradley was speechless, and felt as if a lead weight had been dumped into his lap.   His eyes glassed over and he stared, first at the red, carpeted floor and then at the Imam.   How could I live with myself if I am to do what is asked of me, he cried to himself.   Maybe I could convince Baba to disappear and create the appearance of his demise, he considered.   But the Imam has spies all over the place, keeping it under-wraps would be asking for exposure. Finally concluding that there was no way out, he asked, "How should it be done?"

"As discretely and quickly possible," he replied, adding, "today would be good."

Seventy-year-old Imam, Faaroog Awan, had been born in Iran during the Shah's reign. His family, staunch supporters of the fledgling revolution that had ultimately ousted the monarch, had left Persia prior to the Shah's departure, and with a specific goal in mind. They were to establish a cadre of followers loyal to the incoming Ayatollah, and prepare them for a planed uprising within the devil nation, as they had and still do characterize the United States of America.

But plans do not always materialize as envisioned, and the patriarch of the Awan family had succumbed to tuberculosis at the age of fifty-nine. Prior to his demise, however, he had passed the baton to his only son, Faaroog. And given the nature of his malady, the detailed plan had taken many weeks of verbal transfer, as nothing of importance had been committed to print. Faaroog had not been the most attentive student, as the teenager had begun to experience the effects of hormonal surges, further complicated by his peers and their tales of sexual encounters.

On one unfortunate occasion, Faaroog had been caught smoking by his mother, conduct that while not strictly considered *haram* (forbidden) by the Quran, had been prohibited by his parents. And there had been other digressions, the knowledge of which had not found their way to the matriarch. All of these behavioral divergences had been the direct result of the young man's exposure to the Western way of life that he later came to despise.

His repentance and transition to Imam had followed a circuitous course that had involved the intervention of several Islamic scholars and daily appearances at his local mosque. But the title of Imam had been the result of self-ordainment following the death of his mosque's prior holy man.

Faaroog had been called to the Imam's office one late afternoon. The aging Imam had asked him to have a seat, and was about to offer a cup of tea when he'd collapsed in a heap of brocade. Faaroog had been stunned by the event, and had stood above the dead man staring longer than a reasonable person would have deemed appropriate. But during this interval of mindless observation he'd experienced an epiphany ... I will announce to the believers that the Imam has passed, and that it was his dying wish that I become the next leader, he'd decided.

Bradley had left the office feeling like a scolded child. Gone, was the bravado that had been provided by his uniform and Pentagon posting. The Imam's demand had taken him back in time, when he and Baba had ridden their bicycles up and down familiar streets, played games and shared common concerns. He found himself outside of the mosque, morning prayers no longer of importance, and walked mechanically back in the direction of his hotel.

As the well known landscape flashed by, he searched his memory for a verse in the Quran that could justify the killing of another faithful, but nothing fit his predicament. Oh Baba, he mused, you must die so that I may live to fulfill our destiny. But no amount of attempted rationalization appeared capable of calming his anxiety and disgust.

Chapter Fifteen

Sunday, 7 A.M

Battle Mountain, Nevada

Gregory had barely slept, given the stiff block of hay that had been his designated bed. And at a little before 7 a.m. he'd arisen, claimed an empty stall as his restroom and meandered outside in search of a source of water to wash his face and brush his teeth. He found Jeb unsuccessfully hacking away at a small log with a hand axe.

"Need some help?" Gregory asked.

Jeb looked up, shook his head and replied, "Damn axe ain't no longer sharp."

"What do you need the wood for?"

"Electric bill's gettin' out of hand. I use a wood burnin' stove to make my mornin' coffee."

"Let me have a whack at it," he said, reaching for the axe.

Taking aim, with the axe held over his head, Gregory lowered the tool with all of his body weight behind it. The small log split into two equal halves. "Got any more?" he grinned.

"That's all I need for now."

"I could sure use a cup of that coffee."

Jeb signaled for him to follow, and together they entered the house. Gregory took a look around as Jeb loaded the logs into the stove and unscrewed a jar of instant coffee. Jeb's house had seen better days, he noted. The roof is clearly a leaker, he thought, as evidenced by the light penetrating through several boards. And the odor of mildew means that the problem isn't recent. He turned to see the two rocking chairs that filled the opposite side of the room, and aside from the stove and an old cast iron sink, there was little else that could have defined the room as a kitchen. A short corridor led to what appeared to be the solitary bedroom, its purpose suggested by a small section of unmade bed visible from his position. And as he was about to direct his attention back to the now lit stove, the distinguishable portion of the bed moved.

"Do you have a houseguest, besides myself?" he asked.

"Yeah. My brother's wife stays here when they get to beatin' on each other."

"So there's another bedroom?"

"Nope. Just one," he said, bending over to stoke the fire.

"Where do you sleep?"

Jeb rose with a big grin on his face and jauntily replied, "With her."

Sleeps with his brother's wife, Gregory said to himself. That's weird. And he was about to ask how his brother felt about that arrangement, when the large breasted young woman padded into the room wearing only a black thong.

"Coffee ready?" she yawned, ignoring Gregory, who stood only inches from her mostly naked body.

"Almost?" Jeb replied.

"Good, 'cause I got to git on home."

"Not before my mornin' howdy," Jeb said.

The unnamed woman took Jeb by the hand and directed him back toward the doorless bedroom, from where Jeb called out, "Help yourself to a cup of Joe ... I got some pleasurin' to do."

Gregory was dumfounded. If this isn't the most screwed up situation, I don't know what is, he told himself, as he searched for a cup.

The grunting and moaning echoing down the corridor had proven to be overwhelming, and Gregory took his crappy black coffee in to the open air, where he waited. During the sleepless night in the barn he'd cobbled together a rather flimsy plan of approach to the desert cabin. And he needed to square the details with Jeb. He was fearful that that his host might represent one of the many weaknesses in the scheme, and it was paramount that it be dealt with in advance. But one thing had become painfully clear; Jeb was a certifiable imbecile. The initial quest had been presented as a search for a government employee working in an underground facility, he reasoned. And now, for some inexplicable reason, Jeb has decided that the current venture is an expedition for treasure. Well, if that floats his boat, it works for me. But I have no idea how he'll react if the metal plate is actually covering the entrance to my lab and nothing of perceived value is revealed. And even worse, the helicopter could return and take us away.

Twenty sweaty minutes later, the log that he'd been sitting on beginning to cause a throbbing in his posterior, Jeb emerged with a big grin.

"Rang her bell twice," he gloated.

"Good for you," Gregory replied, and was about to ask about his brother but refrained.

"You want some? I think she'd be OK with that."

Gregory shook his head with a, no. " We need to talk about tonight."

"The front loader will be ready to go after dark."

"Your friend's not coming, correct?"

"Yeah. He's afraid of gettin' fired if the loader don't come back before mornin'."

"We'll need some heavy rope or chain to wrap around the metal plate."

"Thought about that, and got him to give us two forty foot lengths of heavy chain."

"Front loaders don't move very fast…"

"I know. They transport an' store it on a truck."

"Can you drive it," Gregory asked, as the young woman, now clothed in a halter top and overly abbreviated shocking pink shorts, exited, gave them both an exaggerated smile and walked off.

"She's hot as steam, ain't she?"

"The truck, can you…"

"Yeah, I can handle it."

***

9 P.M

They'd parked the truck five hundred feet from the shack. Gregory had gambled that the alleged ground sensors hadn't been placed that far away. But there would be no way to disguise the thumping and bumping of the front loader as it approached the target, so they would have to be quick with the plate removal. Jeb mounted the machine as Gregory guided its departure from the truck bed. The chains were already sitting in the loader's bucket, one end of each attached to its left and right sides. The strategy involved wrapping the chains around one end of the plate and joining them with an open link, allowing the loader to pull/slide the slab from the presumed opening. Gregory had gauged that the metal's thickness would prevent the chains from slipping, since it was too heavy to lift and allow for a proper attachment. They wasted no time positioning the machine directly in front of the entrance, which was roughly in line with the plate. Jeb's excitement was palpable, the anticipation of incalculable riches driving him onward with determination. Gregory, on the other hand, was counting the minutes until the militia's arrival.

It had taken longer than anticipated to drag the heavy chain into the cabin and join its ends. Once completed, Jeb fired up the loader's diesel engine and began tugging. At first, there was resistance, but then the loader backed away without restriction ... the chain had slipped over the plate and Gregory ran to inform. Once again, they dragged the chain back inside. The initial pull had succeeded in uncovering less than two inches of the opening. They were both in a sweat, their faces barely visible in the darkness of the unlit shanty, as they reseated the chain and fired up the loader. Black smoke belched from the machine's vertical stack, as it roared in reverse, dragging the metal plate away from the opening and halfway through the front entrance. Gregory leaned into the breach and groped around with an outstretched arm. At first, a blast of stale, cool air was his only finding, but as he leaned downward his hand brushed across yet another metallic structure. He thumped it with a finger. It's hollow, he said to himself. Must be the elevator, as he chided himself for not bringing a flashlight. Just then, Jeb walked in.

"Can you see it?" he asked, excitedly.

"See what?"

"The treasure, man."

"Got a flashlight?"

"Nope. Got this," he said, handing over his cell phone, with its flashlight app enabled.

He aimed the light at the metallic structure below, confirming his initial impression. The elevator was less than a foot below the opening, and on top was an emergency hatch. He stared at it for a few seconds, wondering what to tell his assistant.

"Any tools in the truck?"

"There's a tool box up against the cab. Don't do nothin' 'til I get back," he shouted, as he ran from the shack.

He didn't require any tools to open the hatch from the outside, but he needed the extra alone time to force it open. And unlike residential and commercial elevators, where the hatch is often not large enough for a human's passage, the special purpose lift's opening could easily accommodate same without the risk of activating a kill switch. The scientists at the lab had been instructed about proper escape procedures in the case of emergency that had included passage to the surface. With Jeb's glowing phone in hand, he lowered himself into the elevator, searched for the control board and flicked the interior light toggle. The recessed lighting sputtered to life. That's a relief, he thought, at least the elevator is still powered. But as he was contemplating pressing the button that would take him farther beneath the surface, the familiar, deep thumping sound of an approaching helicopter echoed in his chamber. He extinguished the overhead lights, shoved Jeb's phone into a pocket and waited. With any luck, the promise of riches will prompt the idiot's silence regarding our presence, he hoped. But he realized that the heavy metal plate protruding through the front door would be their ticket to ruination.

The beating noise had been replaced with loud voices

shouting unintelligible commands. He remained still in the elevator.

Gregory had initially feared that the newcomers would attempt to recover the opening, sealing him inside for all eternity, but then realized that it would take a crew of six or more men to move it, something that the average helo could not provide, and that the front loader could not be used to push the plate without destroying the entire structure. So he waited to learn his fate. Heavy, booted steps were heard overhead, and he backed into the elevator, beyond its trap door. A beam of light penetrated the opening and illuminated the floor below the hatch, lingered for a few moments and then disappeared. Now what, he wondered, still terrified to move or allow his lungs to fully expand and deflate. The beating sound returned, as a blast of sand entered the cabin and trickled into the elevator. But the rhythmical sound of helicopter blades quickly became less audible, and Gregory hoisted himself out of the lift and carefully looked about. As he inched his way toward the exterior and mounted the metal slab, the moonlit front loader caught his eye. But Jeb was nowhere to be seen. They must have taken him, he told himself. I hope he keeps his mouth shut, or they'll be back in a flash.

He returned to the elevator and hit the button that

would take him below the surface. Whether the equipment could be powered up was still an unknown, and he wasn't certain that doing so would be a good idea, given the amount of energy required and the likelihood that its use would make his presence known. But he could at least have a look around to see if there were any clues to his apparent blackout. He had no doubt that the posse would return to close up the entrance, so he would have to be quick.

Chapter Sixteen

August 6, 2017

Monday, 2 A.M.

Gregory had exited the underground facility a little past midnight. The government had left just enough power in place to illuminate the entire laboratory, but the giant breaker that had supplied power to the accelerator and ancillary devices had been removed. There was no way he could reproduce the event responsible for his current state of affairs without that breaker. But as he walked from room to room, searching for anything that might explain the nature of his accident, he noticed a large metal cabinet that hadn't been there before. It was locked. He ran for the toolkit that had been kept near the commissary and removed a long screwdriver and pry-bar. Back at the metal cabinet he tried to mangle the lock with the screwdriver but it resisted. Next came the pry-bar, and following a few fruitless attempts the cabinet door finally gave way. To his surprise, its only inhabitant was the somewhat scorched, weighty, breaker switch. He was certain that a crew would return to reposition the steel slab, and he needed to be out before that took place. He closed the metal cabinet and returned to the elevator.

Back on the surface, with the key still in the ignition, he boarded the flatbed and headed back toward town. As he drove, he pondered his ever-evolving predicament. I'll leave the truck just outside of town and walk the remainder of the way, lest I be accused of theft. Jeb, on the other hand, is probably knee deep in shit. Hopefully, he'll go with the treasure hunting story. If the uniforms arrive at the same conclusion as I regarding his lack of intelligence, he said to himself, they might just buy it and turn him loose. As for myself, at this hour, I have no place to go other than his barn. But my primary objective still remains just out of reach. However, this little expedition has not been without merit. I now know where the lab sits, and that the main power supply is probably still intact, or they would not have removed the breaker. And that's an indication that there are plans to reactivate the site at some point. I have to figure out a way to bypass the surveillance, so that I can get back in without the fear of immediate capture.

It was three-thirty a.m. when he was startled by a pair of blue, flashing lights coming from the general direction of Jeb's house. He approached cautiously, and from a distance of a hundred or so feet he could clearly make out the source of the strobing lights; a pair of military Humvees were blocking the path leading to the dwelling. Four camouflage attired people were coming and going from the interior, carrying out what appeared to be cardboard boxes. They placed them in the back of their vehicles, extinguished the strobes and quietly departed. Gregory waited behind a fat tree-trunk until the last of the vehicle stirred dust had settled, and then approached the barn. He hopped up on the bed of hay and thought, what could they have found interesting in his house? He can't be a spy, as dumb as he is. And I can't imagine that he's a national security risk. On the other hand, the pizza business didn't appear to be a money maker … drugs, he wondered. Well, a few hours of sleep and then I'm outta here. I don't want to be around when Jeb returns, so I'll have to find another place to plan my next foray into the underworld.

Chapter Seventeen

Monday, 8 A.M.

Detroit, MI

The day prior, Bradley Duke had left the mosque in a daze. The Imam had given him a kill order that had violated his personal code of ethics, as well as everything that he'd learned from the Quran. He'd understood that the holy book allowed for exceptions, but he failed to see how Baba had met the requirements. And while he'd been told to complete the task almost twenty-four hours earlier, he'd needed the time to reconcile with the proposed deed. Due to the anxiety associated with the Imam's directive, he had not discussed the issue of his religious charade and the need for some form of documentation, but he'd resolved to return to the mosque following his visit with Baba.

He waited until almost nine a.m. and dialed his friend's cell phone.

"Baba?"

"Yes."

"It's Akil. I trust you have been well?" he said, a lump forming in the back of his throat.

"Yes. It is good to hear from you."

"I am nearby, can we meet?"

"My wife is out and I am tending the children. But she will return shortly. Can you wait until ten a.m.?"

Children, he thought. This is going to be more difficult than I'd imagined. "Yes, ten will be fine. You still live at the housing project on Grand Boulevard?"

"Yes. But I will meet you in the street, my wife knows little of my past."

"I will look for you," he said, wondering if Baba would recognize him. He terminated the call.

During his conversation with the Imam, the holy man had slid a black handled switchblade knife across his desk. And Bradley ran a finger over its smooth surface where it sat within his pocket. Basic training had taught him proper blade technique, but he had never actually killed anyone, nor had he been in combat of any nature. The bulk of his career had been spent in various administrative positions, all leading to his now tenuous posting at the Pentagon.

He checked his timepiece and realized that he had time for breakfast. But the thought of slashing his old friend's throat had soured his appetite, so he settled for a cup of tea at a local diner. Years had passed since he'd last visited the housing project, his parents long deceased, and as he sipped the tepid liquid he searched his memory for a place that would allow some level of seclusion. He recalled an alley where children used to hide, and where teenagers had brief, but torrid encounters with the opposite sex. That should work, he thought. I will tell Baba that we need to speak in total privacy, and hope that no one sees me enter or leave.

He arrived fifteen minutes before the appointed hour. A group of four, hoodlum attired young men eyed him up and down as he approached, but he stood his ground and kept walking toward the front of the building. The neighborhood has changed since my last visit, he thought, noticing the litter and empty beer cans strewn about. He gazed upward, toward the apartment window from which, as a young boy, he'd viewed the outside world, and sighed. Life had been much simpler as a child, he pondered. And then he caught a glimpse of his old friend, as he walked toward him munching on what appeared to be piece of bread.

"Akil," Baba shouted.

Bradley shook his head in acknowledgment.

"Good to see you, old friend."

Bradley tried to smile, but his nervous gut intervened and he grunted a version of hello.

"You have spoken with the Imam, I suppose," Baba said, swallowing the last of his toast.

"Yes, and that is what we must discuss, but in private." Bradley said, gesturing toward the group of four.

"Let's walk."

Bradley nodded his agreement, but steered Baba in the direction of the alley.

Baba grinned when they had reached the depths of the narrow, dead-end passage. "Remember how we would tiptoe in the dark and watch, but mostly listen to the elders having sex?" he said.

Bradley cringed inwardly, grasped the knife in his right hand and pressed the button that would release the gleaming blade. He waited until Baba had turned to gaze at a used condom lying suggestively on the concrete and, with one sweeping move from behind, slashed his throat from side to side. More blood than he'd anticipated flowed from the gash, as Baba gurgled in an attempt to speak, his eyes bulging in disbelief. But Bradley stood motionless, the knife still clutched between his tremulous fingers, as the urge to retch took him by surprise. He watched, while Baba's life ebbed away and his body slid to the ground. All he felt was a sense of numbness, but he had the presence of mind to wipe the knife's handle clean and drop it beside his friend's lifeless body. Stepping over blood and his own vomit, he turned once, offered a silent prayer, and walked away.

Two hours later, after aimlessly walking the streets trying to justify his ungodly act, he found himself back in his room, tears flowing down his cheeks before he could even close the door. Is this the life I was meant to lead, he asked of Allah. If this is all there is, please take me, take me now.

And as expected, there had been no response, and Bradley fell back on the bed and closed his eyes. But he could not expunge the image of his first kill, his closest and likely, only friend. So following a cold shower, he'd resolved to return to the mosque, hopeful for the Imam's comforting words.

It was still late morning when he'd arrived back at the mosque. He entered, took note of a few worshipers standing in a huddle arguing about something he could not discern, and marched toward his mentor's private office. He knocked.

"Enter," a voice called out.

Bradley stood by the still open door, speechless. A young boy, his lips glistening, tried but failed to hide his face as he ran past and into the corridor.

"You have news?" the Imam, completely unashamed, asked.

Bradley was torn between running off himself, confronting the holy man, or pretending that nothing out of the ordinary had just transpired. He chose the latter.

"The task is done," he said.

"Good. But you are uncertain of what you've just witnessed?" the Imam taunted.

"I saw nothing," Bradley lied.

"The young man is a student of Islam," he explained, ignoring Bradley's statement.

Bradley had hoped to brush aside the immoral act that he'd just observed, but the Imam had chosen to fan the flames.

"Yes, I understand."

"I fear you do not."

"What is it you wish of me?"

Imam Awan looked away, straightened his robe and rose. He began to pace the room, repositioning various shelved objects as an obsessive compulsive might, and then, with a flick of his wrist, said, "You may go."

Bradley was hardly satisfied with the abrupt dismissal, and he stood his ground and asked, "Will there be repercussions from my actions?"

"Only those of your own creation."

Given the Imam's penchant for parables and

metaphors, he assumed that to mean his conscience.

"Have you other concerns?" the Imam asked.

Bradley hesitated, a moment too long, and the Imam urged, "I sense that you are conflicted."

He wanted to spit out that he'd just murdered a childhood friend, and that of course he's troubled, but he held his tongue. Instead, he said, "There may be a problem with my primary mission."

The Imam bristled and replied, "What kind of problem?"

"My security clearance has been revoked."

Faaroog's piercing black eyes bore down upon him, a pair of missiles that appeared ready to penetrate his own, and he stuttered, "I..I think it will blow over."

"You think, you think," Imam repeated, as he returned to the seat behind his desk.

"It's just a silly misunderstanding."

Faaroog shook his head knowingly, and inquired, "How quickly will it be resolved?"

Bradley realized at that moment that he'd painted himself into a corner, but he had to say something, so he fibbed, "Within the week."

"Our benefactor's plans depend upon it," he shouted, the emphasizing fist smacked against the desktop releasing a small cloud of dust.

Bradley furrowed his brow and said, "There is someone other than yourself guiding my actions?"

Faaroog cradled his face in both hands, his skin momentarily ridding itself of its many folds and creases, and took a deep breath. He poured himself a small glass of water from a crystal pitcher and replied, "I am not alone in this quest."

"Who?"

"The Shia."

Bradley's face took on a puzzled expression, and the Imam clarified with, "Iran."

"The Ayatollah is pulling the strings?"

"Look around, Akil," he said, gesturing with outstretched arms. "It takes a great deal of money to appease the believers and support this sacred structure."

"And it all comes from them?"

"Yes."

"I am confused."

"Complete your mission, that is your only responsibility."

"But I never agreed to work for them."

"The cause is just, and in the name of Allah we will get it done."

"But..."

"Your path is clear."

"I will do as you wish."

"They, as well as I, will be expecting results."

"It will have to wait for the hold on my security clearance to be lifted."

The Imam raised his eyebrows.

Bradley took note and said, "If you're implying that I should steal from my superior, I could be tried for treason."

"Whatever is necessary."

"But..."

"You may leave."

As if the blood on his hands had not been enough to upset his equilibrium, the Imam had just made an impossible demand.

Without my clearance, he mused, I will not have access to anything of value. Areas of weakness, he's said, he wants me to find fragile links in the chain of command. Right now, that would be me. But I am no more part of America's military machine than the dog who'd left that pile of shit, he said to himself, passing a rather odorous deposit on the sidewalk. The best I can do is stall for time.

Chapter Eighteen

Monday, 11 A.M.

The Pentagon

Office of General Louder

The General had just lowered his telephone receiver when two dark suited men entered his office without notice. One man stationed himself at the door, while the other stared stone faced at the flabbergasted General Louder.

"What the hell's going on," Louder protested.

"Stay seated and listen," the man demanded.

"You know who I am?" Louder blurted, his hand moving toward the alarm button that would summon armed guards.

"Place your hands on top of the desk," the man barked.

Louder slowly complied and said, "Who are you?"

Ignoring his question, the man replied, "You've made a verbal agreement to safeguard a certain project, and you've been negligent."

It was gradually becoming clear who these men represented, and an icy shiver went down Louder's spine. "In what way have I been neglectful?" he asked calmly.

"You've removed the standing security from the

facility."

"It was my understanding that it had outlived its usefulness."

The man's face turned crimson, and he thrust his clenched fists against the desktop. "Who told you that?" he hissed.

"My sentries watched as your people buried the entrance."

"Are you aware that there have been trespassers?" the man growled, his face now leaning across the desk.

"No."

"We have one in custody."

Louder swallowed hard. "One of our citizens?" he asked, hoping that it was not a foreign agent.

The man retreated to the middle of the room without replying.

"What can I do to make it right?" Louder said.

The man turned to gaze at his partner, as if the General's question had not been anticipated, and replied, "We'll get back to you."

"I'm not your pawn," Louder said, his bravado returning, as he continued with, "tell your people that unless they read me in, they can forget about Pentagon cooperation."

"Not sure that'll fly."

"The alternative is me spilling what little I know to the Joint Chiefs," he spat, pointing at the door.

The men left without another word, but Louder sat in his chair rehashing the threat. I've heard of those people causing the untimely disappearance of those they fear or dislike. Maybe I should have kept my big mouth shut but, on the other hand, I have what they want.

***

2 P.M.

Louder had just returned from lunch, and was in the process of unlocking his office door, when he heard the phone ring. Running and reaching across the desk, he stifled a belch and lifted the receiver.

"This is General Louder..."

An unfamiliar voice interrupted his introduction and declared, "I understand that you have disregarded our arrangement."

"Who is this?" he barked.

"We haven't met, but I know you quite well."

"I repeat, state your name," he demanded.

"Under threat, you've made a request to be read into a

particular project."

"Oh, I see that my message has reached its target."

"We don't respond to threats," the voice remarked.

"And I will not deploy my assets without good reason."

"Then I will provide you with one. Be at the Four Seasons bar at 6 p.m. Wear a suit and tie, no uniform."

"How will I recognize...," he tried to ask, but the call had ended.

Louder eased into his chair, painful hemorrhoids still on the forefront, and pondered the upcoming meeting. I could take a position of strength with the unknown caller, but that might put him off. On the other hand, he might respond to feigned subservience.

The rest of the day dragged on, and the more he replayed the brief conversation, the angrier he got. I'm a Goddamned three star general, he thought, and no friggin' spook is going to treat me like a child, as the clock approached five.

Dressed in a gray suit, white shirt and red stripped tie, he surveyed the bar's chatting guests, hoping to catch a glance of someone who appeared out of place, suddenly realizing that spooks are trained to blend in. At exactly 6 p.m., he approached the bar and took a seat. Moments later, an attractive young woman pulled up alongside and ordered a club soda with an olive and a slice of lime. Louder lowered his shot of Johnnie Walker Black and, stifling a chuckle, said, "That's and odd combination."

"Perhaps," she said, toying with the skewered olive.

Louder returned to his drink, wondering if the hot number beside him was a working girl. But he reminded himself that sex was off the table until his leaky hemorrhoids improved. Every now and then he turned in his seat, waiting for the unknown caller to approach him, but ten minutes had passed and the anticipated man in black had not surfaced. Suddenly, the club soda drinker lowered her now empty glass and deftly passed a small square of paper beneath Louder's bar top resting hand. He flinched, and gazed in the direction of the young woman, but she had already departed. Suspecting that the paper contained a telephone number to be called for a "good time," he laughed inwardly and and flipped it over. His brow furrowed.

The message said, *walk out of the hotel exit and enter the waiting black SUV.* So she's the spook, he said to himself in amazement. He immediately exited the bar, casually walked to the exit and spotted the described vehicle, its rear door open invitingly. He hesitated, looked about for anything else out of the ordinary, and stepped into the backseat of the Chevy Tahoe. The car pulled slowly away from the curb, as the male, front seat passenger announced, "Your desire to be read in has been considered and denied. You will uphold your original pledge."

What the fuck, Louder thought. "You do realize who you're dealing with?" Louder blustered.

The man chuckled and replied, "I ask the same of you."

"I'd made it crystal clear to your errand boys, that without an understanding of what I'm guarding..."

"It appears that you falsely presume a position of superiority," the man cut in.

"My agreement was with a senator, who the hell are you?"

There was no response from the front seat, just a billow of smoke from a freshly lit cigarette. And then a demand, as the car came to a halt fifty yards from a bus-stop, "You can get out now, but remember, contractual breeches have consequences."

"What contract and what consequences?" he called out to the departing vehicle.

He called a taxi to take him to his highly leveraged, million dollar plus condo on 15th Street NW. As the cab rolled through traffic he began to consider his plight. I'd assumed that the senator had set me up for the NSA, but if the jackass who'd just kicked me out of the car was NSA, he would have said so, and the same for the Company, he mused. This has to be dark shit, very dark. I've heard rumors and conspiracy theories about something called MJ12 (Majestic Twelve), but if it had existed, it would go back to the days of Truman. And even if such a group had been formed, what are the chances that it's still in play today, he wondered. Well, the intel's also suggested that nosey people have been made to disappear, and I'm not ready for that, so I'd better pussyfoot around the topic.

The taxi let him off at his condo. He checked the mailbox, nodded to the concierge and took the elevator to his unit. Despite the building's significant age, Louder had hired a decorator to transform the dull and lifeless apartment into a modern, clean environment. It had cost more than he'd budgeted for, but she had achieved the desired effect, with black granite tiled floors, high gloss white kitchen cabinets and a colorfully appointed living room. The single guest and master bedrooms had been supplied with similar, black epoxied furniture that emitted an unusual glow when struck by sunlight. Louder took a deep breath, and sighed. This was his sanctuary, away from the demands of the job, the ignorant masses that occupied the lower levels of the Pentagon, and Bradley Duke, the man who'd been the recent precipitator of ill-defined nightmares. He kicked off his shoes and walked into the kitchen for a glass of water. And that's when he saw it. Seated on the countertop was an envelop. He'd almost overlooked it, as at first glance it had appeared to have been an optical illusion precipitated by the bright, LED, overhead lights illuminating the white quartz surface. He checked the calendar that he kept programmed into his cell phone. This isn't the housekeeper's day, he thought. How did this get into my locked apartment, he wondered. With his gaze aimed at the envelope, he filled a glass from the refrigerator's water dispenser, took a gulp and reached for the intruder. It hadn't been sealed, but inside was a single sheet of paper, that by touch and visual inspection appeared to have been created on an old time typewriter. In all capitals, the brief message warned:

WATCH YOUR SIX.

Louder stared at the off-white sheet of paper. It contained no letterhead, nor any indication of its origin. But its mere presence in his locked home spoke volumes about the sender's abilities. And with the message still in hand, he eased onto the electric blue living room couch and began considering a list of possibilities. Watch my six? he repeated to himself. Sounds like it came from a jock (Navy slang for a pilot), or at least a pigeon (a member of the Air Force). Who do I know that would give two shits about my wellbeing, he wondered. He searched his memory for another ten minutes, and then made his way back to the kitchen. Frowning at the collection of frozen dinners stacked up in the freezer, he grabbed one and tossed it into the microwave. He considered calling for a Pentagon security detail, but decided against it. So I'm a target, he thought, good luck with that.

Chapter Nineteen

Monday, 5 P.M.

Battle Mountain, Nevada

Gregory had spent most of the day wandering about town, going in and out of stores while pretending to be shopping for specific items that the shops did not carry. He'd made several passes by the unopened pizza shop, hoping to catch a glimpse of Jeb, but suspected that either the fellow had soured on the business, or was still in the custody of some branch of the military. And by four p.m. he still had not configured a plan of action, nor found a place to spend the night. But his journey had taken him past the Royal Inn, and to pass the time he'd meandered through the lobby. The Inn had set out a meager breakfast bar that the staff had yet to clear away, and he'd managed to stuff a few almost stale pastries into his pocket and escape without being noticed. And with a poor excuse for a meal in his stomach, he set about to find a place to bed down for the night and plan for the lab's invasion.

During his aimless jaunt he'd come across a house for sale on Broad Street. It had been clear from his two passes that the house had been unoccupied and, with no other options in sight, he decided to throw caution to the wind.

After all, he thought, the government already has me tagged as a criminal. And by the time he'd reached the one story house the sun had begun to set. He had no tools, nor the knowhow for lock picking, but the realtor had left a lockbox hanging from the front door handle. The street was quiet, and the front door was set back aways. He gazed left and right—making certain that he was not being observed—and began kicking at the handle. His goal had been to break open the digitally locked box, but the aging handle gave way and the box hit the deck. With the box in hand, he searched for anything that could be used to pry it open and, finding nothing suitable, he walked around toward the rear of the house. Separate from the house was what appeared to be a shed, its door secured with cheap padlock and latch. He used the lockbox to break the latch away from the wooden door and entered. Rusty old tools were strewn about the dirt floor, but he seized upon a large screwdriver and, with some effort, managed to gain access and remove the key.

The house was indeed unoccupied and devoid of furnishings, but the appliances had been left behind, and the power and water were still available. This should work for tonight, he said to himself, as he scouted out a satisfactory place to rest his bones, finally settling on a carpeted bedroom floor.

Sometime after midnight he'd been awakened by loud voices echoing from within the house. He arose with a start and crawled to the door that he'd partially sealed before closing his eyes. A beam of light, probably a flashlight, he thought, was casting a shadow on the only visible wall. Assessing the banter more acutely, he determined that the interlopers were speaking in a mixture of Spanish and accented English. And there was no doubt in his mind that they were talking about drugs, specifically, heroin. He gazed about the windowless room, looking for an escape route. The only way out of this place is through either the front or back doors, and that means that I'm stuck here.

Rather than remaining where a curious set of eyes could easily find him, he quietly opened a closet door and slid inside. In the darkness, he'd failed to notice the large, black plastic trash bag that occupied one half of the storage space and, reaching inside, his hand was met with yet more plastic bags containing a compressible, powder-like substance. Shit, he cried out to himself, this must be their stash. If they find me, they're bound to conclude that I'm here to steal ... I need to find a way to distract them.

The closet no longer a safe place to hide, he'd crept to

the door and, with it slightly ajar, he'd maintained a vigil. Bleary eyed, he spotted an empty Tequila bottle rolling across the carpeted living room floor. Maybe they'll pass out drunk, he thought, noting that the incessant chatter had ceased. The sound of the bottle striking a wall had brought no response from the trespassers, so he'd assumed that they had indeed nodded off. He had no idea of their numbers, but his initial assessment had indicated at least two, and that was two more than he'd been prepared to tussle with. So he'd advanced toward the living room on all fours, thankful for the sound deadening nature of the carpet, and peeked around the corner of a barrier-like wall. There were three of them, all dressed alike, with well-worn jeans and gang style, brown and blue vests. But they were stretched out on the floor; two on their backs and one on his stomach. Gregory had not had much experience with gang paraphernalia, but he knew from newspaper articles that the blue and brown colors were indicative of the Latin Mafia Familia Crips. And nothing that he'd read about them had spelled, friendly. Still on his knees, he'd crept toward the front door, reached up and turned the knob. A blast of cool air entered the room and his head jerked rearward, hoping that the breeze had gone unnoticed. With the trio apparently oblivious to the outside world, he wormed his way to the front landing, rose, and ran like hell.

So much for a good night's sleep, he thought, now a half-mile down the road and sprinting farther. When he'd reached what he'd considered to be a safe distance, he stopped and allowed his breathing to normalize. A pickup was parked a few paces away, and based upon the moon's position in the sky he'd figured that sunrise was several hours off. So he climbed into the truck's bed and closed his eyes.

A barking dog awakened him, and he peered over the side of the vehicle. Despite the darkness he could make out the reflective eyes of a large animal staring at him with something in its mouth. What is that, he wondered, realizing that the dog had managed to capture and kill a hefty rat.

"Nice doggie," he whispered.

The German Shepherd dropped its prize and licked it muzzle, but his gaze remained locked onto Gregory's face.

"Go home, doggie," Gregory whispered.

But the dog stood its ground. Seated, the tall animal's head not far from his own, he could feel a puff of warm breath as it panted rapidly. Tentatively, he reached over and patted the dog's head, gratified that his fingers had remained intact, and felt around for a collar. OK, he said to himself, you're out alone and without any ID. And that's when the dog stood on his haunches, placed his two beefy paws on the edge of the truck and slobbered across Gregory's face with his rat coated tongue.

Ugh. Just what I've been lacking, he thought, as he slowly eased his way to the ground and began casually walking away. But when he looked back he noticed that his new found friend had been following a few paces from behind. I've always wanted a pet, he reminded himself, but the timing is off.

"Go away," he shooed, but the dog gazed up at him lovingly, its tongue lolling out of the left side of its mouth. Well, I guess the timing is right for him, or her, he said to himself, as he continued his jaunt with no particular destination in mind.

Chapter Twenty

Tuesday, August 7th

7 :00 A.M.

The Pentagon

Troubled by the warning received the night before, General Louder had arrived at his office earlier than usual. And his mind was still racing through past encounters and possible enemies when he noticed an envelope on his desktop marked, urgent. He rose, poured himself a cup of black coffee that he'd ordered to be brewed before his everyday appearance, and returned to the desk chair. Staring at the envelope, he lowered the cup and broke the seal with a letter opener that had been made in the likeness of a Ka-Bar knife. It contained a detailed surveillance report from the Pentagon security officer he'd tasked with following Colonel Bradley. By the end of the first paragraph he'd all but forgotten about his own well being. The officer had followed the Colonel to Detroit, and had witnessed his entrance into the mosque, as well as the aftermath of his not so friendly visit with Baba. He lowered the single sheet of paper to the desk and pushed back in his chair. I've got a murderer and a possible spy on my staff, he said to himself. Should I confront him and put him in shackles, or should I continue to observe and see what he has planned, he debated. He put in a call to Officer Ryan Keith, with whom he'd been on a first name basis. The officer was the son of an old friend, and he'd willingly agreed to keep an eye on the young man's career.

"Ryan? Louder here."

"Yes, sir. You saw the report?"

"Are you on the premises?"

"Been here since 3 a.m."

"Come by my office, ASAP."

Ryan knocked on the door less than ten minutes later and entered.

"Coffee?" Louder asked, rising to refill his cup.

"I've already had more than enough."

Louder shook his head knowingly and slid onto his chair.

They stared at each other for a few seconds, as Louder lifted the single sheet of paper and shook his head back and forth in dismay, finally saying, "This is a bombshell."

"Yes, sir."

"I assume that you've left nothing out?"

"Well, he spent a good deal of time inside the mosque. And there was no way I could follow him inside without setting off someone's alarm. But I was able to have a look inside when the door remained open for a group of worshipers ."

"And?"

"He wasn't there to pray. I mean, he wasn't kneeling with the others."

"What do you make of that?"

"My intel suggests that the mosque is the sometime home of a well known radical Imam."

Louder shuffled through a few red folders, flipped one open, and replied, "Oh yeah, that guy's a real pisser."

"Do you want me to shut him down?"

"The Imam?"

"No, the Colonel."

"I'd like to frag (fragmentation grenade) 'em both, but taking out the religious guy would set off a political firestorm. As for the Colonel, his actions tell me that he's got an agenda, and we need to determine the ultimate goal."

Louder drained the remains of his coffee cup and lowered it thoughtfully to the desktop, adding, "Let's keep him on a tight leash for now and see what he has planned. However, he's been privy to some classified info, and he'll need to be terminated with extreme prejudice down the road."

"Shouldn't he be held accountable before a tribunal?" Ryan asked, with a troubled expression.

"Wouldn't look good for your's truly. Besides, you're aware of the penalty for treason, and my guess is that the Colonel is headed in that direction. So we'd simply be saving the taxpayers money."

Ryan gazed at his wristwatch and announced, "The Colonel should be here shortly. Should I alert the force?"

"Not unless you require backup. The status is *need to know* and, right now, you're on point. I'll inform your chief that, until further notice, you've been detailed to me."

"Yes, sir," Ryan said, as he rose to leave.

"One more thing," Louder added, "I want a record of everywhere he goes and everything he does. If he takes a crap, I want it recorded ... got it?"

Ryan nodded his understanding and left the office.

***

Louder had waited until the noon hour had passed to summon Colonel Duke to his office. He'd decided to carry on as if all had been normal, although he'd already stripped the Colonel of security clearance. The Colonel knocked and entered.

"Sir," he saluted, as he stood just inside the doorway.

Louder tilted his head in surprise, as the salute had been out of character for his subordinate. And it had been telling, like a child embracing a parent after having spilled spaghetti sauce all over the new couch. But he let it go. "At ease," Bradley, he ordered, continuing with, "have you resolved the issue at hand?"

The Colonel had a puzzled expression on his face that had not been missed by the General, who clarified, "The alleged religious conversion. You'd taken leave to obtain proof."

The Colonel grimaced and fibbed, "I'm afraid that the documents had been lost in a fire."

Nice try, but no cigar, Louder thought. "What do you propose we do with you?"

The Colonel shrugged.

"Well, I suppose we could send you off to active duty," Louder said, rolling a fountain pen between the fingers of his left hand.

The Colonel showed little emotion, and said, "I'm at your disposal."

Louder had no intention of allowing him out of his sight, even if it meant continuing the charade that had begun only hours earlier. But he advised, "I'll find something for you that does not require clearance, but I need to know if there are any other cracks in your background that I might trip over."

"None that I can think of, sir."

"In that case, you can take the rest of the day off."

The Colonel rose, saluted one more time, and left.

Louder sat staring at the closed door. There goes one cool character, he thought. But he and his radical buddy are going down, just as soon as I can figure out what they're up to. And the political nonsense I'd fed Ryan will not prevent that ideological nut-bag's demise.

He gazed longingly at the various bottles of liquor lined up on the metal cart like soldiers at attention. But an instant before rising to pour himself what he called his daily tranquilizer—a double shot of Johnny Walker Black—lunch came back to haunt. He nixed the alcohol in favor of the men's room and what he anticipated to be painful journey, given his active hemorrhoids.

Forty minutes in the head brought to mind the NSA quagmire, and he pondered a response. Watch my six—somebody cares what happens to me, he reminded himself, and that's refreshing. But who is that person, and what do they know, he wondered. I doubt that an NSA operative would break ranks for the likes of myself, so it didn't come from within. And it can't have been that asshole senator, the guy's afraid of his own shadow. It has to be someone I know, someone who has nothing to lose or— something to gain.

He returned to the office, locked away the Duke surveillance documents, and thought about the day he'd agreed to take Colonel Duke on his staff. So much for diversity, he thought. Never fails, nice guys always end up taking it in the ass.

Chapter Twenty-one

Tuesday, 6 A.M.

Battle Mountain

Gregory awakened to a tongue bathed face. For some inexplicable reason, the dog had taken a liking to him and had stood guard while he slept behind a Mexican restaurant. He wiped his face with the back of one sleeve and patted the shepherd's head. The grumbling emanating from the animal's midsection mirrored his own needs, and he said, "I'll bet you're hungry," as he stretched and stood. And as he gazed about, it became apparent that the alley where he'd spent the night served as the rear exit for a number of establishments, including the Owl Club Casino and Restaurant. They walked toward the rear of the establishment and were momentarily startled by a Casino employee tossing an armful of black plastic bags into a dumpster. The man ignored the duo and returned to the building, but the heavy steel door remained slightly ajar.

"What do you think, sport, should we dumpster dive, or see what we can find inside?" he asked of the dog.

The dog, of course, did not respond, but he did follow the command to sit and stay, as Gregory passed through to the restaurant's kitchen interior. Inside, a handful of people were mulling about. Some were flipping omelets, others were chopping vegetables, and a few stood around doing nothing at all. Nobody appeared to notice the stranger standing in their midst. A loaf of bread sat by itself on a stainless steel counter, and Gregory helped himself to the entire package, along with a stack of salami and cheese. He stood motionless for several seconds to see if his pilfering had been observed, but nobody seemed to care about his thievery. He turned and headed back to share the bounty with his new found-friend.

With breakfast out of the way, Gregory set his sights on revisiting the desert shack. He felt it important to determine whether the place had been refortified, thereby potentially denying him access. With the dog—whom he'd christened as, Sport—at his side, he headed out of town.

It had taken longer than anticipated to reach the site, and rather than stroll right up to it, he stationed himself a reasonable distance away. The structure, save for an obvious repair to the front door, seemed unchanged. But he knew that things weren't always what they appeared to be, and the ground sensors could have easily been enhanced.

OK, Sport, he thought, this is where you begin to earn your keep. He took a piece of bread from his pocket, wrapped it around the two remaining slices of salami, and squashed it into a ball. Holding it in front of the dog's nose, he threw it as close to the shanty as possible. "Go get it," he said.

Sport took off running in a straight line, retrieving and consuming the target with ease.

Now we wait, he said to himself, as Sport returned to his side for the anticipated, congratulatory pat on the head.

One hour later, as the night cooled sand had begun to heat up and the dog started to pant, Gregory searched the sky for incoming aircraft. But all remained quiet, and he wondered if the sensors had been deactivated, or if the dog had been too light to set them off. He began walking in the dog's tracks, hoping that Sport had somehow evaded the sensors, but roughly ten feet from the cabin the familiar sound of thumping helicopter blades could be heard approaching from the distance. Shit, he thought, I probably didn't wait long enough. He turned and ran back to his observation spot with the dog in tow. The pair hunkered down behind a sand covered boulder and waited. He knew that if the chopper was headed his way and circled, both he and Sport would stand out from the beige background, but there was nowhere to run that wouldn't present the same risk.

The large helo set down a distance away without circling, and Gregory thought that he was home free. But he had neglected to consider their use of thermal imaging; they'd suspected a human presence even before touching down. Sport grew wary, and began to whine and growl, as the pilots exited the helo and walked toward the shack. Gregory hugged the animal around the neck to quiet him and received a few licks in exchange. But something had changed. The helo's markings were different than before, and the pilots did not appear interested in the structure. With guns drawn, they walked straight toward his refuge.

"Come out with your hands behind your head," one pilot shouted.

Gregory hesitated, but complied. Sport, on the other hand, had a different plan in mind, and jumped at the gun holding hand of the nearest pilot.

"Call him off," the man cried out in pain.

"Sport, come here," he called out.

With his jaws locked onto the man's wrist, Sport's eyes turned in his friend's direction. And after a few tense moments, he let go and padded back to Gregory's side.

The second pilot moved forward and said, "Show me some ID."

"I don't have any at the moment," he replied.

The aviator took out his cell phone, snapped a photo of Gregory's face and returned to the helo, while his injured partner stood guard.

Gregory continued to stand with his hands over his head, while beads of sweat began to form on his brow as the sun rose higher.

"He's coming with us," the photo snapping pilot called out.

"What about my dog," Gregory complained.

"Not my problem."

"He'll die out here on his own."

There was a brief pause, during which the man appeared to bring the phone to his mouth, shook his head and shouted, "OK, he comes with us."

***

Nellis Air Force Base

To Gregory's surprise, his hands had not been secured and he sat with Sport in the aircraft's most rearward position. Sometime during the flight he'd fallen asleep—the rhythmical beating blades proving soporific—and had awakened as they were about to land.

"Where are we?" he called out, but he had not been

given a headset and the pilots could either not hear him, or had chosen to avoid the question.

He could see a parade of military aircraft, with jet fighters and a few tankers off in the distance, but the helo set down near a dark, isolated hangar from which poked the nose of a small, sleek passenger jet. Just inside the hangar, two men stood—in partial darkness—with their hands behind their backs. One wore a dark suit and tie, the other a decorated uniform.

"What's happening?" Gregory asked, as he was told to exit the craft without receiving a reply.

As his feet touched the tarmac, the suited man motioned for him to come forward.

"Dr. Gregory McCraken," the man said.

"Yes," he replied, tentatively.

"You will come with us."

"Who are you?"

There was no reply.

"Am I under arrest?"

"Not exactly," the man said, as he nodded toward the ladder leading to the aircraft's interior.

"Then what?"

The man did not respond but remained behind, as Gregory and the dog climbed into the jet.

Moments later, the dark suited male entered, closed the hatch and signaled for the already seated pilots to depart. Gregory started to open his mouth to ask about the absent uniformed officer, when the suit motioned for him to secure his and the dog's seatbelts and took a seat at the front of the plane, away from his captive.

Chapter Twenty-two

Tuesday, August 7th

6 P.M.

Washington, DC

The unmarked corporate jet touched down at Washington's Joint Base Anacostia, as a black SUV pulled alongside to the sound of the jets engine's fan blades whining to a stop. The suited man directed Gregory and Sport to the waiting vehicle and disappeared. The SUV's door locks clicked shut and the silent driver put the car in motion.

With Sport's head resting upon his lap, Gregory sat back for the ride to an unknown destination and fate.

The vehicle came to a stop behind what appeared to be an unoccupied warehouse on Bladensburg Road, Washington DC. The driver motioned for his passenger to exit and drove off, leaving the canine and master standing beside a ramp leading to a pair of black painted doors. Suddenly, one of the doors cracked open and a waving hand beckoned for him to approach. Gregory hesitated, thinking that he could run, but the ongoing cloak and dagger routine intrigued him and he cast caution to the wind and moved forward.

"Walk to the end of the corridor," a voice called out.

Gregory moved ahead slowly, careful not to trip on any unseen objects in the poorly lit passageway. But a bright light accosted him at the end of the hallway, and he stopped.

"Enter and take a seat," the same voice advised.

Gregory complied, forcing Sport to the ground in the process. A bright lamp, shining directly at his face, obscured the opposite side of the room where the presumed inquisitor sat. So he adjusted his position on the wooden chair and waited. Before him, on a small serving table, sat a pitcher of water, a cup and a bowl. He leaned forward, poured some water into the bowl and lowered it to the ground in front of Sport. And he was about to do the same for himself, when the voice filled the room with, "As the head of LightSpeed you are privy to its objective, correct?"

"Who are you?"

"Irrelevant."

"What you're asking about is highly classified and I'm not the head."

"Also irrelevant."

"Why am I here?"

"Patience."

"OK, I've got all day."

"Why the attempted break-in?"

Good, he thought, he doesn't know that I'd actually made it inside. "I needed to retrieve some personal items," he fibbed.

"Try again."

Gregory had been caught off guard. Telling the truth, he realized, would inadvertently reveal the nature of the project. And he'd been sworn to secrecy. On the other hand, he was once again under someone else's control and needed leverage. "Something happened to me in that place," he said.

"And?"

"I wanted to determine the cause."

He heard the shuffling of paper, and then, "Describe what happened."

"I blacked out."

"Are you prone to blackouts?"

"No."

"Withholding data is unacceptable."

"Who are you?"

"Asked and answered."

"I was told that I'd been burned."

"Has that been confirmed?"

"Not sure."

"What was the nature of your project?"

"I told you, it was classified."

Just then, the bright light was extinguished and the room went dark. A few seconds later, Gregory felt a stream of warm breath near his right ear, and then a whisper. "I'm going to take a guess and say that you are an honorable man," the inquisitor said.

"Yes, yes, I am," he replied anxiously.

"I have a proposal. If you refuse, you will disappear without a trace. If you accept, your loyalty will be to me and me alone. Understood?"

The quintessential offer I can't refuse, he thought. "You give me no choice."

"As intended."

The room went silent, and then a overhead light revealed the presence of a middle aged male dressed in a gray business suit and tie, whose face very much resembled the uniformed officer he'd seen at the airport.

"Have we met before?" Gregory asked.

"Not formally. But I know about you."

"What do you want?"

"Something mutually beneficial."

"Meaning?"

"I need to know the nature and purpose of your

project, and you need to know what transpired."

"But it's classif..."

"Let me worry about that," the man interrupted.

"Are you a spy?" he asked, knowing that if he was, the answer would not be truthful.

The man laughed, and said, "That's hilarious. And the answer is a resounding, no."

"How can I be certain?"

The man hesitated an instant and replied, "One can never stake claim to another's thoughts. In other words, I can offer no meaningful assurances other than my word. But time will prove my point."

Gregory pretended to swallow what he felt to be double-talk, but the man's threat appeared real. So he had little choice but to go along with the plan. After all, he thought, I'm already a government outcast. And then he had an epiphany, "If I do as you ask, can you get me out of the country?"

The man offered a quizzical expression and asked, "Why?"

"I'm a wanted man."

"I know of no criminal record."

"I'm on the run from the people who found me after the accident."

"Perhaps *they* were spies."

"They took me to an Air Force Base."

The man began to pace the room, rubbing his chin, as if deep in thought. He stopped, turned to face Gregory, and said, "You will be under my protection. No one will touch you."

"There's another problem."

"The dog?"

"Well, yes, but something far more daunting."

"I'll make certain that the dog is cared for while you're away. And the other?"

"There are ground sensors all around the place and a steel plate, or more, blocking entry."

"My problem, not yours."

"OK. When do I start?"

"Remain in this room until I depart. Someone will be around to collect you within the hour. They will take you to a safe house where you'll find a change of clothes, food for yourself and the dog, and a place to sleep until you're needed. You will not leave the residence, other than to briefly walk the dog. Understood?"

Gregory was about to reply, but the man had already turned and walked off. He looked down at the dog, who'd begun to whine, and frowned. Sport then rose, walked to the opposite side of the room and calmly lifted his leg, releasing a yellow waterfall that cascaded down the wall.

Sport came back to his side and took a seat. And as Gregory set about to gently pet the dog's head he began to wonder why fate had led him to the edge of a cliff.

Chapter Twenty-three

7 P.M.

General Louder had returned home, hung up his business suit, and poured himself a stiff tumbler of Johnnie Walker Black. As he stretched out on the living room couch he contemplated the day's events. Watch my six, he thought, recalling the day prior's warning. After today's little show, a three-sixty might not be enough. I'm guessing that the first heads-up referred to the men in black who'd visited my office the other day. Well, they'd asked for it by refusing to read me into their project. They want my people to guard their hole in the desert, he mused. It ain't gonna happen without me taking a look-see at what they've got going on down there, but one of their own is going to help me figure that out. He was about to make arrangements for a flight to Nevada, when his encrypted cellphone came to life. He withdrew the government issued device and hit the talk button.

"Louder," he announced.

"This is Raymond Washburn, are you alone?"

"Yes, Senator," he replied, not overzealous about the call from the man who'd placed his life in jeopardy.

"I need your help."

"No can do."

"Please, sir. I'm being followed, and I think it's related to our project."

"Call the Capital Police."

"You know I can't do that."

"Let's get something straight. You conned me into guard dog duty, and now the men in black have targeted my ass."

There was a moment of silence, and then, "I don't know what to do," the Senator sobbed.

"Hire a body guard."

"Wait, why are they after you?" Washburn asked.

"Not your problem," the General growled, as a thought popped into his head and he rose to check the street below. What he saw made his pulse quicken. A black SUV was sitting in a loading zone across from his building. The tag was not visible from his perch, but despite the plethora of black utility vehicles in DC, this one had agency written all over it.

"General, are you there?"

"Afraid that I've said all that I can," he hissed, and then he had a thought. If the same people are watching us both, I might be able to use Washburn as bait to draw them out, continuing, "I meant, all I can say over the phone.

You know where I live, come right over and I'll meet you in the street."

As he waited, Louder periodically checked to see if the SUV had moved, but it hadn't. Fifteen minutes later, he watched as a taxi came to a stop in front of his building. Smiling, he lowered the refilled shot glass and waited. Sure enough, a dark suited male with matching sunglasses exited the passenger side of the SUV and crossed over toward the Senator. A few minutes of what had appeared to have been animated conversation followed, and then the suited man walked back to his vehicle and stood by the opened door.

They let him go, Lauder mused, vigorously scratching his scalp. Has he turned the table on me, he wondered, reaching for his cellphone and dialing Ryan's number.

"Ryan, Louder here."

"Yes, sir. I still have eyes on the subject."

"Not calling about that. I'm at my home and I need an escort back to my office, riki tik," he said, realizing that they couldn't touch him at the Pentagon."

"I'll send a car to get to get you."

"Have them come around back to the service entrance," he advised, hitting the end button, thinking,

Washburn can stand out there all night for all I care.

**

* * *

The Pentagon, 8 p.m.

The General walked the mostly empty hallway to his office, entered and locked the door. He'd missed dinner, and his stomach was demanding food. But all he had in the office were a few power bars and a tray full of whiskey and cognac. The Pentagon had a food court and a few sit down restaurants, but they'd all closed at least an hour earlier. He was desperate, and the quick trip back to his office had transpired without much forethought. So he called the security desk.

"This is General Louder, and I have an unusual request."

"Yes, sir?"

"I'm stuck in my office this evening, and I seemed to have missed the food court closing."

"Yes, sir."

"Do you have someone you could send to get me a burger and fries?"

Louder thought he heard laughing in the background, and then a gruff, "Not allowed to run personal errands, sir."

"You can make an exception for a grateful Flag Officer," he said.

He heard the man exhale, and then, "Burger King or McDonalds?"

Thirty minutes later there was knock at his door. He rose from the desk, turned the lock and was greeted by a female officer carrying a paper bag with the Burger King logo. Louder reached into his pocket for a few bills, but the officer shook her head and said, "Came out of petty cash."

"Thank you," he replied, and closed the door.

He took a deep breath and returned to his desk. But upon removing the wrapped burger a handwritten note fell to the blotter, that read, *You can't hide.* He reached for the phone and redialed security.

"This is General Louder. The female officer who'd delivered my food, put her on the horn," he demanded.

"Sir, there are no female officers on duty tonight."

"Then I want to speak to whomever made the run to Burger King."

"I'm afraid that his shift had ended with your request."

"Give me his home number," he barked.

"Against protocol."

Louder slammed the phone into its cradle, knocking a few fries to the floor. No reason to spend the night in a chair, he thought—taking a bite of burger—I may as well go home. But as he swallowed the remains of his dinner, something struck him as odd, and he reached for the message. The hamburger grease had soaked through a portion of the paper, revealing a series of reversed numbers on its opposite side. He sat back and stared at the numerals. The woman who'd delivered this is likely a spook, he thought—noticing that the numbers could only be seen from the message side of the paper—and they avoid the obvious. She, or someone else, had gone to a lot of trouble to print these numbers so that they could be read correctly through the paper, as opposed to the side upon which they'd been written. It was definitely meant for my eyes. And a greasy hamburger was the perfect catalyst for their chosen method of print. I have to admit, they're good. Seven numerals makes it a likely candidate for a telephone number. And the absence of an area code suggests that it's local. He thought about using his encrypted phone, but realized that they probably already had his private cell number. So he reached into his pocket, removed the phone and dialed.

It rang three times and then a raspy voice said, "Yes?"

"Who is this?" Louder asked.

"You dialed me."

"Of course."

"How was the burger?"

"Just OK. Why the cloak and dagger?"

"These are dangerous times."

"I'm assuming you wanted to talk?"

"We have to meet."

"Not until I know who you are."

"Can't."

"Then no meet."

The phone went silent. "You still there?" Louder asked.

No reply.

I hate these God damn game players, he said to himself, as he rose from the desk, tossed the burger bag into the trash can and prepared to leave his office. But the cell phone began to vibrate in his pocket, and he reached for it.

"Yes?" he said, in a pissy tone.

"We've met before, you'll recognize me," the same raspy voice advised.

Louder considered his options. I can hang up and forget this ever happened, or I can feed my curiosity. "Alright, where and when?"

"Franklin Square, the fountain, 10 p.m., tonight. Come alone."

Louder was about to ask where they'd met, but the call had been terminated. I'm sure as hell not going into a park without backup, he thought. But an intelligence agent will be on the lookout for company. And the only one I can trust right now is Ryan, and he's busy babysitting the muslim murderer. But he punched in the numbers for Ryan's cellphone.

"Ryan, it's Louder."

"Yes, sir."

"Catch you in the loo?"

Ryan laughed. "No, sir. Just eating dinner in my car."

"Anything to report on our subject?"

"The phone tap is live, but he hasn't made any calls. And he hasn't left his apartment."

"Sorry about the twenty-four hour shift thing."

"It's my job, sir."

"It'll all come to a head soon, and you'll be back to normal."

"Yes, sir."

"I've got a question."

"Sir?"

"I have to meet someone and give the appearance of being alone..."

"Understood," he cut in, adding, "you need invisible backup."

"Exactly."

"I can have one of my buddies send up a drone."

"Hadn't thought of that," he said, realizing that he might want deniability, and that the drone driver would negate the possibility.

"I'll give it some thought," he advised, adding, "I need a ride home."

He'd arrived home and changed into a more causal outfit. The drone suggestion, although appreciated, had been discarded as too risky. And since reinforcement was no longer a viable option, he'd retrieved a small 9mm semi-automatic pistol from his nightstand and slid it into a pocket. And when the departure time had arrived, he called for a taxi and was let off within walking distance of the park.

At exactly 10 p.m., Louder approached the Franklin Square fountain. He could hear the lapping of running water before he saw it, and he waited before venturing out into the open. A few seconds later, a person in a dark running suit passed in front of the fountain and stopped, seemingly entranced by the cascading water. Louder watched, as the individual stretched and waved its arms, but stood its ground. As there was no one else about, Louder advanced. When he was within earshot, the runner, with its back still turned to the General, said, "Come closer."

Louder hesitated, as the voice was distinctly female, and clearly unlike that of the caller. "Who are you?" he said.

"I'm insulted. You really don't recognize my voice?"

"No."

"And after all the time we'd spent doing the nasty."

"Veronica?" he said, in astonishment.

The woman turned to face him with a smile that even the darkness could not hide.

"Long time no see, Nucky."

"You're supposed to be…"

"Dead?" she interrupted.

Yes, he nodded.

"My cover had been blown, I had to go deep."

"Why surface now?"

"Your name came up."

"And?"

"It wasn't for a commendation."

"Oh."

"So, you're the grim reaper," he said, fingering the 9mm in his pocket.

"No, I'm here to help."

"I've got the Joint Chiefs behind me, what more can you do?"

"They can't help you, but I can."

"Just to be clear, who's targeting my ass?"

She moved closer and placed her arms around his waist, but he interrupted what most would have considered an endearing embrace, and said, "I'm not wired, if that's what you're looking for."

"You haven't changed," she whispered.

"And you haven't answered my question."

"They don't have a name, but they're powerful."

"CIA or NSA?"

"The latter."

"Well, that's no surprise."

"We need to find a way out for you."

"Like you did?"

"That would work."

"I can't go dark, I've got responsibilities."

"They think you're a liability."

"How so?"

"Too inquisitive."

"Glad you're among the living, but I gotta go."

"Not even a kiss good-bye?"

He paused, and leaned in for a kiss. And that's when the sky began to spin.

The LIght Speed Project

Chapter Twenty-four

Tuesday, August 7th

10:25 P.M.

Colonel Duke had been feeling edgy. The aftermath following the murder of his childhood friend had not been easy, and sleep had been all but impossible. And added to that was a thread of paranoia that had him tagged as the assassin.

No one saw me, I'm sure that I'd gotten away clean, he told himself, as he paced the living room floor in his bare feet, every now and then drawing aside the curtain covering a window with a view of the street. But the presence of a strange vehicle parked across from his residence had added fuel to his delusional thoughts and panic had begun to take hold. Under ordinary circumstances, the presence of an unrecognizable automobile would not have been cause for alarm, as it could easily have been the property of a guest, but Bradley had convinced himself that the police were on his tail, and he had to run. He'd left the lights on in the condo to give the appearance that he hadn't departed, slipped into a pair of shoes, and wrapped a long raincoat about his casual clothing clad body, as he headed for the emergency staircase.

The main level exit door led to an alley behind the building, and he pushed the steel door open just enough to gaze out into the evening darkness. A shadow caused him to retreat, but a second look had revealed that it had belonged to the ever present trash dumpster, and he slowly slithered out into the moonlit passage. As he reached the edge of the building facing the street, he took a brief glance at the rear of the suspicious car and quickstepped in the opposite direction. He had no particular destination in mind, but the wad of cash in his pocket would gain him entry to a hotel for the night, while he planned for his next move.

A distant hideout would have been advantageous, but Bradley had been on foot and his mindless jaunt had taken him across from the Comfort Inn Pentagon City. He'd entered and paid cash for a one night stay. He knew that a decent police search could reveal his location, but he felt confident that his absence from the condo would go unnoticed long enough for him to try for a few hours of rest. He locked the door to his room and braced it with the angled back of a chair. Following a shower, he sat in his skivvies on the edge of the bed and prayed for a restful night, but his cellphone dinged, alerting him to an incoming email. To his horror, the message was from

Baba's wife, informing him of her husband's demise. Baba had claimed that his wife did not know of me, he thought. Maybe she'd come across my email address while going through his belongings, but it is suspicious. He considered a sympathetic response, but was suddenly overcome by intense guilt and a few unexpected tears. I could send flowers, or food, he pondered. How absurd, gifts and words of remembrance from the murderer. In my mind I'm a sinner, but the Imam has said that the Quran allows for such events, and who am I to question the word of a learned man.

He drifted off to sleep with the cellphone by his side.

Sometime during the night the hotel's fire alarm began to clang, and Bradley jumped from the bed. The power had gone out, and as he searched for his slacks in the darkness he was caught off guard by a furious knocking at his door. He opened it ajar.

"Follow me, there's a fire," a bellhop shouted over the raucous clanging.

"I have to dress."

"No time, you come now."

Bradley ran from the room in his underwear, the cellphone still in hand, and followed the beam from the bellhop's flashlight, as he ran down the corridor knocking and shouting. Moments later, he found himself on the street, surrounded by a handful of similarly attired guests, all waiting for a chance to return to their rooms. But destiny had not been on their side that night, as two long fire trucks came barreling down the street, horns honking and sirens screaming. Firemen jumped from their trucks and began unraveling hose and gazing skyward. It was then that Bradley took note of a thick blanket of dark smoke arising from an upper floor. The reality of his personal belongings and cash becoming unavailable brought him to the brink of hysteria, and he grabbed a fireman by the sleeve.

"I have to get my things," he screamed.

"Not tonight, buddy," the man said, as he shrugged away from Bradley's grip.

"But..."

The fireman had already disappeared into the building, leaving the Colonel with only one option; return to the condo.

As is oft commonplace, several police cars arrived on scene. And as Bradley began to walk—barefoot—in the direction of his apartment, one of the cars began to follow from behind. He'd gotten no farther than the end of the street when the cruiser stopped and a uniformed officer exited and called him aside.

"Where do you think you're going?" the policeman asked.

"Home."

The cop laughed. "In your underwear?"

"I was at that hotel," Bradley said, gesturing toward the burning building.

"Where is home?"

"Just a few blocks from here."

The cop turned toward his partner, who was now leaning against the cruiser's front fender, and said, "This guy claims to live nearby, but he decided to stay at the hotel. Make sense to you?"

The partner grinned, and shook his head, no.

"I think you should come with us," the policeman said, reaching for Bradley's left wrist.

"I work at the Pentagon," Bradley said, indignantly.

"Right. And I'm the President's butler," he replied, slapping a handcuff over Bradley's wrist.

"Call General Enoch Louder, he'll vouch for me," he screeched, as the cop dragged him to the car's rear door.

"I don't think so," the man laughed.

"Where are you taking me?"

"To a place for people like you."

They strapped the Colonel into the rear seat and aimed for the George Washington University emergency room.

Chapter Twenty-five

Wednesday, 7:30 A.M.

Gregory had spent the night in a Pentagon safe-house—a condo on Arlington Ridge Road—not far from Pentagon City. He had arisen twice to take the dog downstairs in the elevator for his bathroom needs. The condo had been stocked with canned and frozen provisions, as well as a last minute addition consisting of a large bag of dried dog food. He'd spent the waking hours watching television and flipping through outdated magazines.

He had already taken a shower, spent time playing fetch with Sport using a balled up pair of men's socks that he'd found in a chest of drawers, and had consumed three cups of strong coffee, along with four slices of toast and cheese that he'd first defrosted in the microwave. He had no idea if a housekeeper would be provided, so he'd washed and dried the dishes himself. He had just finished drying the coffee pot when he heard two knocks at the front door, followed by its abrupt opening. A new face came into view, catching him off guard.

"Who are you?" Gregory inquired, backing toward the kitchen counter that housed a few sharp knives.

"We work for the same person," the man, dressed in a

beige casual shirt and slacks advised.

"And that would be?"

The man gazed at him quizzically, and replied, "You're joking, right?"

Gregory shook his head, as if to say, no.

"It's time to go."

"I'm not going anywhere until I know whom I'm working for."

"I'm fairly certain you already know."

Gregory hesitated and dialed his memory back to the image of the uniformed man standing just inside the airplane hanger. And while there was some similarity between that man and the one who'd provided the safe house, there'd been no confirmation. But he ventured a guess, by saying, "A high ranking military officer?"

"Bingo. Now, let's go."

"What about my dog?"

"What's his name."

"Sport," he replied, as the dog's ears perked up at the sound of his name.

"He's going to a good home."

"Wait a minute, that wasn't the deal," Gregory said, angrily.

"You'll get him back when you're finished."

He locked gaze with Sport, and asked, "Can I say good-bye?"

"He's coming with us as far as the airport."

A black, GMC Sierra was waiting beside the building's rear exit. The man gestured toward the back seat, as Gregory and Sport took their places.

Forty-five minutes later, the pickup pulled through the guard gate at Joint Base Andrews. The unnamed man turned in his seat and said, "Say good-bye to Sport, your ride awaits."

"What's your name?"

"Not important."

"How will I get my dog back?"

"He'll be waiting when you return."

But Gregory was thinking, you mean, *if* I return. He ruffled the fur on top of Sport's head and said a tearful farewell, as the door swung open and he exited. Sport lurched forward, as if to follow, but the unnamed man held him in place with an arm around his neck.

***

2 P.M.

Elko Regional Airport

Elko County, Nevada

The government owned Gulfstream 550 touched down at Elko Regional Airport slightly more than four hours later. Gregory had hoped for a few hours of reflection time, but when he'd boarded the aircraft he'd been surprised to find four BDU (camouflage) clad male soldiers already seated. And they'd been a chatty group, both among themselves as well as with the physicist. Initially, they'd introduced themselves and then had begun a lengthy interrogatory regarding the topography of the target site. The group leader, who'd called himself Tom, had done most of the questioning.

"Any cover out there?" Tom had asked, downing the last of a meat filled hoagie, balling up the wax paper and stuffing it between his body and the seat.

"Just a few dunes," Gregory had replied.

"And the ground sensors?"

"Never saw them, but they're out there."

"We've got some tech to neutralize them."

"Good, because I sure don't want to see that chopper again."

"Helo?"

"I guess the sensors had alerted them."

"Military?" Tom had inquired.

"Not sure."

Tom had nodded his head knowingly and had breathed, "Spooks."

"Can you get me in?" Gregory had asked.

"Affirmative."

"Are we going right in when we arrive?"

"Zero dark thirty."

"Huh?"

"After midnight."

They sat in the parked plane until a white utility van arrived with its rear doors opened wide. The four men quickly humped their gear into the van, as Gregory was guided into the front seat with the driver. He closed his eyes for the roughly one hour drive to Battle Mountain. While he'd harbored some trepidation about the return trip to the desert location, he'd reasoned that the four men in the back of the van would provide some level of protection. But he had no way of knowing that their arrival had been been part of a plan to both placate the originators of the dark project and extract intelligence.

At 3:15 p.m., the van stopped alongside of a mobile home sporting a *For Rent* sign. The Driver exited, stood at the home's entry door for several minutes, scanning the desolate street, and then gestured for his passengers to enter. It was a sparsely furnished affair that wreaked of formaldehyde, but it was theirs for only a few hours. The driver joined them inside and, together, they sorted through the operation's required equipment.

"Is that really necessary?" Gregory asked, as he watched them loading their Sig Sauer M11 handguns and M4 Carbines.

"We're always prepared," one of the previously silent soldiers replied.

Gregory shrugged. "I don't suppose there's any food around?"

One of the men reached into a large rucksack and tossed an MRE at Gregory.

"Beef. Any good?"

"Only if you're really hungry," the man grunted.

Gregory tore open the package and downed its contents, as he continued to scrutinize the various pieces of equipment being uncovered. "What's that?" he asked, as two men assembled an oddly shaped device.

"This is the sensor killer."

"Looks like a funky metal detector."

"Close."

"How does it work?"

"Shorts out the sending unit."

"Got any more of those?"

"MREs?" the supplier asked.

Gregory nodded a, yes.

"Living dangerously," the man grinned, as he tossed an apple turnover into his lap.

"When we get in, I'll need electrical assistance."

The food tosser nodded at the man on his right and said, "He's your guy."

"Good. Wake me when its time to go," he mumbled, leaning back on the brown couch.

"If I were you, I'd take a trip to the head, ricky-tick," Tom advised.

"I don't feel the need."

"If you don't do it now, it ain't gonna happen later."

Gregory grimaced and headed off to find the bathroom.

"Not sure he understood," Tom said, "but when he can't shit, he'll get the picture."

"Gotta love those MREs," the driver cut in.

Chapter Twenty-six

Wednesday, 11 A.M.

Arlington, Virginia

General Louder had awakened with a headache and sour taste in his mouth. The bed was his own, but he could not recall how he'd gotten there. He rubbed his eyes and tried to rise, but his body felt heavier than usual, and he fell back into the bedding. Light was streaming through a slit in the drawn curtains and he gazed at the bedside clock. Eleven o'clock, he thought. I've never been late to the office. But as he made a second attempt to leave the bed he became aware of something odd. He was not alone. Reaching into the nightstand's single drawer, he grasped his aging military sidearm—a 45 .cal semiautomatic—and ripped the comforter away from the bed. What he saw caused him to withdraw in horror. A young woman, naked and as pale as a ghost, was lying on her back with a note taped to her immobile chest, that read: *stop your inquiry and she disappears, or you're next.*

For the first time in his career he'd encountered something that had rocked him to the core. The Bradley Duke affair could cause me some real grief, he said to himself, but a dead body in my bed, that's a game changer.

I can't believe that they'd killed some poor innocent just to make a point, his anger rising, as he quickly dressed in an attempt to distance himself from the scene. And as he entered the kitchen, he concluded that the entire fiasco had been carefully planned, and that the only one he could finger for the op was Veronica.

He placed the pistol on the granite countertop and filled a glass from the faucet. Hmm, there must have been something in her lipstick, because we'd had no other physical contact. And while it had always been my impression that she'd worked for the Company, it appears that I've been mistaken, she's NSA. It makes perfect sense to have used her, given our past relationship. But now I'm beginning to wonder if there ever was a relationship. I've been played, and it doesn't feel good.

Dressed in his uniform, he was about to leave the condo, when he was suddenly overcome with a feeling of sadness for the nameless person whose life had been taken by a ruthless organization, an act that they would likely justify with a cry of National Security. I'm almost ashamed to be wearing this uniform, he thought. But that's not what I stand for. And then he had an idea. What if there were no body, he wondered. I'm sure they have photos, but without the body it would be a tough sale. And I doubt that they'd want the existence of their black project to be dumped in Congress' lap by yours truly. But who could I trust to sanitize my apartment and make it all disappear. He closed the bedroom door and sat down on his couch. I would love to turn the tables on that bitch, Veronica, and while I could out her, I'd prefer something a tad more personal to rock her boat. Who do I know at the CIA that owes me a favor, he pondered. And then he recalled the son of a section chief who he'd managed to have recalled from Afghanistan. He searched for and found the small notebook that contained the contact information for people he'd kept apart from his job. It was the satellite phone number for Arthur Montgomery, the CIA Brussels station chief. He checked the time difference, and decided to call.

The phone rang several times before a voice asked, "Who is this?"

"Remember Afghanistan?" Louder said.

"What is this about?"

"Quid pro quo."

There was a moment of silence, and then, "This is about my son?"

"Before I begin, no names."

"Understood."

"I need a cleaner."

"I don't have access..."

"Of course you do," Louder interrupted.

The station chief exhaled loudly, "Your mess?"

"No, your arch enemy's."

"That's a hornet's nest."

"I need it done ASAP."

"Where is the trash?"

Louder winced at the man's choice of words, but he replied, "My nest, key under the mat."

"We'll take care of it."

"How soon?"

"Usually within the hour."

"You have the coordinates?"

"The cleaner will. This clears my account?"

"Yes."

The station chief terminated the call.

Louder locked the door and left the apartment. He wanted to be long gone when the crew arrived, so he headed for the garage and his personal vehicle. If anyone asked about his late arrival, he would blame the miserable headache that throbbed with his every step.

***

* * *

The Pentagon

1 P.M.

The General had stopped at the food court for lunch, but the image of the pale corpse lying on his bed had dulled his appetite. And realizing that the bed would be a constant reminder, he called a mattress store to order an exact replacement. That accomplished, he lowered his half eaten veggie wrap to the paper plate, chugged down the remaining soft drink, and headed for his office.

He passed the room often occupied by his subordinate —Col. Bradley Duke—and frowned. I've been coasting with this one, I'd better be more decisive before he does something irreparable. He made a mental note to call Ryan later on that day, but when he entered his office there was a sticky note on his desk pad that read: *Colonel Bradley has been admitted to George Washington University Hospital*, signed RK.

He recognized the initials as those of Ryan Keith. Hospital, he wondered. He reached for the phone and dialed.

"Ryan Keith," the voice announced.

"I got your message. What the hell's going on?"

"He's in the mental ward."

"Seriously?"

"The cops found him wandering in the street in his underwear."

"Doesn't sound like the Colonel."

"I checked, there was fire in a nearby hotel where he stayed the night. The residents had been told to vacate ASAP. He'd apparently advised the arresting officers of what had happened, but they hadn't bothered to check his story."

"What the hell was he doing in a hotel?"

"Unknown."

"He must be royally pissed."

"They've got him under sedation while they wait for the shrink. Want me to spring him?"

Louder considered his options, and replied, "Let him simmer for awhile, but put a few of your people at his door and take the day off. And make certain that he speaks with no one other than the hospital staff."

Louder smiled. One problem temporarily tabled. He gazed at the brass clock in the shape of an anchor that sat at the end of his desk. The Battle Mountain team should be in place by now, he mused, but they won't have a green light until sometime after sundown. I'm guessing that the men in black now consider me neutralized, so they won't be anticipating an incursion at their site. And if they do get wind of it, I'll simply explain that I've supplied the security that they'd requested. Not a rock solid excuse, but it should be good for some negotiation.

Chapter Twenty-seven

Wednesday, August 8th

2 P.M.

Imam Faaroog Awan had been calling Akil's (Colonel Bradley Duke) cellphone to no avail, until, following the fifth attempt, a female voice had responded.

"I am seeking the owner of this telephone number," the Imam had said.

"He is currently indisposed," the nurse had replied.

"Are you a friend?"

"I am a registered nurse."

"Had there been an accident?"

"No."

"Then what is your function?"

"Are you a family member?"

The Imam hesitated, and had replied, "No, I am the spiritual adviser."

"Sorry, I can't help you."

"Wait ... where is he located?"

"For purposes of visitation?"

"Yes, of course."

"Visitors are not allowed at this time."

"May I send a gift of solace?"

"Send it to the George Washington University Hospital," she'd said, and hung up.

The spiritual leader sat back in his heavily embroidered chair, scratched a growing bald spot on the top of his head with a spindly finger, and frowned. I must know the nature of his illness, he thought. The visitation restrictions suggest a contagious illness, severe physical dysfunction, or... The disposal of his friend should not have been destabilizing, after all, he's a soldier of Islam. But Akil has been among the devils longer than anticipated, perhaps he has become less dedicated than I require, or worse, has been seized by an attack of conscience. His role is of paramount importance. I will immediately dispatch an envoy to uncover the truth.

The Detroit mosque had served as the Imam's base of operations, and he'd rarely left the building, except for a few hours of sleep in his nearby apartment. But it was the middle of the afternoon, and despite the fact that prayers were not long off, he walked out into a light rain heading for his second most trusted disciple.

Jaafar Mowad worked as second in command at an auto repair shop not far from the mosque. When they'd first met, during one of Jaafar's infrequent visits to the mosque, the Imam had endeavored to improve the middle aged man's attendance. Jaafar had explained that his job required that he be present during the daytime hours and often beyond. Maintaining a rigid prayer schedule was not possible. The Imam had invoked the name of Allah, but Jaafar had indicated that food and a roof over his head took precedence, and they had parted ways without animosity. But that had been several years earlier, and while Jaafar's appearance at the mosque had been sporadic at best, he had relied upon the Imam's council on several occasions for matters of personal importance. The holy man had taken a liking to the mechanic, and had brought his own aging vehicle to the shop for repairs. Jaafar had never accepted payment for his services and, over time, they had established an unlikely friendship. It had become apparent to the holy man that his friend harbored a sense of dedication and willingness to support the Islamic cause. And following a work related altercation, Jaafar had considered leaving the country to join several militant family members in Syria, but the Imam had warned against such a decision. He'd made it clear that the cause could be best served by redirecting his nascent militancy in a more local fashion.

The Imam approached the entrance to the shop and found Jaafar sitting under an overhang, eating a hoagie.

"That is not a ham sandwich, I hope," he joked.

Jaafar swallowed, and rose from the ground.

"I did not intend to interrupt your lunch," the Imam said.

"Vegetable hoagie, and it's awful," he replied, lowering his head.

"Is it safe to speak?"

Jaafar gazed about, and said, "Inside, I am alone today."

They entered the shop and passed beneath a lift, on top of which sat a 1970 Oldsmobile. A weakening stream of oil was trailing from its engine into a floor standing bucket, and Jaafar warned, "Watch that you don't get soiled," as he led the way to the 6'x6' office.

He offered the Imam the only chair, a torn swivel affair covered with faded, black vinyl. Jaafar took a seat on the edge of the metal desk, as his friend and mentor cautiously lowered his body onto the chair.

"I have need of your services," the holy man said.

"Do you need a tow?"

"No," he smiled, "one of our own has taken ill and I need to comprehend the circumstances."

"How can I help?"

"I understand your commitment to this place," he

said, waving an arm about the room, "but the person I speak of is in a Washington hospital."

The mechanic scowled. "There is no one to take may place."

"When will the proprietor return?"

"Late tonight."

"Then you will depart in the morning," he advised, removing an envelope from his pocket and placing it on the desktop.

"What is this?"

"The name of the person to be investigated, his location and money for your trip."

"But..."

"You are wondering why I could not have accomplished this task over the telephone, I assume."

Jaafar nodded his agreement.

"Apparently, it is not a simple illness. And only family can be told."

"I am to be a family member?"

"It appears so."

The Imam left the shop and headed back to the mosque. Jaafar waited until he'd disappeared from view, then tore open the envelope, pocketed the cash and memorized the unfamiliar name. That accomplished, he shred the envelop and the message within and plopped into the chair recently vacated by the Imam.

Gazing briefly at the dark blue Oldsmobile, with its prominent rust spots and grease encrusted undercarriage, he decided to dip into the package of chocolate licorice that the shop's owner kept in a bottom desk drawer. Ripping off a sizable piece, his purplish, rubbery lips forcing it into the depths of his mouth, he considered the Imam's demand. I've never been to Washington, he mused. I will need a map. And I am to pose a the man's relative, he thought, running a few fingers through his long, black beard. Well, I guess I could be a cousin.

Chapter Twenty-eight

8 P.M.

Battle Mountain

With darkness came the green light.

Gregory followed the four soldiers and squeezed into the rented Jeep Grand Cherokee. The car had come from a local rental agency and provided a level of anonymity not offered by a military vehicle. It took slightly more than an hour to reach the sandy perimeter surrounding the shack, and upon arrival the men cautiously exited the car and stood by its side surveying the area with night vision goggles.

One of the commandos nudged Gregory and asked, "Anything different?"

"I haven't been here in the dark, can't see a thing."

The man removed his goggles and handed them to Gregory. And after demonstrating how to adjust the device, he repeated the question.

"Looks like the front door has been boarded, but otherwise all else is the same," he whispered.

The goggle lender signaled an OK to the remaining three, and together they removed the pair of EMP (electromagnetic pulse) devices that they'd assembled in the safe house.

The identification and destructive process took almost two hours, but their efforts had resulted in a clear path to the front of the shanty. Gregory followed from behind, trying to make out their boot prints with starlight as his only source of illumination. And as he approached, two commandos pried loose the boards covering the entrance, resulting in the release of a blast of heated, foul smelling air.

"Man that stinks," Tom observed.

"Smells like death," another said, as he inched his way inside.

"Found the source," Tom called out, as he lit a small, but powerful flashlight and aimed it at a decaying body. With his booted foot, he rolled the maggot infested corpse over and said, "We've got a problem."

"What's up, boss?"

"This guy's been shot."

Gregory, who had remained at the entrance enjoying the cool night air, and had heard only the word, *shot*, stepped inside and asked, "Who'd shot whom?"

Tom waved the flashlight for him to approach the body and he asked, "Familiar?"

Gregory recoiled from the repulsive odor, but there

had been something about the remains of the person's face. He held his breath and took another look. Oh shit, he said to himself, Jeb.

"Well?" Tom insisted.

Gregory backed off and replied, "It's the owner of a local pizza shop."

"Makin' deliveries out here?" he guffawed.

"He'd helped me move that metal plate," he gestured, adding, "the one thats covering the entrance to the elevator."

"And you shot him?"

"Hell no. The helicopter guys took him for trespassing, but left me behind."

"And why would they do that?"

"I have no idea," he breathed.

"You two," Tom said, pointing at his men, "get this carcass outta here, ricky tick, an' come right back. We got some heavy lifting to do."

When the five men had managed to slide the steel plate far enough to gain entrance to the elevator shaft, Tom sent one man outside to stand sentry, and turned to examine what should have been the top of an elevator. "They sure don't want no visitors," he spat.

"What's wrong?" Gregory asked.

"Look for yourself," Tom said, passing the flashlight to the physicist.

Gregory felt as if he'd been kicked in the gut. "Where did it go?" he wailed.

"Probably at the bottom of the shaft."

"Now what?"

"We rappel down."

"I was never good at rope climbing."

"No problem. If it's functional, I'll bring the elevator up."

Tom and two others unraveled a long length of climbing rope and secured the top end to a thick metal ring that hung from one end of the recently moved steel plate.

"Will that support your weight?" Gregory asked.

"It will if you all stand on it," he grinned, as he lowered the loose end into the darkened shaft. When the entire length had disappeared below, he eased himself over the side and, with a flashlight held firmly between his teeth, began the descent. Since those remaining above were standing a distance away, adding weight to the plate, they could not see Tom as he released the elevator's top hatch and slid inside. Five minutes later a humming sound filled the room, as the top of the lift rose flush with the flooring. And then, Tom's head popped out of the top and he called out, "All aboard."

The functional elevator had already proven that at least some power had been left alive, and Gregory encountered no difficulty locating the first of many light switches. Tom activated his radio to check with the sentry above.

"Are we clear?"

"Roger that," the sentry replied.

"Probably gonna lose signal down here, so drop a flash-bang down the shaft if there's trouble."

"Fuckin' A."

Gregory showed the three men the location of the large circuit breaker, and the one with the greatest electrical expertise took hold if it, along with a few nearby tools, and followed the physicist to its insertion point. It had taken thirty precious minutes to install the breaker without, as the installer had said, getting fried. But when the final connection had been made, a loud horn echoed throughout the interior.

The installer jumped back from the breaker panel and shouted, "What's that?"

"It's telling us that the plasma generator is in standby mode."

"Standby? Then why the horn?"

"If the generator were to be accidentally or intentionally initiated, and the plasma it generates were not contained, it could exceed ten thousand degrees," Gregory informed.

"That ain't fryin', that's incineration."

"We'll follow your cue," Tom advised.

Gregory nodded his approval and cautiously entered the generator room. "This is where I allegedly got burned," he said.

Tom shrugged, as if he had no knowledge of Gregory's accident.

"I'm going to fire up the generator ... you might want to leave the room."

"Is it safe?"

"We'll find out."

The commandos left the room and stood outside looking through the three inch wall of thermal glass that separated the lab from the corridor. With his hand on the switch that would set the machine in motion, he turned to make certain that he was physically alone, and flicked it upward. At first, nothing happened, and Gregory scratched his head, wondering if his so-called accident had damaged the device. But a few seconds later the room lights flickered and the familiar sound of a turbine spooling up—a cooling fan—filled his ears. He gave the anxious observers a thumbs up.

The team had not set a specific schedule for their subterranean time, but it had been clear from the leader's constant clock watching that time had been of the essence. Gregory had left the room several times to explain that there was no way he could speed up the process, but Tom began pressing him for the information he'd been instructed to obtain. "OK, we got you down here. Tell me what this is all about," he demanded.

"You're in a highly classified facility..." Gregory began to explain.

"Cut the crap, and tell me what I need, or I'll make sure you never leave this place."

Gregory was taken aback. My demise hadn't been part of the deal, he said to himself. But right now I have no choice. "I've already told you about the plasma. It's not a naturally available commodity on this planet, and it has to be created with a great deal of energy."

"OK, so you create some hot shit that goes ... where?"

"Into that ceramic composite cubicle at the end of the room."

"What's it for?"

"Plasma can be weaponized, and it would be

unstoppable."

"So it's a weapon?"

Gregory shook his head and replied, "We were never told its purpose."

"So the weapon thing is your theory?"

"Pretty much."

"Anything else it can do?"

"Maybe."

"Don't jerk my chain, spill," he menaced.

"Some physicists have theorized that with enough energy one could warp time and space."

"What the fuck does that mean?"

"Time travel, worm holes and more."

Tom's eyes glassed over, as he processed Gregory's words. "You're kidding, right?"

Gregory shook his head, no.

"Science fucking fiction," Tom said.

"No, it's all theoretically possible."

"And this machine can do all that?"

"I don't know."

"OK, I got what I came for ... time to go."

"But the machine is barely up to full power."

"Not my problem."

"I must find out what happened to me."

"Again, not my problem."

"Then leave me here, but send the elevator back down."

"No can do."

"I had an agreement," he argued.

"And I have my orders."

What followed was a two minute stare-down, during which Gregory had come to a decision. I'll tell him to leave the room while I wind down the generator, he told himself, but I'll lock the door from the inside. Three inch glass is probably somewhat bulletproof, and I'll have enough time to bring the generator back to the state that caused my alleged accident.

Three men were banging on the glass and kicking at the door, before they sent a few high velocity rounds at the glass. But aside from a series of nasty pockmarks, the glass held. Suddenly, the room was filled with an etherial appearing blue-green light, and Gregory could no longer see the three men who were standing outside, mystified by the spectacle. As a scientist, he was thrilled by what he'd created but, as a human being he was terrified. He reached for the switch that had started the process, but while the large titanium lever was clearly visible, his fingers passed through it as if it were a hologram, rather than a solid object. Oh shit, he thought, its happening. This is the light that I'd witnessed before I'd passed out, I need to shut this thing down. A big red failsafe button protruded from the wall opposite the control panel, and he reached for it, but it too had no tactile substance. And then the blue haze began to fade and he found himself on the no longer cool, concrete floor. They were at it again, three men were furiously banging on the door. He crawled to it, reached up and released the lock. They opened it but refused to enter.

"What the fuck was that?" Tom barked.

"The future," Gregory rasped, adding, "did you do something?"

"We pulled the power."

"Thank you," he exhaled.

Chapter Twenty-nine

George Washington Hospital

Thursday, 5 A.M.

Colonel Duke awakened in a stupor in a multi-bedded room. He had been visited the night before by a psychiatric medical resident who had disregarded his story, concluding that it had been a confabulation. And despite Bradley's repeated pleas to corroborate his narrative with the Pentagon, he'd been prescribed antipsychotic medications, as the psychiatric attending had not been due until the a.m. He'd promptly drifted off to dreamless slumber. But while the effect of the medication had lingered—his next dose due at 7 a.m.—he'd come to the realization that he might not be able to convince the staff to release him. So he began to plan his escape.

At 6:45 a.m., a male nurse arrived to check his vital signs and administer medications, and while the man was leaning over his body, Bradley grabbed him behind the neck and forced his body to the ground. The stainless steel tray that the nurse had placed upon the bed contained an intramuscular dose of Zyprexa. Bradley grabbed the syringe and jammed the needle into the buttocks of the unconscious man. As he praised Allah for the absence of any roommates, he removed the nurse's clothing and donned the ill fitting apparel. The medication had left him somewhat unsteady, and after checking the outside corridor for onlookers, he made a serpentine dash for the elevator. To his dismay, the lift was full of medical staff on their way to make rounds, but he kept his face down and avoided eye contact, as the elevator stopped at various floors on the way to the lobby. With his head feeling like it had been filled with mud, he hadn't planned beyond the actual escape, and he was fairly certain that the fallen nurse would soon be discovered. And as the elevator reached the lobby, the door slid open to the sound of a blaring alarm. Assuming that the alert was related to his ongoing caper, he quickstepped to the exit, flashed a smile at a security guard, and trotted out into the cool, morning air.

His first misguided thought was to take a taxi to the Pentagon, but he had no cash, no identification, and to make matters worse, he was dressed as a nurse. While he had no idea how he would enter his apartment without a key, he aimed his undersized shoes in that direction. The roughly five mile trek took several hours, and he arrived at his building's front door at ten a.m. He struggled to recall the code for the rear entry door, but after a few tries he succeeded and took the empty elevator to his floor. The

Imam had instilled in him the importance of being prepared for any emergency, and as his head began to clear he was thankful that the warning had prompted the installation of a small, hollow, brass nameplate to his apartment door, behind which a key had been glued. He pealed away the plate and the pried loose the key. He downed a few aspirin and went to bed.

Chapter Thirty

Thursday, 7 A.M.

The Pentagon

General Louder had returned to his condo several hours following the removal of the dead body and shortly after the new mattress had been installed. Sleep had been fitful that night, given the new bedding and the fact that his head had been filled with a thousand unsavory thoughts. But with his internal alarm clock chiming, he rose, filled a mug with coffee that he'd set to brew the night before, and reached for the newspaper that had been delivered to his front door. With his mouth full of coffee he nearly choked when his eyes met with the front page headline: *MENTAL PATIENT ESCAPES FROM GW SECURE WARD.* But it had been the accompanying photograph, revealing an unmistakable face, that had caused his near apoplexy. Hell's bells, he thought, I'd almost forgotten about that lying piece of crap. This photo is going to cause a shit storm at the office that'll vector itself straight to my desk. He'll have to be dealt with, and if I want to avoid the same, Court Martial is off the table. No, extreme prejudice is the only viable option, but it will take some careful planning, now that the cat's out of the bag.

He finished his coffee, a sense of burgeoning heartburn on his personal radar, donned a freshly pressed uniform, and headed for the condo's garage. Despite the fact that he lived in a secure facility, he found Ryan leaning against his car when he'd approached.

"How'd you get in here?" Louder asked, his brows deeply furrowed.

With a shrug, Ryan grinned and replied, you really should have a talk with the condo commandos.

"Never mind. What's up?"

"Seen this?" he asked, holding up the front page of the local paper.

"Yeah," he breathed.

"Is it time to act?"

"Think so," Louder said, unlocking his black, GMC Yukon.

"Got a preference?"

"It has to be done before the local PD gets a bead on him."

"He's holed up at his apartment."

With his shoes still planted on the concrete garage floor, Louder stared into the vehicle's dark interior. If we do something in town it might look suspicious, he mused. "How about some time off?"

"Sir?"

"I can arrange for some vacation time."

"I could sure use a vacation."

"How does Nevada sound?"

"I've never been to Las Vegas."

"And that's not gonna change. But I've got some jar heads out there on a mission, and they can make our problem disappear."

"How soon?"

"It's now 0730 hours," he said, gazing at his wristwatch, adding, "go to his condo, tranq (tranquillize) him, and take him to Andrews. I'll make the arrangements."

"He lives in a secure building, sir."

"That shouldn't be a problem for you," he smirked.

Ryan shook his head with an, OK.

Louder drove out of the Arlington condo, automatically taking his usual route to the office. He'd yet to come up with a plausible disposal story for the marines, but he was due to make contact with them regarding their mission results.

Halfway to the Pentagon, a black SUV, similar to his own, pulled alongside at a stoplight. The male, front seat passenger made a gun gesture with his right hand, the make-believe muzzle pointed at louder's head. The General hit the button to lower his window, but the light had changed and the vehicle had moved on. Looks like they're not done with me, he thought. I can't fight off the entire spook community, but I can do something about Veronica. I'll just have to come up with a fittingly nasty scheme. And the first step will be to find the rock beneath which she sleeps. Hmm, with Ryan heading to Nevada I'll have to my own sleuthing.

***

8:45 A.M.

He slid the security card into the office door's lock and headed straight for the comfortable chair behind his desk. With a temporary reprieve from his hemorrhoids, he was now able to appreciate the costly seat that the government had unknowingly provided, and he pushed back, savoring the aromatic Italian leather. But the vision of a dead body in his bed, coupled with the finger pointing rider, kept nagging at him and his anger began to build. He glanced over at the rolling beverage cart, thinking, it's a tad early for a drink but I sure could use one. Shaking his head, he reached for the phone, preparing to begin his search for

Veronica's lair, when a locked desk drawer began to chirp. It was the encrypted satellite phone that was stored within.

"Speak," he said.

"Striker(Nevada team leader) reporting in, sir."

"What have you found, Major?"

"Are we secure?"

"We're both encrypted, but I suppose the damn NSA could be listening."

"Maybe I should go secret squirrel (top secret)."

"That big, Tom?"

"And then some."

"All wrapped up?"

"Not exactly."

"Explain."

"The scientist wants to go back."

"Purpose?"

The Major hesitated.

"Tom?"

"Yes, sir. Something strange occurred."

"Remember, listeners."

"Do we have green light for another go?"

The General scratched his chin and gazed out of a deeply tinted window. This op has been risky, not sure I want to press my luck. On the other hand, he mused, it sounds like the men in black are up to something really dark. "Risk assessment?" he asked.

"Moderate."

"Are your crotchers (marines) up for it?"

"Roger that."

"You have green, but there's something else."

"Sir?"

"I'm sending you a package for deep disposal."

"Oorah."

"Courier en route," he said, hitting the end button.

Louder placed the phone back into the drawer and keyed the lock. There are an untold number of bodies buried in the desert, one more won't make a difference, he said to himself. He rose, walked over to the coffee urn and filled his regimental mug. As he turned, his gaze locked onto the liquor cart and he hissed, "Oh, what the hell," as he mixed in a shot of Jack Daniels.

The morning hours passed quickly, with multiple calls from his secretary regarding the scheduling of meetings, her need for time off, as well as an urgent message from Senator Raymond Washburn. And around noon, when he'd completed the morning's to-do list, he buzzed the secretary, "Get me the Senator."

"Washburn?" he said, when the Senator's cellphone

had stopped ringing.

"We need to meet," Washburn's voice quivered.

"I thought we were done."

"Something's come up."

"Probably indigestion."

"Seriously."

The guy sounds scared out of his wits, he thought, maybe they put a stiff in his bed too. "OK, I've got some free time around 1400 hours. Come by my office."

The Senator had arrived without fanfare, and had been waiting a good forty-five minutes before the appointed hour. At 1400 hours he was escorted to the General's office.

Louder avoided the usual pleasantries and motioned for the man to have seat. Rather than his customary posture of superiority, the visibly shaken Senator took his place in front of the General's desk and waited.

"So, what's the emergency?" Louder asked, now sipping from a shot glass.

"I can't go home, I can't drive my car, I can't do anything without being followed, " he whined.

"Sure it's not paranoia?"

"I'm not crazy."

"OK, OK. Who do you think is following you?"

"You know who."

Louder took a deep breath and said, "This office is swept every morning, there are no bugs. Say what's on your mind."

Washburn fidgeted in his chair, wiped a bead of sweat from his brow, and replied, "It's that fucking project. I think they're getting ready, as they say, to clean house."

"They're not going to kill a sitting senator," Louder guffawed.

"Do I have to bring up the Kennedy affair and that laughable commission investigation."

Louder rolled his eyes and downed the remainder of the Jack Daniels. But an image of the pale, lifeless body in his bed popped into view, and he grew concerned. "Has the project reached its goal?" he asked.

"How the fuck would I know. I'm just their errand boy."

"What do you want from me?"

"Protection."

"I'm a flag officer, not a mafioso," he said, with a smile.

"There must be something you can do."

"Call the Secret Service."

"And tell them that a no name NSA division wants to

silence its puppet?"

Louder shook his head in agreement.

The two men had sat in silence for several minutes, when Louder said, "You look like you could use a drink."

"A double, of anything strong."

Aside from the Senator's nervously bouncing leg, and the clinking of ice cubes as Louder refilled a larger tumbler, the room was quiet. And with a mouth full of ice, the General broke the hush, and said, "I need something from you."

"Anything," the man gushed.

"An address. I need the home address of a spook."

"How would I get that?"

"Not my problem. But do it, and I'll look out for you."

Washburn lowered his head, and then looked up and downed the remainder of his drink. "Give me the name."

Louder swallowed the melting cubes and thought, it may not be the snake's real name, but it's a starting point. "Veronica Moltz."

"Agency?"

"Start with the Company."

"You're not sure?"

"She used to be with them, but now it's not clear."

"Free agent?"

"Possibly, but she may be with your benefactors."

"Fuck me. It'll be difficult and dangerous."

"You've already got one foot in the quicksand."

"And my problem?"

"It gets resolved when you bring home the bacon."

Washburn rose and headed for the door, but turned and said, "If you never hear from me again, you'll know what happened."

Chapter Thirty-one

Thursday, 9 A.M.

The Imam had dispatched Jaafar Mowad to investigate the state of Akil's (Colonel Bradley Duke) physical being. He had arrived in Washington the night before, and had checked into an $85.00 per night room at the Kellogg Conference Hotel. His meager luggage had consisted of a small overnight bag containing a change of underwear, a Quran and a rolled up prayer rug.

The following morning, after two steaming cups of tea, he'd headed out to the hospital. He had never been inside of a medical facility of its magnitude, and had no idea what kind of security he might encounter, so he had prepared a fabrication in order to ease his way in. The bus had let him off a distance away, and he'd used the walking time to rehearse the story. When he'd passed through the entrance he went straight to the information desk, but as he stood before the austere looking hospital employee he realized that the Imam had provided only the target's Islamic name. What if he is not registered as Akil, he wondered. But with no other option, he smiled and said, "I am a relative of a patient in this hospital."

"That's nice," the matronly woman replied, as she

shuffled papers around her desk.

"I would like to know his condition?"

"Does he have a name?"

"Akil," he replied.

"I'm gonna need more than that."

The Imam had provided the Americanized family name of Duke. Jaafar had thought it strange, given the target's Islamic origins, but he went with it and replied, "Duke, Akil Duke."

With a quizzical expression on her face, the woman asked, "Do you have some identification?"

Jaafar rummaged through his pockets and produced a driver's license which he slid across the counter.

"And how are you related?"

"First cousin," he fibbed.

"Sorry, I can only speak with immediate family."

"But I am his only living relative," another lie.

The woman glared at him, and then turned to tap a few keys on her computer's keyboard. "Nobody here by that name."

Since Bradley, aka Akil, had been found wandering in his underwear, he had not been able to provide any form of identification. And for that reason, he had been registered as a John Doe. But neither the Imam nor Jaafar had been privy to that information.

Jaafar was speechless. The Imam would not have sent me on a fool's errand, he thought. Something odd is going on.

"If that's all," the woman said, "you'll have to move away from the desk."

"I know that he was here, I was told that a nurse answered his cellphone," he complained.

"Perhaps it was another hospital," she droned.

"No, I am certain it was this one."

"Move away from the desk, or I will have to call security."

The utterance of the word, security, had been enough to put a damper on his bravado, and he backed off. But as he approached the exit, a discarded newspaper caught his eye. While he had never met Akil, the Imam had shown him a photo taken during Akil's recent visit to Detroit, and the image of the disheveled man occupying the front page bore a striking resemblance to the person he sought. If Akil has escaped, he thought, I will never find him. But it must mean that he is no longer ill. I will call the Imam, he said to himself, as he removed his cellphone and punched in the number.

"As-salamu alaykum," the Imam said.

Jaafar repeated the same, adding, excitedly, "Akil has escaped."

"Escaped?" the Imam said, with a tone of incredulity.

"I saw his picture in today's newspaper. It says that a mental patient escaped."

"Akil, a mental patient? I find that hard to fathom."

"What should I do?"

If Akil has truly lost his mind, he is a liability, he told himself. Only Allah knows what he may have revealed. He must be dealt with. "Find him," the Imam demanded.

"Where should I look?"

The Imam rattled off his last known address.

"A man on the run does not return home," Jaafar suggested.

"A crazy man might."

"And if I find him?"

"He can no longer be trusted."

"I understand."

Jaafar placed the phone back into his pocket. He had understood the Imam all too clearly. In the past, he had been called upon to perform various menial tasks for the Imam, some of which had required the threat of violence. But murder was an act reserved for infidels, and Akil was a true believer. He was deeply troubled by the unusual request, and for the first time in his life considered disobeying the order. But first he had to find Akil and get a feeling for the man's devotion to Islam, only then could he make a rational decision. After all, he thought, I do not wish to sully my chance for paradise.

Chapter Thirty-two

Andrews AFB

Thursday, 11 A.M.

Despite several unanticipated obstacles, Ryan had managed to overcome the condo's security measures and had found his way to Colonel Duke's apartment. His plan had required the element of surprise, and to that end he had made his way to mark's floor with a folded wheelchair and hid in a utility closet until he'd been certain that the corridor had been empty. He then set about to pick the Colonel's front door lock. It hadn't taken long, and he'd entered the unfamiliar space with a filled syringe in hand. The colonel, still feeling the effects of the medications that he'd received at the hospital, had apparently passed out on his bed. Without hesitation, Ryan had jabbed the needle into Bradley's neck and pushed the plunger to its depths. With his eyes glued to his luminescent wrist watch, he'd counted off the five minutes that he'd been told it would take for the medication to become effective, and heaved Bradley's limp body onto the chair, layering a blanket across his torso.

As promised, a small, government owned corporate jet was waiting at Andrews AFB when he'd arrived. The pilot and copilot helped him carry the unconscious Colonel into the cabin, where they strapped him into a rear seat and proceeded to spool up the engines for takeoff.

***

Battle Mountain, Nevada

Straw-buyer obtained safe house

5 P.M.

"That the package?" Tom, aka Major Striker, asked of Ryan, nodding at the still lifeless body in a wheelchair.

Ryan smiled and said, "It's all yours."

"Is there a story that goes with it?"

"Does it matter?"

"Guess not," Tom admitted, adding, "you here for the show?"

"What show?"

Tom grinned and said, without explanation, "Welcome to weirdsville."

The Major introduced Ryan to his team, saving Gregory for last. "This guy over here," he said, motioning toward the physicist seated a few feet away, "is the ring master."

Gregory snarled at the announcement, but extended

his hand, and said, "You might want to stay behind tonight."

"Not a chance."

"It's gonna be dangerous."

Ryan shrugged, as if he could care less.

Tom motioned for Ryan to follow him into the safe house's kitchen, where they both took a seat. "Got any preference for disposal?"

"Just as long as it's permanent."

"We don't enjoy fragging civilians."

Ryan was about to explain that the lump heaped into the wheelchair was not a civilian, but decided against it, and replied, "National security issue."

"I've got something in mind," he chuckled.

"Just as long as he disappears."

"Oorah."

They settled into a cacophony of small talk and a few bawdy jokes to pass the time, as they awaited the return of the coin toss loser who'd been tasked with carrying food back from the Ming Dynasty Chinese restaurant.

At eleven thirty p.m. the Major announced that it was *go time*, and the group's demeanor quickly morphed into that of a well trained killing machine.

"Game faces," Tom called out, as they checked their

weapons and assorted gear.

"Expecting resistance?" Ryan questioned, surprised by the assorted weaponry.

"Always prepare for the unexpected," Tom said.

"In that case, I could use..."

Tom caught Ryan mid-phrase by pressing a Heckler & Koch MP5 (9mm submachine gun) into his midsection.

Ryan grunted, examined the weapon and complained, "Are you expecting close on combat?"

"Borrowed that from a Seal unit, it's our only spare. Know how to use it?"

"I've trained with one, so, yeah."

"Time to mount up."

Earlier that day, realizing that the Jeep had been a tight squeeze for his men and their equipment, Tom had replaced it with a GMC Yukon. The men, along with the unconscious Colonel Duke, piled into the large vehicle and drove off into the night. Little to no conversation had taken place during the journey, but as they approached the cabin's perimeter, the Major turned toward the rear seats and announced, "Get the blasters (EMP devices) ready, we need to clear a new path."

"Mines?" Ryan said, a slight quiver to his voice.

"Pressure sensors," replied a solider seated by his side.

Ryan babysat the still unconscious Colonel, while the team mapped out a safe route. Bradley had moaned a few times, prompting Ryan to administer his remaining dose of tranquilizing medication. And rather than carefully provide just enough to keep the man under, he'd decided to give him the entire syringe, thinking, makes no difference if he dies now or later.

With the path safely marked by small, luminescent flags, one man returned to the Yukon, heaved the Colonel over his shoulder, and motioned for Ryan to follow.

Everything was as they had left it.

At the time of their last foray, to avoid the appearance of an unwanted visitation, Tom had sent the elevator back down to the bottom of the shaft. And now, he pointed a finger at his second in command, handed him a coiled nylon rope, and said, "Do the monkey."

The man secured the line and rappelled down the shaft to the top of the lift. A few minutes later, the familiar whirring sound accompanied the motorized box's rise to floor level. Two men dragged the Colonel and literally dropped his body through the opening in the elevator's roof. He hit the bottom with a bang, as the remaining team members lowered themselves through the access door and inside.

The large circuit breaker had been removed at the time the of strange event that they had labelled as *weirdsville*. Two men set about reinstalling it, and when they'd finished, they backed away slowly and called out, "The show's yours, doc."

Gregory took a deep breath, scanned the glass enclosed room from the outside, and then opened the door and entered. He took great care in examining every inch of the room and its equipment lined walls. Special attention was paid to the ceramic composite cubicle that sat at one isolated end of the room, whose external dimensions were roughly six feet high by ten feet wide and deep. But due to the thickness of its walls, the interior was barely large enough to accommodate an average height, weight, and fetal positioned human. Convinced that all was in order, Gregory was about to hit the start button, when Tom began pounding on the glass wall. Gregory lowered the hand that was prepared to begin the ignition process, and opened the door.

"What?" he snapped.

"That box over there," he said, gesturing toward the ceramic affair, "what does it do?"

"It's the plasma receptacle."

"The hot stuff?"

Gregory nodded, yes.

"Does it have a door?"

"On its side."

Tom's expression turned into a devilish grin, and he said, "BBQ anyone?"

The soldiers standing off to the side broke into raucous laughter, but Ryan and Gregory stood by stone-faced. The levity had been lost on the uninitiated Pentagon security agent, while the full intent of Tom's suggestion had yet to dawn on the scientist. Major Striker, still grinning, but recovering from his attempted humor, and recognizing the apparent confusion, said, "Can you think of a better disposal device?"

"Are you serious," Gregory screeched, "you want to put that unconscious man in the box?"

"Exactly," Tom replied.

"This isn't an execution machine," he shouted.

"It is tonight," he declared, turning to and addressing Ryan, "you got a problem with that?"

"Works for me."

"I have no idea what a human presence will do," Gregory complained.

"Guess we're gonna find out," Tom replied.

"The box was designed to capture the plasma and

prevent its escape. With something else filling its volume, anything could happen. Remember the last time?"

"Yeah, what was that?"

Standing just inside the lab, Gregory's mind flashed back to the inexplicable event that had occurred slightly more than twenty-fours hours earlier. I have no idea what really transpired at the moment that everything outside of this room had become invisible to me, he thought. I hadn't discussed it with them, so I don't know if I'd been invisible to them. But if I had to venture a wild and out of this world guess, I'd say that for a fraction of time, this room had entered into another dimension. I can't tell them that, they'd label me as insane, but I'm beginning to get a feel for the nature of this project. However, I have to come up with something.

"I think that the intense heat had caused the glass wall to momentarily become opaque," he explained, congratulating himself for the on the fly confabulation.

"What about the blue light?"

"Probably plasma," he shrugged.

"But you said that the box contains the hot stuff?"

"It's supposed to."

Tom tilted his head, his square jaw set, as if he was about to call Gregory's bluff, but he backed off and called to his men, "Get the package."

Chapter Thirty-three

Midnight

Washington, D.C.

He had failed the Imam, and Jaafar was in a panic.

Following his visit to the hospital he had returned to his hotel room. He had considered numerous approaches to the problem, but none of them had resided within the realm of possibility. He'd made a promise to call the Imam, and it was now past midnight and he had nothing positive to report. There had been rumors regarding the holy man's temper and his lack of restraint that had, according to followers, resulted in the death of the person or persons to whom his wrath had been directed. I do not wish to die, Jaafar had told himself, paradise can wait. But he still had to deal with the Imam and there was no way around the truth; Akil was nowhere to be found.

He had managed to circumvent the security surrounding Akil's condominium and make his way to the apartment door. But he'd found the door ajar and no one within. He did not have the resources to trace Akil's steps, nor search the combined districts of Washington and Arlington. And then there was the possibility that his target had flown the coup and had left the country. It had been a fools errand from the beginning, he'd told himself, and he'd begun to wonder if the Imam had set him up for failure for some unknown reason. Nevertheless, the call had to be made, and he gritted his teeth and punched the number for the Imam's personal cellphone.

"Speak?" a sleepy voice, followed by a yawn said.

"It is I, Jaafar."

"You have news?"

"Not good."

"He is dead?" the Imam said, his voice tinged with hope.

"I have failed," he droned.

"What does that mean?"

"I could not find him."

An uncomfortable pause was followed by, "Did I misplace my trust?"

Visions of a sharp knife being drawn across his throat from behind danced before his eyes, and he replied, "As Allah is my witness, I have done my best."

"Where did you look?"

"His home."

"And?"

"The door had not been fastened, the bed had not been made, and he was gone."

"Akil would not have left the door unlocked but, then again, perhaps he is a crazy man."

"Maybe the police will find him."

"That is what I had hoped to avoid."

"What do you wish of me?"

"Return home," the Imam growled, and terminated the call.

Jaafar sat at the edge of the bed with the phone still in hand. While he had a return ticket, he was considering altering its destination. My children would miss their father, he said to himself, and my wife ... well, she would probably celebrate. But where would I go, he wondered, and how would I pay for my expenses.

In the end, he'd packed his bazaar purchased overnight bag and prepared to leave on the first morning flight back to Detroit.

Chapter Thirty-four

Friday, 5 A.M.

Home of General Louder

Louder had been awakened five minutes before the programmed alarm clock by the cellphone lying on his nightstand. It had begun to vibrate and dance across its black granite top. He scratched his crotch and reached for it.

"Yeah?" he rasped, assuming it was a call from the office.

"I've got the goods," the voice said.

He turned on the bedside lamp and glanced at the phone's LCD. It was blank, no caller ID. "Who the hell are you?" he bellowed.

"The address you asked for," the voice said.

Shit, he thought, that idiot senator is playing spy games. "Cut the cloak and dagger crap and give me what you have."

"And my protection?"

"You'll have it, God damn it."

The senator rattled off the address, as Louder scribbled the information on a yellow legal pad. "That it?"

"She jogs at 6 a.m, everyday, rain or shine, and

frequently after dark."

"What time at night?"

"Between eleven and midnight."

"The address, an apartment or house?"

"Condo."

"Front or rear?"

"What?"

"How does she leave the building?"

"Oh. Front entrance."

"Are you home?"

"Yes."

"Stay there, someone will be by to take you to a safe place."

"But my office will be looking..."

Exasperated, Louder exhaled and said, "You want protection or not?"

"I'll do what you say."

Louder slid the phone back to the nightstand and rose from the bed. Following a hot shower, he'd dressed, poured himself a cup of coffee from the automatic brewer, and called to make arrangements for the Senator's safekeeping.

Rather than going straight to the Pentagon as usual, he'd taken a detour to scope out Veronica's Arlington condo.   It was a modern appearing high-rise on Key Boulevard, and he'd parked with the engine running, as he tried to imagine the street activity at six o'clock in the morning. He'd stared at the building a few minutes longer than necessary, but with reconnaissance completed, he'd put the car in gear and headed for the office. As he drove, he strove to conjure a plan for revenge. I know that the body in the bed thing had not been all her doing, but she could have put the kibosh on the caper, if she'd wanted to. That means that she doesn't give two shits about her old lover. And while I can't go after her superiors—hell, I don't even know for whom she works—I sure as shootin' can make her life miserable, or more. But she's a crafty witch, and I have to make certain that she doesn't see it coming.

A mountain of messages awaited his arrival at the office, and he temporarily tabled the Veronica affair. But by midmorning the mental image of their last visit had returned to haunt and he was back on track. I need to deal with her ASAP, and I've already missed the morning opportunity, he told himself. That leaves tonight. The Senator is the only one in the loop, but while he is under my protection he is to be considered sequestered. After that, I'll have to think of some way to keep him quiet, whatever it takes. But Veronica is the real problem. I can out her, but she'll just bug out and disappear and that won't solve anything. Her keepers will simply find another troll to keep me in line. Nope, I have to send them a message, one that says don't tread on me. Hmm, that means Veronica has to meet with extreme prejudice. And that presents a conundrum. How do I neutralize that bitch without getting caught, while at the same time making it clear to her people that I'm responsible. The departure of an operative will never make the evening news, the spooks keep those kind of events to themselves, but the locals could be a real problem.

The clock had yet to reach the noon hour, but he rose and poured himself a tumbler of Johnny Walker and returned to the chair. Let's consider the options, he thought. A suppressed weapon fired from my car could catch her off-guard, but I could never effectively remove the gun powder residue that would inevitably imbed itself into the upholstery. If the cops ever decided to look at me for the deed, the car would put me in the slammer. And that leaves out a rental, he thought, squirming in the chair, trying to silence his reignited hemorrhoids. I could grab her from behind with a garrote, but she's more agile than I, and my oversized belly might get in the way. Hit and run is off the table as well. Shit, I'm sure that those bastards have a thousand clandestine ways to accomplish what I need. He emptied the tumbler and, out of frustration, began to drum his fingers on the desktop when a thought came to mind. It's noiseless, quick and final, he mused, recalling the employment of a tranquilizing dart-gun during an African safari.

Some years prior, he had set out with a guide to hunt Kudu, when they'd run into a herd of rhinos. And rather than kill the lead animal, the guide had chosen to use a powerful tranquilizer. I nearly shat my pants that day, he said to himself and, to this day, I'm still convinced that the guide should have shot the beast. But I'd survived, and I guess that's all that counts. Anyway, a dart-gun is an easy find—the drug is another issue. No doubt that the MIB (men in black) have a variety of sophisticated drugs, but I don't have access to anything of that nature. However, I don't need to reinvent the wheel, do I, he mused. The Pygmies used curare, and Tricare (Pentagon's Dilorenzo Tricare Health Clinic) might have some in their storeroom.

***

2 P.M.

With a concocted story, Lauder had managed to acquire a small quantity of d-tubocurarine. But it had not been without significant risk and a promise of future reciprocation. Furthermore, the malleable pharmacist's assistant had informed Louder that the container had been lying around the storeroom since the 90's because *"no one used it anymore."* The General had convinced his naive benefactor to not log the distribution—under the guise of national security—a direct violation of the clinic's protocol and an omission that could be used to the General's advantage if the need ever arose.

An hour later, having told his secretary that he was leaving early due to a severe headache, he purchased a dart gun from a firearms distributer and headed for his condo to practice. The acquisition had come with several, solid, metal tipped darts, as well as two darts capable of releasing, and thereby injecting, a liquid agent. Once at home, he sacrificed a bright yellow throw pillow and used it as his target. After an hour of dry-runs, he felt confident enough to load the two hollow darts and store the gun back into its carry case. The next several hours were spent polishing the details of his planned, nighttime caper.

Chapter Thirty-five

Friday, 2 A.M.

Nevada

Gregory McCraken had put up a good fight, advanced by his unwillingness to use the machine for nefarious purposes. He had argued for hours with the marine Major, with Gregory refusing to start the initiation sequence and the Major threatening to put him in the hot box with the package. In the end, the marines had prevailed and the unconscious Colonel Duke had been folded into the restrictive confines of the ceramic box.

"How long will it take to get up to speed," Tom asked.

"In a rush?" Gregory sneered.

"We've wasted too much time already."

"Close the door and wait outside."

The glass door latched and Gregory raised the lever that supplies power to the device. A few seconds later the room began to vibrate, mildly at first and then more vigorously. McCraken's facial expression turned dour, and he quickly lowered the lever and cut the power. Once the vibration had ceased, he unlatched the door.

"We've got a problem," he announced.

"Just get it done," Tom demanded.

"Your package is unbalancing the system."

"And that means?"

"Did you feel that vibration?"

"No."

Gregory frowned, recalling that the lab's flooring had been structurally isolated from the walls. "My room began to resonate seconds after power had been applied," he explained.

"Worse case scenario?"

Gregory shrugged.

"Take a guess."

"It could explode," he said, hoping that the specter of disaster would remove the Colonel from the equation.

"We've got to RTB (return to base) before sunup ... I'll risk it."

I didn't come down here to die, Gregory said to himself, but I've got a feeling that I'm doomed either way. He relocked the door and flipped the power lever to the on position. The vibration returned, and Gregory backed away from the control panel in a sweat, as he waited for the unknown to occur. Fifteen minutes later, the vibration—which had reached a feverous pitch—had begun to subside and Gregory relaxed. But as he turned to give the marines a thumbs up, an odd odor began to appear, along with the hint of a bluish haze. The fog continued to build, and at one point the people outside of the glass enclosed lab were no longer visible to the scientist. Is it the haze that's obscuring my view, he questioned, as he walked to the usually transparent wall and pressed his face against it. Imagination and terror took front and center, as the emptiness beyond the wall became all too real. "What's happening," he screamed, into sound deadened space. Gregory reached for the power lever, but his fingers passed through it as if it were merely a hologram. In a panic, the blue haze now enveloping him like a shroud, he leapt for the door and its handle. It too offered no tactile response, and Gregory began to suspect that death was about to smack him in the face. He slid down to the warm floor, covered his eyes with open palms and wept. "I warned you," he sniffled, wiping his dripping nostril across a sleeve and scanning the room. Most of the equipment was visible through the mist, but the ceramic box was no longer discernible. With his scientific curiosity overcoming fear of the unknown, he rose and walked a few feet closer to where the box should have been. Did it disintegrate, he wondered, realizing that the conduit connecting it to the generator was gone as well. But then something even more bizarre came to light. The two thick grounding cables, that traveled along the floor from the generator to the box, were suspended in the air where they would have ordinarily made contact with the enclosure's connectors. He kicked at one with his shoe, but it had the same effect as his hand had when it'd passed through the power switch. "Am I the only real object in this room?" he mumbled, "or has my reality been altered?"

And then a horrific notion popped into his head, and he wondered if the machine had killed him, or, if he'd been correct in his prior assessment regarding a dimensional shift. It's over for me, he lamented, there's no way I can reverse the process and, unless someone pulls the main breaker again, everything in this room will eventually... He was stopped mid thought by the return of intense vibration within the isolated flooring, along with a gradual dissipation of the haze. Suddenly, frantically waving hands and barely discernible faces could be seen through the previously opaque glass, and he relaxed, recalling the last time he'd been saved by the marines. He slid to the floor, nervously exhaled and crawled to the door and its now tactile lever.

"What the hell happened?" Tom shouted.

"Same as the last time, only worse," Gregory breathed.

"Where's the box," Tom's second in command asked,

nodding toward the end of the room.

"I don't know."

"Well, at least the package is gone," Tom sneered.

"But to where?" Gregory cautioned.

Ryan, who had been standing off to one side, mystified, pushed forward and asked, "Are you certain that it's gone?"

Tom looked at him with an, are you FUBAR expression on his face, and Ryan backed off.

Gregory wasn't certain that he should verbalize what was going through his mind, but the notion was so intriguing that he let go with, "It could still be in this room."

"Seriously?" Tom mocked.

"It may be straddling another dimension."

"Don't go all spooky on us, doc. It's gone—that's all I care about."

But Ryan, an avid science fiction fan, moved closer and asked, "This dimension stuff, is it real?"

Gregory scratched his formidable chin stubble and replied, "Until a few moments ago it'd been entirely theoretical, but the box is proof enough for me."

"C'mon, you said yourself that the plasma could reach thousands of degrees," Tom cut in, "maybe it incinerated your box."

"Incineration would leave behind a residue of sorts."

While they had been arguing, Ryan had inserted himself into the room and was now kneeling where the box had been. "Clean as a whistle," he called out.

Gregory gazed up at Tom and shrugged.

"Like I said, the package is gone," Tom announced.

"This is the scientific discovery of a lifetime, I can't stop now."

Tom shook his head and said, "BAMCIS."

"What?" Gregory replied.

"Mission complete," he explained.

They've got me by the short hairs, Gregory admitted to himself, as he followed the team down the corridor toward the elevator. But the scientific implications of what'd just transpired are mind blowing, and there's no way I'm going to walk away from it—I'll be back.

Chapter Thirty-six

Friday, 4 P.M.

Detroit, Michigan

Jaafar had taken the first available flight out of Washington. His last conversation with the Imam had been less than pleasant and, as he'd crossed the Detroit Metropolitan airport, his thoughts were a blur of possible scenarios. Defeat had not been an option for the holy man, and Jaafar knew that the Imam's largess could disappear in a heartbeat. There were no apologies that he could proffer, no words of solace that could soften the blow of his mentor's rage; he was terrified for himself and his family.

With the mission's remaining cash he took a taxi that, at his request, had let him off a short distance from the mosque.

He'd loitered outside of the mosque for more than thirty minutes, but there had been no avoiding the inevitable, so he'd marched though the heavy entry doors and made his way to the familiar office and knocked.

"Enter," a voice called out.

Jaafar hung his head, as he waited several feet from the Imam's desk.

"Your task had been simple," the Imam declared.

"I have no excuse for my failure."

"Akil is a potential problem," he said softly, followed by a shouted, "it is unacceptable."

Jaafar, still standing, cringed and mumbled, "I understand."

"He is no longer your responsibility."

"But..."

"Another will perform your task."

"I assure you, I'd looked everywhere. You will not find him."

"Insolence," the Imam shouted, emphasizing his rage with a fist thrust in the air.

"What shall I do?" Jaafar whispered.

"Get out of my sight, go back to your shop."

With moist eyes, Jaafar retreated from the office and left the building. I cannot face that man again, he said to himself, as he walked the street aimlessly. I will take my family and disappear, move to another state. But then he passed a homeless man seated on the bare concrete humming an unrecognizable tune, all the while running a handful of grimy fingers through a long white beard. A sign perched by his side read, God is great. Jaafar stopped and stared at the sign, the man no longer of interest. Allah is my guide, he mused, not the Imam. He deserves no allegiance.

With a renewed sense of purpose he took a seat on a lonely bench and waited for a bus that was nowhere in sight. And feeling fatigued from the flight and his stressful meeting with the Imam, he dozed off. But suddenly, his neck was on fire and he gasped. He tried to call out, but something was closing about his throat like a vise, making speech impossible. Fighting for his breath, he grabbed at the thick length of leather but his fingers could not get behind it, and then two shadows stood before him as light began to fade. An instant later, his lifeless body slumped forward.

Three bearded men gazed about, checking for onlookers. Assured that they had not been observed in their broad daylight attack, the more muscular of the group rolled the leather belt into a ball, shoved it into a pocket and, without a word, quickly left the scene. Without looking back, the remaining two took off in different directions, oblivious to the horrific screams unleashed by the women who had arrived at the stop and had encountered Jaafar's body.

Chapter Thirty-seven

Friday, 11 P.M.

Louder had arrived at ten forty-five, found a parking place near the front entrance to Veronica's condominium and exited. He had been practicing with his dart gun and was fairly confident that he could hit his intended target, as long as she didn't run serpentine. He'd abandoned his usual garb in favor of an old pair of oversized bluejeans and a black, long sleeved shirt. His face had been camouflaged in commando fashion—green and black—and he'd taken up a position that would give him running access to Veronica no matter which direction she'd taken. The street was relatively quiet at that hour, save for a few dog walkers. And while his outfit was not entirely out of the ordinary, his facial makeup was, and he did not wish to be spotted by an overzealous 911 caller. He checked his wristwatch and thought, eleven-fifteen, she's late. But Washburn did say that she runs between eleven and midnight.

He had to scoot around a parked pickup truck to avoid one of the poop scooping dog walkers, but aside from the curious, whining poodle who was straining at its leash and sniffing in his direction before being yanked away by its owner, he was home free.

A wraithlike form emerged from the condo's front entrance at eleven-thirty. Bingo, he said to himself. He'd hoped that her run would have taken her away from his hide, providing a chance to approach from behind, but after crossing the road she'd begun to run directly toward him. He waited, gauging her speed, and with the rear fender of a Toyota Camry supporting his forearm, he prepared to fire a dart as soon as her neck came into view. She was almost upon him, and he held his breath, the pistol now in a two handed-grip, but as the moment arose he withdrew, an inner voice shouting, abort, that's not Veronica. "Shit," he breathed, as the wraith passed by without the faintest notion of what had almost transpired. I hadn't considered the possibility of other joggers.

Another twenty minutes had gone by, and he was getting antsy. I'm pressing my luck by hanging around this long, he mused. But as he was about to approach his car and accept a failed mission, a second runner exited the building. It was dressed in a gray running suit with an iridescent band of bright green surrounding its midsection. He removed a pair of mini-binoculars from his pocket and tried to focus on the runner's face, but darkness had obscured all but one feature, its nose. Veronica's nose had been badly damaged as the result of a fall that she'd sustained during an operation gone sour, and it had been surgically reconstructed to perfection. I'd know that nose anywhere, he told himself, game on.

The runner took off, her back facing Louder, but suddenly changed direction and began trotting his way. He took cover behind the pickup's roadside rear fender and waited, dart gun at the ready. Holding his breath as she approached, he fired. The dart missed the intended target —her neck—but penetrated the fabric covering her right shoulder blade. She stopped one car length beyond the pickup and winced. The projectile was just beyond her reach, but Louder watched as she frantically tried to dislodge it. For an instant, he felt the need to assist, but the illogical thought dissipated and he gradually distanced himself from the scene. I'm not sure how I feel, he said to himself, as he stood alongside his vehicle. I should be elated for the successful payback, but I'm not feeling joyous. Did I go too far, he wondered, as he watched her steady herself against a parked auto and then slide to the concrete. An inner voice told him to get into his car and drive off, but he was fighting the desire to see the event through to its anticipated end. And then a thought came to mind. She's a spook. She must have a way of contacting her people around the clock, and that means she's got a cellphone on her person. He entered his car and drove off, taking one last look as he passed her crumpled body.

***

Saturday, 1 A.M.

Louder had returned to his condo in a quandary. I have no way of knowing if she's out of the picture, he pondered, while walking to the liquor cabinet to pour himself a nightcap. He took a seat on the couch and thought, it'd been clear that she, or her controllers, had been out for blood. Will her demise take me off of their radar, probably not. The best I can hope for is to convince them that I'm not a pushover. And now, some part of me wishes that things had been different with her, but she knew the risks, always had. Tonight's escapade may turn out to have been a mistake, but there was no misunderstanding the dead body message. I had to derail the train, didn't I, he reassured himself, as he drained the glass.

He left the tumbler on an end table and headed for the bedroom. Thirty minutes later, when sleep would not come, he continued to second guess his course of action as a possible impulsive response. I probably killed her, he pondered. She would have done the same to me, and even tried to years in the past, but I'd forgiven her and I can't remember why. Well, one way or another, I've sent a message and I guess only the future will tell how well it'd been received.

Chapter Thirty-eight

Battle Mountain, Nevada

Saturday

11 P.M.

Major Thomas Striker had closed up the desert shack to resemble its initial appearance. His men had removed the flags that'd been used to mark the path to and from the building and they'd brushed away their bootprints. Aside from the mysteriously absent ceramic box, the facility had been made to appear untouched. Gregory had kept silent during the ride back to the safe-house, but he'd been seething mad after being admonished by the Major for initially refusing to depart.

"Everybody out," Tom shouted, as they pulled into a covered parking space at the safe-house. One by one the marines silently slithered from the vehicle, but Gregory remained within.

Tom turned and hissed, "You can sleep in there if you like, but watch out for the coyotes."

At the sound of the word, coyotes, Gregory begrudgingly exited and followed the team inside.

When the door had been closed and locked, Tom turned to the team and announced, "Store your gear, we're outta here."

"Oorah," the men shouted.

"We're outta here at 0500, so get some shut-eye. And you," he added, aiming an index finger at Gregory, "are no longer my problem."

"You're gonna leave me here?"

"This place is off limits after 0500," Tom advised, leaving Gregory seated on a metal chair, as he disappeared with a satellite phone in hand. And once out of earshot from his team and the physicist, he punched in the General's phone number.

Louder was still trying to suppress a building sense of guilt, when the encrypted sat phone came alive. He reached under the bed where it had been clasped in place, and yanked it free. "Yes?" he rasped.

"The package has been disposed of," Tom said.

"Good. Anything else?"

Tom hesitated, a second too long.

"You still there?"

"Yes sir."

"Then answer my question."

"There was some strange shit, sir."

"Explain."

"Not sure I can."

"Gimme a hint, son."

Tom sighed, "You're gonna think I'm fubar, sir, but the machine made the package disappear."

"That was the idea."

"No sir, I mean really disappear."

"What are you saying, Major?" Louder croaked, now sitting at the edge of the bed.

"McCraken spoke of a dimensional shift."

Now it was Louder's turn to pause, as he removed the phone from his ear, quickly replacing it and shouting, "What the hell does that mean?"

"He thinks that the box is still in the room, but in a different dimension."

"So the package is still there?" Louder shrieked.

"Yes and no."

"Unacceptable," he bellowed, adding, "I need a concrete answer."

"Sir?"

"Get your ass back there and confirm."

"But..."

"That's an order, Major."

Tom slipped the phone back into a pocket in his fatigues and stood in the dark room deciding how he was going to withdraw his departure statement without loosing his team's respect. But he'd been given a direct order and he had no choice other than to go forward. The marines were still mulling about the main living space when he'd returned and signaled for them to gather around.

"Change of plans, we're going back."

"Back home, sir?" the lowest ranking man on the team asked.

"No, back underground."

Gregory grinned from ear to ear.

***

Zero dark thirty (12:30 A.M.)

The Yukon rolled to a stop in the desert where it had parked only a short while ago. The team set upon remarking a safe path to the shack, while Gregory remained in the rear seat conjuring a plan of action.

I don't know what had actually occurred earlier, when the box became invisible, Gregory thought, but if there had been a dimensional shift we won't be able to find any evidence of its existence. A rent in the time space continuum—is it really possible, he wondered. There are all kinds of theories being thrown about that suggest it's a possibility, but by every account it would require a lot more energy than our machine is capable of. However, I'm going by the data that had been provided at the beginning of the project, and we all took it for granted that the info was accurate. What if we'd been lied to, he considered. The gauges could have been rigged to show a lower than actual output, hell, a few giant resistors could have accomplished that task. Well, there's neither the time nor the equipment to make that determination, and one thing is clear, something odd had happened to the box and its cables.

Three short bursts of light, a prearranged signal for Gregory to follow the flagged pathway, caught his attention and he exited the vehicle. The steel plate has once again been repositioned, and the elevator had been brought to the surface. Tom nodded toward the opening in its roof and Gregory slid inside, followed by the rest of the team.

"We're here to confirm the absence of the package, nothing else," Tom announced, glaring at the physicist, as the elevator reached its destination.

Gregory had remained silent until they'd reached the glass enclosed lab, and then said, "What we'd witnessed earlier could be the discovery of a lifetime, it could have unimaginable military implications."

Tom stopped short of opening the glass door and turned to face Gregory. "I have my orders," he replied.

"But we're the only ones here, who would know?"

The Major surveyed the anxious faces of his speechless team members, his jaw set firm, and asked, "What are you proposing?"

"We crank it up again and see what happens."

"Doesn't sound very scientific."

"I agree, but this is unchartered territory and there is no benchmark."

"Go on."

"If this machine can truly open a door to another dimension, well, imagine what it could do for space travel, warfare and God knows what else."

"Are you suggesting that we try to bring the package back?"

"From where?"

"Good point. But the box is gone…"

"Maybe not. Take a look at those fat cables hanging midair," he cut in.

Tom put his nose against the glass barrier, scratched his head and replied, "I see what you're saying."

"So, is it a go?"

"Reinstall the breaker," he called out to his men.

Fifteen minutes later, Gregory stood before the familiar bank of switches and levers. He'd been given the go ahead by the team's electrician and he engaged the power supply. As before, the room began to hum and vibrate, but moments before the machine had reached maximum power output the suspended cables began to glow bright white, quickly shifting to light blue. Tom and his crew were still visible through the glass, as Gregory moved his sweaty hand across the main power lever. His fingers did not go through it as before, and he nudged it as far as it would go. Suddenly, the end of the room that had previously housed the ceramic box grew dark, as a murky, blue-green mist began to fill the previously well lit lab. Gregory called out to the marines, but his voice appeared to go no farther than his quivering lips. This is it, he told himself, this is when it had happened. And with that thought still in mind, an image of the ceramic box flashed into view and then disappeared. He fought the urge to walk toward where he'd just seen the box, not knowing what would happen. Would he move into another dimension as well, he wondered. And where was the superheated plasma that normally filled the box. No, this is close enough, he warned himself.

Outside, Tom and company had been watching anxiously. They too had seen the box flash into view and then vanish. But unlike the time before, they could not see the physicist through the mist, nor could they hear him banging on the glass to get their attention.

Gregory had tried to grasp the door's lever, but once again his fingers had failed to seize the composite material ... it had been as if it too had moved to another dimension. The control lever had suffered the same fate and there was no way for him to power down the machine, it had to be done from the outside. As he slid to the ground, not knowing if he as well would be lost like the box, the significance of the project had become crystal clear. Nothing that he'd been told had been true, the current event had not been accidental and this had indeed been the intended outcome. Myself and my colleagues were never meant to survive this experiment. And if we had, by some extraordinary stroke of luck, made it through, we could not have been allowed to carry the knowledge of this success back to the world we had known. A line of tears trickled down his cheeks but, without warning, the light began to return to the lab and the mist commenced to dissipate. He breathed a sigh of relief, thinking, there may be a tomorrow.

The door flew open and Tom came crashing through. "The box, is it gone or not?" he shouted.

Gregory took the offered hand and rose from the

floor.   He focused on the end of the room where only moments ago the box had flashed into view and replied, "Look at the cables, they're lying on the ground."

"So it's gone."

Gregory nodded, yes.

"And you're scientific breakthrough?"

"Historic."

"I assume that it's classified?"

"If word gets out, we're all dead."

Tom frowned and asked, "Who do you work for?"

Gregory shook his head, as if to say, I don't know.

"How could you not know?"

"Government research is all we'd been told."

"And you hadn't been informed?"

"It was need to know."

"But you must have a suspicion."

"I don't know for sure, but my best guess is that it's the NSA."

"What about your paycheck?" Tom asked, with an expression of incredulity.

"My account, as well as everyone else who'd worked here, received a monthly direct deposit that originated from different named companies."

Tom gazed back at the still lit lab and remarked,

"They're gonna know that someone was here."

"Unless they've replaced the allegedly damaged cameras, they'll be scratching their heads."

"Pull the breaker an' make it look like it hadn't been touched," Tom barked to his men.

Chapter Thirty-nine

Sunday, August 12th

4 A.M.

Louder had barely fallen asleep when the sat phone beneath his mattress began to chirp. He rubbed his eyes, rolled over, and pulled it away from the bed frame.

"Yes," he yawned.

"Striker here, sir."

"This better be good."

"It's gone."

"You certain?"

"Affirmative."

"The physicist, he needs to disappear."

"Sir?"

"He's been witness to a disposal."

"Sir, I think that you should talk to him first."

"What for?"

"He's got something really important to share."

"You realize what you're risking?"

"Yes sir."

"Again, you're sure about this?"

"Affirmative."

"Ok, bring him back with you but keep eyes on him

and call me when you've landed. I'll tell you where to meet up."

Louder replaced the phone but remained seated at the edge of his bed. What could be so important, he wondered. This guy could bring us all down, but if what he has to spit out isn't useful I'll put him back on the plane and have the marines drop him over water. He glanced at the bedside clock, the room's only light source, and thought, it's 04:30, no sense in going back to sleep. He rose, crossed the darkened apartment and, in his skivvies, headed for the kitchen for a glass of water. But what he saw caused him to gasp. Out from the blackness of the living room, a green dot traveled from his bare foot up his torso to someplace between his eyes. Finding his voice, he called out, "Go ahead, pull the trigger, I don't give a shit."

"Not yet," the electronically altered voice replied.

"What's this about?" he hissed.

There was no reply, but he could hear heavy breathing coming from somewhere near the couch.

The green dot began to travel once again, this time settling near his groin. "You used to be pretty good with that," the voice declared.

Despite the relatively cool room temperature, Louder began to sweat. This is no stranger, he thought. Whom did

I mess with that's capable of this, he asked himself. And then, it struck him like sledge hammer. "Victoria?"

"Bingo."

The sound of a suppressed round hitting the marble flooring near his right foot made him jump, the shards striking his thighs.

"That miss was intentional," the voice said.

"Can you stop with that silly voice?"

"No, thanks to you."

"How did I..." he began to say, realizing that it could be related to his attack.

"You need to feel the helplessness that overwhelmed me."

"But you've survived."

"Barely."

"How..."

"A fellow jogger," she interrupted.

"It was you own fault."

"The stiff was just a warning."

"You should have anticipated the response."

"They wanted you to squirm."

"They ... being?"

"You already know."

"It wasn't enough that I did their bidding?"

"You weren't supposed to ask questions."

"I'm a curious guy," he said, sidestepping a few feet to the left.

"And that's where the story ends."

A second round whizzed by, striking the wall behind where he'd been standing. He leapt in the direction of the kitchen, hoping to make his way to an exit door that led to the emergency staircase. But the sound of a third round smashing into a dish cabinet caused him to duck behind a center island. Suddenly, a beam of light from a handheld flashlight began to intermittently pan the unlit room at the same time that the fingers of his right hand wrapped themselves around a pairing knife that had been resting on the countertop. Victoria's rubber soled shoes made an occasional squeak on the polished tile floor, and he crept around the island as she came closer. By now, his vision had dark adapted, to the extent that the limited light emanating from the oven's LCD had made the back of her neck visible, the rest of her body cloaked by a dark garment. It's now or never, he shouted to himself, as he rose, came up from behind and drove the knife into the side of her neck up to its hilt. As warm blood coated his right hand, she groaned, letting loose with another aimless round, followed by the sound of her body slumping to the floor with a thud.

He knelt down and held the knife in place until he was certain that she could do no harm, and then rose and switched on the room light. His hand and forearm were bathed in red, as were the kitchen countertop and flooring. He let out a deep breath, kicked the suppressed pistol away from her lifeless hand and leaned against the refrigerator wondering how he was going to clean up the mess.

The guilt that he'd wrestled with earlier had been eradicated by the attempted assassination, but her presence had made it clear that he was still a prime target. But whose? Had she been out to avenge his attempt on her life, or had the Agency sent her to silence a loose end, he asked himself. Only time will tell, he reasoned, but I've got a feeling that it ain't over.

After thirty minutes of deliberation he'd decided to call PFPA (Pentagon Security) and tell them that he'd subdued an intruder that was now dead, and that he would need a cleanup crew. He had considered calling local law enforcement, but realized that it was bound to result in unwanted questions and newspaper coverage, all of which he sought to avoid.

Later, there had been a few questioning glances when the security people had discovered that the invader had been a female, but the suppressed weapon had corroborated the General's explanation. They'd placed her body in a black, zippered bag, had performed a reasonable job of cleaning the room with peroxide and liquid chlorine, and had left without further adieu. Louder had made it clear that discretion was of the utmost importance and, after a lengthy discussion regarding their duty to report incidents, they'd agreed to dispose of the body, along with all other evidence. Protection had been offered, but Louder had insisted that it had been an isolated event and had declined.

***

7 A.M.

Having spent more time in the shower than had been necessary, scrubbing blood from his hands, he'd gotten dressed and driven to Bob & Edith's Diner for breakfast. Sunday had been his day to relax and contemplate the future, but the present had appeared more meaningful these days, and the usually savory bacon and eggs had barely tickled his tastebuds. His thoughts were torn in different directions. On the one hand, he was concerned that the agency could make another attempt and that luck might escape him, and on the other was what ever had transpired at the underground facility that had prompted his trusted marine major to disobey a direct order. Over a third cup of black coffee he mused about the past, when life had been simpler, right and wrong had been clearly characterized, and the path to the future had been well defined. But things had changed, he thought. Just a few years back, if I'd been told that I was destined to kill a onetime lover it would have been considered nonsensical. But that train has already left the station. And why in the world I'd ever have agreed to babysit a secret underground project calls into question my sanity.

With a go cup filled with black coffee he drove back to his condo, parked the car in the usual garage spot and rode the elevator to his floor. As he opened the door, he could hear the subdued chirp from his sat phone, and he rushed into the bedroom to retrieve it.

"Yes?" he said, the now empty coffee cup still in his left hand.

"We just hit the tarmac," Major Striker announced.

Louder lowered the cup to his nightstand and his butt to the edge of the bed. He exhaled and said, "Keep the scientist on the aircraft, and make sure he doesn't escape."

"He's anxious to speak with you ... I don't think he'll

bolt."

"Good."

"What about my men?"

"You and one other stay with the plane until I get there, the rest can be relieved."

Chapter Forty

Sunday, 7 A.M.

Seventy-year-old Imam Faaroog Awan had slept little the night before. His plan to extract information from the Pentagon had gone south, and while he'd been considered by his disciples to be a man of power, there were others pulling his strings, and they were not happy. He'd received a message—via diplomatic pouch—from an Iranian businessman housed in Moscow, that had clearly originated from the Ayatollah. It had suggested, metaphorically, that his foreign account would not receive the promised funds if he did not provide the requested information. And there was no way that neither he nor his mosque could survive without those funds.

He'd stumbled through morning prayers like an automaton and, now, he stared at the cooling pot of tea that sat to one side of his office desk, while the fingers of his right hand toyed with the fabric of his silver and gold brocade robe. There are few whom I can trust, he said to himself. Akil had been my shining star, my most promising weapon, but his mind had failed him. I cannot allow that to happen again. Time, I need more time to mold another and somehow insert him into a position of trust, he thought, reaching for the pot and filling a waiting cup. With the liquid barely swallowed, he mused, I am old. My body resists the demands of life and I wonder if it will allow me to fulfill my duty to Allah. He swallowed, and then did something entirely out of character by smashing the ornate cup against the desk, causing tiny shards of fine china to fly across the room. "I've done as ordered," he cried out in a whisper, as he rose and began to pace, the broken pottery crunching beneath his slippered feet. There must be some way to appease him. Perhaps if I could speak with him face to face I could explain the difficulty of my situation, he thought. But we have never met, and I doubt that such an arrangement would be permissible. Only one option remains, the man whom Akil served, he would be privy to the data that I require ... he must be taken.

Chapter Forty-one

8 A.M.

Joint Base Andrews

General Louder had shortened the forty some odd minute drive to the Joint Base by exceeding the speed limit. And after passing through security, he'd aimed his car toward the familiar, distant hangar. The doors had been partially closed, but the aircraft's nose was visible on approach, enhanced by the reflection of the bright yellow sun. He parked the car off to one side and entered. The stairs had been lowered and Major Striker stood just at its edge. He saluted when Louder approached.

"He inside?" Louder asked.

Striker nodded.

Louder mounted the stairs and made his way to the jet's interior with the Major in tow.

Gregory was eating a ham and egg breakfast sandwich and crunching on potatoes chips when Louder took the seat opposite.

"You got something to say to me?" he said.

Gregory raised his right hand, as if to say, allow me to swallow.

Louder waited impatiently.

"The people I worked for never told..." Gregory began to say.

"Cut the bullshit, just the facts," Louder interrupted.

Gregory gazed about the aircraft, his eyes locking onto those of the Major, looking for the support that was not forthcoming, and said, "I made something disappear."

"Oorah," Louder exclaimed, sarcastically.

"OK. I think that the experiment was meant to create a portal..."

"A what?"

"A doorway into another dimension, or another place."

"Explain."

"I won't bore you with the theory behind it, but if you could generate enough energy you might be able to open an Einstein-Rosen Bridge, also called a wormhole, or a rent in the space time continuum."

"And?"

"I think we might have done it."

Louder leaned toward Gregory, his chin now resting on the palms of both hands, as he contorted his face into a quizzical expression. "Do I look like an idiot?" he shouted.

"No, sir," Gregory replied, "but neither am I."

"I've been told that we do not have the technology to

accomplish that."

"Guess what, we do."

Louder rose from the white leather seat and walked to the front of the aircraft, turned and faced the physicist. "The thing you made disappear, where'd it go?"

Gregory shrugged.

"That's your learned reply?"

"I don't know where it went, but I can say, with conviction, that's it's gone for good."

"This wormhole thing, what can it really do?"

"If we did actually create one, and I have no way of proving same at this moment, it could take us to places that we'd never dreamt of."

"Is there another explanation for the object's disappearance?" Louder asked, changing direction.

"Since there was no residue suggesting high energy destruction, I have to assume that it was transported elsewhere."

"Any idea where?"

"None."

Louder shot a troubled glance at the Major, and said, "So it could turn up just about anywhere, correct?"

After a moment's consideration, Gregory replied, "I guess so."

"And that anywhere could be in the middle of Time Square."

"Sir, I think that it's more likely to be another galaxy."

"You're back to the wormhole theory again," Louder growled.

"If we really did create one, and we could learn how to control it, we'd be space travel pioneers."

"How so?"

"By warping time and space—basically folding space in upon itself—we could travel across our galaxy in short order. We would not need the powerful rocket engines of this day, or those currently conceived of."

Louder turned and walked to the back of the cabin. Fact or fantasy, he wondered. What the physicist is describing could turn out to be the discovery of a lifetime, or a grand pile of shit. On the other hand, it is a black project, and I wouldn't put it past the NSA to hide something of this magnitude almost in plain sight. But it is their baby, and while the potential implications are incredible, I'm not sure how I could make use of it without their knowledge. But...

He returned to face Gregory and asked, "Could you reconstruct the laboratory elsewhere?"

Gregory offered up a quizzical expression, thought for

a moment and replied, "Maybe."

"Yes or no."

"Well, if I had the funds and a few engineers to help, I think so."

"Were you involved in the initial construction?"

"Yes."

"Were there blueprints?"

"We'd only been provided with what had been needed for a given day of construction."

"And you recall enough to duplicate the machine?"

"I have an eidetic memory."

"What about engineers?"

"I have two in mind."

"Can they be trusted?"

"The company that had hired us thought so."

"It could be dangerous," Louder advised, knowing that the NSA was likely to get wind of his intentions.

"Not my first rodeo."

Louder smiled, as he began conjuring a plan of action. If I can steal their project by duplication, he mused, it'll make the crap that they've put me through worthwhile and represent the best revenge of all time. I can probably dig up the initial funds from our own, undesignated projects account. But location and construction will be difficult to hide from those snoops, and that could create a problem. Hmm, there is an empty hangar here at Andrews (Joint Base Andrews), and it does have an underground compartment used for storing maintenance equipment. Wonder if it would suffice, he pondered.

Having never been to the NSA lab, he asked, "How much room would you need to make it work?"

Gregory made a mental computation of the existing lab without the living quarters and small dining area and replied, "About eight hundred to a thousand square feet."

"Could you do with less?"

"The power supply takes up most of the space."

"What if it were external?"

"Then I could make it work with five hundred. But the space should be well isolated from anything of value."

"Why its that?"

"Remember, I made a box disappear."

"So you're suggesting deep underground?"

Gregory nodded.

Louder withdrew a handwritten note from a pocket and approached the Major. Striker had been sitting a distance away from the physicist, and had for the most part ignored the conversation. He stood at attention when the General approached and ordered, "Take him to this address and post a sentry. I'll have someone provide clothing, food and whatever else he needs, but he doesn't leave unattended."

"Oorah."

He then turned to Gregory and said, "You understand what you're signing up for?"

"Yes."

"OK. I'll need a detailed list of all required equipment, parts and supplies to get us up to speed, as well as any personal items that you might need. I also require the names and addresses of the two engineers that you spoke of."

"They might need some convincing," Gregory advised.

"My specialty."

"There could be one small problem."

"Go ahead."

"We're going to need a lot of electrical power to run the machine, and unless we can get our hands on a custom storage capacitor like the one in Battle Mountain, we might cause a major outage."

"I'm not sending my people back there to steal it, so you'd better come up with an alternative," Louder barked, as he made his way down the stairs, his voice echoing throughout the hangar.

Gregory went back to his unfinished sandwich and thought, I should have asked about my dog.

Chapter Forty-two

Detroit, 10 A.M.

The Imam had been searching though his files for a few loyal disciples. And realizing that the assignment could turn deadly, he had to be certain that the chosen did not have families to weaken their resolve, or other factors that might undermine their dedication. He had narrowed the potentials down to three, one of whom he'd discarded due to a prior altercation. The two remaining were still on the premises and he summoned them to his office individually. The first to enter was Faisal Halabi, a six-foot tall brute with a flowing brown beard, piercing black eyes and a harelip.

"Please, take a seat, Faisal," the Imam offered.

Faisal stood for a moment and then acquiesced.

"Your persistent attendance has not gone unnoticed ... you're devotion to Islam is commendable."

Faisal nodded his approval.

"And you are a man of few words, but can you keep a secret?"

"Na'am (yes)."

"Are you ready to serve Allah?"

"Na'am, Imam."

"And you will do so without question," Faaroog said, more a demand than a question.

Faisal nodded, yes.

The Imam dismissed the man, requesting that he wait outside while he spoke with another. And when Faisal had exited, Omar Botros, a thin, medium height male with a black beard and an unruly head of hair entered and stood just inside the threshold. The Imam stared at the large black mole occupying a good portion of the man's right cheek, and then motioned toward a chair. The same abbreviated conversation followed with an identical result. The two men had been more than willing to undertake the yet to be defined assignment in the name of Allah.

Alone at his desk, with the chosen pair waiting patiently beyond his closed door, he pondered the envisioned mission. Would it be prudent to provide the purpose behind the operation, he wondered, or should they be told only of the sequestration. The information that I seek is not for publication, and while I am willing to trust them with the abduction, a slip of the tongue could prove disastrous. He called them back into his office together.

"You are familiar with each other," the Imam asked, once the men had taken a seat before the desk.

"On occasion, we have shared a cup of tea," Faisal

said.

"The job I have in mind will require a joint effort."

The two men nodded their approval.

"You are curious about its nature, no?"

"We are at Allah's disposal."

Imam Faaroog pushed back in his chair, the springs squeaking from the effort. He rose and approached the breakfront, upon which sat a sterling silver tray sporting a tea kettle and several small cups. Filling three cups, he handed one to each of the men, placing his own on the desk blotter. The two men waited until the Imam had taken a sip and then followed suit.

"There is a man with whom I must speak," the Imam advised.

The disciples nodded but continued to sip the warm tea.

"He resides in another town, and may not be a willing participant."

They lowered their cups simultaneously, as if waiting for the punchline.

"You are to bring him to me by any means necessary."

"Here, to the mosque?" Omar inquired.

"No. To a location that I have yet to determine."

"Will there be danger?" Faisal asked.

"Perhaps, but Allah will guide you."

"Will we require weapons?"

The Imam had not considered that possibility and, realizing that some form of forceful persuasion might prove necessary, he said, "Only for inducement, he is not to be harmed."

The two acquaintances gazed at each other, as they awaited the location of the intended target and the details, but the Imam waived his hand as a gesture of dismissal. And then, as they rose to depart, he advised, "This conversation is not to be shared. You will be contacted later this week with the specifics. A travel stipend will be provided. You may go."

With his hand poised on the door lever, Faisal hesitated and inquired, "The weapons?"

"You will purchase ordinary kitchen knives at your destination," the Imam replied.

The two would-be kidnappers left the mosque, while the Imam pondered his decision. Those two are not the brightest among us, he thought, but I have little choice and even less time to please my benefactors.

Chapter Forty-three

Sunday, August 12, 2017

Arlington, Virginia

11 A.M.

Safe House

The single family home had been purchased by a straw buyer who'd presented a relocation fable to the seller's realtor. Years had passed since the completion of that transaction, and until this very day the house, although looked after by a property maintenance company, had remained mostly unoccupied.

Gregory had caught only a brief glimpse of the bright, white, wood clad single story structure, before he'd been hustled through the rear door into its musty interior. Major Striker had transferred the responsibility to Pentagon Security, under the watchful eye of Louder's, Ryan Keith. Ryan had taken a seat on the living room's faded maroon couch, while Gregory explored his new residence. When he'd staked his claim on what he'd determined to be the master bedroom, he'd returned to the living room and stood before Ryan.

"Now what?" Gregory asked.

"This is your home for the foreseeable future," Ryan

advised.

"What about transportation?"

Ryan grinned, handed him a cellphone, and said, "You call for what you need."

"I'm a prisoner?"

"Sort of."

"That sucks," Gregory replied, plopping onto the couch beside Ryan.

"I gather that you won't be lonely for long."

"Meaning?"

"Your two engineer colleagues."

"They've agreed?"

"The General can be pretty persuasive."

"When?"

Ryan shrugged, as if to say, I don't know.

"I'll need some clothes, food, toiletries..."

Ryan reached into an attache case that he'd placed on the carpet, and withdrew a yellow legal pad and a box of number two pencils, and said, "Make a list of everything you need, and I mean, everything."

Gregory took that to mean the equipment required to mimic the Nevada facility, an inventory that he'd already begun to mentally construct. He accepted the writing materials and Ryan rose to leave.

"What about keys?"

Ryan shook a keychain in the air and replied, "I'll be locking you in. If anyone rings the bell, ignore them."

"What if I want a pizza?"

"The cellphone that I gave you, you can't buy one like that. You'll notice that the buttons are functionless. Press talk and I'll answer. "

Gregory took a close look at the phone and complained, "What the hell is this?"

"It's a phone that has only one function, that being, to communicate with me and no one else."

"What about the General?"

"He'll contact you through me, when he needs to."

"And the pizza?"

Ryan groaned, "Call me with the order and one of my people will bring it."

Gregory heard the door being locked and he returned to the couch. The blinds had been closed in all of the rooms, except for one, the kitchen, and in the gloom of the living room he began to contemplate his future. I don't think that my hair can get an grayer, but I'm not sure that this prisoner status is any better than what the military had subjected me to after the Asian mixup. But maybe the General will allow me to disappear if I can successfully build the machine, he thought, his gaze locked onto the blank, yellow pad. Hmm, those custom high energy capacitors are going to be a problem. I can recreate the transformers from commercial sources, but unless the engineers can come up with a means of chaining a load of the largest capacitors available, we may run into a roadblock.

He kicked off his well worn athletic shoes and rubbed his sore toes. I used to be a tad over six-feet tall, but age is catching up with me and I'm shrinking, he mused, as he stretched out on the couch. Pushing on the sofa to make himself more comfortable, his left hand slid down behind one cushion and came into contact with something cool and metallic. He leapt from the couch and flipped the fabric covered mass of foam to reveal a forty caliber, Heckler & Koch P2000 pistol. Ryan wasn't visibly carrying a gun, he thought, and if he had been, he wouldn't have left it behind. He lifted the pistol and dropped the magazine to reveal that it was full. Despite his limited knowledge of firearms, he was familiar with the danger of accidental discharge due to the presence of a live round in the chamber, so he racked the slide and out popped a forty caliber bullet. Maybe the last inhabitant had left it behind, he mused, aiming the now empty weapon at a blank wall.

But a gun isn't something you easily forget. Well, no use trying to figure out where it'd come from, but it may come in handy down the road.

***

3 P.M.

Not having had the energy or inclination to make up the bed in his chosen room, Gregory had fallen asleep on the couch with the pistol resting by his side. Suddenly, he was awakened by the sound of the front door slamming shut. He gripped the pistol, whose chamber was now empty, and fell to a crouch beside the sofa with the weapon pointed at the two people who had just entered the darkened room.

"Easy doc, I see you've found it. But lower the weapon," Ryan advised.

Gregory did as requested.

"I brought you a playmate," he chuckled.

"Iliana?" Gregory exclaimed, visibly surprised.

"Hi Greg," she replied.

"I wasn't certain that you'd ever talk to me again, no less work with me."

"The General made me an offer I couldn't refuse."

"So you're on board with the project?"

"Looks like it."

Gregory shifted his gaze to Ryan and asked, "And the other engineer?"

"Workin' on it."

Ryan lowered the suitcase that he'd carried into the living room and said, "I trust you will show Ms. Franks to her assigned room.   One more thing, the General has assigned a few low profile sentries to keep an eye out for you ... 24/7."

"So we don't escape?"

"For your protection.   This house has been unoccupied for a long time, and *you know who* is bound to get wind of the activity."

"What are you talking about?" Iliana asked, a tinge of fear in her high pitched voice.

"The doc will explain it to you," as he turned to depart.

Now I understand the gun, Gregory thought, as he grabbed hold of Iliana's suitcase and carried it to one of the two unassigned bedrooms.

"What was that all about?" Iliana asked, as she kicked off her pink athletic shoes and pumped the mattress, checking its resilience.

"Our former employer."

"The General said that what we're going to do is on the up and up," she breathed, patting the mattress, an invitation for him to take a seat.

"He said that?"

She shook her head with a, yes.

"You might want to reconsider, because we're about to hijack the NSA's experiment."

"Are you shitting me?" she shouted.

"Keep it down, don't want to alert the neighbors."

She lowered her head, a lock of intensely red hair falling over one eye, and said, "The General had made it painfully clear that, like the Mafia, once you're in there's only one way out."

"Great. In that case, welcome to castle McCraken."

Gregory had left Iliana to freshen up in the en suite bathroom, as he retired to his own room to prepare the bed for a good night's rest. The strange cellphone was in his pocket, and he had every intention of using it to call in their dinner order when hunger presented itself.

An hour had passed since Iliana's arrival and there was much to discuss, but the past was just that, he pondered, and the project at hand requires our most diligent attention. With the bed made, he knocked on

Iliana's closed door.

"You decent?" he called out.

"Are you looking to borrow another dress?" she giggled.

I had hoped to sweep that under the carpet, he said to himself, as he smiled and replied, "Not today."

She opened the door to reveal that she'd changed into a pair of abbreviated denim shorts and a white halter top. Shoeless, she beckoned him to approach.

"Time for a proper hello," she said, pressing her lips to his without warning.

With his eyes still closed, he said, "I've missed you."

"She backed away and replied, "That's all you get for now."

"Understood. I know that I'd left things unsettled back at that military base."

"That was my favorite skirt, you bum."

"I wish I could tell you that I'd saved it, but it did save me."

"Where the hell have you been?"

"Trying to get some answers."

"And?"

"I got more than I'd bargained for."

"I assume that's the reason we're here?"

He nodded, yes.

"What did you find?"

"You'd better take a seat," he grinned.

"Ok, spin your yarn."

"Think, Einstein-Rosen Bridge."

"W-h-a-t?" she shrieked.

"Looks that way."

"I can't believe that we'd been duped."

"Not really. I don't recall an exact description of the endpoint."

"We all thought that it had something to do with a killer satellite design."

"Not sure where you'd gotten that from. Frankly, I had no clue, but the pay was good."

"Tell me about it."

"It almost got me killed. But remember the ceramic box at the end of the lab?"

She nodded, yes.

"It isn't there anymore."

"Holy shit."

"I don't know for sure if it'd disappeared through a wormhole or a dimensional shift, but either way, it was a monumental event. Shook me to the core."

"We're gonna need a shit load of power," she advised.

"That's where you and Jacks come in."

"Geronimo Jacks is joining us?"

"I hope so. We can't do this without him."

"He hates the government."

"But he likes money, and I think that he'll jump at the opportunity to stick it to our former employer."

"Why?"

"They'd treated him like a second rate citizen."

Chapter Forty-four

Sunday, 4 P.M.

The Rye Bar, Rosewood Hotel

Washington, D.C.

General Enoch Louder, dressed as a civilian, stood before the mirror in the Rye Bar's restroom.

I'm getting older by the day—wait—change that, by the hour, he told himself, as he tried to envision his face without its collection of wrinkles. I didn't sign up for all this cloak and dagger crap, but I'm up to my knees in it, nevertheless. What kind of legacy will I leave behind, he wondered. I have no family to speak of, no real friends, but plenty of enemies. I'm just a tired old man trodding through a squalid maze of treacherous creatures that some call, life. He took one more look at the mirror and, interrupted by another entrant, returned to his seat at the bar and an unfinished tumbler of Michter's 20 year-old bourbon that he'd paid a fortune for. Swiveling to face the room he realized that, except for a young couple seated at the opposite end, he was alone. Well, so much the better, he thought. I didn't come here for conversation. Hmm, I've made some questionable decisions in my career, and this revenge project of mine might take the cake. However, unlike those secretive assholes, I might be able to do some good if we're successful and I can keep it beneath the radar long enough to reach fruition. But McCraken did say that it could take down the local electric grid, and that would be a definite red flag. I hope that he and his buddies can overcome the power obstacle.

Five o'clock had come and gone, and Louder had switched to a more economical bourbon that had not benefitted his evolving inebriation. At six-thirty he swiveled off of the stool and stumbled to the men's room, where he promptly deposited the contents of his stomach into the nearest basin. And as he washed the remnants of vomitus from his lips, checking for completeness in the mirror, he noticed the presence of a dark suited male standing by the door, effectively blocking his eventual departure. He pretended to ignore the figure, spending more time than was necessary washing and drying his hands. In no mood for a physical confrontation, he turned and asked, "Can I help you?"

The man smiled and replied, "I've got a thing about privacy, and I was waiting for you to leave."

Louder breathed a sigh of relief and offered, "It's all yours, friend."

Back in the bar, it was apparent that the guzzlers and

sippers had been arriving en mass, and while his seat had remained unoccupied, he'd decided to vacate the premises and head for home and a much needed shower.

***

7 P.M.

He'd parked his car in the garage and taken the elevator to his floor, but as he walked the short distance to the front door he found Ryan Keith leaning against the wall, reading a hunting magazine.

"Is there a problem?" Louder asked, from ten feet away.

Ryan rolled the magazine into a tight tube and replied, "Maybe."

Louder frowned and unlocked the door, motioning for Ryan to follow him inside. "Take a seat," he offered, walking into the living room, still feeling the effects of the alcohol.

"The Indian's changed his mind," Ryan advised.

"That can't stand, fix it."

"How?"

Louder gazed over at his stocked bar, his usual response to a stressful situation, but altered course, and replied, "By any means necessary."

"You want me to threaten an American citizen?"

"You're right. Make him a better offer."

"Frank's was promised a quarter of a million, you want me to go higher?"

"I need him onboard."

"OK, I'll give it a try."

"Make it happen ... today."

Ryan nodded OK, and left the condo.

Louder tossed his clothes onto the bed and ran the shower. And without waiting for the usually slow to arrive hot water, he slipped inside. With the cool beads cascading down upon his head, he wondered if he'd done the right thing by placing so much trust and responsibility upon Ryan. He could blow me out of the water, he thought, taking a mouthful of the now warm liquid and spitting it against the white, polished tile wall. Then again, he's never given me reason to believe that he's anything but loyal. But who knows how he'd react if the MIB (men in black) got hold of him and cranked up the pressure. Well, that train's left the station with him fully knowledgeable and somewhat in control. He grabbed a bar of soap and began lathering up when a thought came to him. Geronimo, he was an Apache, and this Jacks guy is from the Lakota tribe.

Is that some kind of Indian joke, he wondered.

He dried off and dropped, naked, onto his California King bed. Sleep had come without effort and it was almost nine p.m. when the encrypted phone beneath his bed came to life. He groaned, a throbbing headache reminding him of the afternoon's excess, and reached for the phone.

"Yeah?"

"He's agreed."

"How much?"

"Three hundred."

"OK. Get him to the safe house tonight."

"Can't it wait till morning?"

"Don't want him to hold out for more."

"Understood."

"Is there a family to deal with?"

"No, he lives alone."

"Good. Help him pack some things and lock him in with the others, and then take some time for yourself," and as an afterthought, he added, "You're due a bonus for all you've done."

There was a moment of silence and then, "Thank you, but money's not my motive."

"I know, but you deserve it," he said, and terminated the call.

Shit, he thought, I may have insulted the guy. And with all of the things that could go wrong with my scheme, the last thing I need is for Ryan to be pissed off.

He fell back onto the bed, but sleep defied him. So he rose, put on a robe and walked into the living room to surf the cable channels. As usual, there was little to pique his interest, so he hit the off button and sat staring at the dark screen, wondering if McCraken and his colleagues had completed their wish list. He knew how to contact the cellphone that Ryan had provided, but he wasn't certain that it was as secure as he'd like it to be. He toyed with the idea of making a surprise visit to the safe house, but suspected that his travels were being monitored by his adversaries.

The underground maintenance pit at the Andrews Air Base was scheduled to be modified to the specifications provided by McCraken. He'd made certain that the Air Force contractor was aware of the excavation's secret nature, and it was to begin Monday morning. It had been estimated that it would take a month to accomplish the task, but Louder had used his clout and insisted on a two week timeframe. The contractor had balked, but in the end, under threat of lost business, he'd agreed to put more people on the job to meet the deadline. But he had no idea how long it would take for McCraken and his engineer buddies to build the machine, and it left him feeling powerless.

He made himself a ham sandwich with sour pickles, belched for an hour afterwards, and hit the sack, anticipating a restless night.

Chapter Forty-five

Safe House

11 P.M.

Ryan had dropped Geronimo off at the safe house and had locked the trio in for the night. There had been a brief sense of bonhomie, as the three exchanged pleasantries for the first twenty minutes. But when the reality of his semi prisoner status had become apparent, the electronics engineer—Geronimo—became irate.

"What right do they have to lock us in?" he shouted.

"It's part of the agreement," Gregory said.

"I didn't sign any agreement," Geronimo cried out adamantly.

"But you're being paid well."

"I guess, but it's more about getting back at our prior employer."

Iliana, who had kept quiet as she sat on the couch filling her fingernails, cut in with, "You never told us why you hated them so much."

Geronimo flipped his long, black ponytail over one shoulder and lowered his five foot, six inch frame to the end of the couch. He grimaced and said, "They seemed to have had an issue with native Americans."

"What do you mean?"

"At my initial interview, one asshole asked what I was doing off the reservation. He later said that it was meant in jest, but I didn't think so."

"That sucks," she admitted.

"Listen," Gregory said, from across the narrow room, "we don't have a lot of time to put this thing together. We have to create a list of the absolute essentials, and we need to do it tonight."

"Why the rush?"

"I've been through hell arriving at this point, and I don't want to be roadblocked by any government agency."

"Who appointed you the leader?" Geronimo sneered.

"Your new employer."

"Anyone else coming to this party?" he asked.

"We're it."

"OK, gimme something to write on."

By three o'clock in the morning they had compiled a several page long list of the required items. But as suspected, an adequate power source had remained the limiting factor, a problem that both Geronimo and Iliana had theoretically resolved following a heated discussion involving complicated calculations. The remedy consisted of chaining together a few dozen of the largest and most efficient, commercially available capacitors, in order to duplicate the charge released by the custom array at the Nevada facility. Their calculations had been accurate, but the chain's ability to discharge uniformly, thereby releasing a cumulative charge, had remained a troubling unknown.

"OK, time for us to get some rest," Gregory suggested.

Iliana, from her prone position on the carpeted floor, posed a hypothetical, "What happens if it doesn't work?"

Gregory yawned, scratched his chin and replied, "Don't wanna think about it."

"Power is the rate limiting feature, and there's no guarantee that our proposal will bear fruit," Geronimo advised.

"We don't have the time to test the power supply, it will have to work."

Geronimo rose from the couch, where he'd been sitting shoeless in a pair of bright red shorts that he'd changed into upon arrival, pointed a finger at Gregory and said, "I think it's time you spilled the beans."

"Beans?"

"The machine. Something brought us to this point and I, we," he said, gesturing toward Iliana, "need to know what it is."

"I already know," Iliana cut in.

"Then I'm the only Indian without a clue?"

Gregory laughed, fatigue taking the forefront, and said, "Sorry, should have told you from the get go. What would you say if I told you that the machine may have opened an Einstein-Rosen Bridge?"

"Holy shit."

"Exactly."

"How is that even possible?"

"As the theory goes, it should have required a lot more power than we'd had available, but it made the composite box disappear."

"I could buy disintegrate, but vanish..."

Gregory shook his head with a, yes.

"You think that our employers knew?"

"I'm beginning to think so."

"This is enormous. But if we're stealing their experiment, we could be in deep shit."

"We have the military behind us, but who knows what *they'll* do with us if we succeed."

"And if we don't," Iliana smirked.

"If you're thinking sabotage, forget it. I'm fairly certain that it wouldn't turn out well for us."

"So we present the list and keep our fingers crossed that it goes as planned," Geronimo groaned.

"There is one thing that I haven't mentioned," Gregory frowned.

"What's that?" Iliana asked.

"It's possible that our's wasn't the only experimental facility."

"What are you implying?"

"If I were a giant, secretive, government agency with a project of this magnitude, I wouldn't trust its success to one group of scientists."

"Makes no difference," Geronimo hissed.

"Perhaps, but it would explain why they've left the Nevada site untouched since my alleged accident."

"My turn to play devil's advocate," Iliana chimed in, continuing, "if I were them, I'd have a dragnet out for you."

"Why?" Gregory asked, a slight quiver to his voice.

"If what you think happened down there is verifiable, you're knowledge makes you too dangerous to be on the loose."

"Hmm, I hadn't considered that possibility.

"And now we all carry that risk," Geronimo said.

"No point worrying about that, we've got work to do."

"Yeah, if we live long enough."

***

* * *

Monday, 6 A.M.

With less than an hour of sleep behind him, groggy, McCraken rolled out of bed and reached for the phone that Ryan had provided. It rang a few times before a sleepy, almost unrecognizable voice responded with, "What do you need?"

"We have a shopping list for you," Gregory announced.

"There's food in the kitchen," was Ryan's reply.

"It's not for food."

"Oh. OK, I'll be by to pick it up before eight."

He ran a cold shower and jumped in. Finished, and not knowing if the others were awake, he wrapped a towel around his damp body and padded into the kitchen to put on a pot of coffee. Standing at the sink filling the carafe with water, he'd caught a glimpse of movement through the kitchen window. Lowering the pot to the counter, he moved closer for a better view, but all he saw was a tree and a poorly maintained hedge. But as he was about to turn back to the coffee machine, it had appeared again as a man in camouflage sporting a bullet proof vest with a short barreled rifle held with both hands. Panic began to set in, and he was set to rouse his housemates, when he recalled that Ryan had posted a pair of sentries outside of their house. I hope he's one of our's, he thought. But it occurred to him that the man was moving very cautiously, as if he was trying to avoid recognition. Is there someone else out there, he wondered. I can't keep this to myself.

Quietly, he opened Iliana's unlocked door and approached the bed. She was on her side, facing a blank wall, with a comforter drawn over her shoulders. Recalling that she was a light sleeper, he nudged her gently. There was no response. Well, she was up all night, he thought. But something made him linger a moment longer, and it was then that he'd noticed the bluish line about the exposed portion of her neck. He shook her more violently, and when she did not respond, he turned her face up. He gasped in shock. Her opened eyes were bloodshot, her lips were blue and she was not breathing. He felt for a pulse and found none. He tried to shout for Geronimo, but the horror before him had momentarily paralyzed his vocal cords. Still clothed only with a towel, he ran for the front door hoping to alert a sentry, but realized that they'd been locked inside, Ryan having taken the keys that he'd initially dangled before him. Frantic, he ran to Geronimo's room.

"Get up, get up, Iliana's been murdered," he shouted.

"What?" Geronimo moaned, still half asleep.

"Get outta bed, we're in trouble."

Geronimo, wearing only a pair of boxer shorts, followed Gregory into Iliana's room.

"Look," Gregory screamed, "they must have come through that window beside the bed."

"She's dead?" Geronimo said, still not fully grasping the spectacle before him.

"Get dressed, we have to get outta here."

"We're locked in," Geronimo shouted, pulling on his jeans and a T-shirt.

"Ryan's on his way."

"What about Iliana?"

"She stays."

"Who did this?" Geronimo growled through clenched teeth.

"Has to be our former employer, we know too much."

"Hoka hey."

"What?"

"Something Crazy Horse had said before going into battle. Means, let's go, it's a good day to die."

"I'm not dying today, or any day soon," Gregory grunted, as he slipped into his shoes and reached for the pistol that he'd hidden under his mattress.

The front door slammed shut with such force that the

drywall above it cracked, sending lumps of the popcorn ceiling to the carpeted floor. The two men crouched beside one bed, as Gregory aimed the gun into the corridor beyond.

"It's me, Ryan," a voice called out.

Gregory continued to point the pistol outwards until he could confirm that the voice matched the face. When Ryan was within arm's length of the bedroom's threshold, Gregory lowered the pistol and motioned for Geronimo to get off of the ground.

"Iliana's dead," Gregory tearfully croaked.

"Shit," Ryan moaned, "I should have gotten here sooner."

"You knew about this?"

"I think we have a mole at the Pentagon."

"Now what?"

"One of my sentries had his throat slit."

"And the other?"

"He's called for reinforcement."

"We can't stay here."

"There's another option, but you won't like it."

"Anything's better than waiting for another strike," Geronimo said.

Ryan grimaced and offered, "It means going

underground again."

"Nothing new for us," Gregory said, gazing at Geronimo.

"It also means putting the General's project on hold."

"There's no project without us."

"Agreed."

"So?"

"We wait for the reinforcements. In the meantime, you stay low, with your pistol aimed at the window, while I guard the front entrance. Shoot anything that approaches from the outside."

"What about me?" Geronimo asked.

"Grab a few kitchen knives and wait."

"Oh, sure, why not a bow and arrow."

Ryan thought about his complaint, and lifted the cuff of his slacks revealing a stainless steel, snub nosed revolver held in place by an ankle holster. "Here," he said, removing the gun and handing it to Geronimo, "know how to use it?"

"You bet."

Chapter Forty-six

Monday, August 13th

7 A.M.

Ugh, what the hell was I thinking, Louder said to himself, as he awakened with the residual taste of sour pickles and headed for the bathroom to empty his bladder. But so deep had been his sleep, that he had not responded to the intermittent chirping of the phone beneath his bed. And he'd first become aware of the oversight when his foot had struck the device and it was inadvertently dislodged from its clasp. What did I miss, he wondered, as he realized that the only two important people who had his number were Ryan and Major Thomas Striker. Standing in his skivvies, he pressed the sequence that would redial the caller's number and waited.

"Ryan here, sir."

"Sorry, I missed your call."

"We have a problem."

"Go ahead," Louder said, his face now set in stone, as he plopped to the edge of the bed.

"One of the scientists is dead, and my sentry has been neutralized."

Louder paused, dead, he thought. "What happened?"

"She was strangled."

"By one of her own?"

"No, intruder."

"And your sentry?"

"Throat slit by a pro."

I was afraid this could happen, he brooded. "Got an ID?"

"Probably a competitor."

"Those bastards."

"One more thing."

"Go."

"I think we have a mole."

Louder's eyes widened at the sound of that word, and he asked, "You got proof?"

"One of my out of the loop people made an off the cuff remark about the safe house being used."

"Think he's the mole?"

"It's a she, and no. Said that she'd heard it on the grapevine."

"This requires an immediate, internal investigation."

"I'll notify my superior."

"Sure it's not him?"

"No."

"Where are you?"

"In place, with the remaining scientists, waiting for reinforcements."

"If there's a mole, assume that you've been compromised. I'll send the marines."

"It'd better happen ricky tick, because they're still out there."

"Hang up, I'm on it."

Louder dialed Major Striker who, along with three of his squad members, had been preparing to leave for maneuvers at Andrews. The Major answered on his personal cellphone.

"Striker here?"

"It's Louder."

"Yes, sir," the Major said, automatically and unnecessarily coming to attention.

"Need your help," he said, as he went on to cryptically describe the situation at hand.

"Oorah. On my way," Striker bellowed, motioning for his men to come nearer.

While Ryan and the two scientists awaited the General's trusted soldiers, they watched, as several heavily armed masked beings passed by the windows, communicating with hand gestures.

"It won't be long now," Ryan speculated.

"It's broad daylight, the neighbors will notice," Geronimo advised.

"That's assuming that they haven't already been dealt with."

"And they called us savages."

Ryan shook his head in agreement.

Gregory, who had been guarding the window in Iliana's room, took a momentary break to adjust the sheet that they'd draped across her body, and turned back just as a wraithlike figure peered through the closed window. In response, he thrust the muzzle of his pistol against the glass and cocked the hammer. The wraith nodded knowingly, taunting his prey by brandishing an MP5 submachine gun. Gregory jumped back, his pistol no match for the raider's weapon, and he called out, "They've got automatic rifles."

"No surprise," Ryan shouted.

"What are they waiting for?" Gregory wailed.

"Don't know, but the longer they wait, the better our chances are."

Almost forty minutes had passed, and Gregory had counted no less than five different, black and camouflage clad bodies crossing his line of sight. Aside from the taste of fear in the back of his throat, his body was drenched in nervous sweat, and he was ready to accept his fate as a massacred loose end, when he saw one of the attacker's fall to the ground for no apparent reason. "One down," he called out.

"The Marines have arrived, back away while they do their thing," Ryan advised.

Gregory put some distance between the window and himself, and moved to the corridor just outside of Iliana's room. Suddenly, the window began to split into a giant spider like affair, while a bullet hit the doorframe just inches from his face. Seconds later, the entire window fell to pieces and a rush of outside air entered the room. He moved forward once again and took a position alongside of the absent window, his gun holding hand shaking like an unbalanced washing machine.

"All clear," Ryan shouted.

"You sure?" Gregory croaked.

"Yeah, we're sure. Lower your weapon," Major Striker said, as he stepped into the corridor and leaned against the doorframe.

Gregory exhaled and handed the gun to the Major, "Thank you," he breathed.

"Follow me."

"Where we going?"

"You'll know when you get there," Striker replied.

It had taken the Lincoln Navigator slightly more than thirty-five minutes to reach the entrance to Joint Base Andrews. After passing through security, they drove to a distant hangar where an unmarked corporate jet sat just outside awaiting its passengers.

Gregory leaned toward Ryan, who was seated in the front of the vehicle, and asked, "Is that for us?"

Yes, he nodded.

"When you said that we were going underground, I assumed that it was here, in the maintenance pit."

"Negative."

"Then where?"

"You'll be told when we're airborne."

He turned to this seatmate, Geronimo, with a confused expression. Geronimo simply shrugged, as if he was prepared to go with the flow.

Fifteen minutes later, the Gulfstream 550's wheels had left the tarmac and were quickly retracted. The Major and his men had been asked to accompany the flight to its final destination, from which they would immediately be flown back to Andrews. When the pilot had extinguished the seatbelt light, Ryan rose and approached the two scientists.

"You're going to Cheyenne Mountain," he advised.

"Where the hell is that?" Geronimo asked.

"Colorado."

"Is it safe?"

"About as good as it gets."

"And then what?"

"We'll see."

"And our project?"

"Above my pay grade."

"So we just sit around and watch the soaps?" Gregory complained.

"You'd prefer a bullet to the head?"

"No," he breathed.

"Then chill out and wait for the General's next move."

Neither of the two men had had the time to repack their clothes, and all of their belongings had been left behind at the safe house. Geronimo was wearing his jeans and T-shirt, while Gregory had on a pair of green shorts, a faded blue polo shirt and a pair of athletic shoes. Their attire was no match for the aircraft's full cool mode air-conditioning.

Ryan had returned to his seat, and was speaking on a telephone when Gregory approached.

"Excuse me," he said.

"Just a minute," Ryan replied, the phone still pressed to his right ear.

"In a minute I'll be frozen solid."

Ryan groaned, lowered the phone and said, "Ask the steward for a blanket."

The Steward appeared to have read his mind, as he reached into a cubby and withdrew two blankets, along with something that looked oddly familiar.

"Get back to your seat," the steward demanded, the black machine pistol's muzzle pointed down the isle toward the marines.

"What the fuck," Ryan called out, attempting to strike the man with the phone, but was thwarted with a backhanded wallop to the head.

"To the marines in the rear," the steward barked, "you may try to overtake me, but these three will die before you leave your seats."

"What do you want?" Gregory managed.

"Shut up."

"If it's about money, we can make some arrangement in Colorado," Ryan urged, pressing his handkerchief to a bloody gash on his forehead.

"We're not going to Colorado."

"What is it you want?" Ryan asked.

"Shut up," the gunman demanded.

The forward passengers fell silent, but the marines seated in the rear of the aircraft were, with the seat backs hiding their activity, communicating among themselves with hand signals. Major Striker gazed down at the short barreled M4 CQBR resting on the floor by his feet, with its 30 round Stanag magazine attached. He had removed it from his rucksack after boarding the plane with the intention of temporarily detaching the delicate, custom made optical sight that he'd had installed by a gunsmith. Neither the steward nor the pilots had been aware of its existence, the other team members having placed their rucksacks in the baggage hold. The marine seated nearest the Major nodded his approval, as Striker kept an eye on the hijacker, hoping that he maintained his forward vantage point. He knew that it would take only a second to acquire the target, but the act of leaning to retrieve the weapon might prompt the man to investigate. He needed a diversion, something to cause the hijacker to look the other way. He'd noticed how the man had turned to shout at Ryan when he'd asked a question, but he had no way of prompting Ryan to repeat the act. There were risks in all forms of combat, but close quarter battles were the most perilous, and this qualified as the worst scenario possible.

"Gotta take a leak," Striker called out.

"Do it in your seat," the man replied, his gun aimed steadily toward the soldiers.

"C'mon, that ain't cool," he replied.

The man ignored his plea.

"What about somethin' to drink?" the marine beside the Major asked.

"You can drink his piss."

Gregory, either aware of the purpose of the discourse, or simply in need, called out, "There must be something to eat aboard this plane."

The gunman, with a mean expression, spun to face the scientist, presumably hell bent on providing a violent response, when Striker saw his opening and brought the rifle to rest on the seat back before him. Without a moments hesitation, he acquired and double tapped the man, causing his head to explode like a watermelon dropping from a skyscraper. White hair, chunks of skull and brain matter clung to the elegantly appointed aircraft's interior, while its owner's body lie in a crumpled mass blocking the aisle. The cabin filled with the dense odor of spent ammunition, but the rifle's report had not gone unnoticed by the pilots. And while one round had traversed the hijacker's skull to lodge itself in the bulkhead separating the cabin from the cockpit, the other high-powered round had grazed the co-pilot's left shoulder, endings its travels in a noncritical section of the instrument panel, and he came running with a Glock 9mm pistol gripped by the fingers of his right hand. He stopped by the second row of seats and glared down at the headless carcass.

"You'll pay for this," he growled, stepping over the body and heading for the marines and the dissipating cloud of spent gunpowder.

Striker had already lowered the M4, its muzzle pressed against the forward seat back, and as the man approached, he took a chance, flicked the selector switch to burst automatic mode and pulled the trigger. The co-pilot's face took on an expression of shock, as he staggered forward a few paces and collapsed with a large red stain extending across the front of his white shirt, the Glock sliding down the aisle toward the rear. In an instant, the Major rose, marched across the dead man's body and aimed his rifle in the direction of the cockpit. Ryan and the scientists, who had remained seated with heads down throughout the very brief encounter, ran forward to assist the Major. They found him ensconced in the right seat, with the rifle's muzzle firmly pressed against the pilot's head, and were just about to back off, when they heard him say, "Set course for Colorado."

Chapter Forty-seven

Monday

7 A.M.

The Imam's chosen kidnappers had been called back to the mosque on Sunday evening. Following their initial visit to his office, the Imam had concluded that time was of the essence, and he had been on his way out of the restroom when the two men had entered the empty building, late that night. He'd motioned for them to follow him to the office.

"Please, be seated," he'd said.

"Are we no longer needed?" Omar Botros had inquired.

"We need to act sooner than anticipated."

"I mean no disrespect, Imam, but earlier you had indicated that we would have a few days before departure," Faisal Halabi whined.

"You will leave tonight. I have made travel arrangements, and this will cover your expenses," he'd advised, sliding two yellow envelopes across his desk.

"And our mission?" he'd asked, assuming command of the duo.

The Imam had provided a newspaper file photo of the

General that had been taken some years earlier, when he had been in considerably better physical condition. On the back of the photo he had written Louder's last known home address and his position at the Pentagon. Prior to his disappearance, Akil had furnished Louder's approximate daily schedule and habits, and this too had been added to the narrative.

"You must understand the importance of this assignment, failure is not an option. You will contact me via cellphone when the abduction has been completed and I will supply the drop-off location. Understood?" the Imam had barked.

"If he resists?"

"He most certainly will."

"And our response?"

"He is not to be harmed, but a few bruises would be acceptable."

"If that is the case, what is the purpose of the kitchen knives?" Omar had asked, before receiving a jab to the rib cage from his assumed leader.

"Self defense only," the Imam had replied.

"How much time are we allotted?"

The Imam gazed at the glass encased, brass clock that sat at the edge of his desk, and replied, "You will have forty-eight hours."

***

They'd arrived on the last flight out of Detroit and had checked into the Arlington Days Inn by Wyndham. The Imam had provided each with five-hundred dollars in cash, more than enough to cover the cost of the single room that they'd shared, as well as food and required transportation. Prior to leaving the airport they had purchased a map of the city and had outlined the desired route to Louder's condominium. The Wyndham did not offer a true dining facility, and other than the free breakfast that came with the room, they were on their own.

"Where will we purchase our knives?" Omar whispered to his accomplice.

Faisal gazed about, grabbed two butter knives, and replied, "This will do."

"It barely slices through my cake," Omar complained.

"We will sharpen them on the concrete," he breathed, as he stretched his cheeks with an entire blueberry muffin.

Omar stopped chewing, checked his wristwatch and said, "We must leave now."

Faisal grabbed one more muffin and followed his

partner to the street.

The information provided by Akil, via the Imam, had indicated that the General's condo departure time generally hovered around eight a.m., but that he occasionally left earlier. Their scheme was simple. They would take a taxi to a point one block before the General's building, exit same, and walk the remaining distance. The Imam had left the planning entirely up to the duo, who had decided to use a direct approach. They would penetrate the securitized garage with the code acquired by Akil. There, they would wait in hiding a short distance from Louder's vehicle and grab him—with one in front and the other from behind—when he approached. If he resisted, and they'd been advised that he most certainly would, they would wield their sharpened butter knives to subdue him. But there was an unanticipated fly in the ointment. Due to the various and presumed NSA threats, the General had taken to carrying a concealed weapon—a forty-five caliber semiautomatic pistol—on a daily basis. Neither Akil nor the Imam had been aware of this change in habit, a modification that had rendered their butter knives almost laughable.

They'd entered the garage and had hidden behind an older, dark green Lexus that had been parked several feet from the General's SUV. At seven fifty-five, out of the peacefulness of the concrete tomb that was the garage, they heard approaching footsteps. They'd stiffened and readied their weapons. The General, unaware of their presence but cautious nevertheless, stopped a distance of ten feet from his vehicle and surveyed the surrounding automobiles. He'd taken to watching his six ever since Ryan had demonstrated the penetrability of the garage's security measures, and this time something had raised his concern.

Out of the corner of his eye he'd noticed a slight sense of movement from beside the green Lexus. Is that the tip of a shoe, he wondered, as he sidestepped a few feet and wrapped the fingers of his right hand around the gun's grip, releasing the safety as he gently slid it from the holster. Not noticing any further activity, he cautiously approached his SUV with the gun's muzzle aimed forward, and that's when all hell broke loose. On cue, both Omar and Faisal leapt into the air, the overhead florescent lighting reflecting off of their knives, and made it to within two feet of the General when his own right foot stubbed against his vehicle's front tire and his hand jerked. The weapon fired, with its ear shattering report echoing off of the concrete walls and ceiling. The round had struck Omar in the solar plexus and he screamed in pain, gasping for breath, as his body slumped to the ground, his gray sweatshirt turning red. Faisal, having never been witness to the horrific vision before him, was stupefied, and he stood motionless, like a deer caught in oncoming headlights.

With a second round sitting in the gun's chamber, the hammer cocked and ready, Louder stood his ground and shouted, "On the ground, face down. Do it, do it now."

Faisal, still in shock, complied mechanically, as a growing puddle of urine began to stream from beneath his body.

"Who sent you?" Louder demanded.

"Allahu Akbar," Faisal shouted.

"One more time, who sent you?"

"No one."

"Try again, or I'll splatter your brains across the floor."

Faisal hesitated, and then replied, "The Imam."

Louder squatted beside the man and pressed the pistol against the back of his head. "I need a name."

"He will have me killed," Faisal whimpered.

"I'll save him the trouble ... the name."

"Faaroog Awan."

Louder rose and scratched his head, trying to place

the name, but he drew a blank. "Where can I find him?" he growled, stepping over the yellow puddle that had formed beside Faisal's torso.

"Detroit," he stuttered.

"What does he want with me?"

"Don't know," Faisal breathed, with his lips pressed to the concrete.

Louder glared at the man on the ground and wondered what he was going to do with him and the dead body lying a few feet away. Ryan's off to Colorado, he thought, so I may have to play this one by the books and call the cops. On the other hand, that's gonna lead to a shit load of questions that I can't answer, and if they decide to hold me I won't be able to figure out what the damn Imam wants. And then he had a thought. Ryan's initial dossier on Colonel Duke had mentioned something about an Imam, and Duke had come from Detroit. There has to be a connection. He stepped back a few yards and scanned the wall and ceiling of the garage, looking for cameras. His security people had informed him that the garage was the building's weak spot. And he had complained to the condo board about the lack of adequate surveillance near his assigned parking space but, to the best of his knowledge, they had yet to respond. Should I chance it, he pondered.

Noticing that no visible cameras had been added since his last certified letter to the board, he approached the sobbing Faisal and said, "Stand up and give me a hand."

Faisal hesitated, apparently anticipating a bullet of his own, but rose and looked away from his accomplice.

"Help me push this body under that car," Louder demanded, gesturing toward the green Lexus.

"I will be in defiance of Islam."

"You'll be dead if you don't. And, oh, you can forget about paradise, it ain't gonna happen."

Faisal's eyes locked onto the gun in Louder's right hand, the gun that had ended Omar's life, and began dragging the body backward. Together, they shoved Omar beneath the car's chassis, leaving behind a large, red stain on the concrete floor. There's no time to deal with it, Louder realized, deciding to make it less visible by having Faisal knock out the florescent light above that area, with the hope that the blotch would initially be taken for transmission fluid. Unfortunately, any forensics intern would recognize it as blood, he thought, but it should buy me some time to come up with an alternative solution. He ran his hand across the Lexus' engine hood and came back with a palm full of dust. This car hasn't been driven for awhile, he thought, so there's a good chance that the body will go undiscovered until it begins to stink, and I should be able to have it removed before that happens.

Faisal was now standing with his back against a cement column, nervously pulling on his dark beard. He ran the back of one hand across his moist eyes, and said, "You're going to kill me now?"

Louder had considered that option, but had concluded that one dead body was more than enough to deal with. Furthermore, he had a plan that involved a live participant. But there was some unfinished business to be dealt with first.

Chapter Forty-eight

Cheyenne Mountain

El Paso County, Colorado

Monday, August 13th

11 A.M.

The Gulfstream had landed and taxied to a secure location, where the aircraft could be sanitized and the hijacker's bodies removed beyond the scrutiny of onlookers. A pair of black, unmarked SUV's had been waiting nearby for the two scientists, while the Major and his men remained on the plane. The vehicles—one containing Gregory and Geronimo, the other occupied by four military police—sped off in tandem to their mountain destination. Both Gregory and Geronimo sat silently in the rear seats expecting some form of friendly conversation from the driver and the armed passenger, but all they'd received was an uncomfortable hush.

Gregory, still disturbed by the lingering sense of foreboding arising from the attempted hijacking, leaned forward, and asked, "How long 'til we get there?"

The front seat passenger ignored the question, unwrapped a piece of chewing gum and shoved it into his mouth.

Gregory leaned back and frowned at Geronimo, who was busy scrutinizing the passing landscape through the overly dark, tinted windows. "Looks like we're prisoners ... again," Gregory whispered.

"Better them than the hijacker," Geronimo replied, still facing the window.

Both men had dozed off, but had been awakened when the car came to a abrupt halt at the mountain's security gate. The rear doors opened and a uniformed guard snapped, "Out."

They followed the nameless front seat passenger through a cavernous corridor, where they were hooded and led to their sleeping quarters. Once through the steel door, their hoods were removed. And before they'd had a chance to survey the surroundings, their guide droned, "Someone will be around to bring you a change of clothes and food. There is a bathroom and shower through that door," he advised, gesturing to the right of their beds, "and if there is anything else that you require, press that green button near the door."

"What should we call you?" Gregory inquired.

"You won't see me again."

"Will we be allowed some fresh air?"

The man smiled and replied, "The air inside the

mountain is purified, it's as fresh as it gets."

As he departed, they could hear the lock click shut.

"This sucks," Gregory moaned, as he dropped onto the bed of his choice, adding, "I have a feeling that boredom will be our biggest enemy."

"Not for me, I can meditate."

As Gregory kicked off his athletic shoes and stretched out on the bed, he turned to face Geronimo, who was seated on the near bed with his back against the wall and said, "I'm curious, care to tell me something about your childhood on the Reservation?"

Geronimo let loose with an energetic guffaw, and replied, " It was a real blast."

"C'mon, I'm serious."

"It wasn't all fun and games. Pine Ridge is in South Dakota, on the Nebraska border. The average high temperature is in the mid 50's, not exactly bathing suit weather. We lived in a rusty old trailer that had no electricity, and we got our power, what little we had, from refurbished car batteries. Get the picture?"

"Sorry."

"Yeah, it was horrible. I still have a younger sister who lives on the Res."

"What about your parents?"

"Dead."

"You sister lives by herself?"

"She's a druggie. Sells her body for the habit."

"Can't you help her?"

"Tried. But she wasn't interested."

"You're PhD. How did that happen?"

"Funny story. I snuck off the Res one night and made it all the way to Whiteclay ... that's Nebraska. Anyway, there's not much to do on the Res, so I'd spent countless hours teaching myself how to play chess. So here I am, walking around in the dark, and I stumble upon a cafe and I walk in. The place was empty, save for one guy dressed in cowboy attire, seated at a table staring down at a chess board. I walk over and tell him that his queen is about to be taken, and he tells me to sit down and play. That's how it happened."

"Details, I need the details."

"OK. I beat the pants off the guy—twice. Turned out that he was the major liquor supplier for Whiteclay. I told him about my shitty life on the Res, and he tells me that each year he pays for a scholarship for a deserving student. Says that it's a tax write-off. I get suspicious and begin to wonder if he's after my ass, but then he shows me photos of his most recent recipients—three girls. He said that educating me would be his biggest achievement, if I didn't let him down. End of story."

"That's quite a narrative."

"What about you?"

"My parents came over from Scotland when I was just a few months old. But as a teenager, I became curious about my heritage, visited the homeland and ended up at the University of Edinburgh, graduated and came back to get my PhD."

"Rich boy," Geronimo mumbled.

"My parents were comfortable, but there were no fancy cars in the garage."

Without warning, the door to their room opened, bringing with it a blast of cold air. A woman in military fatigues entered carrying a bundle of clothes, toothbrushes, liquid soap and a few bottles of water. She lowered them to the nearest bed and announced, "Sandwiches are one their way, and the mess hall will be open for dinner at 1700 hours. I'll be back to escort you there at 1650, be ready." Like a practiced ballet dancer, she spun on her heels and departed.

Geronimo grinned and said, "White girl pretty."

"Huh."

"Great, so you know how to say, yes, in Lakota."

Gregory mimed an exaggerated grin, grabbed a toothbrush and headed for the bathroom.

They passed the time discussing the original project and the feasibility of same in the absence of Iliana. Despite their current sequestered status, Gregory wasn't ready to give up on the discovery of a lifetime. And Geronimo had caught the bug as well, as evidenced by his knowledgable contribution to the debate. But the safe house attack had changed everything, and the pair weren't certain that they'd be allowed to continue, since the General was the key to their quest and he'd been conspicuously absent from the get go.

The female military escort arrived punctually, as promised, and they marched in silence to the mess hall. The two men were surprised to find themselves completely alone, save for the soldier who'd approached and had taken their orders for the day's special—meatballs and spaghetti.

"Where is everybody?" Geronimo asked of the soldier, the female having already departed.

He gazed up at a clock and replied, "You have until 1800 to finish up and leave."

"And then what?" Gregory asked.

"Your escort will return," he said, lowering the steaming plates to the metal table.

"I guess that's when everybody else gets to chow down," Geronimo whispered.

"They're isolating us, like lepers."

"Yeah. I wonder whose behind that nasty game."

They dined in silence. And ten minutes before their deadline, the server returned and cleared Geronimo's plate from the table, leaving that used by Gregory conspicuously behind. Gregory called after the man, but he'd already disappeared behind a counter. But as he leaned against the table in the process of rising, his plate shifted forward, revealing a small square of green paper. He stared at it for a second or so, and then brought its closer to his face.

"Do you believe this?" he breathed to his dinner partner.

"What is it?"

"Says, check behind the toilet tank."

The two men glared at each other, not sure what to make of the note, but Gregory pocketed the paper square and pretended that nothing had transpired, although it was obvious that the server had known about it, and had probably placed it there himself.

The chaperon arrived at the appointed time and escorted them back to their room. The sound of the lock clicking shut was their cue to follow the message's direction. And sure enough, taped to the back of the commode was an envelope that contained a single, printed sheet of paper and a key, but no signature.

"What are we supposed to do with this?" Gregory said, to his stupefied companion.

"The directions are pretty clear, the sender wants us to escape and has told us how."

"Aren't you curious as to why? And what about the key?"

"You might not have noticed, but the lock on our door is keyed from both sides," Geronimo informed.

"OK. That gets us out, but where do we go afterwards, and who sent this?"

Geronimo shrugged.

"The NSA can't get to us in here, but outside is another story."

"You think this is their ploy?"

"More likely than not."

"Shit."

"Agreed."

Chapter Forty-nine

Monday

11. A.M.

Louder had sealed Faisal's lips and had bound his hands and legs with the silver duct tape that he'd kept in the glovebox for emergencies. And he'd pushed the man into the rear of the vehicle and weighted him down with two heavy comforters that had been marked for disposal, leaving him in the parked and locked car. He'd been awaiting a call from Major Striker regarding the successful handoff of the scientists and he had to get back to the encrypted phone, the nearest device being located in his condo. He was anxious, and he ground his teeth as the elevator crawled upwards. The lift came to an agonizingly slow halt, the door slid back and he flew into his apartment.

The LCD revealed that an incoming call had been missed. He hit redial and waited.

"Striker here, sir," the voice returned.

"Report."

"There was a problem."

Louder groaned.

"Sir?"

"Listening."

"There was a hijack attempt."

"And?"

"Neutralized."

"Origin?"

"Unknown."

"Casualties?"

"Theirs."

"The packages?"

"Delivered."

"Oorah."

"Orders?"

Louder thought about the kidnapper locked in his car, and considered involving the Major's team, but needed more time to think it through. "I'll get back to you," he said, hitting the end button.

He reattached the phone to bed frame and took a seat. He knew that his secretary would be calling soon, as he was hours late for the office, so he used his personal cellphone and called to inform her that he was feeling under the weather and would not be in.

The dirtbag in my car claims to have been sent by an Imam, he thought. And the fact that both the Imam and Colonel Duke have Detroit in common tells me that both he and mosque man were somehow in cahoots. So, do I drag that bearded piece of shit with me to confront the man, or should I dispose of him and move on, he pondered. Hmm, taking him along poses too many logistical issues, but a photo of him trussed up like a ready to roast pig should be convincing enough.

He dislodged the encrypted phone and redialed the Major.

"Striker here, sir."

"I have two to go."

"Destination?"

"Deep six."

"Oorah."

"Cleanup?"

"Minor."

"Where?"

"My twenty."

"Be there in thirty."

He ended the call and headed back to his vehicle. Faisal was squirming about, trying to rupture his bindings but having no success. Louder removed his cellphone and snapped a few defining photos of his captive, and then checked beneath the green Lexus, pleased to see that the corpse had not been discovered. And exactly fifteen minutes later, Major Striker and three men made their way through security and into the garage. Louder nodded as they approached.

"One under that car," Louder said, gesturing toward the Lexus, "another in here," he advised, pointing at his own vehicle.

The Major stood by the General, as one of his men poured hydrogen peroxide over the blood stained concrete, while a 5 gallon can of full strength muriatic acid stood by his side. The other two began bagging the corpse and, when finished, dragged Faisal from the back of Louder's car and placed his thrashing body into a black, zippered bodybag.

"We'll silence this one after we leave, no need to make a mess here," Striker said, nodding at the undulating black bag.

"You can't carry them out, too risky," Louder advised, adding, "use my car and then dump it. I'll report it stolen."

"Affirmative."

Louder tossed the key fob to the Major, turned, and headed back to the condo.

With my project on hold, and the two scientists safely hidden inside the mountain, he said to himself, I can concentrate on my immediate threat ... the crazy Imam, and whatever he wants from me. But as the elevator began to rise, he wondered if a solo mission to Detroit was a good idea. I should have called Pentagon security after I'd shot the moron, he thought. That would have allowed me to turn the investigation over to them. On the other hand, it would have opened a giant can of worms. I was an idiot to think that I could deal with everything on my own, and I hate to involve Ryan yet again, I already owe him big time. And speaking of being in debt, Major Striker and his boys can hang me out to dry whenever they choose. I need to think this through.

By later that night he'd decided that whatever the Imam's motive it wasn't worth exposing himself to further danger. He'd already tabled the notion of involving Ryan and or Major Striker, and he'd concluded that traveling to Detroit on his own would not be a good idea. What would I do once I'd arrived, he'd wondered. A confrontation, physical or verbal, would not be a politically sound approach, he'd reasoned, and given that he'd yet to have been questioned about the absence of Colonel Duke, he wanted to avoid rattling anymore chains. He'd decided to see what the future brought.

Chapter Fifty

Tuesday, August 14th

Office of Imam Faaroog Awan

6 A.M.

Following the dawn prayer, Imam Faaroog Awan had returned to his office to await the anticipated call from his two emissaries. Having not heard from them at the appointed time the night before, he'd been concerned. He'd locked the door, poured himself a cup of tea, and was about to take a seat behind his desk, when he'd realized that he was not alone. Two men emerged from behind the red brocade curtains that shielded the room from the outside world. Silently, with catlike steps, they'd taken their positions; one, behind the Imam, the other just before his desk. The Imam, shocked by their presence, tipped the small porcelain cup, spilling the steaming tea across the polished wood surface.

"By what insolence do you invade my sanctuary?" he shouted, a slight quiver to his voice.

The man before the desk simply smiled in response.

"Have you no voice?" the Imam squealed, attempting to rise from his chair but thwarted by the man from behind.

"We come with a message," the man in front announced.

The Imam slowly eased back into his seat, and said, "From whom?"

"Your benefactor."

The Imam swallowed hard. He had only one significant sponsor, and the presence of the messenger duo made his heart beat with fear. All he could muster was, "And?"

"The Mullahs have grown tired of waiting."

"But at this very moment I await the call of success from my operatives."

"Too late."

He took a deep breath and asked, "What do they wish of me?"

"You are no longer in their thoughts."

"But..." he replied, before he was grabbed by the neck from behind and yanked from his seat.

The Imam, always resourceful, and in desperation, seized the gold letter opener that sat near the edge of the desk blotter. Gasping for breath, he jabbed upwards and over his own head, penetrating the would-be assassin's left eye with remarkable accuracy. Screaming in pain, the black bearded man lost his grip and fell backwards. The

Imam rocketed from the chair, but at that very moment the killer's associate flew across the desk and latched onto the Imam's robe, causing his face to come crashing down against the desk. Blood splattered everywhere and documents flew through the air, as the two men struggled for dominance. At one point, the Imam held the upper hand, with his body draped across his opponent's torso. But the man had not come unprepared and, with some effort, removed a jeweled Khanjar (Arabic knife) from the small of his back. With the palm of his left hand held against the Imam's forehead, he forced his head upward, while slashing across his neck with the sharp knife. The Imam gasped, his eyelids flew apart like tiny garage doors, as his breathing was halted by a blood filled trachea. He gurgled, and then grew silent.

The killer straightened his clothes, took note of the large red stains covering his white shirt, and moved to his writhing associate.

"Can you walk?" he asked.

"With assistance," the man groaned, the letter opener still protruding from his orbit.

"This must come out," he said, gesturing toward the shiny opener.

"Do what you must."

The Imam's executioner jerked the blade free, and with it came the man's eyeball, suspended by the still attached optic nerve. He withdrew in horror, as if the image was somehow more appalling than the nearly detached head he'd just left behind.

"May Allah be with you," he said, placing the blood covered fingers of both hands on his friend's neck and squeezing with all his might. He waited until it'd been clear that his effort had been victorious and then released his grip. As an afterthought, he positioned the Khanjar in his accomplice's left hand and exited the office.

Chapter Fifty-one

Tuesday

Cheyenne Mountain

5 A.M.

Gregory had not slept more than an hour. Between the strange message that had been taped to the commode, and Geronimo's jet engine-like snoring, sleep had not been possible. And at 5 a.m. he sat at the edge of his cot wondering if there was a way to contact the General. He gazed at a wall clock that the military had thoughtfully installed just above the doorway and thought, hmm, it's two hours earlier back in D.C. Do I care if I wake him, he said to himself, thinking, not the least. He felt his way to their room's only door in the dark and began banging, at first, with light taps and then with more forceful fist slams.

Geronimo awakened with a start and yelled, "What the hell's going on?"

"I need a phone."

"Pizza, at this hour?"

"Hell no."

"Then what?"

"We can't sit here forever, and that toilet communique had kept me up all night Well, that, and your snoring."

"I don't snore," he said, indignantly.

"We'll debate that another time."

"So?"

"The General put us here, he must have a plan. We need to know what that is."

"I guess he gave you his personal number," Geronimo sneered.

Gregory slouched. "I was planning to call the Pentagon."

"Good luck with that," Geronimo said, pulling the sheet over his head.

"Yeah, that could present a problem."

Geronimo slowly lowered the sheet, shifted to a seated position, and asked, "You up for some adventure?"

"The kind that gets me killed?"

"Maybe. But you want to escape, right?"

"Bingo."

"But we'd already determined that the message is bogus," Geronimo reminded.

"It's supposition, not fact."

"It's risky, but being locked in is no different than living on the Res., although, the bathroom is better."

"It's five-thirty," Gregory announced, adding, "we

either go right now, or wait until tonight."

"I can't wait."

Since they'd arrived with just the clothing on their backs, with the exception of those provided by their hosts, there was nothing to pack or carry. Gregory carefully inserted the key into the double-sided lock, held his breath and twisted his wrist. To his surprise, the door opened without resistance and he peeked out into the corridor. There were a few soldiers standing guard at the far end, but they weren't aimed in his direction. He turned back to Geronimo and whispered, "Do you remember the turns we took to get here?"

"I'm an Indian, that makes me a tracker by heritage."

"But do you remember?"

"Not really," he said, sheepishly.

"We'll only have one chance at this, and the bags over our heads obscured the path most of the way here."

"We'll follow the scent."

"Now you're a bloodhound?"

"No, smart-ass, the scent of outside air."

"It all smells the same to me."

"I'll lead the way," Geronimo breathed, pushing Gregory aside and exiting the room.

They moved slowly away from the soldiers, hugging

the walls as they inched their way into the unknown. The cavernous, brightly lit facility was larger than they had imagined, and the slow pace made their discovery an eventual given.

"Think we should go back?" Gregory muttered.

"What's the worst they could do, lock us up?"

"The toilet message said to head past that bank of computer screens."

"There are three people sitting at those screens, we need to create a diversion so we can get behind them without being spotted."

Gregory reached into his pocket and produced the room key. "What about this?"

"Well, it is pretty quiet in here, but that won't make much noise."

"It might, if I can hit that metal cabinet on the other side of the room."

"OK. Be ready to run if it catches their attention."

Gregory wound his right arm like a pitcher warming up for the last throw of the game, and let go. The key flew up into the air and across the room, landing atop the cabinet with a tinkle. But it was just loud enough to break the room's silence, and the three screen gazers swiveled in their chairs. The two scientists ran as fast as their legs would allow, making it behind the bank of machines an instant before the watchers returned to their initial positions. In a crouch, they continued over and past the thick black and multicolored cables that exited the six-foot tall computer cabinets, on their way to an unknown destination. Beyond the heat emitting machines was a collection of military style vehicles, all lined up as if they'd been waiting for the next showing of Rambo.

"We're close," Geronimo announced.

"You smell air?"

"Nope. But the Humvees tell me that the exit is near."

"Should we take one?"

"Yeah, that makes sense. The noise alone would wake the dead, and I'm not sure what the penalty is for boosting a government vehicle."

"Ok, duly noted."

"There it is."

"Look like heavy steel doors."

"Follow me," Geronimo said, disappearing among the trucks and Hummers.

Gregory followed from close behind, checking his six every few seconds. The motorized steel doors were indeed thick, as evidenced by the lack of sound made by Geronimo's fist against the first one encountered. But twenty feet to the left was a small alcove that harbored its own steel door, and Gregory gestured in that direction.

"An emergency exit," Geronimo hissed.

"Could be wired."

"Yeah, maybe an alarm."

"Do we risk it?"

"We're too close to turn back," Geronimo declared, his right hand grasping the handle.

"Wait, I've seen photos of the entrance to this place. There's no place to hide outside."

"Then we run."

"We'll be out in the open, and you can plan on cameras out there."

"Now you're telling me this?"

"I just remembered."

"OK, you're call."

Gregory furrowed his brow and considered the options. We were captives inside, and if they catch us escaping they'll probably put us right back where we came from. After all, we're not criminals. "OK, we go. But we either run like never before, or we slowly walk out like we're on a mission."

"We're wearing military fatigues, I'm for the mission thing."

"And if this door's alarmed?"

"We're fucked."

They opened the door and nonchalantly walked toward the open air. But the door's silent alarm had alerted the computer watchers, as well as the formidable security detail assigned to the facility. Within seconds, and before they'd reached the exterior end of the entry tunnel, they were being chased by no less than twenty armed soldiers. And since they'd been walking rather than running, they were surrounded in a matter of minutes.

"Just wanted some fresh air," Geronimo offered, elbowing Gregory in an effort to keep him quiet.

"This is as close as you get to it," a solider, who appeared to be the leader of the group, growled.

"We're not criminals, you know."

"Move," the rifle toting man ordered, as he steered them back to the interior.

"Can we have a word with your commanding officer?" Gregory intervened.

Two of the nearby security officers chuckled.

"I guess that's a no."

The rifle muzzle pressing against his back reinforced his conclusion, as he reluctantly marched at a rapid pace.

But the soldiers did not return them to their room.

Instead, they left them in the mess hall with a pair of guards positioned at the doors.

"Now what?" Geronimo whispered.

"Breakfast sounds good."

Gregory rose and headed for a coffee urn that was perched on a counter across the room. He poured two cups, placed them upon a metal tray, and carried them back to the table. And they were about to lift the cups to their lips, when the door flew open, the soldiers jumped to attention and a middle aged man entered wearing a crisply pressed Air-force uniform. He approached the pair and, with a stone-like facial expression, said, "As you were."

They lowered their cups to the table.

"Are you the commanding officer?" Gregory inquired.

"Major General Sean Cooper," he announced, extending his right hand.

"Gregory McCraken," he said, shaking the General's hand.

"And you're Geronimo," the General smiled.

Geronimo nodded.

"You men are here under my protection, and your little excursion was a violation of protocol."

"We meant no harm."

"You meant to escape," The General said.

"Well, sort of," Gregory admitted.

"Here's how it's gonna go down. I'll allow you some freedom within the facility, but no more hanky panky."

Gregory glanced at Geronimo and replied, "Deal. Any idea how long we have to remain here?"

"Classified."

"Is that the standard response to, I don't have a clue?"

The General, who had already turned to depart, stopped in his tracks, pivoted and barked, "I don't tolerate insubordination. You follow orders like everyone else and never question my authority."

After the door had slammed shut, the two men stared at each other, as they sipped their cooling, black coffee.

"That didn't turn out well," Gregory breathed.

"Hoka hey."

"Not for me it isn't."

Chapter Fifty-two

The Pentagon

Office of General Enoch Louder

8:30 A.M.

Louder sat enjoying his spiked morning coffee, proud of the fact that he'd managed to single-handedly save himself from an attempted kidnapping, or worse. And despite his overwhelming desire for revenge against the named Imam, he'd decided to quench the flames with a daily dose of primo alcohol. When the bumbling duo fail to return, he thought, the holy man might forget about me and move on. Anyway, I would have made a lousy hostage, assuming that's what he was after. But I'll deal with him at a later date. I still have those two scientists on ice in the mountain —I'll need to do something with them. I can't risk their freedom, it'll put us all in jeopardy. Hmm, I wonder if I could somehow arrange for them to do their thing in place, he wondered. I could have what they need transported to the facility, and there is some freaky shit going on down there, anyhow. He took another swig from the coffee mug and reached for the telephone.

"Get me General Cooper at Cheyenne Mountain," he demanded of his secretary.

"Yes, sir."

Not more than three minutes later, his phone jingled.

"General's on the secure line, sir."

"Cooper, Louder here."

"Sir," General Cooper said.

"Cut the protocol, no one's listening."

"OK. How are you, Enoch?"

"I'm not living underground, so, pretty good, I'd say."

"What does a Flag officer want with a lowly Major General at this hour?"

"You had a chance to move up, but you wanted the action."

"Yeah, bad choice."

"Still housing dark stuff?"

"You know I can't discuss that."

"Where do you think the funding comes from," he countered.

"Nevertheless, it's classified."

"No doubt, but I've got a little project that needs a home."

"What kind of project?"

"The kind you don't wanna talk about."

"Sanctioned?"

"Does it matter?"

"I can't lose my stars."

"Won't happen."

"Dangerous?"

"Maybe."

"How many people?"

"For starters, just your two houseguests."

"Equipment?"

"Leave that to me, but we'll need an enclosed and secure area."

"The whole damn place is secure, but I may need some time to build out the space. How big?"

"Ask the two scientists."

"Don't think I made the greatest impression with them."

"Let them do their thing and they'll be happy."

"How much time do I have?"

"You have until yesterday."

"Great," the General moaned, as the line went silent.

Louder leaned into the chair and sighed. Looks like I'm back on track, he thought, as he dialed Ryan Keith's cell number.

"Sir?" Ryan said.

"The two packages that were shipped to Colorado are about to be activated."

"That's good, sir."

"You still have the list that they'd prepared?"

"Yes, sir."

"Bring it to me ASAP."

Ryan showed up at Louder's office fifteen minutes later and was motioned to a seat before the General's desk.

"This everything?" Louder asked, reviewing the several page inventory.

"According to the ... packages."

"This room's been swept, no need for code."

"Yes, sir."

"I'll arrange for the acquisitions, but I'll need you to escort the shipment when it's ready."

Ryan nodded OK.

"Remember, this is just between the two of us. It's secret squirrel (top secret)."

"Oorah."

"Once a Marine always a Marine," Louder said.

"Oorah," Ryan saluted, and departed.

The next few hours were spent arranging for the purchases to be made from a multitude of government suppliers, and paid for with Pentagon funds that had been earmarked for *memorial projects*. This was money— several billion dollars—that Congress had approved, despite the nebulous nature of its destination, and with the likely knowledge that it would be used in a classified fashion. The power source had proven to be problematic, as the General had limited knowledge of its specifics, other than what had been explained by the scientists, and the supplier had asked questions that had been unanswerable. In the end, the General had agreed to several versions of the requested capacitors, hoping that at least one of the options would suffice. The entire order was to be delivered, in non revealing cartons and crates, to Joint Base Andrews by the end of the week. A bonus had been offered for the order to be fulfilled within the desired timeframe.

It was now 12:45 p.m., and Louder had just finished the last bite of the tuna salad sandwich that he'd ordered delivered to his office, when his desk phone came to life.

He wiped his greasy lips on the tiny napkin that had come with the sandwich, reached for the receiver and grunted, "Yeah?"

"Senator Raymond is on the secure line, sir," the secretary announced.

Shit, what the hell does he want, Louder thought. But he was in a good mood, so he said, "I'll take it."

"I'm still alive, General," the Senator said.

"Nice to hear."

"I think that you can call off your security detail."

Should I tell him that I'd already done so, Louder wondered. Nah, not worth the bother. "Will do."

"I'm in the clear, right?"

"If you say so."

"But..."

"You got into bed with a thorny bunch, Senator. Their attack dogs could be waiting for the right moment, or they could have moved on."

"Then I'm still in danger," he whined.

"I really don't know."

"What should I do?"

"Get you're house in order," Louder advised, as he lowered the receiver, thinking, that ought to put the asshole in a permanent tizzy.

Now that I know the significance of the NSA project, I'm fairly certain that neither myself nor the Senator will ever be in the clear, he mused. And my attempt at duplication will certainly raise their ire. Yeah, I'm in the shitter for life. But I've defied the grim reaper before and I'll do it again.

The intercom buzzed and he hit the talk button.

"Yes?"

"Major Striker is on line one."

Uh oh, that can't be good, he thought, replying, "Got it."

"Sir, I have some intel that may be of importance."

"Go ahead."

"Secret squirrel."

Lauder exhaled, "OK, I'll meet you at Clarendon Central Park—outside of the Metro station—in one hour. Come in civvies."

"Oorah."

***

Metro Station

2 P.M.

Louder had changed his clothes at the office and arrived by taxi wearing a pair of black, dress slacks and an open collared, white short sleeved shirt. The sky was cloudless, and the afternoon heat had reinforced his sartorial decision. The Major was already present, leaning against a bicycle rack, dressed in a pair of camouflage shorts and a red, Mickey Mouse T-shirt.

"Interesting outfit," Louder remarked, as he came near.

"Sir, it was a short notice affair," Striker replied.

Louder nodded with a grin. "What have you got?"

"We'd disposed of the trash as requested, but before...," he halted to scan for listeners, continuing, "before we'd neutralized the squirmer, he'd tried to buy his way out with intel."

"Anything useful?"

"He named an Imam as the sender."

"Yeah, already got that from him."

Striker withdrew a piece of paper from a rear pocket and said, "Have you seen this?"

It was a computer screen shot of a breaking news report from a Detroit station, that read: *"Worshipers at a local mosque have discovered the bodies of their Imam and one other, unidentified male. Police have yet to determine motive, but have identified the Imam as Faaroog Awan, a long term resident of..."*

Louder smiled. Good news, for a change. Saves me the trouble. "You have relatives in Detroit?" he asked.

"No sir. But the squirmer's statement made me curious, and bingo, there it was."

"You'd make a good detective, son."

"Anything else I can do, sir?"

"Forget any of this ever transpired."

"Oorah," he whispered.

The two men walked off in different directions.

Chapter Fifty-three

Cheyenne Mountain

6 P.M.

Following the dressing down in the mess hall, Gregory and Geronimo had been escorted back to their room. They had all but resigned to their continued prisoner status, and had passed most of the day moping in silence, when their door opened abruptly and in walked Major General Cooper.

"Stay seated, gentlemen," he said.

"What are we being accused of now?" Geronimo droned.

"I may have been a little too hard on you guys, but it looks like you'll be back in business in short order."

"Meaning?" Gregory piped up.

"Your project is back on track."

"Are we leaving?

"No. You'll be billeted right here. But I need to know how much space you'll require."

The two men conferred briefly and Gregory replied, "A 20'x20' space would suffice, but the power supply could be an issue."

"That so," the General said.

Gregory explained that the electrical energy required

would likely equal or exceed that of a large city. The General frowned and left the room, promising to return after conferring with his engineers.

"He has no idea what he's getting involved in," Gregory said.

"He didn't appear concerned."

"We'll see what happens when the lights start dimming," he chuckled.

"There's something else," Geronimo breathed.

"Go ahead."

"I'm not sure we can assemble the system by ourselves."

"We'd promised the General that we could."

"There were almost a dozen people at the Nevada site."

Gregory scratched his head and replied, "I'd thought about that back at the safe house. But it'd appeared that our lives depended upon getting it done."

"And it might still be the case, but I've got a feeling that failure isn't an option."

"OK. But this place must have all kinds of technical and mechanical knowhow, we'll ask for help with the heavy work."

"And questions will be asked."

"Do we have a choice?"

Geronimo shrugged, as if to say, guess not.

The Major General returned forty minutes later, entered, and closed the door. "We've chosen a location that meets your needs. It's isolated and far from daily foot traffic. But I need more data regarding the power requirements."

Gregory rose from the cot and said, "We basically need all that can be supplied."

"That's not very helpful," the General admonished.

"It's hard to define a finite requirement, since the device will use as much electricity as is available."

"No way I can allow that to happen."

"What if we draw some of the power from outside."

"Not possible, we're completely self-contained."

"There must be a way," Geronimo groaned.

The General's expression turned dour, and he barked, "That's your problem to solve."

"You have backup power, correct?"

"Yes," the General replied tentatively.

"Does it duplicate the internal power system?"

"Has to."

"Can we tap into that system?"

"I'd have to discuss that with the Pentagon."

"We wouldn't be online very long."

"Like I said, I'll look into it."

He turned to leave, but Geronimo stopped him short when he said, "There is one other thing."

"Go ahead," he replied, his hand resting on the door's lever.

"When the equipment arrives, we'll need some muscle to help with setup."

"That can be arranged," he said, on his wait out.

The two men stared at the closed door for several moments following the General's departure. Geronimo was the first of the pair to show some element of relief, as he dropped onto the bed, face down.

"That's it, you're going to sleep?" Gregory snapped.

"Nothing else to do."

"We could go over our notes and be ready to jump when the stuff arrives."

"We have no idea when that might be."

"My guess is sooner than you think."

Geronimo groaned, rose, and took up position at the edge of his bed. "Have you given any thought to our status post project?"

"No."

"I have."

"And?"

"The best we can hope for is a bullet to the back of our heads."

"What, no ticker tape parade?"

"We won't even have existed."

"Thanks for spoiling my day."

"You must have thought about it," Geronimo pursued.

"Yeah," he exhaled.

"Then why so gung ho?"

"Keeps my mind off the inevitable."

"There might be a way out," Geronimo sneered.

"Listening."

"The Einstein-Rosen Bridge."

"You can't be serious."

"I'd rather deal with the unknown than certain death."

"I can't guarantee that what I created was a Bridge."

"If not, then what?"

"I don't know."

Geronimo jumped to his feet and said, between gritted teeth, "Are you shitting me? You dragged me into this mess for a guess?"

Gregory shrugged.

"Sure, burn the Indian, he ain't worth much."

"I'm in as deep as you, and Iliana gave her life."

Geronimo slid back onto the bed, his head in his hands, and replied, "OK, time for rational and analytical thought. You said that the Nevada box disappeared into a blue light."

"More or less."

"Don't tweak out on me now," he shouted.

"OK, yeah, it vanished."

"Where did it go?"

"I don't know."

"As I see it, there are three options. One, it disintegrated. Two, it passed through the Bridge thing. And three, it shifted to another dimension."

Gregory had been gazing at his bare feet, but he looked up when Geronimo went silent, and suggested, "If I had only one choice, I'd go with a dimensional shift."

"And the Bridge?"

"It's theoretically possible, but I don't think we had enough power to make it happen."

"It's just a mathematically derived theory, it could be wrong."

"You mean the power requirement?"

Geronimo nodded a yes.

"Shit, I don't know."

"Mind you, the multidimensional theory has no

greater basis than the Einstein-Rosen Bridge."

"You're right," Gregory whispered.

"But remember, something quite unusual happened in the Nevada lab."

"Yeah, but what?"

"I don't think it really matters."

"Explain."

"You made something of substance dematerialize, that's what counts."

"How is that going to advance science?"

"Fuck science, I'm more concerned about survival."

"You're suggesting that we subject ourselves to the same unknown fate as the box?"

"Beats the bullet."

"I'm not sure about that."

"Well, we have some time to decide. And the longer we procrastinate, the longer we get to breathe."

Chapter Fifty-four

Wednesday, August 15th

7 A.M.

Major Striker had followed orders and had disposed of the bodies contained within the General's vehicle, as well as the car itself. That had left General Louder without personal transportation, a minor issue that he'd planned on addressing with his insurance company, after reporting the car as stolen. A phone call had delivered chauffeured conveyance to his front door, courtesy of the Pentagon. And as he sat at his desk drinking coffee and fantasizing about a new car, a small, yellow Post-It note caught his eye. *Call RK,* was all it said.

Hmm, he wondered, what could Ryan want at this hour. He dialed Ryan Keith's cellphone.

"Sir," Ryan said.

"I got your note, what do you need?"

"I assume that I'm to be the go-between for the facilitator?"

"Yeah, is there a problem?"

"No, sir. But he'd called and said that there might be a delay with the capacitors."

"Unacceptable."

"What should I do?"

"I'll handle it," Louder barked, as he hung up.

Without lowering the phone, he dialed the facilitator's personal number. It rang four times and then a voice inquired, "Hello?"

"This is General Louder," he announced sternly, adding, "we had a solid agreement, everything to be delivered by the end of this week."

"Yes, sir, I know, but my supplier claims that the high value capacitors are backordered."

"From where?"

"China, I believe."

"God damn it," he shouted, "isn't there an American supplier?"

"Yes, sir, but they're much more costly."

"I don't recall haggling with you on price, get it done, and on time."

"But today is Wednesday..."

"I don't care if you have to fly the fuckers to Colorado yourself," he interrupted, adding, "just make certain that the entire order arrives safely and on time."

What is it with people today, he grumbled to himself, they don't take the initiative to get things done. Well, if the asshole lives up to my schedule I'll have to make my way to

Cheyenne Mountain by the end of the week to jump start the project and give ol' Sean Cooper a good boy pat on the back.

An hour later, eight-thirty a.m., the intercom buzzed and he cursed at it. He'd been hoping for a brief respite so he could contemplate the new automobile that he'd been considering. He knew that he'd be receiving flak for buying a non-American car, but he didn't really give a crap. The tricked out, shiny, black Range Rover that he'd eyed at the dealer was calling to him, and he wanted it. But he frowned and hit the talk button.

"Yes, what is it?" he called out.

"Major General Cooper is on line two, sir," the secretary yawned.

Ugh, he thought. "OK, I'll take it."

"General?" Cooper said.

"It must be six-thirty in the morning where you are," Louder exclaimed.

"You've forgotten what it's like to be a soldier, sir."

"Yeah, guess so. What can I do for you?"

"We've got a bit of a dilemma with your project."

"How so?"

"Electrical power, sir."

"OK, you've got my attention."

"I'd asked about your project's requirements and was told that the sky's the limit."

"So?"

"We don't have unlimited resources, sir."

"Give 'em what they need," Louder barked.

"That would mean a shut down, and you know I can't do that."

"Options?"

"We have a parallel backup system, but it's designated emergency only. Your people want to use it."

"So?"

"I can't take that responsibility on my own."

"I get it, you need a fall guy in case it goes south."

"Hate to admit it, but, yes."

"OK, I'm your guy."

"Thank you, sir. There is one other thing."

"Speak."

"Your people have requested physical assistance from my staff, and questions will be asked."

Louder considered the General's statement and replied, "Do what you always do, tell 'em it's classified."

"Not an easy sale in a close knit society like this mountain, sir."

"It'll have to do until I can come up with a plausible

fable."

"Fable?"

Louder winced at his poor choice of words, and said, "This project is so secret, that if it'd been feasible, I would have shipped it off to a moon base, that is, if we had one."

"Does that leave me out of the loop?"

"Afraid so."

"That could be a problem, sir."

"Trust me, Sean, you're better off in the dark."

Major General Cooper hesitated, and there was a moment of uncomfortable silence, but he came back with, "So we're talking black project."

Louder exhaled noisily, to the extent that it was likely heard on the other end. "I've said enough already, Sean. Believe me when I repeat that you do not want to wade into this murky pond."

"What do I say if unexpected guests decide to pay us a visit?"

"Point them in a different direction."

"Sir?"

"Give those nosey Congressional wonks something they'd understand, like coloring books and crayons."

Major General Cooper laughed, and replied, "Yes, sir."

"Oh, and Sean, you should expect a delivery by the

end of this week."

"We'll be on the lookout."

He gazed longingly at the liquor caddy sitting by its lonesome beneath the tinted window, an amber glow emanating from a fresh bottle of Grand Marnier calling to him, as a ray of morning sunlight pierced the dusky orange liquid like a flaming arrow. I really need to do something about my drinking habit, he thought, but hey, some people take tranquilizers and pain pills ... I drink, and it works for me. He filled a mug with hot, black coffee and, with a huge grin of satisfaction, added two fingers of the sweet elixir.

Now, if the MIB (men in black) decide that I'm no longer worth their bother, he thought, life could be good. On the other hand, since I'm likely still on their radar, my equipment requisitions are bound to trigger an alarm. And that's when my life will turn to the most vile form of shit one can imagine. Once again, he reached for the bottle of Gran Marnier, removed the cap, pushed the coffee mug aside and chugged down a few gulps of the sweet, alcoholic beverage. Hmm, about that new vehicle, he pondered.

Chapter Fifty-five

Wednesday, 7 A.M.

Fort Meade, Maryland

The Nevada desert shack had languished in a dormant state since the marine visitation, but despite its black origins the proprietors had not been in the dark. The unnamed NSA department charged with its operation and surveillance had been monitoring the incursions via their satellite placements, and had been made aware of the scientist's activities with the aide of discretely placed, secondary and tertiary cameras located throughout the underground facility. The intruders had been completely unaware of their existence, as they had been disguised to mimic common, everyday objects, such as a door handle. The voice and video recording devices had been in place since the laboratory's inception, and had dutifully transmitted their live feeds directly to a secure, underground office at the NSA, located at Fort Meade, Maryland.

"Any further activity?" the supervisor, known only by his last name, Bucky, asked the young man seated at a computer.

The young man removed his headphones, swiveled on

a metal chair, and replied, "Nada."

"Good."

"Will we be shutting it down?"

"Just as soon as the secondary site is back in operation."

"I'd received some traffic from Denver one hour ago, sir."

The supervisor moved closer, his nose almost colliding with the young man's forehead, and he growled, "Why the hell are you telling me now?"

"Sir," he stuttered, "you weren't on the premises."

"Gimme the fuckin' communique," the supervisor snapped.

The young, nameless man handed the single printed page to his boss and waited, like a wagging dog.

The supervisor read and reread the brief document, and then turned to depart.

"Orders, sir?"

"There's a problem."

"Sir?"

"We have a competitor," he hissed, as he left the secure room in a huff, and disappeared.

The supervisor, in anticipation of advancement within the organization and fearful of any missteps, rushed to convey the news to his boss. And after running down a lengthy corridor, he stopped at a secretarial desk and urged, "I need to speak with him."

"No can do, he's in a meeting," the young man lisped.

"It's important."

The civilian dressed twenty something fiddled with his hot pink tie, and replied, "That's what everyone says."

"I'm not everyone," he snarled, as he reached for the door to the meeting room and knocked.

Suddenly, the door opened slightly and a voice barked from within, "Did I not make it clear? No interruptions."

"It's Bucky, sir."

"Not now."

"It's about Nevada, sir."

Bucky stood by the partially open door, a steady stream of warm air trickling from within, and realized that there more than two voices beyond the door. He'd heard rumors about a super secret group that controlled many aspects of his own no name organization, but he'd written it off to the usual gossip mill nonsense. But since he was privy to his boss' daily schedule of meetings and activities, this particular event seemed rather odd, since it had not been listed on the daily itinerary.

The door closed with a click, and Bucky stood by it

like a dog awaiting a treat.

The secretary's intercom buzzed and he called out, "You're to step away from the door."

Bucky was confused, but complied, and moved back the ten feet it took to reach the young man's desk. A moment later, the superior exited, his face flushed, and he grumbled, "What the hell, Bucky?"

Bucky motioned for him to step away from the secretarial desk and, when he'd reached an unoccupied section of the corridor, Bucky whispered, "There's been suspicious traffic, sir."

"I don't have time for code, Bucky, spit it out."

"Looks like parts are being ordered to duplicate Nevada."

"Has that been confirmed?"

"Affirmative."

"And we know who's behind it?"

"The calls came from a Pentagon number."

"OK. This stays right here."

"Understood."

"Anything else?"

"Destination might be Colorado."

"Might be?" he thundered.

"It was a passing reference, sir, not a definite

location."

"I need to know by the end of the day."

Chapter Fifty-six

Arlington, Va.

5 P.M.

Louder had spent most of the day in his office, sleeping off the morning's alcohol excess and ignoring the stack of documents requiring his approval and signature. But by the time the clock had begun its pendulous swing toward the five-o'clock hour, he'd congratulated himself for negotiating a personally beneficial deal for the black Range Rover. He'd been waiting for a call from the dealer's service department, where the vehicle was being detailed, and he was getting antsy. Using his personal cellphone, he dialed the salesman and had been informed that the car was ready for retrieval, assuming that he arrived with the promised payment.

The taxi let him off at the Arlington dealership and he trotted inside, admiring the shiny new automobiles that were scattered about the showroom. A nattily dressed older male was seated at a well worn wooden desk and he smiled as Louder approached.

"May I help you?" the gentleman inquired.

"I'm here to pick up a new Rover."

"Oh, yes, the manager told me to expect you."

"Is he available?" Louder asked.

"No, there was a family emergency."

"Sorry to hear that."

"Allow me to accompany you to the finance office," the man said, rising from his desk.

"I'd like to inspect the vehicle beforehand."

"Of course, but it's late, and there's a mountain of paperwork to be filled out," the man frowned.

Louder hesitated, and the man said, "But if you insist..."

"I insist."

The man led the General through the showroom and into the unoccupied service area. And there, parked in a distant bay, was a brand new, black, Range Rover Sport. With a big smile, Louder trotted toward his new ride, with its tightly sealed, dark tinted windows and gleaming black paint. But as he was about to open the driver's side door, two men sprung from the opposite side and grabbed him. The taller of the pair clamped his formidable right hand over the General's mouth, while the other zip tied his hands behind his back and removed the .45 caliber pistol that was shoulder holstered beneath his navy blue sport coat.

"Be a good solider, and we won't cause you pain," the shorter of the two demanded.

Louder tried to bite the fingers of the large handed man, but just as quickly as he'd covered his mouth, he'd withdrawn.

"What the hell is this about?" Louder rasped, as they shoved his back against the new car.

The two men moved off a few feet, as the fake salesman approached, and said, "Nice vehicle."

"Who the hell are you?" Louder seethed.

"Let's not play this game, you know the answer."

Louder did a rapid search through his mental archives, and the only thing that rang a bell was the NSA. "What do you want?"

"It's too late for cordialities, I'm afraid."

"Yeah, I get that. So what do you want?"

The man shook his head, as if searching for a convincing reply, and said, "You're so deep in the quicksand that there's little else to do."

"What do you mean?"

"You're a liability."

"How so?" Louder asked, knowing exactly what the old man was implying.

The man jabbed his right index finger against the Generals skull and said, "It's in there."

"Can we stop with the metaphors."

"OK, you do not have clearance for the information that you've been privy to, no one does."

"And what information is that?"

The old man nodded toward the pair off to the side, and the taller of the two stepped forward and launched a roundhouse punch into the General's abdomen. Louder doubled over and coughed up his last night's dinner, along with remnants of the chocolate croissant that he'd eaten that morning.

"I'd warned you, no games," the old man cooed.

Louder raised his head and grunted, "Give me a minute," as he attempted to straighten up. "You're going to kill a flag officer?" he breathed.

"I see no other option."

In most other situations, Louder held a trump card, but at this inopportune time his deck was empty. There was no plausible way out, even though there were others who had assimilated the same data, he was then one on the hook, so he stalled for time. "What can I do to make this right?" he breathed.

"You can put that forty-five to your head and pull the trigger," the man said, solemnly.

"What else have you got?"

"I'll leave you in my assistant's very capable hands,"

the old man remarked, as he walked away with the shorter thug in tow.

The nameless assistant, the same one who'd recently imbedded his fist in Louder's belly, waited until the old man was out of sight, and then produced the General's .45 cal. pistol. He removed the magazine and thumbed off several rounds, save for one that he chambered, while carefully releasing the hammer. He then cut the zip tie and offered it to the General, muzzle first.

Louder hesitated. Feigning excessive abdominal pain, he pretended that he couldn't reach far enough forward to grab the gun. The ruffian moved in closer, and that's when Louder's right hand darted forward and twisted the pistol from the man's right hand, while kicking him in the groin with a pointy toed left shoe. The man grimaced, bent forward and moaned, while the pistol now occupied the fingers of Louder's shooting hand. Rather than alert the old man with the sound of gunfire, he slammed the heavy pistol against the base of the man's skull. The dazed male fell to the ground, face forward.

The ignition key fob was lying on the dash of the brand new Rover. Louder jumped in, started the vehicle, hit the accelerator and took off with a squeal. But the outer service bay door was closed. Taking a cue from countless action based movies, he aimed for its center and gunned the engine. Rather than shattering, the entire door broke free from its tracks and flew off to one side, allowing the now severely damaged Rover to exit unimpeded.

He'd driven less than two miles before coming to a stop behind a parked moving van. Whew, that was close, he said to himself, as he sat with the engine idling. And my beautiful, new vehicle is a twisted mess ... good thing I hadn't paid for it. However, one thing is painfully clear, he thought, rubbing his sore abdomen. The NSA has a hard-on for my ass, and they've passed the threat stage. Shit, I have no idea how long my luck will hold out, since it's clear that my name is on their hit-list. Wait a minute, he thought. The old guy seemed most concerned about the information that I'd been privy to, but he'd made no mention of my hijacking of their project. Is it possible that the all knowing agency is unaware, he wondered. Or is there something else goin' on? I'd suspected that the idleness of the Nevada site had indicated the presence of a duplicate elsewhere, but unless they've moved beyond the capability implied by McCraken, there'd be a another strike team searching for my scientists. So that must mean that they're ahead of the game, and my little project is old news. Well, two can play at that sport.

Chapter Fifty-seven

Thursday, 7 A.M.

Cheyenne Mountain, Colorado

General Louder had arranged an unscheduled flight aboard a military transport that had departed from Joint Base Andrews at 2 a.m. in the morning. He had sent a text message to his secretary and a colleague indicating that he required some downtime, and that he anticipated a return to office by the beginning of the week. In reality, his recent and enlightening encounter with the NSA had triggered unfathomable rage and a burning desire to leapfrog whatever had been accomplished at the Nevada laboratory. To that end, he wanted to meet with the scientists and be on hand when the equipment arrived the following day.

A car had been awaiting his arrival, and the driver, along with an armed security guard, whisked the General off to the secure, Mountain installation.

It was 0700 (7 a.m.) when the General exited the vehicle, smoothed the wrinkles from his uniform, and watched the driver carry his go-bag into the depths of the facility. Major General Cooper was on hand to greet with a cheshire grin. They shook hands and walked toward the mess hall.

"Breakfast?" General Cooper asked, as they took a seat in the mostly empty room.

"Yeah.   Scrambled, black coffee and dark toast," Louder said, to the solider standing beside their table.

"So, what brings you to my home?" Cooper inquired.

"You're joking, right?"

"I didn't think that you were a hands on kind of General," Cooper chuckled.

Louder gazed at him askance, and replied, "Then you don't know me very well."

"No offense, sir."

"And you can cut the sir crap when we're alone."

Cooper nodded his agreement.

The food arrived and the two officers dined in silence. When Louder had drained his coffee cup, he announced, "I need to speak with my scientists."

"They're probably back in their room, I'll take you to them."

As they walked, Louder asked, "You're not treating them as prisoners, I hope."

"Not at all, but I can't allow them the freedom of the base."

"Understood."

General Cooper knocked on the door and Gregory

unlatched it, staring in astonishment when he recognized General Louder. Cooper walked off and Louder entered the room.

"Good morning gentlemen," the General bellowed, as Geronimo sprang from the bed and stood at mock attention.

"Sorry for the lack of seating," Gregory said.

"I've seen worse. But I'm not here for a reunion, and I'm sure you've already guessed that."

"Are we going ahead with the project?" Geronimo asked.

"Hell yes," Louder said, leaning against the door.

"And you're here to oversee the startup?"

"And the end."

"The end?"

"When you were working at the underground lab, was there ever an indication that yours was not the only site?"

"There was no reason to suspect another, until they'd sealed up the Nevada location," Gregory droned.

"And what made you suspicious at that time?"

"The so-called accident that I'd sustained, it was a phenomenal breakthrough. With that knowledge, I couldn't imagine that any research organization would simply close down their site, unless there'd been a backup elsewhere."

"Excellent deduction," Louder said.

Louder toyed with the idea of sharing his most recent experience with their prior employer, but decided that it would only serve to frighten them, and he needed them as sharp as tacks, not hobbled by fear.

"Your equipment should be arriving tomorrow, how much time will it take to get it up and running?"

"We still haven't resolved the power issue," Geronimo admitted.

"Taken care of," Louder announced.

"Then given our past experience, and if we can gain some physical assistance from within ... a week or a little longer."

"Let's make it a little less."

"Less than a week," Gregory screeched.

Louder nodded a, yes.

"Not possible."

Louder had been accustomed to demanding more of his people than most would have considered feasible, but these were not military men, he reasoned. And they weren't building a simple Quonset hut.

"OK, a week, and I'll arrange for as much muscle as you require."

"It'll mean day and night?" Geronimo whined.

"Whatever it takes," Louder said.

"We'll do our best," the two men replied in concert.

"Oh, one other thing."

"Sir?" Geronimo inquired.

"The bridge that you've spoken of."

"Yes?"

"Where do you envision going from there?"

"Not sure I understand?" Gregory indicated, now seated on the edge of his cot with an anxious expression.

"Scientifically, is there something more that you can do with the equipment?" Louder asked, considering the possibility that the NSA's secondary team may have accelerated beyond their desert installation.

"First off, we should clarify our position on the Einstein-Rosen Bridge. We're not really certain that we'd created one."

"Then what in tarnation happened down there?" Louder shouted.

"We're not sure. But according to theory, the amount of energy required to open a wormhole should have far exceeded what we had available."

"But it's theory, and theories can be wrong."

"Of course, but we're talking Einstein,   he hadn't

made a lot of mistakes."

"Did you, or did you not make something disappear?"

"We did. But where it went is a mystery."

"Alright. Get it up and running. We'll deal with the unknown when the time comes," Louder said, as he turned and exited the room.

Louder had passed into the outside corridor, but he'd left the door slightly ajar to eavesdrop on the two scientists. He'd had the distinct feeling that they'd been holding back regarding the missing article. And as he stood on the opposite side of the door, he listened.

"What do you think he was getting at?" Geronimo said.

"About what comes after?" Gregory asked.

"Yeah."

"Maybe he's expecting more breakthroughs."

"Or perhaps it was about where a wormhole could take us."

"There is no answer for that. But he seemed interested in other potential applications for our device."

"He's a military guy, and those people think weapons."

"Not sure how the machine could be weaponized," Gregory breathed.

"If we actually succeed in creating an Einstein-Rosen Bridge, and can figure out how to control it and keep it open, it could mean instantaneous travel from one end of this planet to the other."

Gregory shrugged.

"You don't agree?" Geronimo asked.

"If we're going to fantasize, I see it more as a boon for space travel. But there are those who've theorized that humans could not survive a wormhole."

"What about your original thought regarding a dimensional shift?"

"I've given that further consideration, and I can't see how it can be proven."

"Explain."

"If there are indeed multiple dimensions, meaning, various realities, or parallel universes that to some extent mimic our own, we would require the ability to travel back and forth in order to prove their existence."

"Quantum theory tends to give credence to their existence."

"Are you willing to take the trip?" Gregory asked, jokingly.

"For science? Maybe."

"You can't be serious."

Geronimo simply smiled in response and walked off to the bathroom.

General Louder gently closed the door and walked off in a daze. The conversation that he'd overheard had been perplexing and troublesome. The usually decisive Flag Officer could not fathom how he would respond to a request from a team member—in this case a scientist—to be the first live human to go where no man had gone before, with no chance of return. But on the other hand, he thought, it might eliminate one potential liability.

Chapter Fifty-eight

Friday, August 17th

Cheyenne Mountain

6:45 A.M., D Day (Delivery day)

Louder had been billeted in a self contained, one room apartment that had been constructed for VIP guests. And from his observation it hadn't been used for quite some time, as an undefinable odor had prevented a restful night's sleep.

The phone call had come at 5 a.m.. The pilot of the cargo aircraft had called to provide an ETA. The project's equipment had arrived later than anticipated at the Baltimore/Washington International Airport, a non military facility that had been chosen to avoid scrutiny, but by flying at a higher altitude than typical, he'd explained during his rather chatty conversation, no time had been lost. Louder rushed to dress, his normal early arousal schedule thrown off by the unfamiliar surroundings. He'd made his way to the mess hall, downed two cups of black coffee, scrambled eggs and toast, and marched off to locate Major General Cooper's office.

The Cheyenne Mountain facility is quite large, and Louder lacked the level of familiarity required to find his way around, but several servicemen had been helpful in that regard. The General's office was located in a secluded corner, and Louder stopped when he'd reached the closed door. He'd thought about knocking, but he'd already been marginalized by his need for directions. Feeling the urge to exercise his superiority, he barged right in and was about to announce himself, when a very surprised Major General Cooper sat speechless with his pants around his ankles. Between his legs knelt a young, attractive service woman who immediately released a now flaccid penis from her mouth, while attempting to hide her face. Louder was embarrassed to have exposed the pair in the midst of what amounted to a major violation of military code. And as he stood motionless, like a deer caught in a pair of oncoming headlights, General Cooper struggled with his uniform slacks that were lodged beneath the servicewoman's shoes. The space where the act had taken place was quite cramped, and Louder realized that under different circumstances the entire scene would have been hilariously comical.

"Sir, I don't know what to say," Cooper stuttered, as the young lady seemingly attempted to fade into the wall.

Louder threw up his hands and said, "There's nothing to say."

But as the last word exited his clenched lips, he'd realized that he now had leverage that could be used to his advantage. He shook his head and left the office, taking a position a few feet away from the door, in order to allow the servicewoman to escape. With the palms of both hands covering her face, the woman ran down the corridor as if chased by a pack of wolves. He reentered the office and stood by the closed door.

"I know you have to report me," Cooper moaned.

"Let's consider the options," Louder said, sternly.

"Options?"

"This has been a most egregious infraction, and I assume that this isn't the first time you've been serviced."

"No," Cooper said, solemnly.

"Well, according to a prior commander in chief, a blowjob is not sex."

"But we've..."

Louder raised a hand and said, "I don't want to hear it."

"Yes sir."

"I have a proposition, a quid pro quo."

"Sir?"

"My project does not, and has never existed. My two scientists, and any other personnel that I may deem necessary, were never here and you know nothing of them, understood?"

"Yes," he said, and vigorously nodded, adding, "but my people have seen them."

"That's your problem, and I trust that you can convince your partner in crime to keep her mouth shut?"

"Of course."

"Then I will as well."

Cooper breathed a sigh of relief, fastened the belt around his waist and began to rise. Louder motioned for him to remain seated and remarked, "I'd change those slacks, if I were you."

Cooper gazed at this crotch and, noticing the large stain that had caught Louder's attention, plopped back into the chair.

"There's an eighteen wheeler on its way here," Louder announced, adding, "I'll expect you to alert your people to offload the cargo and move it posthaste into the appointed area."

General Cooper nodded affirmatively and Louder left the room.

Louder chuckled to himself, as he walked the corridor heading toward the main entrance. That was both entertaining and fruitful, he thought. But pornography was never my cup of tea, I prefer the real thing. However, I could be convinced to change my mind.

***

10:00 A.M.

The two scientists were on hand to receive the delivery, and spent several hours checking the inventory as the truckload of boxes were transported into their new laboratory. Large, capped, power cables protruded through one wall of the recently created room. The once empty space was quickly becoming a crowded environment, as crates were rapidly emptied and servicemen carried the detritus away.

"Looks like it's all here," Gregory announced, checking off the last line on his clipboard and surveying the room.

"Now comes the hard part," Geronimo said.

"The real heavy lifting has already been done."

"We have to fill the racks and complete the wiring," Geronimo frowned.

"I know, the allotted time is unrealistic."

"Do we have a choice?"

"Nope, let's get started."

Lunchtime had passed and the dinner hour was quickly approaching, when the two men took a seat on the floor and reviewed their progress.

"Did you label your cables?" Geronimo yawned.

"Yeah, but good luck with my handwriting."

"I've only completed about ten percent of my cabinet."

"That's eight percent more than mine."

"Shit. We'll never make it," Geronimo breathed.

The two men fell silent, but were startled by a knock at their solitary door.

With some effort, Gregory rose and asked, "Yes?"

"It's Louder," the General bellowed.

Gregory opened the door and quickly closed it as the General passed through.

"Make any progress," Louder asked.

"Some," Geronimo replied, gazing askance at his partner.

"Remember, we have a tight schedule," Louder advised.

"It's just day one," Gregory groaned.

Louder checked his wristwatch and said, "Take a break, get some food and then back to work."

"Earlier, you'd advised us to keep to ourselves, but the mess hall will be full of soldiers," Gregory noted.

"Point taken. I'll have something brought to you."

"But that person will know about us."

Louder exhaled. "I'll shoot him afterwards."

"Seriously?" Geronimo said.

"Of course not. He'll leave it at the door and knock."

"There is one small problem," Gregory observed.

"Speak."

"They've already seen us about."

Louder smiled, shook their hands, and marched off to the mess hall to find someone to do his bidding.

Chapter Fifty-nine

Saturday, August 18th

6 A.M.

They had worked through the night, stopping only for coffee and the snacks that had been brought to and left outside their makeshift laboratory. Both men had fallen asleep on the floor, and were awakened by a knock at their door. General Louder had instructed that they not make themselves visible until they were certain that no one was about.

"You gonna open it," Geronimo asked, rubbing his sleepy eyes.

"Sure," Gregory replied, as he cracked the door to a slit and peeked into the corridor. Assured that the coast was clear, he lugged the heavy tray into the room.

Geronimo reached for a plate of scrambled eggs, filled a Styrofoam cup with steaming coffee, and asked, "Don't you think that the delivery person has questions about the recipients?"

"Probably, but I'm sure the General has threatened the soldier with court-marshal."

"Frankly, I don't care what they know."

"Ditto," Gregory mumbled, crunching on a strip of

bacon.

Geronimo wiped his lips with a paper napkin and sat upright. "We'd made some progress last night, I think we might just make the deadline."

"Yeah, if the damn thing doesn't blow up and kill us."

"OK, I'll admit that I'm not a soldering expert, but I didn't see any cold joints."

"Hope you're right, because if there are any it'll take more time than we have to find them."

Gregory checked the corridor and shoved the empty tray outside with his bare foot, careful to lock the door afterwards. The two scientists stretched, and got back to work.

By two o'clock in the afternoon, following a progress check by General Louder, they had reached an impasse.

"My end of the power supply is almost complete, but I can't find a way to connect these damn capacitors," Geronimo groaned.

"Hmm, the connectors are really short," Gregory observed, turning one over with both hands.

"The soldering gun's heat could destroy them."

"Here's an idea. I'll heat sink it with my pliers, while you solder," he suggested, holding up a needle-nosed pincer.

"That'll work."

There were more than twenty high-value capacitors that required connections, and the team effort took time away from Gregory's allotted responsibilities. But almost two hours later it had been completed and the men took a break.

"Still considering the disappearing act?" Gregory joked.

Geronimo hesitated, and replied, "Yeah, I am."

"You're nuts."

"Maybe, but I could be the first native American to visit another galaxy."

"Or to be vaporized."

"Yeah, there's that," Geronimo breathed, "but I'm still deliberating."

"My money is on a no-go decision."

"You know, this being a stolen project, we're expendable."

"We've already covered that ground."

"And that's why my travel plan is not so absurd."

Gregory gazed at him askance, as if to imply a lack of understanding.

"I'll clarify," Geronimo said, continuing with, "when we hand over the keys to the general, he'll likely view us as dead meat, since we'll be a liability. Therefore, if we're destined to meet the great one, we should be the ones to decide when and how."

"But what if you're mistaken? After all, he's gonna need someone to operate the thing, perform upgrades and repairs."

"All that presumes that our prior employers will condone his existence."

"C'mon, he's a general, they're not gonna kill him."

Geronimo shrugged, and said, "But they might decide to make *us* disappear."

"OK, I can see that. But getting fried by our own creation? Not my idea of a fun time."

Geronimo craned his neck to check the clock fastened above the doorway. "Break's over," he exclaimed.

"Another sleepless night, I suppose."

"And many more until we finish."

Chapter Sixty

Friday, August 25th

8 P.M

The week had dragged on laboriously. Both Geronimo and Gregory had taken turns working on a short ladder in order to complete the wiring and installation process. In all, there had been several electrical burns, a few bruised knuckles and one slip from the ladder's second level that had resulted in a call for first aid. General Louder had returned to the Pentagon towards the middle of that week, leaving Major General Cooper as their only source of support. To that end, he had supplied them with a wireless phone capable of direct communication with his own, but blocked to the outside world.

"Whew. Another hour or so of inspection and we should be finished," Gregory announced.

Geronimo took a break, slid to the concrete floor, wedged his back against the only free space on the near wall, and replied, "My eyes are burning. You can inspect all you want, but I need some rest."

Gregory lowered the continuity tester that he'd been using to examine the circuitry. "I could use a full night's sleep myself," he yawned.

"Let's drop it for tonight."

"Can't, I might forget where I'd left off."

"Shit," Geronimo hissed, as he hoisted his body from the ground, adding, "lemme help with that."

Three hours later they stepped back into the only remaining free space in the cluttered room and smiled at their masterpiece.

"We've met the deadline," Gregory gloated.

"It's the *dead* part of your statement that has *me* worried."

"The jury's still out on that."

"Right," he replied, sarcastically.

Gregory gazed sheepishly at his partner and nodded toward the machine. "Should we give it a go?"

"I'll wait in the bathroom," Geronimo joked.

"If this thing blows we're both getting fried."

"Should we call the Major General?"

"Not sure he gives a damn."

"He'd never explained the auxiliary power source, it might not be enough," Geronimo revealed.

"This mountain is designed to self sustain for long periods of time, I doubt that we're talkin' about conventional fuel."

"Nuclear?"

Gregory nodded, yes.

"Wow. If that's true, an overload could bring down the mountain. And you can expect consequences."

"Yeah, the death of everyone inside, including ourselves."

Gregory rubbed his hands together and approached the ignition button. He hesitated, as Geronimo stood by his side breathing heavily. Tentatively, he reached forward and said, "You can do the honors if you like."

"I'm OK as a bystander."

He grimaced, as his right hand pressed the large red button. An orange glow began to emanate from the control panel and they backed away and waited.

"I don't smell anything burning," Geronimo grinned.

"Looks good to go."

"So?"

"I'm gettin' to it," Gregory breathed, as his sweaty hands approached the power levers and began to ease them upward.

Unlike the Nevada facility, there was no composite box at the end of the lab, rather, the entire room assumed its function. Lack of space and time had dictated that decision, but with it had come the risk of everything in the room joining in the disappearing act. And as such, Geronimo's decision to go-no-go could become moot. They had both recognized the potential hazard, despite Gregory's constant ribbing of Geronimo's desire to venture *where no man had gone before.*

"We're coming up on fifty percent power," Gregory said, his hands still glued to the levers.

"Keep going."

"I'm trying, but it won't go any farther," Gregory complained, his knuckles turning white from the pressure against the control levers.

"Here, lemme try," Geronimo urged, shoving his partner aside and grasping the controls.

"See what I mean?"

"Yeah, they're stuck in mid-position."

"I don't know what could cause that."

"Beats me."

"Shut it down and we'll take it apart."

"There goes the deadline."

***

* * *

At that same moment in time, but two hours later, General Louder was seated in his living room watching a televised National Geographic show, when the concierge rang his apartment. He grunted and walked to the wall mounted intercom.

"Yes?"

"General, there's a senator here to see you."

"At this hour?"

"Yes sir."

"What's his name?"

"Senator Raymond Washburn, sir."

"Fuck me," Louder whispered to himself, shaking his head and adding, "send him up."

He stood by the door and waited, hoping that whatever Washburn had in mind could be dealt with at the threshold, rather than suffering through his chatter in the apartment. The knock came a few moments later.

"Yes?" he called out.

"Its Raymond Washburn."

Louder mouthed an expletive and opened the door, effectively blocking the Senator's entrance with his robe enshrouded body. "What the hell do you want at this hour?"

"Sorry to disappoint, but I'm still alive," Washburn

gloated.

"So?"

"Can I come in?"

Louder hesitated, but realized that whatever the man had to say would be better heard in privacy, so he moved aside and watched with displeasure as the Senator marched straight to the couch and took a seat.

"It's late, Senator, get to the point," Louder growled.

"I'm just a messenger…"

"Like I said, spit it out," he interrupted gruffly.

"The organization is extremely unhappy."

"And who would that be?"

Washburn raised his eyebrows in silence.

"This place is clean, it's swept on a regular basis."

"OK, the same people whose project you were guarding."

"And do they have a name?"

"None that they've chosen to share."

"So we're still talking NSA dark," Louder said, as he remained standing before the Senator, hoping to abbreviate the conversation.

Washburn nodded his agreement.

"What are they pissed off about?"

"They said that you'd know."

Louder turned, thinking about pouring himself a drink, but abruptly changed his mind. Only two things of recent note come to mind, he said to himself. The hijacked project, and the flunky that I'd pistol whipped at the new car dealer. "What do they want?" he asked.

"A sit down."

Louder smiled. "Those their words or yours?"

Washburn shrugged.

"And if I refuse?"

"They didn't say."

"Tell 'em I'll think about it."

"Not sure that'll work."

"It's the best I can do at this hour," Louder advised, gesturing toward the door.

The Senator rose, but stopped short of the exit, and said, "You know that I'm just the delivery guy."

"Yeah, next time bring a pizza," he replied, gently shoving the Senator out into the corridor and locking the door.

Louder retired to the living room couch. He stared at the blank TV screen and cursed his self-destructive life. This all my own fault, he thought. I didn't need the aggravation but, then again, I enjoy living on the razor's edge. But somewhere along the line it'll be my ticket to the bought and paid for mausoleum.

He rose and perused the liquor cabinet, the usual choice glaring back at him. He ignored it and reached for a four hundred dollar bottle of Rey Sol Anejo Tequila. Returning to the couch, he took a swig, switched the TV to a news channel, and promptly dosed off.

Chapter Sixty-one

Saturday, August 26th

5 A.M.

Following another sleepless night, the two scientists awakened on the makeshift laboratory's cold, concrete floor. Breakfast had yet to arrive, and they'd secreted their way through the corridor to the nearest bathroom, careful not to alert the sentries patrolling the premises. Once back in their secure space they reviewed the night's progress.

"One little piece of loose solder, hardly enough to cause a problem," Gregory breathed, scratching his chin.

"I'm ready for another go," Geronimo declared.

"I've run the levers up and down fifty times without power ... smooth as butter."

"So?"

He vacillated. "OK, let's power up."

The now familiar, low pitched hum of the transformers filled the room, as Gregory gently moved the levers closer to the midpoint. And this time they continued along their track until the three quarter mark, when one of them froze in place.

"Shit, we're stuck again."

"Lemme try," Geronimo urged, as he stood before the machine and used the palm of his right hand to hammer the reluctant lever. Suddenly, a two foot long spark flew from the space between the lever and its housing, causing Geronimo to lurch backward. He lost his balance and fell to the floor, his head contacting the concrete with a thump.

"You alright?" Gregory shouted, reaching for Geronimo's extended hand and assisting him to his feet.

"Yeah. I'm a tough old savage."

"Now what?"

"Obviously, whatever caused the short is restricting movement."

"But only when powered?"

"The transformers may be creating some magnetism, causing something to shift into the lever's path."

"That means another day of dismantling."

"No choice."

There was a knock at the door, followed by the sound of retreating footsteps. Gregory cautiously opened it and retrieved the food tray. "We eat, then we dismantle," he advised.

By the time they had disassembled the power supply, the floor space was littered with delicate parts that they had carefully placed in the order in which they had been removed.

"You see anything unusual?" Gregory inquired.

"Nothing."

"What about your magnetic theory?"

"Aside from that flat cable that's still attached," he said, gesturing toward the middle of the open cabinet, "there's nothing that could obstruct movement."

"Let's zip tie it as far away from the levers as possible and put this thing back together."

Three hours later it was complete, and the two men crossed their fingers as the main power switch was engaged.

Once again, the familiar hum materialized as the room's temperature began to climb. And Gregory had nudged the levers beyond the halfway mark without resistance, when Geronimo called out, "Stop."

"What's wrong?"

"We haven't discussed our endpoint."

"What are you talking about?"

"This thing has made stuff disappear. So if we go to the max we could follow the same path, and that would empty the room."

Gregory quickly removed his hands from the levers and then, without hesitation, cut the power. "What the hell were we thinking," he said.

"Not clearly, that's for sure."

"We don't have the time or materials to recreate the Nevada box. This entire room is, in essence, the box."

"We could, if time would allow, rig a remote for the power."

"I don't think the General would jump for joy if we made all this expensive equipment vanish."

"What do you suggest?"

"How long would it take to build a remote?"

"We don't have the parts for wireless, but I could build a hard wired setup from spare parts in a few hours."

"Do it."

"What are you thinking?"

"Assuming that everything works as planned, the General should be here to witness the event."

"I'll call our keeper and ask him to make the call."

***

2 P.M.

The lunch tray had been removed minutes before Major General Cooper opened the lab's door without warning. Startled, the two scientists recoiled to the only free space available beside the main equipment cabinet.

"You can come out now," General Cooper grinned.

"Any reply from General Louder?" Geronimo asked.

"Stand down."

"Are you serious? We've been working like animals and now he wants us to stop?"

"It's a temporary hold," Cooper said.

"How temporary?"

"That's need to know."

"And of course, we don't need to know," Gregory moaned.

"Affirmative."

"Are we free to go?" Geronimo inquired, hopefully.

"Negative," Cooper advised, as he turned and departed.

"That sucks," Geronimo spat, as the door slammed shut.

"Agreed. We may as well crank this thing up and see where it takes us," Gregory hissed.

"I'm game."

"I'm not."

"Might be our only way out."

"I'm not ready for the great unknown."

Geronimo grabbed a voltmeter from their collection of

testing equipment and walked to the back of the machine cabinet. "Take a look at this," he called out.

"So we still have power, big deal."

"It *is* a big deal, especially if they neglect to cut it."

They locked eyes and grinned. "We keep going," Gregory said.

"The remote is almost ready."

"There is one last thing that's been bugging me," Gregory revealed, scratching his chin stubble.

"Yeah?"

"Running the remote's cable out to the corridor will leave the door slightly ajar. And that might effectively extend the reach of the machine's effect."

"We could drill a hole in the wall and pull it through."

"The wall is corrugated steel, and we don 't have a drill."

"Then we risk it," Geronimo frowned.

"But we could be putting the entire base in jeopardy."

"Doubt it."

"Well, the good news is that if it happens, we won't be around for the punishment."

The remote's construction had taken longer than anticipated, and at five-thirty p.m. there were several rhythmical knocks at their door. Assuming that the food tray had arrived, Gregory, who had just returned from the corridor restroom, opened it ajar, and that's when all hell broke loose. Two, suited men, accompanied by a pair of automatic weapons bearing soldiers, pushed their way into the cramped room.

"What the hell's going on?" both he and Geronimo shouted.

The men made no attempt to respond, and began surveying the large cabinets, while the soldiers held the two scientists at bay. One of the men finally opened his mouth, turned to his partner and said, "Think we can drag this shit out?"

"Negative. Orders are to neutralize."

Hearing those words, the two scientists began to tremble, since it wasn't clear just what was to be neutralized. Suddenly, Gregory found his bravado and shouted, "This is government property."

One of the suits nodded at a nearby soldier who promptly shoved the butt of his rifle into Gregory's abdomen, causing him to double over and wretch.

"You're a dead man if you touch those cables," Geronimo called out to the suit standing behind auxiliary powered cabinet.

"That so?" the man said.

"Extremely high voltage," Geronimo explained, eyeing the overzealous soldier and hoping to avoid a gut punch.

The man stared at the thick, black cable and stepped back. "You do it," he ordered.

Geronimo glanced at Gregory, who had recovered from the blow, and smiled. "I first have to put the machine in neutral," an outright fabrication, he advised, as he approached the main power button with his outstretched right hand and pushed it inward, while at the same time slamming the power levers into their maximum detent.

"What the fuck," the man hollered, as the usual, low pitched hum filled the room and his eyes widened in terror. The entire team of invaders stood behind the main cabinet, looking for a way to dislodge the power cable, while a split second later Geronimo and Gregory escaped through the partially open door.

"Have a nice trip," Geronimo shouted, just before he slammed the door shut.

Not realizing that the door only locked from within, the two soldiers began unleashing a volley of automatic fire at the handle. But it was too late, as the machine had rapidly reached its most critical stage. And instead of following the path of the Nevada box, with the disappearance of its unfortunate occupant, the two suits and their military escorts were instantly fried to a crisp. Had the scientists been able to witness the event, they would have been shocked by the damp, smoke filled lab and the horrendous odor of charred flesh. But they had run to a point farthest from the lab in the hope of encountering Major General Cooper and gaining his support. While the General was not visibly present, a marine, shocked by the appearance of two apparent civilians, escorted them to his office. They knocked feverishly.

"Come," a voice demanded.

The two men entered the office and stood at attention before the General's desk.

"This office is off limits to you," General Cooper advised.

"Our lab has been invaded," Gregory rushed to explain.

"Invaded?" Major General Copper chuckled.

"Two men in suits and two uniformed soldiers," Geronimo clarified.

The General's demeanor shifted to concern, and he rose from behind his desk. "How did they get through security?" he barked, reaching for the phone.

"Not our problem, but they claimed ownership of our

machine."

General Cooper rattled off a series of harsh orders and smashed the receiver back into its cradle. "Show me," he said.

As they exited the base commander's office they were met by a team of six heavily armed servicemen who led the way back to the lab. But as they trotted onward, Geronimo sped alongside of the General and said, "If its a pow wow you're aching for, sir, it ain't gonna happen."

"What do you mean," Cooper barked, as they continued their rapid pace.

"They've probably disappeared."

"Not without my men observing their departure."

Geronimo slowed his stride, and whispered to Gregory, "He hasn't got a clue."

They had reached the closed door and stopped.

"Something smells bad," General Cooper announced.

Geronimo sniffed his right armpit and shrugged, "Isn't me."

"Not that kind of odor," Cooper grimaced, adding, as he nodded to the nearest soldier, "open the door."

A greasy stench oozed from the darkened room, as they stood just outside in the corridor. All present began to gag, some more intensely than others, but the Major

General managed to regain composure and ordered, "You men find the source."

Four soldiers entered the room, the bright beams of light projected from their automatic rifles reflected back by a dense cloud of smoke. Moments later, the men exited, coughing and choking.

"Report," Cooper ordered.

The team leader apparent replied, "Two metal cabinets and some black, charred material on the floor, sir."

Gregory faced Geronimo with a stupefied expression, and whispered, "The machine is still there?"

"Not what I'd expected," he replied.

"Notify security, ricky tick, intruders at large," he demanded of the team leader.

But as the soldier ran off to follow his commander's orders, Geronimo placed the palm of his right hand over his nose and mouth and slipped into the lab. And as his eyes adapted to the darkness, the lab lit only by a trickle of light coming from the corridor's overhead fixtures, he noticed that the machine, from all outward appearance, was intact. The charred material—several isolated piles of it—on the other hand, bore an odd resemblance to the contents of an urn that he'd knocked over as a child; his grandmother's ashes. And as he gently kicked about the cinders, his foot came into contact with the thick, black power cable that had remained attached to the control cabinet's rear. He walked back into the corridor and drew a deep breath. "Where's the Major General," he asked.

"Took off with the soldiers to find the intruders."

"He won't find them."

"So they did disappear."

"Nope, they're still in the room, but not in their original form."

"What?"

"Think—incinerated."

"Are you serious?"

"Deadly."

"How...?"

Geronimo shook his head, as if to say, I have no idea.

Chapter Sixty-two

Saturday, 3 P.M.

The Pentagon

Senator Washburn's sudden appearance had been unsettling for Louder. And he had tossed and turned throughout the night in an attempt to conjure a plan of action. But there had appeared to have been no way of escaping the all seeing and knowing NSA. With those thoughts still rambling around in his head, he guided the rental car via a circuitous route to the Pentagon, hoping to avoid detection. Once in his office—which he'd deemed to be the safest place in town—he locked the door, poured himself a tumbler of Johnny Walker Black and eased into his chair. He had recently been blighted by a repeat performance of hemorrhoids—the full Monty—complete with intense burning and itching, and he was not a happy camper.

Not sure what to do about Washburn's warning, he thought, sipping the soothing elixir. And if I agree to meet with them, whomever *they* might be, what could I possibly say ... sorry? That'd be like pissing in the wind. The truth is, I stole their project and they have a right to be unhappy. The real question is, what would, or could they do about it.

I'm guessing that the experiment is so black that they wouldn't risk exposure, but that doesn't bode well for me. So if I agree to a meet, I might end up sleeping with the fishes. Not an option. He gulped down the remainder of his drink and leaned forward to rest the tumbler on the desk pad, when he observed a previously unnoticed yellow sticky attached to the telephone receiver. He ripped it away and read the brief note: *Call Major General Cooper, ASAP.*

His brow furrowed and he wondered if there'd been a problem related to his stand down order. Gazing at his wristwatch, he reached for the telephone. Cooper answered his private line immediately.

"What's going on?" Louder asked, while performing a side-to-side in dance in his chair, in an attempt to squelch the itch.

"We've got a problem," Major General Cooper said.

"Explain."

"You're little secret is out."

"Which one is that?"

"We've had some intruders, and they'd known exactly what they'd been looking for and where to find it."

Louder exhaled loudly. "Identified?"

"No."

"They escaped?" he blurted, loud enough to be heard through his two inch thick office door.

"Not exactly."

"Just cut to the chase."

"They were carbonized."

"English, Cooper, English," he growled.

"Burned to a crisp."

"How?"

"Your machine."

"And my people?"

"They're scared shitless, but OK."

Louder moved the receiver a few inches from his mouth and thought, that wasn't supposed to be a operational possibility. What the fuck happened, he wondered.

"You still there?" Cooper asked.

"Affirmative."

"Orders?"

"Secure the scientists and wait 'til I arrive."

Without lowering the receiver, he dialed Ryan Keith's cellphone and ordered him to arrange for a chartered flight to Colorado. Ignoring the empty tumbler resting on his desk, he reached for the Johnny Walker, took a swig directly from the bottle, scratched his ass and left the office.

***

5 P.M., local Colorado time

General Louder arrived with his go bag in hand and was immediately escorted to Major General Cooper's office.

Following a quick, perfunctory handshake, Louder barked, "Where are my people?"

"In their quarters, sir," Cooper replied.

"What the hell kind of an operation are you running?"

"Sir?"

"This is supposed to be a secure base, but you had unannounced guests."

"It's under investigation."

"That's all you've got?" Louder yelled.

"For the moment."

"I'm sure that the Joint Chiefs will be overjoyed with your response. Hell, I need a drink."

"Sir?"

"Whiskey, I know you've got some, give," he demanded with an outstretched hand.

Hesitantly, Cooper reached into a bottom desk drawer and removed a fresh bottle of Highland Park 18 Scotch, along with two shot glasses. He uncapped it and filled the glasses, sliding one of them to the outer edge of his desk. Louder reached for it and finished it off in the blink of an eye.

"That's better," he breathed, adding, "I want to see my men."

Cooper, without any conversation, escorted the General around the many twists and turns to the scientist's quarters. Once there, Louder advised, "I'll take it from here."

He stood in the doorway assessing the two surprised and haggard appearing men. Gregory rose from his cot and offered the General a seat, but he declined.

"Are you men OK?" Louder asked, with genuine concern.

"A little shaken, but OK," Gregory said, accompanied by an agreeing nod from Geronimo.

"What happened?"

He repeated the account that they'd provided for General Cooper, as it pertained to the suits and soldiers.

"Had they identified themselves?" Louder asked.

"No."

"The soldiers, describe their uniforms."

"They wore what I think were Army fatigues."

"Hmm, you can buy those in any surplus store. Anything else?"

Gregory shook his head.

"I understand that there was a fire?"

"Not your typical inferno," Geronimo explained.

"Meaning?"

"It appeared to have been a high intensity electrical burn."

"Leaving no remains?"

"Pretty much."

"You've met the deadline," he smiled.

"Well, we'd finished, but it hadn't functioned as planned," Gregory moaned.

"Any thoughts?"

"Yes. We think that the space was too large."

"I don't follow," Louder admitted, leaning against the closed door.

"In Nevada, the machine's output was concentrated into a box, but here, the entire lab received it. The power yield wasn't enough to produce a disappearing act, but it was enough to fry a human."

"You're both convinced?"

The two men nodded, yes.

"It's not entirely clear, but the intruders were

probably sent by your former employer."

"What now?"

"They know its here, we have to move it."

"Won't they come looking for their people?" Geronimo asked.

"Questionable. They broke into a secure facility, and its unlikely that they'd be willing to admit to the incursion."

"Move it where?" Gregory added.

"Get some rest, I'll get back to you," he suggested, as he turned and left the room.

"We're dead meat," Geronimo lamented, with the sound of the door's closure.

"Agreed. The NSA will never allow us to go free."

"We need a way out."

"Yeah. It's clear that we're not safe here, and if not here then where?"

Geronimo's lips contorted into a Cheshire grin.

"Not a chance. Even if we could recreate the box scenario, I'm not going in."

"Might be our only escape."

Gregory walked to the restroom, splashed cold water on his face and returned. "OK, we'll try to build a large box, but it gets used only as a last resort. And that's assuming that the General doesn't rush to relocate the equipment."

"Glad you're on board."

"Not yet. Just keeping my options open."

"I've been giving the construction some thought, and I'm not convinced that we need the composite material."

"That's good, since we don't have any," Gregory said, putting on a fresh pair of socks.

"But we do have an empty aluminum cabinet sitting outside in the corridor, and a box of insulation."

Gregory shook his head and frowned, "So you want to build an oven?"

"Ouch, that could be a problem. But if we could get some heat shield material..."

"And why would they give us that?"

"Think, Gregory. General Louder wants us to relocate, not shut down. So we use the electrical burn event as an excuse to request high-tech insulation."

"Why not ask for the whole enchilada?"

"The composite box?"

Gregory shook his head, as if to indicate, yes.

"He might go for that."

"It'll mean more time before we're up and running, but it should give us a duplicate of the Nevada machine."

"Sounds like a plan."

* * *

***

9 P.M.

General Louder had not returned to provide relocation information, but the two scientists had been busy sketching out a schematic for their box design. They had communicated with Major General Cooper regarding their requirements, but he'd remained under the impression that the stand down order was still in effect.

"Sounds like our General hasn't shared his plan with Cooper," Gregory said, dropping a pencil and stretching out on his cot.

"That leaves us hanging."

"Is the schematic workable?"

Geronimo shook his head with a, yes.

"Maybe we can scrounge up some of what need around the base."

"Unlikely."

"So we sit here and stare at the ceiling?"

"I don't see an option."

Gregory glared at his partner, clenched his jaw, and reached for the cellphone that General Cooper had provided.

"General Cooper, this is Dr. McCraken and..."

"What do you want?" General Cooper growled, clearly annoyed by the interruption.

"It appears that General Louder has kept you out of the loop."

"What?" Cooper blurted.

"He told us to fix our problem?" he lied.

There was an interval of prolonged silence, following which Cooper replied, "I'll get back to you."

Gregory lowered his body to the edge of the cot and, with the phone still in hand, said, "I may have screwed the pooch."

"Meaning?"

"I wasn't thinking, the words just escaped my lips, but I may have upset the apple cart."

"You told him the truth."

"Maybe it was need to know information."

"Too late."

"What do we do?"

"We wait and see where it goes."

It hadn't taken long, before Major General Cooper appeared at their door and barged in without notice.

"What kind of game are you two playing?" he barked, with the screech of a drill sergeant.

"No game, sir," Geronimo said, trying to cover up the fact that he was clad only in a pair of boxer shorts.

"General Louder claims to have told you to prepare for relocation, nothing more."

Geronimo was about to reply, when Gregory raised his right hand and interrupted with, "We'd assumed from his relocation order that the General desired to have an operational device in another location, otherwise he would have had us dismantle or destroy the machine, sir."

"This is the military, we don't assume, we interpret orders literally."

"But we're not military."

Cooper chewed on his lower lip and replied, "Affirmative, so it appears that we have an operational issue."

"Sir?"

"General Louder is my superior and, as such, his word is law. But your unauthorized assumption has merit. That said, I'm not prepared to question his motives, not directly, that is."

"So?"

"I'll requisition the requested material, but if it ever comes up for review we've never had this discussion, understood?"

"Yes, sir," they cried out in concert.

"How soon do you need it?"

"We're dead in the water without it."

General Cooper nodded knowingly, and took leave.

"Break out your schematic, and let's go over it again," Gregory said.

Chapter Sixty-three

Sunday, August 27th

General Louder's residence

The turnaround flight from Colorado had arrived back at Joint Base at 2 a.m., and Louder had been driven straight home, where he'd plopped into bed without undressing. He'd awakened at 9 a.m., a significant departure from his usual schedule, sat at the edge of the bed and examined his rumpled clothing. I'm getting too old for this shit, he said to himself, as he stretched, rose and tossed his shirt and slacks onto a nearby chair.

Sunday was the day to enjoy a leisurely breakfast at his favorite venue, relax, reflect and prepare for the week ahead. But the week had already begun with the fatiguing trip to Cheyenne Mountain, and his mood was sour. And to add insult to injury, he had yet to decide upon a plan of action for his nemesis, the NSA.

A cold shower had washed away most of the morning cobwebs, and as he wrapped his body in an oversized towel his landline began to ring. Barefoot, he padded his way to the bedside device, glanced at the null caller ID and, anticipating a robocaller, lifted the receiver in silence.

"General?" a gravelly voice asked.

"Who is this?" Louder thundered.

"Your favorite senator."

Not that asshole, he said to himself, before replying, "What do you want, Washburn?"

"You'd never replied to the sit down request."

"Oh gee, and I was so looking forward to it," he replied sarcastically.

"I'm on the hook."

"Guess you're their favorite worm."

"Joking aside, General, my life is in danger."

"No surprise."

"What am I going to tell them?"

Go fuck yourselves, comes to mind, he thought, and answered, "Use your imagination."

"You're signing my death certificate, sir," Washburn whined.

"You signed it yourself when you'd decided to jump into their bed."

There was a deep sigh from Washburn's end and then dead air.

"You still there?" Louder asked.

"Yeah, no place to hide."

"OK, let's play their game. Tell them that I want a list of their questions in advance of any meeting."

"You can't be serious," Washburn chuckled nervously.

"See what they say."

"OK, but if you don't hear from me, you'll know what happened."

"Anyone I should contact?" Louder sneered, but the line had already gone dead.

Why they chose that weasel as the go-between is beyond me, he thought. However, I've already been tested by those assholes, and I'm still on their radar. But I've made it this far, and I'm not about to call it quits. Funny thing is, we all work for the same government, but those fuckers have their own agenda.

Louder drove the rental car to his favorite Sunday breakfast venue, ordered his usual scrambled egg concoction and, following several coffee refills, decided to contact the scientist pair in Colorado. Back in the car, he tossed caution to the wind and dialed Major General Cooper's cellphone.

"Cooper, Louder here."

"Yes, sir."

"In the office?"

Cooper hesitated and replied, "No, the head."

"I need to speak with my boys."

"They don't have a connected phone, sir."

"But you'd provided a contact device, right?"

"Affirmative."

"Patch me through."

"I have to be in my office to comply, sir."

"So?"

"On my way."

Fifteen minutes later, Louder's phone came to life with Cooper on the calling end.

"Go ahead, sir, they're on the line."

"This is classified, Cooper," Louder advised.

"Acknowledged, I'm leaving the room."

"General?" Gregory asked.

"We have a little problem."

"Sir?"

"There are time constraints that will impede relocation," he said, realizing that he had to get the machine up and running before NSA's next move, and since they were already aware of the device's location, the best approach would be to leave it in place. He continued, "That said, I want you to resolve whatever caused the electrical fire and get it going, ricky tick."

"Sir?"

"ASAP."

"We've requested some needed materials."

"I'll make certain that you get whatever you need, but I want to hear that it's working before the end of the week."

"If we can get the supplies by tomorrow, we can be ready for a run-up on Wednesday."

"I'll make it happen."

"Sir, will you be returning to the Mountain?"

Louder lowered the phone, considered that his end of the conversation could, and was likely being monitored by his nemesis, but uncertain about the receiving end, he replied, "To be determined."

He'd terminated the connection and dropped the phone on the front passenger seat, as he chided himself for not providing the men with an encrypted phone. Well, their existence is no mystery to the MIB (men in black), but the call might prompt another attempted invasion, so I'd better warn Cooper.

***

2 P.M.

There were a limited number of individuals that Louder could count on as friends, or acquaintances, and they were for the most part, hangers-on. These were people whose self-images had been enhanced by their association with a Pentagon official, and were rarely available to fulfill his needs. But as a self-sufficient, solitary soul, he'd generally gravitated toward unilateral decisions, while feelings of anger and discontent were deftly stored beneath his steely facade. However, those secreted emotions would occasionally burst free and raise havoc, and an envelop that had been slid beneath his apartment door had served as just such a catalyst.

The letter sized parcel had been shoved beneath his door sometime following his morning departure and his afternoon return. He tossed it onto the kitchen table, kicked off his shoes, and headed for the bathroom. Returning to the kitchen, he examined the parcel. It had neither a return address nor a stamp, and he instantly surmised that it had been hand delivered. Aware that several government officials had, in recent weeks, received questionable unrequested posts containing what had been deemed to have been tainted with the deadly poison, ricin, he'd considered calling Pentagon security. He shook it and held it over a bright light in an attempt to analyze its contents, but there had appeared to have been no movement from within. He donned a pair of rubber gloves that the housekeeper had left behind and cut one edge open with a scissors. Carefully, he shook the slit end over the table, but what dropped into the open air caused him to gasp. It was a photo of a grossly dismembered male that bore a vague resemblance to Colonel Bradley Duke. He flipped it over, looking for a message, but it was blank.

Louder sank onto one of the nearby chairs, the grotesque image staring back at him, and thought, only one place this could have come from. They know that I have no leverage and those sick scumbags are toying with me. But it does reveal a momentous issue; if Duke was allegedly made to disappear, where and how had he rematerialized, he wondered. A kitchen clock revealed that it was 2:30 p.m. Rising, he quickstepped to the bedroom and removed the encrypted phone from its charger and dialed Cheyenne Mountain's secure contact number that rang into the base commander's office. The line existed primarily for national emergencies, but he had no choice.

"Alpha tango X-ray," the voice called out, awaiting a confirmation code.

"This is General Louder, forget the code shit. I have an emergency and I need to speak with my people."

"This line is restricted, sir."

"Oorah."

"You do recall that I'm Air Force, sir?"

"Affirmative, but my order stands."

"Use an alternative."

"I have classified intel that requires conveyance."

General Cooper sighed audibly, and replied, "Ok, but make it brief."

"Put them on the line."

"Call back in five."

Louder lowered the phone to his bed, as he sat at its edge and glared at the bedside clock, watching the minutes tick by. At exactly five minutes following his initial call he hit redial and waited.

"Remember, sir, make it short."

Geronimo had apparently been elected spokesperson and he took the offered phone from Cooper.

"General?" he said.

"Who's this?"

"Geronimo."

"We've got a problem, a big one."

"I'm listening, sir."

"The contents of the Nevada box have reappeared."

There was a moment of silence and then, "What?" Geronimo blurted.

"You heard me."

"Where?"

"Unknown, but I have photographic evidence."

"Oh shit," Geronimo hissed.

"Yeah," Louder agreed, adding, "can you explain?"

"No."

"I've put myself out on a limb for this fubu (fuck up), you'd better figure it out, ricky tick"

"I don't know what to say."

"I don't want words, I want performance."

"I'll look into it."

"You'll look into it?" Louder shouted angrily, but Geronimo had already surrendered the device, following General Cooper's signal to end the call.

Louder was spitting mad, and he punched the mattress with his balled fist. "I'll have that fucking Indian's ass if he doesn't come through," he roared to the empty room.

Chapter Sixty-four

12 P.M.

Cheyenne Mountain

Geronimo had reviewed General Louder's demands with his partner, and together they'd accepted the possibility of failure.

"There's no guarantee that we can pull this off," Gregory lamented, once back in their quarters.

"Cooper confirmed the arrival of our requisition. So we should be able to start the box's construction sometime tomorrow," Geronimo advised.

"It shouldn't take more than a few hours to put it together, but it's not the box that has me worried."

"Then what?"

"If we experience another burn, we're dead."

"C'mon, the guy's not gonna kill us," Geronimo chortled.

"Maybe not, but our prior employers most certainly will. And if we can't come through, the General might just throw us under the bus."

"Hmm, he did imply that his ass was on the line."

"And there's been no mention of what happens to us, success or not."

"Well, assuming that Louder wasn't blowing smoke to scare us, it appears that the machine will not be our way out."

"It did work, just not as I'd surmised."

"So much for the Einstein-Rosen Bridge?" Geronimo smirked.

Gregory rubbed his stubble encrusted chin, and replied, "Not necessarily. There's nothing in its theoretical derivation that requires the bridge to leave this planet."

"You're suggesting that a wormhole could form in its entirety within the confines of this world?"

Gregory nodded in the affirmative.

"Would be nice to know where that body landed."

"Agreed, but from what the General told you, it wasn't intact," Gregory said.

"I had read that there was doubt regarding human survival through a theoretical wormhole," Geronimo suggested.

"How do you think General Louder found out about the body?"

"No clue."

"I have a suspicion, but its inconclusive."

"Let's hear it," Geronimo breathed.

"The suits that invaded our lab appeared focused on

disabling our apparatus, not us. "

"So?"

"We really don't know who they were, or how they got through the tightest security one can imagine, unless..."

"You think it was a dog and pony show?"

"Maybe, but with unintended consequences."

"Big price to pay for a gag, and what would be the anticipated outcome?" Geronimo smirked.

"We can assume that the NSA has it in for the General, and that they're blackmailing him with the body's appearance. Let's also assume that he'd made some kind of a deal to compensate for the hijacking of their project to save his own hide. And that deal involves the destruction of the device."

"You think that he'd sent the men?"

"Maybe."

"Then why insist upon getting it up and running?"

"The suits didn't come with sledgehammers, did they?"

"No."

"They were concentrating on removing the power source, which is hardly destructive."

"Agreed ... oh, I get it. They weren't really here to take it down, just to make it look like they'd tried."

"And that would explain how they'd penetrated security, it'd been prearranged."

"Sneaky."

"And smart."

"But it ain't gonna work," Geronimo suggested.

"The ruse, why not?"

"Unless the NSA has an inside source, they'll have only the General's word to go on. And that won't fly."

"And if we're able to recreate the box scenario, who knows where it will set down."

"That puts us between a rock and hard place."

"Well, we have no choice other than to keep going," Gregory admitted.

***

Monday, 7 A.M.

Cheyenne Mountain

They had prepared the lab for the eventual box completion, eaten dinner in the confines of their quarters, and gone to sleep. They'd been awakened at 7 o'clock in the morning by a knock on their door and, assuming that it was their breakfast tray, Geronimo opened it wearing only his skivvies.

"Put some clothes on," Major General Cooper ordered, as he burst through the door.

Geronimo grimaced and quickly drew on a pair of fatigues that had been seated on a chair near his cot. Gregory, who had raced to the bathroom at the sound of the knock, and similarly attired, opened the bathroom door ajar and peeked into the room. "Be right there," he called out, reaching for the terry robe hanging behind the door.

"Your requisition will be arriving within the hour," Cooper informed.

"Thank you for the heads up, General," Gregory said, from behind the door.

Cooper cleared his throat and added, "There may be a storm on the horizon."

"Sir?" Geronimo asked.

"Questions are being asked."

"Your people?"

He hesitated, and replied with an index finger aimed skyward.

"The President?" Geronimo asked.

"They have no names."

"Shit."

"Affirmative. Came down through channels."

"What do we do?"

"Finish and get off my base," Cooper demanded, as he turned and departed.

Gregory exited from the bathroom, put on a set of fatigues and plopped onto the cot beside his partner. "Is there really any point in finishing?" he droned.

"Yeah, feels like we're approaching a dead end."

"You know, I'd almost considered allowing the machine to take us wherever. But that was before the Colonel's body had reappeared."

"We need an escape plan."

"Agreed. But that's gonna be more difficult than completing this project."

Chapter Sixty-five

Monday, August 28th

Noontime

The requested materials had been piled up outside of the lab and, after dragging them inside, they'd quickly begun the process of assembly. As anticipated, it had taken less than three hours to build a square box with a six by six foot interior dimension.

"Looks larger than the Nevada component?" Geronimo said, standing back to admire their work.

"Might be, it was the only part whose exact dimensions had escaped me."

Geronimo crawled inside, and with his legs tucked beneath his torso and arms folded across his chest, he said, "Can't be that far off."

"Not sure it even matters, since I'd rather not test it."

"Seriously?"

"If the NSA found the product of our last fiasco, whose to say they won't luck out with round two."

"Good point."

"But the ultimate decision rests with General Louder."

They'd slid the lunch tray into the corridor and had notified Major General Cooper that they were ready for

General Louder's final word on the machine. One hour later, as they sat on the floor of the lab dipping into a large bag of potato chips and admiring their handiwork, the single purpose cellphone began to chirp. Geronimo wiped his greasy hands on a pant leg and reached for it.

"General?" he called out, expecting to hear Cooper's voice on the other end.

"I heard the news," General Louder said.

"Yes, sir, we're finished."

"Does it work?"

"We haven't tried, yet."

"Get it done."

"Sir, we have some reservations."

"Put McCraken on the horn," Louder demanded.

Geronimo passed the phone to his partner and grimaced.

Gregory, nodding knowingly, grabbed the phone and put it to his ear. "Sir?"

"What's the delay?"

"We're afraid of alerting the NSA."

"An' I'm afraid of heights," he lied, adding, "but it don't stop me from taking an elevator to the top. I need to know if it works."

"And if the MIB (men in black) return?"

"C'mon, they're a product of your imagination."

"We saw them."

Louder hesitated, and replied, "OK, maybe they're real, but we can't stop now."

"There's one other issue," Gregory said.

"Go ahead."

"If we're recreating the Nevada test we need something in the box."

"Send your dirty undershorts," Louder barked.

Gregory ignored the twisted humor and replied, "The Nevada test employed a corpse."

"You want me to send you a body?" he croaked, with a tone of incredulity.

"No, sir, but..."

"You're in frickin' Colorado, find some road kill, or a God damn side of beef."

"We're prisoners."

"Look, I don't care how or what you use, just fire it up and get back to me."

Louder had not revealed the source of his information regarding Colonel Duke's reappearance, and Gregory had been loathe to ask, but the question had to be raised, so he took a chance and said, "And what if it lands in the NSA's lap again?"

"What do you mean, again?" Louder shouted.

Gregory was stumped. He didn't want to piss of the man who held the keys to his cage, but he felt that the truth should be on the table, so he responded, "Weren't they the recipients?"

"Do what you do best, and leave the rest to me," Louder said, ignoring the dangling question.

"Will you be coming..." Gregory half said, as he heard the line go dead.

"What did he say?" Geronimo asked.

"What do *you* think?" he hissed, sliding the phone across the floor.

"So we crank it up?"

Gregory nodded in the affirmative. "But first we need some meat."

What followed was a marginally humorous conversation with Major General Cooper.

"You need what?" Cooper had gasped.

"A side of beef," Geronimo had repeated.

"You gonna eat it raw?" Cooper had guffawed.

"It's for our machine."

"The machine needs raw meat?"

"No, sir. But General Louder is aware of the requirement."

"So the meat is for him?" Cooper had said, still laughing.

Geronimo suddenly realized that neither they nor Louder had made the Major General aware of the machine's potential, or its functional demands. And he wasn't about to get into a detailed, classified discussion over the phone, so he replied, "The machine requires a large source of protein, sir."

"How large and how soon?" Cooper had asked, in a more sober tone.

"Large enough to fill a six foot square enclosure, and now."

"If you men are planning a BBQ, don't forget to invite me," he chuckled, terminating the call.

"That was fun," Geronimo smiled.

"You sure about this?"

Geronimo shrugged and replied, "We have no choice."

"But if the cow ends up on an NSA table, without a doubt, we're dead meat."

"If, and it's a big if, the Nevada machine had opened a wormhole, its destination would have been unpredictable. Therefore, the likelihood that our beef will end up in their hands is minimal," Geronimo explained.

"Just in case, let's include a disclaimer."

"Like, this meat could be harmful to your health?"

"OK, it was a stupid idea."

"It might arrive already cooked," Geronimo laughed.

***

4 P.M.

A large, flatbed cart was heard squeaking down the corridor toward the lab. The noise ceased and the men waited until they'd assumed that the coast had been clear before opening the door. And as they wheeled the cart into the limited, available space, they grunted and groaned from the weight of the slippery heap of bone and muscle.

"This must have raised a few eyebrows," Gregory said, as he lie on his back forcing the cow parts into the box with his bare feet.

"Yeah, no way this went unnoticed."

"When I kick the last of it inside, seal the box," Gregory croaked.

Gregory withdrew his left foot just as the lid slid down from the top of the box, his heel caught by the closure's edge. "I only have two of these," he complained, rubbing the sole of his foot.

Geronimo ignored his partner's obvious discomfort

and began engaging the activation sequence.

"Shouldn't we wait until tomorrow?"

"What for?" Geronimo replied, his hands spinning dials and eventually falling upon the power levers.

"I think we should pray."

"You're losen' it," Geronimo sneered, as he began to add power.

"If we don't make it," Gregory shook, "no one will know about this."

"Maheo will."

"Who the hell is that," Gregory asked, as the room began to hum.

"Cheyenne God."

The intensity of the low frequency hum increased to the extent that their bodies began to vibrate, and the two men gazed at each other with fear in their eyes.

"You smell something?" Geronimo squealed.

"Can't tell if it's the meat or something electrical."

"Better be the meat, I don't wanna fry."

"What's that on the floor?" Geronimo stuttered, pointing in a panic.

"Cow blood."

"O-o-h shit, it's happening," Geronimo cried out, his eyes shut tight."

There was a pause, and then Gregory called out, "Open your eyes."

"What ... what happened?"

"It's gone."

"What's gone?"

"The box."

Chapter Sixty-six

Monday, 10 P.M.

General Louder's Residence

Louder had been sitting on pins and needles all day awaiting word from his scientists. Major General Cooper's call had come during the early evening hours, and the news had been at once both exciting and troublesome. His people had managed to recreate the NSA's experiment, but he still had no firm understanding of its nature, or how he could harness its power for the benefit of the service. And then there was the very real threat posed by his nemesis. Up until the successful test, his hijacking had put him on the NSA's radar as a problem with an uncertain solution, but success had raised the threat level to an unsustainable limit—his, as well as the heads of his scientists were likely approaching the chopping block, he'd reasoned, assuming, that is, that the NSA has been made aware of their triumph.

It won't take them long to figure out that we've got a working device, if they don't already know, he said to himself, as he downed a tumbler of whiskey. And then comes the realization that I did not keep my promise to destroy the thing. However, they can't get to the scientists, or the machine, while they're under the Mountain, but

Cooper wants us off base, and that's a problem that has no current remedy. So there are two issues, the men and the machine. The machine can be reproduced, but I'd need the Indian and his partner to get it done, so they're not expendable. On the other hand, unless whatever they've sent ends up somewhere on mother earth, the NSA might not be aware, and then who's to say that it wasn't the product of the machine before I'd made my deal with them.

He'd downed another tumbler of the amber liquid and had drifted off to sleep with his shoeless feet dangling from the living room couch.

The much needed repose had been accompanied by a dream-state so apparently real that it had placed him somewhere in the Arctic, seated before a neatly drilled hole with a fishing pole in hand. In his dream, the air was icy cold and crisp, while a few wind driven tears froze upon his cheek. The subzero temperature caused his booted feet to feel frozen and wet and he stirred in his sleep, his overweight body rolling from the narrow couch. He hit the floor with a bang, the impact awakening him to the unexpected. While the dream had been pleasantly relaxing, the awakening had brought forth a sense of pure terror.

"Who the fuck are you?" Louder yelled, as he slid

across the floor, away from the black garbed intruder who was armed with a suppressed handgun.

"Get up," the obviously male voice demanded.

"If you're here for loot, you've fucked up big time," Louder growled, getting to his feet.

"Put this on," the man ordered, withdrawing a black hood from his pocket.

"Fuck you."

"I'm the one with the gun, so..."

Louder clenched his teeth and took the hood in hand, hesitated, then pulled it over his head. "Mind if I put my shoes on?" he asked.

"Shut up and get moving," the man snarled, shoving the General toward the front door.

"The minute security sees you with a gun and me in tow, it's all over."

The man chuckled and sneered, "Taken care of, walk."

Images of the friendly, old security guard, and the slightly younger concierge lying in pools of blood flashed before his mind's eye, and he winced. "What's the plan?" he questioned, once inside the private, delivery elevator.

No response.

And then he'd felt it. A jolt of pain on the right side of his neck, followed by a burning sensation and an irresistible tug back to dreamland. He had no way of knowing, but he had crumpled to the elevator's marble floor in a heap of disarray. When he'd finally awakened, still drowsy and slightly nauseated, he'd found himself seated barefoot on the floor of a concrete cell. He rubbed his eyes in an attempt to sharpen his cloudy vision, but the room was lit by a single fluorescent tube, and was filled with a cold, foggy mist. He tried to reassemble the timeline leading up to his predicament, but no amount of cogitation could adequately fill in the memory gaps.

I've been drugged, he said to himself, as he scratched his head and gazed down at the naked feet that were turning a dusky shade of blue. No windows in this tomb, he thought, as he cautiously rose and paced off the distance from one wall to another. Seven feet, he pondered, and solid concrete, not cinderblock. No way to crash out of this mess.

The room was entirely devoid of furniture, so he lowered himself to the ground with his back against one damp wall. Well, this isn't the desert, he thought, too cold. But, on the other hand, could be a very efficient cooling system. So the desert remains a possibility, that is, assuming I'm somewhere in the good old USA. I've got a pretty good idea who ordered the snatch, and my presence in this box must mean that my death is not imminent. So what could they want, he wondered.

He did not have to wait long, as the steel door sealing his cell creaked open, ushering in a blast of warmer air, followed by a dark suited female.

Louder did not speak at first, and simply glared at the young woman who acted in a similar fashion. The door had been ajar, and the bright light coming from the exterior silhouetted the woman's sharp facial features, a face that was devoid of color. She moved silently to one side of the doorway and, for the first time, spoke.

"How are you feeling?" she said, her voice absent any sign of emotion.

"Well, it ain't the Ritz."

"Sorry about that."

"No you're not."

"You've been a bad boy, General."

"Well, boys will be boys."

"Your snarky humor doesn't work for me."

"If you're expecting tears, forget it."

"We both know why you're here, so cut the shit and get real."

His eyes had adapted to the mixed lighting, and he accomplished a better assessment of his inquisitor. She was probably in her late 30's to early 40's, he reasoned, muscular but lithe. Her dark navy or black business attired slack outfit appeared out of place for the surroundings, but her white athletic shoes fit right in with the program. He yawned, and said, "What do you want?"

"We had an arrangement, but you breached."

"I'm sorry, but you have yet to identify yourself."

"You can call me Sandy," she replied.

"OK, Sandy, who do you work for?"

"You know the answer."

"Actually, it's never been spelled out."

"The agreement..."

"Was made via an intermediary," he cut in.

"Because you'd refused a face-to-face."

"I know how you people work, it still would have been an intermediary."

"Perhaps."

"So, what do you want."

"I'm not here to negotiate."

"What's your demand?"

"It's more of a proposal."

"And if I reject it?"

"It one of those offers that can't be refused."

"Sounds exciting."

"I warned you about sarcasm."

"You sound like an old girlfriend," he said, hoping to trip her up and gain some leverage.

"It has to do with the machine that you've been so intrigued with."

Louder's brow furrowed and his eyes narrowed, as he said, "I'm listening."

"That's all I'm allowed to say."

"Isn't much."

Even in the dimly lit room, her sardonic smile had been apparent, and he pressed onward with, "You're gonna leave me hanging?"

"Afraid so," she breathed, backing up toward the exit.

"You know that I'll be missed."

"And we know that you take frequent, unauthorized trips. It'll be awhile before the Pentagon knows that you're gone."

"And when they do?"

"They won't be looking at us," she returned.

"Hey, how 'bout a pair of shoes...," he called out, as she exited and closed the door.

I knew they'd be pissed, but I hadn't expected this, he thought, rubbing his cold and numb feet. I doubt that I can find my way out of this dungeon, so I wonder where the machine fits into the deal. Maybe they want my copy as a backup, but if that's their angle, why lock me up in this shithole, he pondered.

***

While Louder analyzed his plight, two men and one woman—a subset of a larger group of twelve, formerly known as MJ12 (Majestic Twelve)—sat around a polished, round mahogany table, leafing through the red, bound folders that sat before them. In contrast with Louder's enclosure, their room was well lit with overhead, LED fixtures. The walls and ceiling had been covered with the type of soundproofing material frequently found in recording studios, while the floor, isolated from the subfloor by a wide column of air, had been heavily carpeted. A glass pitcher of water, filled with lemon slices, occupied the center of the table. The room was otherwise bereft of any other furniture. The three occupants were all similarly attired with dark colored clothing, crisp white shirts for the males and a corresponding blouse for the female. The men wore navy blue ties, while the woman sported an opened collar. They addressed each other by number, rather than their given names, monikers that had not been shared.

Number one carefully closed his folder and slid his chair back a few inches. Reaching for the pitcher, he filled a water glass, took a few sips and announced, "Our course is clear."

"Agreed," the female, number three chimed in.

"I'm not," number two contradicted.

"State your objection," number one drawled, drumming the fingers of his right hand on the tabletop.

"We may be autonomous, but we're all part of the same system," he said,

"And the system condones the execution of miscreants," number one instructed.

"This is not an ordinary citizen," number two countered.

"A crime is a crime," three whispered.

"Some might argue that what *we* do is unlawful," two argued, frowning at number three.

"Remember, the greater good," one said.

"Still not convinced. If our action becomes known, there will be an inquiry."

"They will not be able to make habeas corpus."

"We cannot be certain that the body, or some part of it, will not reappear."

"Unlike the reproduction, our device has been proven effective," one advised.

"But the risk remains," two said.

"I'm afraid that you've been out voted," one declared, nodding toward number one.

Chapter Sixty-seven

Cheyenne Mountain

10 P.M.

Ten minutes following the disappearance of their box, and the beef within, Gregory had called Major General Cooper and asked that he relay a message to General Louder. He'd wished to verbally convey their success, with the hope that their benefactor would graciously allow them their freedom. But hours had passed without a response, and when he'd again called the Major General, he'd been informed that Louder had not been available.

"Something's not right," Gregory said to Geronimo, as they sat in their quarters munching on stale popcorn.

"Maybe he's out for the night," Geronimo advised, followed by a train of sneezes.

"You had better not be getting sick."

"Like you care," Geronimo sneered, falling back onto his cot.

"I don't want to catch it."

"Where do you think it went?"

"The meat? No clue."

"Hopefully, we'll never know."

"If the eventual destination is as unpredictable as

we've thought, I fail to grasp its potential military value."

Geronimo nodded his agreement.

"But what if the machine is only part of a system," he said, as his voice trailed off.

"What do you mean?" Geronimo said, his own voice now more nasal.

"Our prior employers appeared to have had no problem tossing aside the Nevada facility. So as we've conjectured, they likely have another, or several others."

"So?"

"They may be many steps, or leaps ahead of us. And if that's the case, they may have also devised a means of controlling its endpoint."

Geronimo grabbed an handful of tissues and sat upright. "Shit, that's the holy grail."

"Imagine, a controllable wormhole that could take you anywhere in the universe."

"Beats standing in line at the airport," he sneezed.

"However, we've already witnessed the side effects."

"But if what you've conjectured turns out to be accurate, they may have improved upon our first generation machine."

"We may never know."

"Well, the good news is that somewhere out there our

side of beef is ripe for a BBQ."

"Unless the recipients are vegetarians."

"We can sit here all night and make light of the situation, but our usefulness is quickly coming to an end," Geronimo wheezed.

"OK.   So unless we hear from General Louder by morning, we need to plot out our futures," Gregory warned.

"There is no future under this mountain."

"And that's why we need to figure a way out."

"And go where?"

"Anywhere but here."

"You do realize that we're in the middle of nowhere?"

"If I recall correctly, this mountain lies within a state park."

"Good point. And parks usually have hiking trails."

"Exactly. All we need to do is evade security and head for the hills."

"What about supplies?" Geronimo said, his voice becoming more nasal by the minute.

"We're not mountain men.   As soon as we're far enough away from this facility, we'll find our way to Colorado Springs."

"That's a good seven or so miles from here, you're suggesting that we walk?"

Gregory nodded, yes.

"Shit," Geronimo moaned.

"You got a better idea?"

"Yeah, find some horses or hitch a ride."

"Never been on a horse," Gregory admitted.

"Hitch it is."

"There is one small potential problem," Gregory advised, taking a seat at the edge of his bed.

"Here we go," Geronimo hissed, hesitantly.

"Cooper might send out a search party."

"Don't think so."

"Explain."

"He hates us."

"No argument there. But we're pretty much General Louder's property."

"But if Louder's incognito, we might be able to put some distance between us and this place before he finds out."

"It's worth a try."

The two men extinguished the lights and tried for a night's sleep.

***

* * *

Tuesday, August 29th

6 A.M.

Geronimo was the first to arise, a fit of sneezing serving as a wakeup for his roommate. Padding off to the bathroom, he took care of his morning necessities, flushed the toilet and returned to bed.

"Get any sleep?" Gregory inquired, rubbing his eyes.

"Hell no. Between not being able to breathe, and the thought of escape, there was little room for snoozing."

"Yeah, me too."

"So, should we check in with Cooper?"

"Let him come to us."

"And when and if he doesn't?"

"We get ready to check out of here tonight."

"Too bad we can't control that damn machine," Geronimo lamented.

"Agreed. But the box is gone and anyway, there wasn't room for two."

"In that case, I suggest that we ration our food trays, save some for the trek."

"Breakfast will be arriving anytime now. After the tray retrieval, one of us should meander out and do some reconnaissance, make certain that the security checkpoints haven't changed."

"That'll have to be you."

"Me?"

"Yeah. My sneezing and sniffling cancels out any chance for stealth."

The trays arrived a short time afterwards. They'd consumed the scrambled eggs and bacon, and saved the toast—four slices each—along with the small, single use, raspberry jam containers, for their journey. By seven-thirty a.m., the trays had been removed and Gregory slipped out into the corridor.

The previously noted computer banks had not been moved, nor had the vehicles that had been stationed not far from the motorized doors. Military guards, carrying shoulder hung automatic rifles, paced back and forth near the portals, apparently prepared to ventilate any uninvited guests. And as Gregory hung back, out of sight, he wondered what their response would be to departing residents. I guess we could try the need for a breath of fresh air ploy again, he thought. I can't imagine getting shot for that. He took a sloth like approach back to his quarters, checking and double checking for anything that might interfere with their departure.

"Well?" Geronimo asked, as Gregory quietly closed the door.

"Same as before."

"That means guards everywhere."

"Pretty much. We have to take our chances."

"Look at it this way, we're not criminals," Geronimo sniffled, blowing his nose and continuing, "if caught, we claim insomnia."

"And that's why we're carrying food wrapped in bedsheets?"

Geronimo, with a mixture of laughter and coughing, responded, "We're eccentrics."

"What should we do about the lab?"

"Nothing."

"It could be a danger to anyone without proper knowledge."

"Not our problem."

"I don't feel comfortable with that."

"Are you suggesting that we disable it?"

"Just enough to make it safe for the uninitiated."

"It's government property."

"Remember what happened the last time it was powered up without the box," Gregory warned.

"Yeah, that was a sticky mess, wasn't it. OK, we'll hit the lab after lunch."

* * *

Ron Wilk

Chapter Sixty-eight

Tuesday, August 29th

8 A.M.

Louder awakened on his cell's cold, hard concrete floor. His head was aching, and an attempt at assuming an erect posture had brought a bout of low back pain acutely to the foreground. And the absence of a window made time determination all but impossible, since his wristwatch had been removed by the abductors. There was no bathroom, not even a honeypot, so he scooted over to the side opposite his chosen rest area and urinated against the wall, thankful that the floor was level, thereby preventing the river of yellow from invading his space.

I've managed to avoid prisoner of war status to end up like this, he thought, shaking his head and scratching his growing chin stubble. The bastards didn't supply a pitcher of water, even the worst criminals are allowed that necessity. The weak fluorescent tube provided limited opportunity to examine his confines, but he could make out scratch marks on one wall, indicating that he had not been the first overnight guest. The barely visible markings suggested that at least one inmate had been confined for more than two weeks, and he wondered whether the poor soul had survived. He pushed back against the wall and tried to mentally remove himself from his predicament.

It might take them a few days, but my superiors will begin to question my absence. And when they do not find me at my home, they'll put out the equivalent of a BOLO (be on the lookout). However, despite my rank, I'm just one disposable hunk of flesh and bones. And given that, along with the obscurity of my location, they could decide to forget about me. That means that I'd better start thinking about escape tactics.

But before he could gather his senses to begin a detailed inspection of the solitary door, it flew open with a bang, along with the simultaneous extinguishing of the singular source of illumination. The outer corridor's bright light attacked his dark adapted eyes, making it difficult, if not impossible to identify the entrant, so he sat quietly and waited, the stench of urine invading his nostrils.

"For a Flag Officer, you appear quite disheveled," the male voice said, in a clipped voice.

"I left my tux at home," Louder sneered.

"Cute," the voice returned, as he leaned against the frame of the still open door.

"Where's the bitch?" Louder asked, hoping to get more than a one word reply.

"It's my turn."

"To taunt me?"

"If you will."

"What exactly do you want from me?"

"In due time."

"You people have a limited vocabulary."

"Don't have a lot to say."

"So take a hike."

The man chuckled under his breath, but at a volume sufficient for Louder to hear. And Louder whispered, "Glad you're having fun."

"Not as much as you're about to have," he replied, and left the room, closing the door with a bang.

Hmm, what the hell was that about, Louder wondered, as he pushed himself off the floor, groaned from a sharp jolt of low back pain, and approached the door.

While the visitor had leaned against the doorframe, the penetrating light had provided a glimpse of the locking mechanism. It hadn't appeared to be anything exotic, he thought, meaning that escape had not been considered an option. He felt around the ground for something that could be slipped between the frame and the latch, but aside from a few clumps of dust, his hands came up empty. And as if an oversight, the fluorescent tube once again came to life with its greenish glow. Standing, he estimated the low ceiling to be about a foot above his head. And at five feet nine inches tall, it put the ceiling at roughly seven feet. Since there was nothing tool-like in the cell, it left the metal light fixture as the only alternative.

I can just about touch the thing, he thought, with his arms stretched above his head. And there's enough light to rule out the existence of obvious cameras, well hidden devices notwithstanding. But it's worth the risk.

Standing on his toes, he reached up and yanked on the caged fixture. Nothing, it didn't budge. But several attempts later the cage flopped to the ground, accompanied by the shattering glass tube. Neither of those elements served his purpose, but darkness now filled the room and he still had yet to dislodge the actual fixture, with its flat, metal surround seated flush against the ceiling. Feeling around for a place to insert a finger, the sharp metal sliced through his flesh, and he withdrew as blood dripped onto his forehead.

C'mon Enoch, you've been through worse, he told himself, as he once again reached above, located a slight opening and pulled with all his strength and body weight. As the fixture came loose, a few sparks briefly illuminated the room and he slipped to the ground. With his back against the wall, and with no light to guide him, he located the flat portion of the aluminum fixture and worked it back and forth. It took what he'd gauged to have been fifteen minutes before a ten inch length of metal snapped free. The finger had continued to leak blood, signaled by a metallic taste on his tongue, but he ignored it, he had a mission to undertake.

No matter how hard he'd tried he could not get the metal strip to dislodge the latch. Finally, he slid to the ground beside the door and wiped his sweaty brow with a swipe of his right forearm. There has to be a better way, he said to himself, the strip still held tightly by his fingers. I would have thought that the NSA, with all their trickery, would have gone for electronic locks, as opposed to this garden variety thing. Well, one more try, and if that doesn't work I'll huff and I'll puff and ... give up.

He tore off a section of his now totally soiled pant leg and wrapped it around one end of the metal strip. Using the door handle as a blind man's guide, he carefully inserted the strip into the narrow space between the doorframe and the lock and slammed the covered end with the palm of his hand. This time the latch moved into the locking mechanism for a few millimeters and he took a deep breath and held it in place. One more shove and it gave, the door popping open with a click. He quickly withdrew his makeshift tool and placed it at the foot of the door to prevent it from re-locking, as he stood with his body against the supporting wall.

Despite my considerable efforts, this was entirely too easy, he mused. They're playing with me, and I can't wait to see what they've got planned for my next hurdle. And I have to assume that they're laughing their asses off watching me via some high-tech device, so I may as well play along, he told himself, as he eased the door open wide enough for his shoeless body to pass through.

The hallway opened in three directions; left, right and straight ahead. He took a few seconds to decide and then, for no logical reason whatsoever, padded off to the right. The floor was grey concrete, similar to his cell, but the stucco walls had been painted a sickly shade of glossy, green. I don't see any surveillance cameras, he thought, but I'm sure that they're trained on me right now. He kept walking until he could see what appeared to be the end of the corridor roughly thirty feet ahead. A dead-end, he told himself, as he kept heading forward. But as he inched closer it became apparent that the hallway jogged to the left, and he kept moving ahead. Halfway down this new passageway there was a break in the wall that led to yet another corridor, and he stopped. This is a frickin' maze, he realized, and there are no obvious doorways. But there has to be a way in and out. Picking up his pace, he trudged onward down the new path and finally encountered a door with an electronic keypad. Now that's more like these jackals, he said to himself, as he tested the pad by punching in a few random combinations, all to no avail. He mentally calculated the odds of stumbling upon a workable series of numbers, and gave up, passing the door and moving onwards.

Chapter Sixty-nine

Cheyenne Mountain

10 A.M.

The original plan had the scientists visiting the lab following lunch, but sitting around their quarters staring at each other had led to boredom, so they'd altered their schedule.

Geronimo disappeared behind the main cabinet and began assessing the power cable supplying the device. He let out a squeal, "Something's not right."

"Meaning?" Gregory asked, removing a sneaker and attempting to clean some stepped in, residual beef blood from its sole.

"What happened to the grounding cables when the Nevada box took off?"

"Initially, they'd remained in place, suspended, as if still attached," Gregory said, walking to the rear of the cabinets with his shoelace untied.

"Well?" he said, gesturing toward the pair of fat cables resting on the ground."

Gregory scratched his head, as if confused, and responded, "OK, that's different than the first attempt, but the box is gone."

"Hold on kimosabe, this changes everything."

"Make your case."

"It was not, and is still not clear whether the Nevada box had gone extra-dimensional, or had passed through a wormhole, right?"

Gregory nodded his agreement.

"The fact that the Nevada cables had initially been suspended suggested a dimensional shift, meaning, the box was still present, just in another dimension. But these cables are grounded, not connected to anything."

"But the Nevada cables did eventually hit the deck," Gregory reminded.

"Yeah, I recall you saying so, and we may have actually opened an Einstein-Rosen Bridge then and now," Geronimo sniffled.

"But that raises the possibility that the dead man in the box never really left the premises."

"In the first instance I agree, but when the cables had been found lying on the floor ... not sure."

"So you're suggesting that they'd either found the stiff dimensionally shifted in the lab, or it had landed someplace accessible to them." Gregory mumbled.

"Exactly, but if it had shifted dimensionally, how do we explain its return from another reality?"

"I can't."

"Yeah, me neither. But chances are that our side of beef won't be returning home."

"That's a good thing, might buy us some time."

"Remember, we haven't got a clue where it'll land."

"Hopefully, off-planet."

"Anyway, with the power cables in their current state, the machine is essentially useless. Our work is done."

Gregory gazed at the clock sitting above the doorway and advised, "We've got a shitload of time to waste before we bolt."

The two men left the lab and returned to their quarters for a few hours of rest and planning.

***

12:30 P.M.

With the machine in an inoperative state, there had been little to do, so they'd each fallen asleep on their respective beds. The usual knock came at half past noon, and they'd awakened and retrieved the food tray, consuming its contents in silence. And after sliding the tray into the corridor with his shoeless foot, Geronimo stood before his seated partner and said, "You know, we have enough material left over. We could build another box."

"What for?"

"You know."

"I'll take my chances in the park," Gregory said.

"Even if we make it to Colorado Springs unscathed, we'll still have to deal with the MIB."

"If they catch us."

"You seriously think that we can evade that bunch, nothing escapes them."

"I'd still rather chance it than get inside that God forsaken box."

Geronimo, having slipped back into his loafers, reached for the door lever and said, "See you later."

"Where are you going?" Gregory asked.

"We've got plenty of time before dark, I'm going to build another."

"You're out of your mind, but if it'll keep you out of my hair go for it."

Two hours later, with nothing to do and no one to complain to, Gregory made his way to the lab. Geronimo was inside, seated on the floor with a half completed box resting before him. "You're not really considering taking a ride, are you?" he said.

"Thinkin' about it," Geronimo uttered, without taking his eyes from the box.

"What about the power cables?"

"I can reconnect."

"And what if you end up off planet in a place that does not support life?"

"I'll be no worse off than if the NSA had caught up with me."

"You don't know that."

"Face it, we're dead men talking," Geronimo stated, running a line of high-tech glue along one edge of the composite slab, and pressing it against its counterpart.

Gregory leaned against the closed door and stared down at his friend. "You're really serious about this, aren't you?"

Geronimo nodded, yes.

"And you're gonna allow me to run through the park by myself?"

Geronimo gazed up with a facial expression that said, you bet.

Gregory exhaled noisily, lowered himself to a crouch and murmured, "Let me help you with that."

By six that evening, with the dinner tray's contents cooling outside of their quarters, they'd finished assembling the second box and power cables.

"Get in," Geronimo suggested.

Gregory frowned, but lowered himself to the ground before the container and crawled inside. Assuming a fetal position, he called out, "C'mon in, the water's fine."

Peering in from the outside, Geronimo knelt before his rolled up partner and said, "No can do."

"Are you fucking kidding me? This was your idea," Gregory growled.

"Not enough room."

"I told you that it wouldn't work for two," Gregory complained, one leg now beyond the interior, preparing to exit.

"I'm claustrophobic," Geronimo advised, pushing Gregory's leg back inside.

"You just figured that out?"

Geronimo shook his head and admitted, "One of us has to power the device, there's no autopilot."

Gregory rocketed his body from the box and remained on the ground, gazing up at his roommate. "This was your plan all along, wasn't it."

"No reason for both of us to suffer."

"And sending me off to the great unknown, in pieces or intact, doesn't imply suffering?"

"I think you'd survive."

"But we don't know for certain. And then there's the minor issue of destination."

"You could be missing the adventure of a lifetime."

"I'm not going."

"Well, I guess it's back to the park."

Gregory stood, slapped the dust away from the seat of his pants, and said, "Now that we've got a fully operational machine, what do we do with it?"

Geronimo grinned, grabbed a sheet of notepaper and scribbled a brief message in large, block letters that said, *catch us if you can.*

Gregory took the paper in hand and remarked, "That's from a movie."

"Correct."

"Funny."

***

At that same moment in time, General Enoch Louder lowered himself to the ground in the small alcove that he'd happened upon while trotting among the vast corridors, and closed his eyes. I must have missed something, he thought, as he mentally reviewed the hallways that he'd jogged through. Except for that one door and its electronic lock pad, I don't recall seeing anything that even resembled an exit. These guys are crafty, so they must have allowed my escape into this maze for a reason. But in all my years, I don't recall ever encountering anything this strange. He swiveled his head left, right, and upwards, in an attempt to release the building tension in his neck muscles, when something caught his eye.

It hadn't been immediately apparent, and it had appeared as a momentary flash of red in his peripheral field of vision, but it was undeniable. A tiny, faint, red bead of light shone through the ceiling right above his head. There it is, he said to himself. I knew that they'd been watching me. He tried not stare at it to avoid broadcasting his awareness, but its presence was mesmerizing. The ceiling appeared to be a solid end-to-end structure, as opposed to the more common drop ceilings seen in commercial applications. And yet the red point of light suggested a degree of transparency. He rose and walked on, mindful of the structure above his head. Sure enough, thirty steps from his last position revealed the presence of another red pinpoint of light. They must be laughing their asses off, he mused. Well, I'm tired of playing their game, time to give them something to think about.

The ceiling was no higher than that of his recently vacated cell, so he made a tight fist with his right hand, jumped upwards as high as possible, and smacked the red dot with a white knuckle. At first, nothing happened, and then it began to flicker on and off until the dot was no longer visible. I don't know how many of these little buggers I can kill, he said to himself, but I'm gonna keep punching until my knuckles bleed, or I get interrupted.

Chapter Seventy

Tuesday, 7 P.M.

General Louder had continued along the passageways doing his best to disable the tiny red dots of light that emanated from the ceiling, pinpoints of light that he'd perceived as video surveillance cameras. He'd counted fifteen dead cameras by the time he'd reached the end of one hallway and had decided to take a breather to rest his blood tinged knuckles. Although he had suspected, he had no way of knowing who had been logging his actions. And as he leaned against one green wall, the team of three were meeting in a secure, soundproofed room several levels above.

"We've wasted enough time," number One announced, sipping from a can of diet Pepsi.

"What do you suggest?" number Three asked.

"Move up the schedule."

"Not sure it's ready," number Two advised, filling a small cup with cooling tea.

"Look at him," One suggested, nodding toward the large television screen illuminating the room from one end, "he's the picture of frustration and despair."

"I agree, he's ready," Three concurred.

"I doubt that anyone would be ready for what we've got planned," Two offered.

"Call our people and tell them to expect a passenger," One said.

"I spoke with them two hours ago, they weren't ready for a guest," Two revealed.

Number one smashed the soda can against the polished wood table and rose. He paced the windowless room for a few seconds and then turned toward his associates and announced, "I don't care, just do it."

***

With the knuckles of his right hand dripping fresh blood, his shoeless feet running a close second in the discomfort department, Louder was beginning to lose hope. From his resting place on the ground, the world was a mass of green and white; green walls, white flooring and white ceiling. The military had taught him to adapt to any situation, but he was no longer the same young man who had joined the force and had climbed the ladder of advancement to a nosebleed level. He was sixty-seven years old, and at that moment he felt somewhat older. How do you adapt to something like this, he wondered.

There's no apparent way out, no one to negotiate with, or fight. This is a prison. Do I deserve this treatment, he asked himself. Well, I did steal something meant to be secret, but they'd made it easy, as if it had been part of a plan. And he had just decided to resign himself to his internment, when the wall at the end of the corridor parted and two armed men in casual attire entered.

"Stand," one man demanded, his MP5 pointed at the General's chest.

Louder sat immobile, his tired eyes fixed on some distant point.

"Get up," the man repeated, now only two feet from where Louder sat.

"Who are you?" Louder managed.

"Doesn't matter," the second man growled, his weapon a sidearm that had remained holstered.

"Water, can I have some water?"

"Do I look like I care," the MP5 man sneered.

"Please."

"When you get to where you're going," the man ordered, motioning for him to move with the submachine gun's muzzle.

Louder struggled to his feet without their assistance, and walked ahead, the MP5 pressed against his back.

"Where are you taking me?" he asked, a few feet from the opening in the corridor wall.

The two men laughed, but did not respond.

"You may as well shoot me here, if that's your scheme."

"Keep moving," the man ordered, as they passed through the wall into a stairwell that led both up and down.

Louder stopped, slipped to the ground and announced, "My legs, they won't hold my weight."

"They'd better, 'cause we ain't gonna carry you."

"I need some help to get up," Louder whispered.

The two men appeared to confer, and then the MP5 toter moved closer, to the extent that his left leg was within Louder's reach. That was all he'd needed. Louder reached out and grabbed the near leg, pulling with all his might. The man, now destabilized, reached for the staircase railing, while Louder spun around and kicked the man's grounded leg from beneath his body. He fell, and began rolling down the staircase. His action had been so quick and unexpected that the partner's pistol had yet to clear its holster when Louder pointed the fallen MP5 at his head.

"I'll take that," Louder shouted, gesturing toward the semiautomatic in the man's right hand.

"There's no escape," the stunned man said.

"Really? Kinda looks that's what I'm about to do."

"This place is a fortress," the man advised.

"And you're gonna show me the way out."

"Or?"

"You'll end up like your motionless buddy at the bottom of the stairs."

"Alright, but they'll kill us both."

"They?"

The man stood closemouthed.

"You're an NSA thug, right?"

"You're a dead man."

"Maybe, and maybe not. Now, which way out?"

With the nine millimeter pistol tucked into his loose waistband, and the MP5 pressed against the back of the man's head, they walked down the stairs, pausing briefly to assess the fallen's status.

"Got any words for your friend," louder sneered.

The man offered a glassy eyed expression and kept moving downward.

Two levels later, voices were heard coming from behind a closed door. "Stop here," Louder demanded, adding, "where does that lead to?"

"Second floor."

"What's there?"

"Cafeteria and sleeping quarters for double shifters."

"And the exit?"

"One level down."

"Guarded?"

"Yeah."

"How many?"

"Too many."

"I need a number."

He hesitated, and murmured, "Four."

"Location?"

"Two inside, two out."

"Remember, if there's a firefight, you're my shield."

The lower level landing was sealed off with a steel door sporting an electronic keypad. Louder reached for it, frowned and said, "Open it."

"I don't know the combination."

"Bull shit. Now, open it."

The man glared at the General, and for a moment Louder considered that he might bolt, but a jab to the gut with the MP5's muzzle had likely erased that consideration and he reached forward and began tapping the keypad.

An instant later came the click of the latch retracting and Louder ordered, "You first."

The door pivoted open revealing two heavily armed

guards seated on either side of yet another door containing a small window in its upper one third. The two, bulletproof vest toting guards, alerted by the approaching movement, jumped from their chairs and released the safety on their automatic weapons.

"It's OK," Louder's prisoner exclaimed.

The guards hesitated a second too long, just enough time for Louder to release two, loud, several round bursts from his weapon. The resultant double taps struck each man in the throat, the vests having been rendered moot by his chosen point of impact, and they fell to the ground, gasping and gurgling.

"Get the door," Louder demanded.

The prisoner gaped at the two guards with horror, but a shove from the still smoking gun barrel resurrected reality and he opened the outer door. The MP5's unsuppressed report had forewarned the exterior sentries, and bullets began to fly the moment Louder's nose commenced to suck in fresh air. The pair retreated back into the building to the sound of an earsplitting alarm.

"Is there another way out?" Louder demanded.

"We'll never make it," the prisoner moaned, the fabric covering his left shoulder turning dark red.

"Staying here won't cut it either, now, move."

"We have to go back the way we came."

They returned to the staircase but did not ascend. On the backside of the stairs was a door that had been hidden from view by the structure itself. The man stood before it and entered the required code. The door unlatched and he entered, and in doing so attempted to close the door before Louder could follow from behind. The door slammed against the MP5's muzzle and Louder, caught up in the moment, pulled the trigger, releasing a long, noisy volley that would ordinarily have been heard from a distance, but had been camouflaged by the alarm. There was a scream and an thud from the other side of the door. Louder wrenched the door open and entered, stepping over his prisoner's lifeless body into a narrow corridor. He started to walk ahead but had an afterthought. Leaning the gun against a wall, he dropped to a crouch and removed the mans boots, inserting his feet into the one size too large shoes. Better than nothing, he thought, wiggling his toes and searching the man's pockets for anything potentially useful. And without a second thought, he rose from the shoeless corpse and began to hunt for a way out.

The abbreviated hallway that he'd entered traveled straight for thirty feet and ended at an unlocked door. Cautiously, he opened it just wide enough to peer beyond and, finding the area oddly unoccupied, he slipped through with the MP5 at his side. Something isn't right, he thought, as he snooped around the corner of a wall that led to what appeared to be a gymnasium, and then realized that the alarm had been silenced. That doesn't make sense, he told himself. By now, the dead sentries have become apparent, and my body isn't among the deceased. The alarm should still be active ... unless. He began to scrutinize the ceiling above and, sure enough, the familiar red pinpoints stared back at him.

Gyms have windows, he thought, ignoring the certainty of surveillance. Maybe I can blow a hole in one and jump to terra firma. He ran through the open door and past a line of treadmills, weights and other equipment, stopping at a large expanse of what at first glance seemed to be glass. Gazing left and right, and noticing that the room was completely devoid of personnel, he emptied the MP5's store of ammo into the window.

"Shit," he hissed, "plexiglass."

The weapon's report brought forth a handful of men and women, their guns all trained on his body. There was only one option; drop the now empty submachine gun and surrender. He stood motionless for a few seconds, until two people approached. The male holstered his pistol, relieved Louder of the gun in his waistband, and wrapped an arm around his neck, effectively placing him in a sleeper hold. With the General's body now supported upright by the forceful male, the female jabbed a one inch needled syringe into his neck and emptied its contents.

When he'd awakened sometime later, he found himself lying on his side on the floor of a brightly lit and excessively air-conditioned room, his hands and legs bound, to the extent that his body had been forced to assume a fetal position. He had no way of knowing how long he'd been there, or how long he'd been unconscious, but one thing was crystal clear, there was no easy escape.

Suddenly, a bodiless voice called out, "Time to go, my friend."

"Go where?" Louder managed.

"That is the question, isn't it."

"Show yourself, you gutless piece of shit."

"Wouldn't change anything."

"What do you want?"

"Too late for that."

"Explain."

"Not gonna happen."

"The Pentagon will be on alert for me."

"They've already been informed that your burned

beyond recognition body had been found at the site of an auto crash."

"They'll want DNA confirmation."

"And they will have it."

Well, that's it, he thought, game over. And then, "I did what you'd requested, I destroyed the device."

"We have satellite imagery that says otherwise."

"Bravo Sierra," he shouted.   "It's under a fucking mountain, you can't see through that."

"When activated, it gives off a distinct signature that is immune to barriers."

"There must be some way we can negotiate?"

"Afraid not. Time is up," the voice said, just as three men entered the room, placed his hogtied body on a wheeled cart, and rolled him out of the room.

Chapter Seventy-one

Wednesday, August 30th

1 A.M.

The two scientists had accumulated as much snooze time as possible in preparation for their escape. At half past midnight they arose, gathered whatever small items they'd wished to take with them, and slithered from their room.

"Got a minute?" Geronimo whispered.

"What for?" Gregory replied in kind.

"Just out of curiosity, I want to check the machine to see if there's been a response."

"To your stupid message?"

"Yeah."

Gregory shook his head in disbelief and murmured, "Go for it."

They walked the short distance to the lab and stopped at the door.

"Hear that?" Geronimo said hesitantly.

"Did you leave it powered on?" Gregory asked, his tone displaying clear evidence of anger.

"No way."

"What should we do?"

"Turn it off."

"But who turned it on?"

"Good question. We're the only ones that know how to activate."

"The only ones *here*," Gregory hissed.

"O-o-h shit. You think that it's been remotely initiated?"

Gregory shrugged, and said, "You were the one who'd claimed that there's no remote."

"To activate on site, as a sending device. But theoretically, it could be activated as a receiver."

"Then we have a problem."

"Think it was the message?"

"Only one way to find out," Gregory said, as he lowered the lever and entered the lab with Geronimo close behind.

"Oh shit, the box is back."

"That can't be good," Gregory stuttered, as he cautiously approached the composite container and gently touched its closed surface.

"What do you feel?"

"It's cool."

"Open it," Geronimo suggested.

"It was your dumb idea to send off a note, you do the honors," he said, backing away a few feet.

"Shouldn't we turn off the machine first?"

"I'll do it, then you open the box."

The familiar hum and vibrations ceased and Gregory called out, "Open it."

Geronimo slowly unlatched the enclosure, and when the door was barely open a crack, he stopped and scrunched his nose and exclaimed, "I think our beef's come back."

"Ugh, stinks like a dead animal," Gregory complained, squeezing his nostrils with the fingers of his right hand.

"Should we just leave it and go?" Geronimo asked, standing a few feet back.

"And forever wonder what it really was, hell no. Open the damn door."

When Geronimo had removed the lid from the enclosure, his eyes bugged open so wide that Gregory thought that they might fall out, and he approached from where he'd been waiting at the lab's door. But Geronimo remained immobile, his voice seemingly absent, while his right index finger wavered in the direction of the box.

"Calm down, Buddy," Gregory said, and then stuttered, "holy, fucking shit. Is that what I think it is?"

Geronimo, still without words, shook his head affirmatively.

"But how...?"

Geronimo had retreated to the opposite end of the lab, while Gregory, still incredulous, attempted to reseal the box. That done, he pushed Geronimo into the hallway and several feet from the lab.

"Deep breaths," he said, patting Geronimo on the back.

"We're dead men," Geronimo groaned.

"You sure that was him, and not a dressed up dummy?" Gregory asked.

"Dummies don't stink like that."

"None of this makes any sense."

"There's a dead General in that box, that's all the sense I need."

"Right, let's get outta here."

***

It had taken more time and waiting than they'd planned on, but almost two hours later they were crunching through underbrush in search of a trail, the darkened sky occasionally appearing through the canopy of trees.

"You gonna make it?" Gregory asked, with Geronimo

several paces behind and breathing heavily.

"I can't get that image out of my head."

"And the odor," Gregory replied as they kept walking.

"Did you see his arms?" Geronimo pressed.

"Yeah, looked like they'd melted."

"Part of his head was missing."

"We really fucked up," Gregory whined.

"How so?"

"Are you kidding, you just saw the results."

"But the body had been sent from somewhere. And don't ask me how, but they'd managed to direct it to us.

"So we really did open a bridge?" Geronimo said with a tone of wonderment.

"Or we'd built a matter transporter, a la Star Trek."

"Those guys are way ahead of us."

"Not surprised."

"Hey, is that a flashlight out there?" Geronimo said, stopping to peer around a tree trunk.

"Get down."

"Think they're looking for us?"

"Shush."

The distant sound of barking dogs could be heard, and Gregory lifted his head from behind a bush.

"The lights have aimed in a different direction, but

we'd better run."

"Run?"

"Dogs, they'll sniff us out, gotta keep moving."

"We need to find water, the'll lose our scent."

"I'll leave that to you," Gregory said, as he trotted along trying to avoid roots and other obstacles.

"Because I'm an Indian?"

"No, because I'm totally out of my element."

"Truth is, I don't have any tracking skills."

"But dogs do, so we'd better find a lake, river or whatever real soon."

"Without a map, and in the dark?"

"I think I read about something called the Helen Hunt Falls out here."

"Good luck finding it."

"If we get close enough, we should be able to hear it."

"I think I heard a dog bark."

"Keep moving," Gregory breathed.

Their trek had taken them ever deeper into the park, and for all intents and purposes they'd lost their way, while the profound darkness had served both as a shield and a curse. More than one dog's barking had been heard when the wind had blown in their direction, but they'd found themselves gaining altitude as they'd attempted to distance themselves from their apparent pursuers.

"There, hear that?" Geronimo whispered.

"Could be water."

"That's the falls."

"But which direction?"

Geronimo spun around, almost tripping on a rock, and replied, "That way," pointing to their left.

They walked for another ninety minutes, the sound of crashing water ever more perceptible, until they both stopped cold.

"There it is," Gregory said, standing roughly sixty feet from its top.

"We have to get into the water to negate our scents."

"You're nuts, I'm not jumping over that, or any other waterfall," Gregory chuckled nervously.

"No, we have to climb down to the calm water."

"You really do have a death wish," Gregory remarked, walking closer to the top of the fall and peering over.

"We have to throw them off our trail."

"I haven't seen a flashlight for the past hour, I think they've quit."

"Or they're waiting for sunup."

"Everywhere I look I see the General's melted body ... can't erase that image," Gregory admitted.

"It was gruesome, but we have to survive."

Gregory sat down on a flat rocky prominence, removed an uneaten chicken leg that he'd salvaged from their dinner tray, and took a bite. Gazing up at Geronimo's barely visible face, he said, "I'm not sure we'll make it out of here."

"Yeah, me too."

"And I have no idea how to get to Colorado Springs."

Geronimo took a seat on the edge of the same rock and reached into their food bag. They sat munching in silence for thirty or more minutes, until Gregory announced, "I think we should stay right here."

"Like, forever?"

"No, until we decide that it's safe to move on."

"It can get pretty cold here at night."

"It's already heading in that direction," Gregory admitted, his body beginning to tremble.

"We can cover ourselves with leaves and branches, that should afford some shelter."

"We'll sleep in shifts, four hours each."

"I'll take the first watch," Geronimo offered.

At six a.m., Gregory watched the sun begin its lethargic rise above the horizon, and he looked over at his partner, his body partially hidden by a mass of brown leaves, and said, "Wake up."

"Huh? Is there a problem?" he groaned.

"Time to make a decision," Gregory said, brushing away some leaves from his friend's face.

"I gotta pee," Geronimo advised, rising quickly and grasping his crotch.

"Stay away from the waterfall."

"Why?"

"Blowback."

He returned several minutes later and took a seat.

"My watch was quiet," Gregory advised, "no dogs."

"Maybe we're in the clear."

"And maybe not. They could be waiting for us to make a move."

Geronimo reached into the food bag, flicked away a few foraging ants, and tore their last piece of bread into two pieces. "This is all we have," he said.

"So that's it, we have to get going."

"Pick a direction."

"I think we should ... did you hear something?"

"Probably an animal."

"Are there bears in these parts?"

"Sure."

Gregory grimaced, and then lowered himself to a

crouch. "I see some movement down there."

"Where, down there?"

"Near the tree line."

"Hikers?"

"Get down."

"Oh shit, I see them now. Must be at least ten people and ... dogs, there are dogs."

"We're fucked. We can't outrun the dogs."

"What should we do?"

"I heard about people hiding behind a waterfall."

"That won't fly. I took a look over the side and, by the way, you were right."

"About?"

"Blowback."

"Forget that, what did you see?"

"It's all rocks down below, and no way to get there from here without jumping."

"I took a long look as well. There's a staircase that leads down, and across the way is a structure of some kind."

"Where's the staircase?"

"Over in that direction," he pointed.

"And when we get to the bottom?"

"We cross over to the building and wait."

"For?"

"It's August, tourist season.   We wait for them to arrive and then get lost among them."

"Good plan, but not a guarantee."

"It's all I've got."

"Hoka hey."

"Not for me it isn't."

"OK, let's go."

They stumbled toward the stairs in a bowed position and when they'd reached them, Gregory raised a hand and whispered, "You go first."

Geronimo did not hesitate, but before his right foot had descended upon the first step he grabbed his chest and stumbled.

"You alright?" Gregory called out, seeing his partner grimace.

There was no response, so he scurried over to the where he'd last seen Geronimo and stared in horror. The Indian's motionless body was strewn across the bottom half of the staircase, his chest a dark, red, bloody mess. He took a deep breath, squelching the urge to scream, and looked about for the source of his partner's demise. There has to be a shooter around here somewhere, he thought, while desperately searching for cover in a area that offered none.   And there it was, a second noiseless round had struck the boulder by his left foot, sending shards of rock into the air.   Shit, he thought, a suppressed weapon. Geronimo was right, we were dead men right from the onset.   I was an idiot to think otherwise, and after seeing what they'd done to the General, I should have realized that.   But my brain wouldn't accept reality ... there's no escape.   We should have waited until the tourists had arrived, their presence would have protected us.

He sat down on the rocky soil and waited for the inevitable.   Two more bullets struck the ground on either side of him, and he wondered why they'd missed.   There's obviously a sniper within range, and they don't miss.   Are they having fun with me, he wondered.   Well, may as well get it over with, he said to himself, as he stood to present a better profile to the shooter.   Nothing.   He waived his arms about, shouted a few profanities, but the kill shot remained elusive.   And then he had a thought.

He turned and headed down the slippery, stone stairs, passing over Geronimo's lifeless body until he'd reached the bottom.   Secure in his new found freedom, he took one last look at his friend and scurried toward the tourist center building.   But as he approached the unoccupied structure, four masked beings grabbed him from behind, lashed his wrists behind his back, pricked his neck with a needle and threw his limp body over the shoulder of the stoutest.

Hours later, Gregory awakened to find himself shoeless, in a damp, windowless, concrete cell, a single fluorescent tube flickering above his head. A pounding headache confirmed that he was still alive but imprisoned. Chiding himself for the false sense of security back at the park, he'd resigned to a lengthy stay in his new residence, when the heavy steel door creaked open and a very pale, middle age female entered.

He looked up and asked, "Where am I?"

"Irrelevant," she said.

"You killed my partner," he seethed.

"And you broke your vow of secrecy."

"What now?"

"The adventure of a lifetime."

THE END

www.ingramcontent.com/pod-product-compliance
Lightning Source LLC
Chambersburg PA
CBHW021835010726
47493CB00005B/1414